Alice, Shaken and Definitely Stirred

Alice, Shaken and Definitely Stirred

Published by The Conrad Press in the United Kingdom 2020

Tel: +44(0)1227 472 874
www.theconradpress.com
info@theconradpress.com

ISBN 978-1-913567-49-1

Typesetting and Cover Design by: Charlotte Mouncey, www.bookstyle.co.uk

The Conrad Press logo was designed by Maria Priestley.

Printed and bound in Great Britain by Clays Ltd, Elcograf S.p.A.

Alice, Shaken and Definitely Stirred

Paula Smith

Dedicated with much love to
Martin, Michael, Thomas, John and Aidan

1

Number 24

'*Scarlett O'Hara was not beautiful, but men seldom realised it when caught by her charm...*' Alice reflected upon the opening lines of her book.

'What a load of old codswallop! She either had large breasts or was very beautiful or probably both. I mean, let's face it, they got Vivien Leigh to play her and she was not only beautiful but a nymphomaniac too by all accounts.' Alice put the book down in great disdain.

Sue protested, 'Oh, I don't know, I mean there are women who you would not call beautiful or striking looking but they just seem to have a certain *je ne sais quoi*. Remember Penelope?'

'Penelope?' Alice reminisced back to her old school days. 'The one with the buck teeth who looked like a llama when she smiled?'

'No! No! you're thinking of Perpetua. Anyway, Penelope played Maid Marion in the end of term production in year ten. If I remember correctly, she was in Robin Hood and His Merry Men in Tights.'

Alice thought back and yes Penelope suddenly sprang to mind, 'Oh yes, Penelope Pitstop we called her. Umm, accidentally kneed Robin Hood out of his manhood in the last scene.'

'That's the one! Yes, she could do those tremendous high

kicks and you know you're right, on that day it had all gone a bit wrong! Now, no one would have called her beautiful but all the boys were round her like a swarm of flies. Great personality and real fun to be with.' Sue attempted to return to her book.

'Yes, and if I remember correctly was about size 38 in the bust region and could do the splits, I think that might have had more to do with it,' Alice insisted.

'You are so cynical, shame on you.' Sue shook her head giving one of her disapproving looks.

'Well, anyway, getting back to our Scarlett she certainly managed to work her way through quite a few husbands, she certainly had something.'

Alice got off the sofa and wondered over to the window and peaked through the blinds.

'Some women have all the luck. I mean that one down there seems to have men on tap.' Alice gestured towards the flat's carpark.

'Oh yes?' Sue tried to sound interested but was reluctant to put her book down.

'Look, there she is again, Number 24, come and have a look!' Alice urgently beckoned Sue over to the window. Sue sighed. She could see the mood Alice was in and trying to read her book was becoming a futile task.

'There!' Alice pointed down to the car park. 'Number 24, there she is.'

Sue begrudgingly got off the warm, cosy place she had just managed to wriggle into the right amount of cosiness, and sneaked a preview through the blinds. Sue's eyes lit up. Number 24 certainly was a vision of loveliness. Tall, brunette with long flowing hair, a tiny waist and, yes, it was true, well endowed.

'Oooh yes. I see what you mean, who's she with?'

'Goodness knows. It seems like a new bloke every two minutes.'

Alice and Sue's eyes grew larger as the tall dark handsome stranger and Number 24 were in a deep, passionate embrace across the bonnet of a Mercedes Benz.

'Oooo! All right for some,' they both muttered looking enviously on.

Alice threw herself back down on the sofa seeming even more fed up.

Sue continued to look through the window. 'When did she move in?'

'Number 24? Oh, about six months ago now, just after…' Alice stopped.

They both looked at each other and after an uneasy pause, Sue sat back on the sofa and gave her friend a big hug.

'It will be fine, Alice, I promise you. When you get back to work tomorrow, life will return to, well, some sort of normality, you have just got to hold on in there.'

Alice knew her friend was right. Being at home allowed her too much time to think, to reminisce. Life had been so difficult this year, losing her dad and then Mark walking out. Work and life had just got too much. Everything had gone into a downward spiral. She got up and wondered over to the long mirror in the hallway. Alice stared at a woman who seemed not to recognise her.

'Too much gin and chocolate,' she mumbled to herself as she held her top tightly over her tum and bottom thinking she really ought to do something about those few extra pounds she had put on. She swept her sandy brown hair behind her ears and looked at her eyes, the same deep blue eyes Mark used to flatter her about. Well, almost the same apart from, perhaps, a few more wrinkles. She sighed again.

Sue studied her friend. She felt sure that, after Alice's lengthy absence from work, it would be good for her to return to the working world again; to get back to some sort of normality and routine would help her friend move on. Alice had spent too many long hours in the flat on her own and she was getting concerned about Alice's reluctance to go out, particularly after that last unfortunate incident in the car park, which no one, not even Sue, had been allowed to mention again.

Sue looked down at her mobile. 'Oh for goodness sake, that can't be the time, I am late for my hair appointment!' Sue gathered herself together as quick as she could and headed for the door, followed in hot pursuit by Alice who had noticed her jacket still parked on the hallway stand. Sue rushed through the door, blew a kiss through the air and hastened down the stairs, 'Don't forget Ben, will you? 3.45 he finishes school today. You won't forget, will you?' In an instant she was gone.

'Have I ever forgotten him? No, no, I'll be there,' but Alice's words were lost as Sue disappeared. Just at that moment, Number 24 was now proceeding up the staircase. Alice admired how any woman could walk so gracefully and balance in four-inch stiletto's without breaking their neck in the process. She certainly had all the *je ne sais quoi* that could be bestowed on a woman. 'How did some women manage to be so well endowed?' Alice thought to herself as she peered down at her own pimples on a pancake and once again sighed. Alice tried to make polite conversation. After all, this woman was her new neighbour.

'Afternoon, settling in okay?' Alice asked politely.

Number 24 gave a hint of a smile, looked her up and down in a rather haughty air Alice thought and glided through her apartment door, shutting it behind her without a nod or even a polite gesture.

'Well yes,' Alice mumbled towards Number 24's door, 'Probably too much effort to engage in a conversation after all that hot passionate sex.'

Alice trudged back into the flat and proceeded into the bedroom, hurling herself on the bed. Her last day of freedom. Life could only get better, surely? She looked across at the wardrobe. Some of *his* clothes were still there. She walked over and reached for one of the sleeves of his jackets. She held it close to her. He would come back, she felt sure of it. He just needed time.

3.45 came and went as Alice sat in St Michael's church. The choir were in full flow under the guidance of an over-zealous choir master, who somewhat reminded Alice of Mr Bean. He kept waving his arms around frantically, as if trying to swat a fly.

There amongst them all was Ben, her nephew. He looked so angelic, in his navy-blue cassock and white ruffled shirt. His huge blue eyes and blonde hair made him stand out from all the other choir boys.

Music filled the church. 'A Boy Was Born' rang out. It reso-nated throughout the perfect acoustics and before she knew it, Alice's eyes started to fill. Christmas would soon be here. Her first one on her own in some years.

She sat and stared at Ben, reflecting on what might have been. There was something about sitting in a church listening to music. Although it was calming it always evoked an immense mixture of emotions in her. She knew it was too late now to have her own child and Ben was the closest she would ever experience to this.

Mark had simply not wanted a family and well, she loved him so much, she had convinced herself that he was right. They could just please themselves he had insisted and enjoy life with no ties. Except looking at Ben would surely have convinced anyone to have wanted a child. He was, as all agreed, a blessing; a real blessing in so many ways. Sue had tried for a baby for years and, having given up after the third IVF treatment, decided it was not to be. Then, one Christmas, the announcement came that Sue was pregnant and, not long after, Ben entered their lives.

The music disappeared. Alice was brought back to the present with the sudden arrival of choir boys running at her from every angle and it wasn't long before Ben thrust his school bag into one of her arms while hurling himself full throttle into the other.

'Double knickerbocker glory, Aunty Alice?' Ben implored with those enormous blue eyes of his.

'Definitely,' Alice affirmed.

'Double chocolate flake?' Ben looked up at her with great expectation.

'Certainly.'

'Extra scoop of strawberry?'

'Could we have it any other way, Ben?'

Both smiled contentedly at each other.

Big Al's across the road from the church certainly knew how to make Knickerbocker Glory's and their speciality was *The Big One*. Almost as big as the Eiffel Tower and twice as thick, they willingly plunged into their favourite treat of the week.

Ben loved his time with his aunt, even more so now *he* had gone. Ben always found him cross and irritable. He had never really listened or seemed interested in anything he had to say. Although Ben didn't like the fact that his aunt now got a bit sad at times, he did like having her all to himself. She had always been more fun when Mark wasn't there and he knew his mum and dad didn't care for that man too much either. He had heard them talking about Mark in their whispery voices thinking he couldn't hear them.

To fix things, Ben felt he now had to find his aunt someone else who could make her really happy. After all, she was very pretty, everyone said so. He looked around Big Al's and thought about the café owner. He had the definite advantage of owning an ice cream shop but, then again, he did look about 84 so Ben thought maybe he was a little too old for his aunt.

Having completed paper, scissors, stone for the last chocolate flake on Aunty Alice's plate, they both sauntered off back home to be greeted by Dad.

'Your home early?' Alice said as she gave her big brother a hug as Ben scampered up the stairs to change into his footy clothes. 'Get the ghetto blaster ready Aunty Alice.'

'Hello there, how's it going?' Alice's brother, Robert, was far too distracted to give her his full attention, he had obviously misplaced his keys, yet again. Alice spied them on top of the key safe and handed them to him.

'Ok, I guess. Each day getting better than the last,' Alice said thoughtfully.

'Good, right… off now to the pub to meet Malcolm and a prospective client for a quick half before dinner, see you soon.'

Robert never knew quite what to say. He was never one for too many words, particularly those awkward chats where feelings might have to be discussed.

'Well, have a good one. Something smells good?' Alice wondered down the hall.

'Yes, Sue's cooking pasta tonight, hope you can stay, see you later.' Robert walked out as Ben hurtled back down the stairs again.

'See you Dad. Ready Aunty Alice?' Ben shouted

'Nearly, just popping in to see your mum. Get it warmed up, I'll join you in two mins.' Alice continued through to the kitchen and was greeted with the usual tempting aromas that always emerged at this time of day.

Sue was arguing once again with the cook book. 'Two teaspoons of parsley, now you tell me.'

'How many times do I have to tell you; you need to check you have all the ingredients first.' Alice proceeded to dip her finger in the sauce, 'Umm – spot on though and love the hair Sue.'

'Ah thank you.' Sue continued to perfect her pasta dish. 'All set for tomorrow then?' she enquired through her misted-up reading glasses.

'Well, as ready as I will ever be,' Alice retorted feeling resigned to the inevitable.

Sue thought some more words of comfort wouldn't go amiss, 'Look Alice, you know Mr Frobersham will be glad to have you back. That place simply can't function without you.'

'Umm, well I'd like to think that's true.' Alice felt comforted by this knowledge.

Alice heard Ben beckoning her to come and join him. She

sauntered off through to the living room to find him on his imaginary air guitar so she grabbed her one too.

'What's it going to be then, Ben?'

'The usual, Aunty Alice,' Ben retorted as they hi-fived.

'Right – here we go – volume up!'

The Arctic Monkeys came on full blast. Sue looked on and smiled. She really couldn't work out at times who was the biggest kid.

Teatime eventually arrived, Robert opened a bottle of wine and the pasta dish arrived tasting as good as it smelt. Alice loved the four of them together around the table. Ben did his usual response on being asked what he had done at school today, 'Oh nothing really,' which Alice felt had pretty much summed up her day too.

After tea, Ben having been banned from the iPad for looking up rude words, was promised a game of *Operation*. However, on discovering the buzzer on the game had stopped working and after everyone had spent a great deal of time trying to find new batteries for the game, Ben decided he would rather play *Monopoly*. The adults, however, were adamant it would simply last far too long, so Ben settled for a quick game of *Pass the Pigs*. It was then time for bed and Alice read the next chapter of Lara Williamson's *The Boy who Sailed the Ocean in an Arm Chair*. Ben had succeeded, as per usual, to wheedle an extra chapter out of his aunt declaring that he would like a pet snail called Brian too and maybe he could search the garden tonight for one?

'Absolutely not Ben, besides you have just had a bath, what would Mum say? No, you know what your aunty says Ben…'

'I know, I know, tomorrow is another day.'

Eventually, after many conversations about all the adventures he would get up to with his pet snail, his sleepy eyes got the better of him and he soon nodded off.

The evening had gone as quickly as it had arrived and it wasn't long before Alice was tucked up in her own bed too. Her stomach was still churning at the thought of returning to work after such a long break but she knew Sue was right, some sort of reality was now needed. She decided to continue to read her novel and it wasn't long before she soon drifted off.

As she was now becoming accustomed to of late, Alice dreamt again that night.

There she was, standing at the bottom of a huge marble staircase. As she surveyed her magnificent surroundings, she realised she was in Tara, the palatial mansion from Gone with the Wind. Amongst all the beauty and opulence of the building she stood there waiting, waiting. Her long, scarlet, velvet dressing gown showed an ample bosom and there, striding towards her, was Rhett Butler. He swept her off her feet and carried her up the long flight of stairs. By the time they had reached the top, however, Rhett seemed to have turned into Mark. He kicked open the bedroom door and hurled her upon the bed. Alice could feel every part of her body tingle with excitement. He was here, he was back, this was their moment…

Sadly, as she had now become accustomed to, her dreams never quite turned out the way she had expected.

As Mark stood there at the end of the bed, he looked as white as a sheet and was panting for breath. Alice was all ready for her passionate encounter but Mark, it seemed, was not. He could barely speak.

'Oh my goodness! Have you put on weight? You weigh a ton! You

haven't been at that biscuit tin, again, have you?' Mark continued to struggle to catch his breath and was now reaching for his inhaler.

Alice couldn't quite comprehend what he meant until she looked down at her dressing gown which was now bulging at the seams. Yes, she thought to herself, maybe she had visited the biscuit tin a little more frequently of late. Perhaps those few extra gins and glasses of wine had also added a few pounds? Alice felt confused. After all, what did this really matter now they were together again. She sat up and moved towards him as Mark continued to take frantic deep breaths from his inhaler.

'But, Mark, I am ready for you. I am all yours!'

Mark looked shocked and appalled at her apparent insensitivity to his current predicament.

'You must be joking! Have you not seen how long that set of stairs is? I am completely knackered.'

'But Mark, I love you?'

However, her plea fell on deaf ears, Mark was already heading for the door. As she called to him, he turned around and looked her straight in the eyes, 'Frankly, my dear, I don't give a damn!' And with those words he slammed the door behind him.

Alice raced after him but, as hard as she tried, she just couldn't open the door. It was firmly locked. Hearing the front door shut loudly, with a huge bang, a wave of panic swept through her body. She needed to stop him. She needed to get him back. She must stop him! Alice ran in haste to the window. Mark (or hang on, was it Rhett?) was walking across her flat's car park followed in hot pursuit by Mr Hughes, that meddlesome, nosey old neighbour of hers. He was complaining at Rhett for having left his horse and carriage for far too long in the guest car parking space and must move it immediately. Frantically, she tried to open the window but to no avail as that was firmly locked too. In frustration, she turned around and hurled herself on the bed.

'Oh, for goodness sake!' Alice punched the pillows.

On raising her head, she looked around the room but now had the strangest feeling she was no longer in Tara. The room was just like the hotel room Mark had taken her to on the anniversary of their first meeting. Yes, the wallpaper was the same, the furniture, it was definitely the same room. But it now felt very cold. She was all alone.

'Oh bugger, I'll think of some way to get him back. That's what I'll do. After all, tomorrow is another day.' Then the room started to fill with music; that very same music from Gone with the Wind resonated around her.

Alice was soon awakened by the clatter of bottles in Howarth Court being emptied by the refuse collectors. Alice yawned and put the pillow over her head. Having not slept well, the bed now seemed very reluctant to give her up. Alice slowly opened up one eye and then closed it only to open the other. After a few minutes she managed to haul herself up, onto the edge of the bed.

'Well, the world of work can wait no longer.' she sighed and before she knew it, she was showered, breakfasted, clothed and was sitting on the usual overcrowded train.

Nothing had changed. Nothing. Well apart from her now being single of course. There was the same bustle of people; the eccentric man with his enormous moustache who insisted on keeping his legs open wider that the actual width of his seat while the steely brimmed, bespectacled woman, sitting next to him, muttered complaints under her breath.

Alice read her paper on her mobile and thought nothing had

much changed in the news either. Politicians still arguing over how the country should best be run. Not being able to settle to read the paper any longer, Alice stared at her own reflection in the window. Her stomach felt like a whole army of butterflies were pirouetting inside. She just had to get the first day done. That's all. It would be plain sailing after that.

Walking down from Oxford Street Station, up past Selfridges, the first drops of rain fell on her newly polished shoes and shiny briefcase. She reached the offices. The lift, yet again, wasn't working so she wandered up the familiar iron spiral staircase to the second floor and opened the door. It was empty. Alice wondered over to her desk. Strange she thought, her leather pencil holder and filing trays had gone? There, on her desk, was a large hairy caterpillar pencil case and a pink fluffy pen? Papers were strewn all over it and there was a large plate of *Kipling French Fancies* lurking under a folder.

Just then, Miss Havisham appeared at the door. Alice was delighted to see her, the ever-loyal, if not rather dotty, employee of some thirty years for the company. Now in her late sixties, Miss Havisham had become part of the establishment. Tall, thin, prim and proper and the kindest woman you would ever want to meet.

'Great to see you Miss Havisham.'

'Oh, Alice. You're back. Goodness! I mean good. You're back. That's marvellous.'

But Alice thought there was something in Miss Havisham's voice that didn't sound that sure?

As Alice was about to park her bottom firmly at her desk. Miss Havisham let off a noise reminiscent of a Pekinese dog being sat on.

'Oooohh! No…well not there… in that seat… hang on… I think Mr Frobersham is waiting for you. Cup of tea, dear – one lump or two?'

Despite Alice having worked at Frobersham's for many years, Miss Havisham could never remember who had what in their tea. Alice had never taken sugar but it made no difference to Miss Havisham because she put it in anyway. Miss Havisham opened Mr Frobersham's door and ushered Alice into the room.

'Ahh, welcome back, Alice. Welcome back. Yes, indeed, yes. Take a seat, take a seat.'

Alice couldn't quite believe her eyes, Mr Frobersham's office had completely changed. Where had the old leather Chesterfield gone? The picture of Mr Frobersham's father and grandfather, proudly mounted on the wall behind him, had now been replaced with a painting of a somewhat scantily dressed couple at the beach. His beautiful solid mahogany wooden desk, that so befitted a man of his age and stature, was now a see-through plastic monstrosity where surely only self-will seemed to be holding it up?

'How are you doing, Alice? How are you doing?' Mr Frobersham enquired.

Alice was about to answer but, as usual, he really wasn't interested in the response and carried straight on.

'Now, one or two changes since you were last here, you know. Yes, one or two slight, yes slight changes.' Mr Frobersham nervously laughed as he clasped his hands together. 'Now…'

But he was soon interrupted by a young red-head who walked over to his desk carrying a large pile of papers. 'I swear pumpkin, she needs to go,' the woman murmured in a high-pitched squeaky voice. 'I can never find anything!'

Alice thought she must have misheard her. Did she say *pumpkin*? Mr Frobersham, *pumpkin*? Charles Frobersham, now in his seventies, simply wasn't a man anyone would have addressed as '*pumpkin*.' This was a man who had been a captain in the army, like his father and grandfather before him. A man who belonged to the distinguished Athenaeum Club. A man whose family had been manufacturing buttons for over 150 years, buttons fit for the Queen. A man not to be trifled with.

This young woman, with legs up to her elbows, seemed to completely ignore Alice as she walked past her and thrust her rather large breasts firmly under Mr Frobersham's eyes. It was now clearly too much for Mr Frobersham to now talk to Alice and concentrate at the same time.

Alice had not seen this woman before. Had she been employed to help Miss Havisham out? She really didn't want to continue her conversation with this woman around. Alice lent forward to catch her eye.

'And you are Miss… Miss?'

'Bond, the name is Bond.'

'Well, Miss Bond, if you would just leave those papers on the desk, Mr Frobersham and I are in the middle of a meeting. Thank you.' Alice felt the sooner she could have a conversation with the man the sooner she could get back to her desk and rearrange it again the way it had always been.

However, Miss Bond looked particularly put out at being asked to leave the room.

'Well, I must say, that is no way to talk to the Dir….'

Mr Frobersham gave a sudden loud, anxious cough.

'Yes. Indeed. Now, the thing is, Alice, we have made one or two changes since you were last here.'

'One or two changes?' enquired Alice, somewhat baffled. This man hated change; he was particularly averse to anything that might upset his equilibrium or anything that might bring Frobersham and Sons into the twenty-first century. This was a man of forty years standing in the field of buttons. Buttons for Harrods, Chanel, Yves Saint Laurent. Buttons fit for the Queen and, as the plaque used to say on the wall behind him, *'Frobersham's buttons, hand-made buttons of distinction, since 1845.'*

'Yes, one or two changes, yes. Just one or two. Indeed, yes. We've gone down a slightly new route. You know out with the old and in with the new, keeping abreast of current trends you know.' Mr Frobersham nervously fidgeted in his seat.

Alice felt the only thing Mr Frobersham was keeping abreast of was the Miss Bond's chest, now being thrust even more firmly under the watchful eye of her boss.

'Design changes?' enquired Alice watching Miss Bond slide around the back of Mr Frobersham's chair and was now starting to massage Mr Frobersham's shoulders in what Alice thought was a rather slow and lurid fashion.

'Yes, well design changes and…' He stopped, almost unsure of how to break the news but was given a sudden boost of confidence by Miss Bond's firm hands massaging up and down his back. He proceeded, 'Clientele.'

Miss Bond interjected, 'Yes, Accentuise.'

'Accentuise?' Alice was somewhat baffled. She must not have heard her properly. 'Did you say Accentuise, that high street chain that makes all those cheap accessories?' Alice convinced herself that she must have been hearing things. Frobersham and Sons had made high quality buttons since 1845. She couldn't quite see what Frobersham and Accentuise could possibly have in common.

'Umm, that's the one. Change. Yes, a change is as good as a rest you know!' Frobersham was clearly now in a different place – obviously heaven. His masseur's hands were now getting firmer and probably, so too, was Mr Frobersham.

'Is it? In what way?' Alice asked.

'Well, in every way. Surely?' Mr Frobersham said in a voice that was not completely convinced himself.

'Titalize,' Miss Bond said.

'I beg your pardon!' Alice couldn't quite believe what she was hearing?

'Indeed, Titalize Tit-Tassels.' Mr Frobersham sneaked a school boyish grin at his masseur.

At this point, Miss Bond reached for one of the draws and pulled out some very strange looking tassels which she clipped, rather inappropriately Alice thought, on to her dress directly over her bosoms.

'Here, pumpkin, fancy another twizzle?' invited Miss Bond to the ever-attentive Mr Frobersham.

At this point Alice needed to pinch herself. This must be another one of her strange dreams, surely? Yes, that was it, she was going to wake up and find it had all been a bad dream.

'Tit-Tassels? But Charles?' Alice pleaded. 'We have made the best quality buttons since 1845. We supply Liberties, Chanel, John Lewis….' she was about to go on but was rudely interrupted.

'Used to!' Miss Bond flashed a look at Alice as if a cat had stepped on her tail.

'Used to?' Alice looked in earnest at Mr Frobersham. Surely

things had not changed that much since she left? Alice was his top sales director, well his only sales director. He surely knew she had been instrumental in building his business back up. She was his right-hand woman. She was the centre, the core of the business. There wasn't anyone else who knew buttons like she did. No one else who could have wooed Mr Chanterelle of Chanel like she did into purchasing their range of superior hand-made silk buttons for his latest collection. No one else who could have helped make Frobersham and Son the top of the button industry like she had.

Miss Bond had now placed herself firmly on the seat next to Mr Frobersham. Through the clear plastic table, Alice could see a hand caressing the parts that were surely best left alone on a man of that age. Mr Frobersham continued.

'The thing is... well the point is Alice... You and I... I and you... Well... We have reached the summit on the mountain... The horizon of our sunset, the depth of our deep blue ocean, the...'

'You're redundant.' Miss Bond interjected.

'Redundant? What do you mean?' Alice felt the like the rush of a tidal wave had hit her.

'Well, it actually means your job doesn't exist anymore.' Miss Bond explained.

'Yes, well thank you for that. I am aware what the word redundant actually means.' Alice snapped. She couldn't believe what she was hearing. I mean who was this woman? Manhandling, well woman-handling, her boss with little more than a pelmet on?

'It's all about Tit-Tassels, you know.' Mr Frobersham lent forward. 'Sales increased by two hundred per cent in just the last two months. Quite an achievement you know. Yes, it's all about being '*Titalized with Tit-Tassels!*' Everyone, everywhere just wants to be Titalized! The whole beauty of them is that you can wear them anywhere, anytime.

Alice still couldn't quite believe what she was hearing.

'Charles, please, this is just a fad. This fad, like many before them, will come and go. They always do. We always said we wouldn't go down the quick buck route. It never works. You know it doesn't. Slow and steady wins the race…'

'Well that's for sure,' said Miss Bond as she leered across at Alice whilst adjusting her Tit-Tassels on her bosoms under the watchful eye of Mr Frobersham. 'Aren't you forgetting something pumpkin?' She continued to look at Alice with a very self-satisfied smirk on her face. Mr Frobersham looked puzzled.

'Our little agreement, pumpkin?' Miss Bond urged him on.

'Ah, yes, quite. Well, yes. Indeed. Miss Bond is our new Sales Director, Alice. It's all about moving with the market you know, can't stand still. Mustn't miss the boat you know.'

Alice had now sunk even deeper into her chair and was lost for words. Titalize? Tit-Tassels? The words kept churning round her now throbbing head. She could not plunge any further into the depths of confusion and utter bewilderment.

'I must protest, Mr Frobersham as Director of Sales this simply won't do.'

'Well, Ex-Director of Sales, I think you will find sweety,' said Miss Bond as her smug smile had now turned into a great big leer.

'Ex? Ex Director of Sales?' Alice turned to Mr Frobersham. She still couldn't believe her ears. 'I have given you twenty years of loyal service. I have helped you put this firm, firmly on the map. I have stuck with you through thick and thin…'

Mr Frobersham now started to protest 'Ah, well sort of. I mean the last six months.'

'For goodness sake!' shouted Alice, 'Considering all that has happened to me! Besides you told me to take the time off! Before then I had never once, not once had a day's sick leave even when my dad was ill. I have stood by your side and we, yes, *WE* have built this business to the grand heights of top button manufacturer of the year. Six months – and *you* told me to make sure I took it too.'

'Now, I know you are going to be a little put out by this but...'

'A little? A little, put out?' Alice screamed. 'For goodness sake man this is my job we are talking about. One that I have devoted many years to and love.' Alice's face was now redder than Miss Bond's dress.

Mr Frobersham felt Alice was now becoming rather hysterical.

'Look, we have a very generous package for you, you won't have to work again, well not for another six months or so at least. I am a very decent, loyal employer and, indeed, friend you know to give you such a great package.'

Alice stood up as Miss Havisham walked in.

'Alice, one lump is it or two?' There was silence. Alice looked Mr Frobersham directly in the eyes.

'Some kind of loyalty. Some kind of friend.' Alice got up and walked towards the door. She looked back but it was to no avail.

Mr Frobersham looked at Miss Bond for some kind of reassurance and she was not slow to respond. She merely thrust her Tit-Tassels firmly under his nose as she collected up her papers. 'She can't give you the sort of benefits I can as Director, pumpkin, fancy another twizzle?'

Unnoticed by the two love birds, Alice removed herself from the office and went back to her desk. Miss Havisham put the cup of tea down in front of her. 'Yes, two sugars isn't it?'

Alice had now lost the will to live and slurping the tea, missed her mouth and spilt it down her new blouse.

Miss Havisham hovered nervously about her. 'I had only taken a day off to go with my friend, Marg, to the races and this temp turns up, just to answer his phone. The thing is, she never left. Now she seems to handle a lot more than just his phone. Well, I didn't know the old fool had it in him? However, if it's any consolation Alice I think I'm next in line, dear.'

Alice felt another wave of sadness come over her. Miss Havisham too had been a loyal employee for so many years. Yes, it was true that she rarely remembered client's names correctly, always misplaced the biscuits and never managed to file any documents in the right places. But Alice loved her. Everyone did. She was the salt of the earth.

'I am sorry I didn't ring you and warn you but...' Miss Havisham went out to reach her hand but seemed to lose courage to hold it.

'Don't worry Miss Havisham, this isn't anything to do with you. I am sure your job will be fine. Besides, anyone would want to snap you up to work for them.' Alice felt the usual tinge of guilt for lying but felt it important to try to reassure her, but Miss Havisham's age and lack of any real administrative or ICT skills would surely be a real obstacle. Miss Havisham gave a resigned sigh and went back to answer the phone.

'Hello, Frobersham and Sons, maker of Tit-Tassels and

more. Oh hello! It's Mr Melon isn't it from Chanel…?' Miss Havisham asked.

Alice mouthed to Miss Havisham 'No, it's Mr Chanterelle…'

'Oh, oh dear, well that is sad news. We will be sad to lose your valued custom Mr Melon, I mean Chanterelle. Are you sure your customers might not like to try the Tit-Tassels?'

Alice didn't need to stay to find out the answer to that question. She threw what was left of her belongings into her briefcase and left.

2

Help!

A lice sat on the tube. To add insult to injury, all she could now see were Tit-Tassels. They were everywhere. She shut her eyes in disbelief hoping it was still all a dream. However, when she opened them, there they were, nothing but Tit-Tassels from every angle. Alice sat in a stupor. Feeling in need of some comfort and knowing Sue would now be at work, there was only one place to go in her hour of need and that was to Mario's.

She had known Mario since she was six. He had been a good friend to her dad and very much like a father figure too. Whenever she had been a bit down or just needed some words of wisdom Mario had always been there for her. She hadn't seen him in the last week or so, so she headed off to visit him.

Mario owned a small coffee shop just around the corner close to her flat. He made the best cappuccino, just the way she liked it with extra creamy froth and lashings of real chocolate sprinkles. This, along with a warmed pain au raisin and Mario's usual words of wisdom, were now urgently beckoning her.

She got off the tube and, after wrestling with an uncooperative ticket barrier, emerged into the light of day. The faint drizzle had now turned into cats and dogs. Alice reached into her brief case for her umbrella.

'Oh, bugger!' The umbrella which always lived in her brief case was no longer there. Her night out with Sue and her friends returned, the one soon after Mark had left her. The taxi had dropped Alice off just outside Howarth Court Apartments and, having had rather a large amount to drink, she felt the need to grab hold of the old Victorian street lamp to regain her balance. Whilst hugging the lamp she had decided to spend the next few minutes singing in the rain, literally singing, *Singing in the Rain.* Her umbrella was reluctant to open but it hadn't deterred her in her rendition of the song, and she really had enjoyed swinging herself around the lamp post and singing it at full volume.

However, after about five minutes, she was rudely interrupted by old nosey parker Mr Hughes, sticking his head out of his apartment window and telling her to '*pipe down.*' This sent Alice over the edge and she told Mr Hughes in no uncertain terms to bugger off and get a life. Mr Hughes, now outraged at being spoken to in such a manner had called the police complaining about the noise.

A few minutes later a policeman arrived at the block of flats. He had, at first, started being quite an amiable and reasonable chap about the whole affair and tried to talk her into going back to her flat and sleeping it off. Alice, however, now had an audience so was game for another verse of her song.

However, as she danced around the lamppost, the previously jammed, automatic umbrella's handle had had now released and had unfortunately found its way into the police officer's important parts, changing his mood somewhat. To top it all, Mr Hughes started shouting out of the window telling her that it was herself who needed to get a life. Feeling tipped over the edge and decidedly drunk, Alice then threatened to put her umbrella *'Where the sun don't shine!'* up her haughty neighbour's bottom. This resulted in the umbrella being confiscated and Alice being marched into a police car, now escorted by a policewoman who was built like a German tank. The rest of the evening was a bit of a blur but her friend Sue and brother Robert had emerged at the police station in the morning promising the police officer that this was just 'a one off, owing to very difficult circumstances etc etc…'

So, no umbrella.

Alice stood on the edge of the pavement waiting to cross the road to get to Mario's. This road is never busy, she thought, and the moment you want to cross, the moment you need to get a simple coffee, it's like Piccabloodydilly Circus. To add yet another insult to injury, the large puddle that had formed just two feet away from her had lured a taxi right in its path launching a tidal wave at her. She stood speechless, well speechless for at least two seconds.

'Bugger, bugger, bugger!' she shouted at the taxi driver who was completely oblivious to what he had done.

Now wet, and decidedly bedraggled, Alice continued to cross the road and having struggled with a damp and now stuck café door managed to eventually hurl herself into Mario's café.

It was almost empty, apart from old Henry who was firmly rooted in his usual seat and slurping the remains of his coffee from his saucer. They both acknowledged each other with the usual polite, friendly nod. Alice walked to the empty coffee bar and plonked her briefcase down beside her. Mario was not in the bar and thought he must be pottering in his office.

'Hello, Hello? Mario?' she called.

Silence. Alice turned round to Henry who repeated the same courteous nod. Alice continued.

'Mario, hello? It's Alice, where are you?'

'Hello Alice,' came an unfamiliar voice emerging from below the counter, 'how can I help you?' A man suddenly sprang up, somewhat startling her.

'And you are?' Alice enquired, somewhat put out by this complete stranger standing before her.

'Ollie,' said the very self-assured man who seemed to have this rather over joyous look on his face.

Alice looked at this tall and broad, but somewhat dishevelled, middle-aged man.

'Yes, I am aware of your name, you have just told me that, but *who* exactly *are* you and *where's* Mario?'

'Ah, yes Mario.' Ollie was not forthcoming on any more information.

'Yes, Mario, the man, who owns this café?' Alice thought this man was very dense indeed.

'Yes Mario. No, he's not here at the moment,' Ollie replied.

'Yes, I am aware of this fact but *where* is he?' Alice repeated. This smiley man's jolly exterior was adding to Alice's agitation.

'He's unavailable,' Ollie replied not really wanting to disclose any more information about his godfather's whereabouts to a complete stranger.

'Yes, I am blindingly aware of this fact, but WHERE is he?' Alice was wondering how many times she could enquire after Mario without this man giving her the slightest bit of information.

Ollie didn't respond to her request but simply put out his hand to shake Alice's. 'Nice to meet you.'

However, his hand was ignored. Alice thought another approach might yield some more information. 'I am a very good friend of Mario's and I know he would not have left without telling me unless it was some kind of emergency. Is he ok?'

'Ah, right...pleased to meet you.' Ollie tried once again to hold out his hand to shake hers.

Alice, however, was not in the mood for any pleasantries. She stood and stared at this man. He had very dark eyes, somewhat shifty she thought. Why on earth would Mario have left his beloved café to *him*? She eyed him suspiciously.

'What have you done with Mario?'

'Done with him? Mario?'

'Oh, for goodness sake. Yes Mario!' Alice's voice was now echoing off every utensil in the room.

'Nothing, he's in Italy.'

'Italy?'

'Yes, Italy, you know the country in southern Europe. Now, what can I get you?'

This man's sarcasm was now like a red rag to a bull.

'What's he doing in Italy?' Alice demanded in complete disbelief. She had never heard Mario talk of an '*Ollie*' chap before? Mario had not mentioned that he was going away and besides Mario hated travelling and hated his family back in Italy even more.

'At a funeral, his brother Antonio's funeral. Very sad – the whole business.' Ollie started to fidget with the coffee machine.

'Right, I see,' Alice muttered. Yes, she did recall Mario had a brother called Antonio. He had run a hairdressing salon in Rome. He was the brother no one talked about in the family because he had run off with a man, called Abramo, from Sicily who turned out to be the son of a mafia super boss. He had taken a shine to the way Antonio had cut his hair and love seemed to blossom from there. Alice remembered she had been amused to find out that the name Abramo, like the related name Abraham, means *'father of a multitude'*. As rumour had it, Abramo had fathered many children before deciding he was gay and running off with Antonio.

'And what connection do you have to Mario exactly?' demanded Alice.

'I am Mario's godson and no, before you ask, I have no idea when he will return. Mario is attending Antonio's funeral. Nasty business, died in a tragic hairdressing accident I believe, all very strange. Poor chap. Mario has gone over to help Abramo with the arrangements. Now what can I get you?'

Ollie purveyed this increasingly angry, very agitated and very wet lady, now dripping over his recently cleaned café floor. The name Alice seemed familiar, had Mario mentioned the name before?

'I'll have my usual,' demanded Alice.

'Right, I see, well, not being a mind reader, you might have to help me with that request.' Ollie threw, what Alice considered to be another one of his self-satisfied grins, towards Henry who returned a snigger under his breath. This, however, went down like a lead balloon.

Sarcastic, self-centred, smuggish and obviously full of himself Alice thought to herself, 'Right, I would like a large cappuccino, skinny, single shot, do you think you can manage that?' Alice felt pleased that she had managed to equally match her opponent's sarcasm.

'No,' Ollie replied continuing to fiddle with the coffee

machine behind the counter.

'Sorry? I beg your pardon? I would like a cappuccino.' Alice was now showing the whites of her eyes.

'No can do, I'm afraid,' said Ollie with a very calm exterior adding to Alice's irritation. She was now feeling very upset, it was all too much.

'Look, I've lost my dad, my boyfriend and now my job in the space of a year, is it really too much to ask for a bloomin' cappuccino? I don't think so, do you?' Alice simply couldn't believe the incompetence of the man.

'That was a bit careless, where did you leave them?' Ollie looked across at Henry who was clearly on the same wavelength and both started sniggering like two naughty school boys. Realising this was not a great joke to relate to a probably recently bereaved lady he backtracked 'No, sorry – the coffee machine is defunct. Sorry.'

Rainwater dripped from every possible crevice in Alice's clothing. She was thirsty, hungry and very tired and now in need for just something hot to drink.

'Right, what have you got to drink then?'

'Tea: Yorkshire, Assam, English Breakfast, Earl Grey, Empress Grey, Lady Grey or Clipper decaffeinated. What do you prefer?'

'Look, just give me a hot chocolate, will you?' Alice snapped.

'Hot chocolate?'

'Yes, hot chocolate – you know the stuff – brown powder then add a bit of milk?'

'No, sorry can't do hot chocolate either. Need the machine for that. Tea?'

'No, I don't want a bloody cup of tea. Forget it, just forget it. I am going elsewhere.' With that Alice turned around and strode towards the door. However, she had forgotten her loyal briefcase waiting patiently beside her and proceeded, rather ungracefully, to hurl herself over it, falling flat on the floor.

Ollie peered down at this woman, now strewn across the floor, 'I think you might just need that cup of tea now don't you?' Ollie's grin had now turned into a full-size Cheshire.

Alice picked herself up. Things definitely couldn't get any worse.

'I don't want your bloody tea…forget it … just forget it.'

Alice stood up, adjusting her now even more forlorn looking jacket and went to open the unwilling door that was refusing to co-operate.

'For goodness sake!' Every muscle in Alice's body was wrestling with it but sadly the jammed door was oblivious to her urgent need to vacate the premises.

Ollie by this time had moved from behind the counter and proceeded to, with very little effort, open the door.

'Easy when you know how. Gently does it, there you go.' He smiled that same, very irritating, self-assured grin.

Alice flashed him her '*Don't mess with me pal*' stare and fled the shop feeling now even sorrier for herself onto what was now a very empty and silent road.

Where was a bloomin' taxi when you needed one?

3

Oliver's army

'To put in in a nutshell, I'm buggered,' Alice repeated for the third time to Sue as she popped another one of Sue's Viennese whirls in her mouth hoping to get some sort of response from her friend who seemed to be not quite understanding her dilemma and was somewhat distracted reading her latest Alliott book.

'These are really good you know. Wonderful biscuits, best batch yet,' Alice said in the hope of some response.

Sue lifted her head from her novel, reluctant to engage in conversation having spent the previous afternoon and evening trying to console her friend but all her advice seemed to fall on deaf ears. Understandably, Sue thought, Alice was distraught. She had had much to contend with in the last few months and she could see that this was the final straw for her friend. Realising that trying to finish her novel wasn't going to happen, she placed the book down and listened to her friend now in full flow. Sue decided it was time for a more forthright, direct heart to heart.

'Look, Alice, now is the perfect chance to start again. You were damn good at your job and you now need to ring round some of your clients and see if they have any openings.'

'What, in buttons? I sell them not buy them!' Alice thought

this bit of advice was very short of Sue's usual wisdom and showed a real lack of understanding of her predicament.

'Chanel, Yves St Laurent my most valued customers don't make buttons Sue. No, they need to buy them. We are one of the few button designers and manufacturers of distinction left in this country or even, Sue, the world.'

'Yes, but...' Sue was not able to finish her sentence. Alice was now in full flow.

'No, my expertise and knowledge are now clearly defunct and what is more, I am too old to start retraining now,' Alice said this as she put yet another Viennese Whirl in her mouth and slurped her tea in utter amazement that her friend was just not understanding the real dilemma she was now in.

'Look, you are hardly too old, for goodness sake! You are a good-looking woman and, quite frankly, not badly off. You are not exactly hard up are you? You earn, or rather earned, a very good wage and, let's face it, never spent it! Now is the time to take time for you, to take stock and take a fresh look on things. Look for a change in direction. It doesn't have to be buttons. You could sell anything to anyone.' Sue looked at her friend's dejected face and came round the kitchen bar to give her yet another big hug.

'You can do anything you choose. You are a talented woman. You have plenty of money Alice. Let's face it you are not on the breadline, are you? You are always saving money – ever the cautious lady when it comes to money.'

'What go into my savings?' Had her friend gone mad? 'No Sue, that is for a rainy day.'

'Well,' Sue slowly and cautiously proceeded 'Don't you think that day may now have arrived?' Sue waited for a response. She could see Alice was now taking this on board and mulling it over.

'You mean not do buttons?'

'Exactly.' Sue's hug got a bit tighter. 'Not buttons. Besides, if the worse comes to the worst and you can't find what you want, you and I both know that Tit-Tassels will be just a seven-day wonder and Mr Frobersham will be back on your doorstep before you know it. Why rush into anything just yet?'

'Umm, yes I can see the sense in what you say.'

Alice cheered up a bit and a smile was trying to get through. She popped another Viennese Whirl in her mouth and was sure that one had been the best on the plate. Alice knew she had always been sensible with money and yes, she could afford to bide some time. What was the point of all those savings if she couldn't use them to buy a little time?

Sue, now confident she could return to her book, picked up her novel and proceeded to read. There was silence... for about five seconds.

'Oh, and another thing. Who is this Ollie man?' Alice enquired.

No, Sue realised, she had picked the book up far too soon and placed it down again with great reluctance.

'Ollie?' Sue's eyes seemed to light up. 'Oh, Ollie! Yes, he is gorgeous isn't he, in more ways than one! A bit of a dish don't you think?' Sue's eyes now seemed to get even larger much to the surprise and somewhat annoyance of Alice. Surely, they couldn't be talking about the same man she had met in the café?

'Yes,' Sue continued, 'He is helping Mario out. I meant to tell you but, well, Mario was anxious you weren't to be worried about the whole business. He felt sure he would be back before you knew it.' Sue pondered over the whole incident 'Yes tragic business, Mario's brother, who would have thought it. So unlucky! Looks like things have got even more out of hand. His body has gone missing from the funeral parlour. The Mafia have it apparently. Abramo is distraught. Mario has gone to negotiate.' By the look on Alice's face, Sue soon realised she had probably said far too much.

'Negotiate, OMG! What exactly?' Alice was horrified that this man, who had been like a father figure to her was now involved with the Mafia.

'To get his body back, of course. They want money for it.'

'Money? How much money?' Alice's eyes were now as big as saucers.

'Oh, I don't know. Mario is sorting all that out. It's a shame, really, Antonio is dead because Mario says there is not a decent hairdresser anywhere at all now in Sicily and Abramo is bereft that he may now have to attend Antonio's funeral with his hair in such a dreadful way.'

'Right, yes I can see how that might trouble him.' Alice, however, couldn't possibly imagine how someone could grieve over a haircut rather than a dead person. 'However, getting back to Ollie...'

'Ah yes, Ollie is Mario's godson.' Sue's eyes lit up again. 'About our age, late forties, I believe.'

'Strange, I never heard Mario mention him?' Alice seemed very put out by this.

'Yes, you have, Ollie is the one that Mario refers to as the *wandering nomad.*'

It suddenly came to Alice who Sue was talking about.

'Oh, my goodness! I didn't realise he was the same man. Yes,

Mario has only ever referred to him as the *wandering nomad* not Ollie. Gosh anyway, better for all if he continues to be a *wandering nomad* and move on.' Alice placed the fourth biscuit in her mouth and Sue, knowing her good friend only too well, was grateful that she had already stowed away a few spares in her biscuit tin for Robert and Ben.

'Ollie is such good company Alice; you should get to know him.'

Alice was alarmed at this and was wondering how her friend had got to know him so well without her knowing about it.

'So how have you managed to get to know him so well then?' Alice enquired with an earnest expression on her face.

'Well, when he first arrived in London, Robert and I invited him to stay a couple of days, just until he found his feet and Mario's spare room wasn't available at that point. He's great with Ben and has many amusing antics to tell from his travels. When you get to know him Alice, you will really like him, I'm sure.'

Alice wanted to put that idea to bed immediately.

'I have never known such a smug, overly confident, man in my life. Good company indeed! Fancy trusting him with Ben, I mean he could be anyone. What do you know about the man?'

Sue brushed aside her friend's comments. 'Oh Alice, don't be ridiculous. He's Mario's godson. I think Mario would know the man by now. The fact that Mario has trusted him with his beloved café speaks volumes, don't you think?'

Alice muttered something under her breath which Sue couldn't quite hear.

'Look, all I am saying is that you never really know anyone do you?' Alice was not to be assuaged on the matter.

'Um, well, that might be said of some, but not Ollie I think.' Sue thought that clearly Alice had never really taken a good look at her own ex-boyfriend to be so judgemental of Ollie. If ever there was a character not to be trusted it was Mark. Alice could see no wrong in Mark, even when he had left her just after she had lost her dad to dementia and her mum the previous year to the same fate. Mark had been, Sue thought, the most selfish, self-satisfying bastard she had ever come across. She didn't like him at Uni and was always suspicious that his need to be admired by all who surrounded him led him to be unfaithful to Alice on several occasions. What with recent events she had surmised these suspicions were fully justified. Alice, however, was ignorant of this and Sue felt, for now, this was for the best. Both her and Robert felt Alice would surely go under again, having lost her boyfriend, her dad and now her job, to be told of Mark's latest antics. After all, Sue knew Alice's stance on it all. Alice had felt sure that Mark would return, some of his clothes were still in her wardrobe. Alice seemed confident that Mark just needed a break. Work had been getting him down and she thought he was having a little mid-life crisis that would soon resolve itself.

Alice was now in full flow, 'I mean, who is called Ollie, for goodness sake. What a name, Ollie indeed!' Alice was clearly not impressed with the name or the man.

'It's short for Oliver,' explained Sue

'Yes, thank you Mr Holmes, I am fully aware it is short for Oliver. Oliver indeed, who is called Oliver?'

'Well, quite a few people actually. Oliver Reed, he was a dish too.'

'Yes, well…' Alice was about to protest but Sue went on.

'Oliver Stone the famous film director, Oliver Platt the famous playwright, Oliver Hudson you know the son of Goldie Hawn and…'

'Yes, well apart from those few. It is not a very attractive name is it and fancy shortening it to Ollie, something a little boy would do not a grown man!' Alice was not impressed.

'Ollie is a great name and you don't really know him Alice. It's not like you to be so uncharitable and to judge people so quickly. He is helping his uncle out and has given up his travels to do so. Mario is very grateful that his business is in such good hands. Besides Ben and Robert have grown quite fond of him. He is great company you know.'

Sue was hoping this might change her friend's opinion but Alice seemed to look most offended at this. Sue's attempts at persuading her friend were given short shrift. Alice was not amused that Ben and particularly Robert, a grown man, had also been duped by this Ollie chap.

'All I am saying is that I would just be cautious when he is around Ben – not giving him lots of unsupervised time, I hope? Trust me he has shifty eyes.' Alice was not to be moved on the subject.

Sue rolled her eyes 'Right, well, I will study those shifty eyes tonight because he is coming round for dinner.'

Alice was clearly shocked and not at all happy with this idea. 'But aren't I going to be here for dinner tonight too?'

'Yes, so you are and so we can both study those shifty eyes, which I think are rather handsome, dark and sparkly.' Sue took one of her own biscuits and was rather enjoying it. Alice reached for the last one but Ben had now emerged and was quicker off the mark.

'Cool, is Ollie coming around? He is even better at air guitar than you Aunty Alice. You should see him! What's more he can play a real electric guitar and…'

Alice felt that words of wisdom were needed from his aunt. 'Ben, a word of caution, don't ever trust strangers, particularly ones with shifty eyes!'

Alice quickly grabbed the remaining biscuit out of Ben's hands and popped it in her mouth. She grabbed him, cuddled him and tickled him much to Ben's great delight. As they started rolling around on the carpet giggling the doorbell rang and who should emerge but Ollie.

On entering the room, Ollie was surprised to see all the jovial antics going on. Ollie purveyed the woman. He had seen her before but where? Ben immediately jumped up and ran straight to Ollie. Alice felt somewhat put out.

'Ollie, come on. Dad has put the new football net up in the garden. Best of ten penalty shootouts?' Ben enquired.

Alice's nose was now definitely out of joint. Ben always did penalty shoot outs with her.

'Yes, go on, I will follow you out Ben,' replied Ollie who was still racking his memory as to where he had seen the lady. However, as soon as Alice got up from the floor, flashing him a look of great disdain it all came flooding back. Once again, a smirk appeared on his face. 'Ah you are the one who flew over her briefcase and…'

'Yes, indeed,' Alice said curtly. 'What a shame to meet someone who takes such delight in another's misfortune.'

Ollie remembered his inopportune comments at the café and decided to change the subject.

'Hello Sue, lovely to see you again. Can I help at all? I bought that wine Robert said he liked, that Argentinian Malbec.' Ollie went over and kissed Sue on the cheek. This rattled Alice and, although she was rather fond of this wine too, she would have rather the bottle had come without the man.

'Oh Ollie, thank you that is so kind and for the wine too.' Sue reached across to return the kiss on his cheek much to the annoyance of Alice who could clearly see Ollie had duped her very good friend into liking him too. False charm had never impressed her. Offering to help indeed and no doubt would fully have expected her to say *no* to the help as well.

'Come on Ollie,' pleaded Ben impatient to get the game going.

Alice grabbed the ball, 'Ben, Ollie is going to be busy help-ing your mother cook dinner, I'll come out and have a kick around with you.'

Sue soon interceded, 'No that's okay. I sorted it all this morn-ing. I've used the slow cooker. It's curry tonight. Your favourite Alice.'

'Oh, right, well…' Alice was unable to finish her sentence.

'I tell you what why don't we all have a kick a round in the garden. You can go in goal Alice and Ben and I can do the first penalty shoot outs. How about that?' Ollie continued to beam at her with that annoying smirk.

Alice was not amused, she eyed him suspiciously. This man was now trying to ingratiate himself with her family. Who was he anyway? No one really knew anything about him she thought. He had wasted his life travelling hither and thither and, from what Mario said, never seemed to have any money wandering about getting the odd job here and there to pay for his next lot of travelling. No doubt he was used to living off other people's hospitality.

Mario and Sue were usually such good judges of character she thought. However, the problem with men like Ollie was the fact they were often good at charming and wheedling their way into people's lives, taking advantage of other people's good nature and living off their generosity. This man had probably never had a real job in his life. One of those layabouts who clearly thought life owed him a living. There was nothing for it, Alice decided she would have to play the long game here. Show him up for what he really was.

'Right, yes. Let's all go in the garden.' Alice gave Ollie the most supercilious smile she could muster.

Well it is true that Ben's aunt had done penalty shoot outs with him before and her goal keeping wasn't bad but Ben knew Ollie was clearly in another league and Ben was keen to show his Aunty just how Ollie had brought his skills on in the last week or so.

'Right, Aunty Alice. In goal you go. Ball here Ollie don't you think?' Ben was clearly looking for Ollie's good opinion.

'No, Ben,' Alice advised, 'a bit too close to the net don't you think?'

'Oh, I don't know,' retorted Ollie, 'looks just right to me,' flashing a smile towards Alice as Ben readily agreed with him.

'Right here goes…' Ben now seemed to go into Ronaldo mode and kicked the ball so hard it flew straight pass Alice into the top right-hand corner of the net. He had not done that move before thought Alice. Umm not bad. It was now Ollie's turn. Alice was ready for the top left of the net. Surely, he would not want to do the same tactic as Ben. She was ready for him. Although he had obviously taught Ben a trick or two, he wouldn't get this one past her. However, much to Alice's clear annoyance, it once again flew past Alice into the top right of the net. This carried on for some time, both managing to evade Alice's goal saving attempts. Now to add insult to injury, Ollie was hi-fiving Ben after each of their goals. Alice thought Ollie was clearly enjoying her humiliation just a little too much and was buddying up and endearing himself to Ben in an excruci-ating manner that did not become a real man. She thought it more than apt that 'Oliver's Army' by Elvis Costello could be heard on Sue's radio. She felt a definite invasion by this man.

'Right, Ollie' said Alice, 'I think it is time for you to go into goal, don't you? Come on Ben let's show him how it's really done.'

Alice was a dab hand at scoring goals, forgetting of course this was when she was up against a seven-year old and not a forty-something-year old. Ben was able to get most of his goals past Ollie but Alice on the other hand couldn't much to the embarrassment and annoyance of both herself and particularly Ben. Ollie was now enjoying her defeat just a little too much for her liking and once again that self-satisfied, smug grin appeared on his face.

Much to the relief of Alice, Sue finally appeared at the patio doors.

'Ben, it's time for bed now,' Sue called. 'Aunty Alice can read you a couple of pages of your book and that is it then Ben, straight to sleep. Big day tomorrow, football trials for Glossly.'

Ben, upset about the prospect of bed and coupled with his embarrassment of Aunty Alice's sad attempts at scoring, kicked the ball hard into the goal and yelled in frustration as he missed it. Alice went to get his hand to lead him in but he turned to

Ollie instead and firmly placed his hand in Ollie's asking him to read his bed time story instead. Alice's face was a picture. However, Ollie so delighted to be elevated to such a place in Ben's affections, clearly enjoyed the adulation at the expense of Ben's aunt. Sue was quick to offer her friend a sympathetic smile. This did not seem to comfort Alice and on taking the first glass of wine downed it rather too quickly, spilling most of it down her blouse.

Later that evening, they all sat and had dinner together, stained blouse and all. Once again, Ollie seemed to be ingratiating himself with his dinner guests.

'This really is delicious Sue, you really have a knack with curry, you must let me have the recipe.'

Sue beamed him a warm smile and topped Ollie's glass up. 'Yes, my friend Nisha is a dab hand at curries, I got the recipe from her'.

Robert asked Ollie about his recent travels to Eastern Europe and Alice grew very bored of hearing nothing but Ollie going on about it. Robert and Sue seemed captivated by it all. Alice just kept downing the Malbec rather too quickly and Robert's attempts to keep the second, now almost empty, bottle closer to him was not working.

'So, tell me Ollie,' Alice enquired, 'how exactly do you manage to fund all of these travels? Notwithstanding, of course, the tax payer's money supplying you with benefits.'

Robert looked extremely embarrassed at his sister's remarks and, deciding to ignore them, went back to their conversation on the Russian underground system. Alice, however, having downed the fifth glass of wine by now was not perturbed by her brother's attempt to skip over her rudeness.

'So, Ollie, where are you staying whilst you are helping out my very special friend Mario?'

'Mario has kindly let me stay at his apartment. Really good of him.'

'Oh, and now living rent free too, very good set up indeed.' Alice muttered under her breath but just loud enough to ensure the man could hear.

Sue flashed Alice her Paddington Bear stare but Ollie knew what Alice probably thought of him. He was used to this.

'I, of course, insisted Mario deduct the accommodation off my wages but you know Mario, ever the generous man and just wouldn't accept any rent. Mario is always so kind but I would never want to take advantage of such a good man.'

'Umm, well so you say,' Alice muttered, once again.

Robert thought it best to change the subject altogether. 'By the way Alice, I have managed to find Miss Havisham a part time job at the office. I have asked her to pop by tomorrow.'

Alice, of course, loved her brother but the few glasses of wine, and his kindness to her old friend, had upped Robert, even more, in her affections. After all, it was so sad that after all those years of devoted service to Mr Frobersham that Miss Havisham should have been fired in such a way. She went round the dinner table and gave him a big hug.

'Oh, big brother, you are the best! Miss Havisham has always wanted to pay her way in life and would never be the sort to accept handouts just to satisfy a need to indulge her pleasures.'

'What pleasures?' spouted Sue. 'I can't imagine Miss Havisham having many of those!' They all laughed apart from Alice.

'Well,' Alice continued, most surprised at her friend's

unkindness to Miss Havisham, 'she has devoted her life to her work Sue that is why. Some people feel to earn a living, scrimp and save for a house, not live off the state and pay their own way in life rather than living off others is the decent thing to do.' Alice continued to slurp her wine, eyes firmly fixed on Ollie with eyebrows raised as if to say put that in your pipe and smoke it.

Ollie knew Alice had been in for a rough ride recently and decided to leave it there. He had heard nothing but great things about Alice from Mario but this didn't seem to be the person Mario had talked about. He didn't want to offend his hosts by challenging her, he would let it go. She clearly wasn't in a good place. After the meal, he said his thankyous and goodbyes and headed for home.

When the door was firmly shut behind Ollie, Alice smiled at her triumph of getting rid of the man. However, Sue's look of utter disapproval said it all. Alice decided it was maybe time for bed as her head was reeling somewhat so she sloped off quietly to the guest bedroom and was soon asleep.

Again, that night, she had another one of her strange dreams.

She was tied up in a chair and unable to move. She was back in that same old hotel room. To the side of her chair was a large bed and on the other side there was a very long window with deep purple curtains that stretched across the whole length of the window.

'Hello, hello, is anyone there? Can you help me!' She started to wriggle back and forth on her chair but it was no good the rope would not budge but, instead, just kept getting tighter.

She felt herself crying uncontrollably. The room seemed very much colder and the long row of curtains started to vigorously blow back and forth. Alice heard the thunder out of the window and lightning flash across the ceiling. Her hair, which was now very long and brunette rather than her short, fair hair, was blowing around her face. She was wearing a long, scarlet Chanel gown with one of her ranges of velvet buttons, encrusted with small, sparkling diamonds. Unfortunately, Chanel had spoiled the gown a little with two Tit-Tassels but, as she looked in the mirror, she could see a woman who looked like a million dollars and somehow years younger than her actual age.

Suddenly, out of the middle curtain who should appear but Sean Connery dressed in black from head to toe. Removing his balaclava, he looked straight at her.

'Shh, don't worry stay very still, I'm here now and I will release you in a jiffy.' He was about to move forward when, out of the other side of the window from behind the curtains, who should appear but Daniel Craig, once again dressed in black. He also removed his balaclava and held up his hand to Sean as if to try and stop him.

'No, it is fine, I think you will find I have this one covered.'

However, within the shake of a nanny goat's tail, Pierce Brosnan then appeared.

'I don't think so gentlemen, this lady is fine with me. I will sort this one. Hello Alice, this won't take long.' Pierce started to walk across towards her.

Alice, now stunned into silence, just couldn't think of a response.

'Look here,' said Sean holding his hand up to stop them both. 'I haven't travelled all this way from Russia to be headed off at the pass, so excuse me gentleman but I'm rescuing this lady.'

'Ah, I don't think so,' exclaimed Daniel. 'Strict instructions from M to take charge of this operation and you know what Judy is like she won't want me to mess this one up!'

At this point, Pierce interjected with a very manly and firm stance, 'Sorry gentlemen but Alice has always preferred me as James Bond so I think this lady is mine.'

Both Daniel and Sean were clearly shocked and not very happy about this.

'Is this true Alice? Have you always preferred Pierce?' Both looking totally bewildered.

Alice looked across at Sean and Daniel feeling very sheepish that they had come all this way but had to admit that, yes, Pierce, was her favourite Bond. However, she really didn't want to offend either of them knowing all the trouble they had gone to. She decided she would have to handle this one carefully.

'As handsome, and as clearly brave and charming as you both are, well yes, I have to admit, I have to be honest, Pierce is my favourite Bond. After all I grew up with him as Bond, so, no offence to either of you. Anyway, Sean you were a little bit before my time and well Daniel you're a bit too rough around the edges, so, if you don't mind, I'd like Pierce to rescue me. But, thank you so much though Mr Bond (looking at Sean) and Mr Bond (looking at Daniel).'

Daniel and Sean did not look very pleased about this at all. 'Well, I have to say this is most irregular and well fancy choosing that Bond,' (pointing at Pierce) exclaimed Daniel.

'Yes, very odd indeed? I was considered to be the best Bond there ever was and the best looking one you know.' Sean was clearly not happy either.

'Well, in that case, we're off, I think we've got better things to do and other ladies to rescue,' announced Daniel.

And with that they both jumped out of the window and

disappeared as fast as they had arrived.

Pierce, looking rather pleased with himself and very flattered at being chosen, gave Alice his warm Irish smile and his eyes sparkled making her tingle all over.

'Now, young lady, let's see if we can untie these ropes and then I think you deserve a long passionate kiss, don't you?'

Now speechless, Alice nodded readily in agreement. Pierce untied the ropes and all Alice could focus on was his beautiful blue eyes and silky hair. Yes, this was her destiny to be kissed by Pierce. It all made sense. She put her lips together and closed her eyes, ready and expectant.

'Excuse me?' A voice came from out of the shadows of the room. 'I don't think you want to do that.'

Alice and Pierce both looked up and who should be standing there but Ollie. He moved forward.

'Definitely not a good idea Pierce.'

Alice was aghast! 'Oh my God, not you! But I am tied up you silly man, I am being rescued, go away,' Alice demanded.

'Yes, go away,' Pierce agreed and held Alice's head firmly between his hands. 'Now, where were we?'

Alice lent forward ready to receive his kiss. She could feel his warm breath on her face and felt a tingling sensation down her spine.

'Like I said, I wouldn't do that.' Ollie was so persistent. 'She had curry for dinner tonight Pierce and you know how that disagrees with you.'

'Curry for tea?' said Pierce. 'Is that true Alice?'

'Well, yes, but…'

'Ah sorry can't kiss a woman with curry on her breath, definite turn off.'

'What!' exclaimed Alice. 'No wait a minute Pierce! Come back.' But it was to no avail. Pierce had already made his way to the window. Waved goodbye and disappeared along with the other Bonds back down the window whence he had come from. All she could feel was sheer anger and frustration.

'How dare you, how dare you!' she shouted at Ollie.

However, Ollie smiled such a smug grin folding his arms and looking at her and shaking his head with real disapproval.

'So, what have you been up to, to get tied up like that then?' Ollie smirked his usual annoying grin.

Alice was livid and started kicking the chair back and forth but just couldn't untie herself.

'Would you like me to untie you?' enquired Ollie.

'You snake, you snake in the grass. Don't you dare come near me! Don't you dare!'

'Right then, well if you don't want to be released, I better be off then.' And with that Ollie waved goodbye and jumped out of the window too.

'What, hang on, wait a minute, you can't leave me here!'

But it was too late Ollie had disappeared.

'You can't leave me on my own!'

Alice woke with a start and, turning her pillow over, thrust her face into it with a huge grunt of disproval. 'That man. He gets everywhere!'

4

Christmas Eve

Christmas was upon them all. It was now Christmas Eve and Alice was glad of the usual invite to go to Sue's for Christmas day lunch. Christmas had always been one of her favourite times of the year but with recent events she knew it was going to be much harder and she just had to keep herself occupied. Christmas, being single, she feared would be difficult because, at her age, most of the people around her either had partners or were married or now remarried and much happier. No matter how much company you are with it can never make up for those feelings of solitude when you are in a room full of couples chattering away, joking or sharing those intimate moments.

Alice had decorated the Christmas tree in her own living room and, as usual, had ordered it from her local garden centre. The delivery man did his usual huffing and puffing to get the tree up the stairs and then attempt to get it through the far-too-narrow door. He didn't understand why she always ordered one far too big for her small apartment but, well, she was the customer and he did always get a good tip from her.

It was only two o'clock and Alice had already got through three of her cherished and favourite movies whilst wrapping her presents. Obviously, it was taking a lot longer than usual with all the distractions of John Wayne in The Quiet Man. She had replayed the scene (several times) where Maureen O'Hara is cleaning his cottage and his arrival surprises her. She is about to run out of the cottage when he grabs her and kisses her long and hard.

'They don't make men like that anymore,' Alice sighed.

Alice then moved on to what must have been her thousandth visit to *Sense and Sensibility* with one of her favourite actors, Alan Rickman, as Colonel Brandon. His performance had been just as she had imagined the real Colonel Brandon to be when she had first read the book. The gorgeous Hugh Grant played the charming Edward Ferrers and the whole feel-good feeling by the end of the film was enough to raise anyone's spirits. This film had then led on to When Harry Met Sally. After a few G&T's, Alice liked to do the pretend orgasm scene which she felt she played a tad better than Meg Ryan. All of these films kept her busy and whiled away the time.

'There, Ben is all done.' She looked pleased at her attempt to disguise the fact that she had bought him the latest Chelsea football kit and posters that he had hinted at so many times and wrapped the kit around a toy giraffe. Mario would be back for New Year and Alice had bought him some new leather driving gloves. Sue had wanted an M&S gift voucher to get some new clothes and Robert always enjoyed a wine voucher so he could choose something for his collection. Miss Havisham had a new scarf to add to her already plentiful supply; her gang of friends and wider family were treated to smellies and Hotel Chocolat. Thankfully Ollie was not going to be there much to the disappointment of Sue who liked how Ollie brought a bit of extra sunshine into the house but Alice certainly didn't have any regrets about that. The usual party games would not have been the same with Ollie around. No, thankfully, Ollie had some other event on and that was going to keep him busy for most of the day. However, just in case he did turn up, like some bad penny, she had bought him a bottle of the Argentinian Malbec, knowing she could drink it herself in his absence.

Alice wondered into the bedroom and started to pack her night bag. She opened the wardrobe door and saw Mark's black suit there. She remembered the last time he wore it was to her dad's funeral. Dad had suffered from dementia and had gone the same way as her mum had only a few years earlier. Was this to be her fate too, she pondered? Dad had started wandering out in the middle of the night, left pans of food burning and by the end of his life seemed to have only a few glimpses of lucidness. She had spent an increasing amount of time being his carer which she knew had placed a strain on her and Mark's relationship. But she had convinced herself that Mark understood. Although Mark had lost his dad when he was very young, his mum had gone exactly the same way and he knew the realities of it all. Alice had been there for him but, when it had come down to her dad's illness, it must have all been too much for him. Perhaps it had reminded him too much of his own loss.

Mark had started to withdraw. It was very gradual at first and then the late nights at work and the weekends away with his friends had become too regular an occurrence. Then the fateful day had arrived. Alice still remembered that day as if it is was only yesterday. He had come home earlier than usual and seemed very surprised to see her, not remembering she had taken the afternoon off to let the boiler repair man in. Mark had walked straight into the bedroom with hardly a word. Alice didn't like to follow him in, no he obviously needed a bit of space. His Man Cave. She didn't think too much of it and thought he had had yet another bad day at the office. However, ten minutes later he appeared, bags packed and he just stood there. At first, she thought he needed to go on another business trip but there was something in his demeanour, his face that told her different.

'I am sorry, this just isn't working for me any more Alice, I can't do this any longer.' Mark couldn't look her in the eye.

She stood in stunned silence. Her head was still trying to take in the packed bag.

'I am really sorry,' and with that Mark headed for the door.

'But I don't understand, look, what are you talking about?' Alice's heart was pounding. 'I know you have been so busy recently at work and you have obviously been under a lot of stress.'

Unperturbed, Mark now having reached the front door, started to open it.

'No wait, just hang on, we can sort this. Maybe you just need a break. That is it, you just need some time, that is fine but don't leave like this, we need to talk.'

Alice remembered how she had pleaded with Mark but he still remained silent. He shook his head from side to side and walked straight through the door. No amount of remonstrating could alter his course. Out he went onto the landing and down to the main entrance. She had followed him like some lost puppy.

'Mark, please let's just talk about this,' but it was to no avail. Mark walked out, across the car park, got into his car and didn't even glance back.

She hadn't seen him since.

Was it just a break he needed? They had spent many years together and she was sure deep down that he would come back. They were made for each other and this was just not like him.

Alice smelt his jacket. There was still his Chanel aftershave lingering. Her mind flashed back to Gone with the Wind. What was it Scarlett O'Hara had said *'I'll go home and I'll think of some way to get him back, after all tomorrow is another day.'* That was her philosophy on Mark. She would get him back. He just needed time.

She finished packing her bag and wondered over to the window to draw the curtains. Yet again, there was Number 24 in the car park. This time with a different man, opening the door for her to his Porsche. She was so very beautiful and elegantly dressed. She had an air of great confidence about her. The handsome man put her suitcase in his boot and off they drove, going, no doubt, she thought to somewhere very glamourous for the rest of the Christmas season. Mark had opened the car door for her at first, but it hadn't lasted long. Familiarity breeds contempt she recalled Sue saying.

Alice carefully checked her apartment and headed for the door. There was always the New Year's Eve party that one of her girlfriends would hold. Perhaps, yes, just perhaps, Mark would be there and everything could go back to the way it was.

5

Ollie

Ollie wasn't keen on Christmas, never had been. His mum and dad had separated when he was quite young and Christmas day had always been full of arguments and disagreements of who was going to have him and for how long.

This resulted in Ollie never feeling comfortable with either of them, particularly at Christmas. His mum seemed to be very busy with a string of male clientele visiting the house which she always claimed was down to the fact she was a sex therapist and yoga instructor but as Ollie got older, he wasn't so sure. Her clients seemed to make a lot of unnecessary noise and the floorboards always creaked so loudly.

Ollie's dad, on the other hand, put all of his passion into cars, spending most of his time either talking about them or fiddling about with them in his garage. Ollie became used to being carted from one house to the other and fending for himself. So much so that, at sixteen, having dropped out of school, he saw an advert in a local paper for fruit pickers in Bordeaux and decided to pack his bags and off he went never to return to either of them.

Wherever he travelled he had always found work whether it was picking fruit, serving as a waiter, a washer upper or packing boxes for a variety of food manufacturers. It didn't bother him.

He just enjoyed the travelling and meeting new people. His godfather, Mario, had been very good to him and very often put him in contact with friends who were able to offer him short-term work.

During the winter, Ollie often went to work at a small ski resort in Innsbruck at one of the local restaurants. He had particularly got on well with the owner's son, Florian, who was as talented as his father at cooking and had gained quite a reputation for himself in his local village. Florian decided to set up his own restaurant in London and had always invited Ollie to spend a few days with him over the Christmas period.

Florian helped a local charity by supplying leftover food from the restaurant and every Christmas, along with a few other local cafés and restaurants, helped run a food kitchen for the homeless. Ollie was always keen to help out and both had spent many a Christmas morning preparing and serving out soup and turkey baps to whoever was in need.

Florian, like Ollie, had always been a confirmed bachelor. However, he had eventually met a woman who he had employed as a temporary front of house member of staff and love seemed to have blossomed between them. Both never looked back and soon settled into married life with ease. Ollie was pleased for his friend's happiness and thought that with their easy-going natures they were well matched.

It was getting to that time in the morning when most of the food had been served and both of them were now glad of a well-earned break. The queue had been relentless and both had been either preparing or serving soup and turkey baps since quite early that morning.

'The two of you make a great couple Florian, she is a lovely woman,' Ollie said as he wondered over to the bench to sit down.

'Ah, yes, Emily is like a breath of fresh air.' Florian's eyes lit up every time he spoke of her.

'And what about you my friend? Still the confirmed bachelor?' Florian knew already what the answer would be but he asked in the hope that maybe Ollie had found that special someone.

'Of course not, you know me, no point settling down, never in one place long enough!' Ollie popped open a bag of crisps and waded in.

'You never, know Ollie. It may just hit you one day; there she will be the woman of your dreams and there is nothing you will be able to do about it!' Florian turned to look at Emily who was engaged in conversation with one of the other volunteer helpers.

'Well, I have to admit looking at you both and then Robert and Sue and their son Ben, you know the family I told you about, I can see how settling down might appeal to some but it's not for me, Florian. Mario doesn't call me the wandering nomad without good reason!' Ollie continued to devour his crisps.

'I like the freedom of travelling, meeting new people and not getting caught up in the usual rush and manic lifestyle so many people lead. I have what I need and life is very simple but good.'

Florian studied his friend. He knew that the relationship Ollie had with his mum had never been very positive and felt this had obviously impacted on Ollie's relationships with women. Ollie never seemed to be in relationships for that long.

62

'Well, my friend, you have never really had a home to call your own and you may find settling down one day is just what you need. There is nothing like coming home to someone who loves you, sometimes you don't know how lonely you have really been until you have someone to share your life with.'

Ollie's experiences of women had generally been negative or short lived or both and besides he had never stayed in one place long enough to have allowed anything to come to any real fruition. No, he had decided he was better off alone.

'Being in a couple isn't for everyone Florian. I know many happy single people who like it that way.' Ollie lobbed the empty crisp packet over his friend's head and it neatly landed in the bin.

'I hope you can stay for dinner tonight, Ollie,' enquired his friend.

'Yes, that would be lovely but, if it's okay with you, after dinner I said I would call in on Robert and Sue tonight. I have a present for Ben and Robert has a great collection of gin which he would like me to sample. The only negative is meeting the rottweiler again.'

'Oh, that doesn't sound like an animal to have around a child?!' Florian sounded alarmed at the prospect of a young child being in a house with a potentially dangerous animal.

'No, not a dog – Alice!'

'Ah a woman, you make her sound scary!' Florian smiled.

'Yes, she is. She's Robert's sister. Let's put it this way - as attractive as she clearly is, she is as mad as a March hare with a bit of a temper. No thank you. Now let's get back to the turkey baps.'

Florian shook his head laughing and followed his friend

back to the serving area. Emily came to join them and they all continued together to serve. Emily liked Ollie and was glad he could spend some of Christmas with them. Although Ollie seemed a confident person, Emily liked the fact he was a very modest man who had a gentle, easy-going manner about him. He had a vulnerability about him. He was so similar to Florian; she could understand why they had both become very good friends.

6

Malcolm

B en flung open the door and jumped on his Aunt's bed.
'Come on Aunty Alice, get up! Mum and Dad won't get
up they say we have to wait yet *another* thirty minutes. Come
on! You and I can start Christmas.'

Alice managed to open one eye and reached out for the
bedside clock. 'Ben, sweetheart it is only five o'clock, give
Father Christmas a chance to get round everyone's house. Now
come in and have a cuddle if you like.'

'He has been! Aunty Alice, he has been!' Ben was now bounc-
ing and jumping on her bed with a little bit too much energy
for a woman who had downed a bottle of Prosecco the night
before. Ben was most persistent, 'Come down with me, come
down now. Everything is under the tree and Father Christmas
has eaten the brandy and mince pie!'

'Ben, you are not allowed downstairs without mum and
dad, you know that.' Alice yawned, still only managing to
open one eye.

Ben looked sheepish. Alice suddenly grabbed him and they
both started playfighting noisily under the duvet. The door
opened.

'For goodness sake!' said Robert 'Who's the biggest kid?
Quieten down the pair of you. No Christmas presents until

7.30 for either of you, you…'

They finished his sentence for him, 'Know the score, George Doors' and they both giggled.

Life couldn't get any better than this Ben thought. Christmas day, Mum and Dad and Aunty Alice and no Uncle Mark! Ben still recalled that time when Mark had shouted at him when he had accidentally spilt his lemonade over his suit trousers. Mark had gone AWOL. He had a fierce temper and really lost it but far worse than Mum or Dad or Aunty Alice ever did. No, he liked it now with just Aunty Alice.

They hugged and Ben told Alice all about his football trials and how he had managed to score more goals than even the best goal scorer in school, Fred Barnett had. He was sure he would get in to the team now.

'However, I think I could play even better if Father Christmas has remembered my Chelsea kit.' Ben's eyes said it all.

'Ah, well, Father Christmas has lots of presents to get at Christmas. Expensive business you know. It might have been some other child's turn to get a football kit, Ben.'

Ben put his eyebrows together firmly. 'Well, Father Christmas always manages to buy Fred Barnett a new kit, EVERY YEAR.'

Alice didn't quite know what to say to that one so she changed the subject. 'So, what did you eye-spy then when you were downstairs?' Alice enquired.

'I think I have a wonky giraffe, Aunty Alice. I hope Father Christmas doesn't think I am still a baby and has bought me a cuddly toy?'

'We must be grateful for what we get, Ben. Father Christmas doesn't like demanding children, you know. Besides it might be a wonky giraffe that needs a good home and lots of love Ben.'

'Umm,' said Ben now feeling a bit guilty. Of course, he would look after the giraffe if it needed it.

'Besides,' continued Aunty Alice, 'I think I spotted a legless Ostrich too, when I went down there this morning.'

Ben now looked really alarmed. Alice smiled a mischievous grin at him and they both started to giggle and the giggles turned into laughter, once again.

As the laughter rang through the house, and Sue and Robert had decided that no more sleep was to be had, they all started Christmas Day.

Alice loved Christmas lunch it was always a treat. Sue was a great cook and Robert was always in his element carving the turkey. This year, much to Alice's surprise, Robert was doing most of the cooking and there was a lot more swearing than usual coming out of the kitchen. Robert could cook but he wasn't as good as Sue and he certainly wasn't as well versed on turning to a Christmas meal with all the trimmings to a deadline. Robert had put the turkey back into the oven three times declaring it would never cook and what was the point of cooking the brussels sprouts for guests who never ate them.

Eventually, only two hours later than planned, dinner was ready and it was a real feast. Sue, being Sue, had invited the usual waifs and strays of the neighbourhood.

Alice looked around the table. There was Miss Havisham sat at the end of the table wearing her new scarf and look-ing as if she may have had too many sherries already. Poor woman, Alice thought. All those years dedicated to that silly old goat, Frobersham. Alice recalled how Miss Havisham had once revealed to Alice that she had been engaged. Her parents didn't approve of her fiancé so she was going to run off to

Skegness with him. Sadly, though, he had gone off with her sister instead. Miss Havisham didn't feel bitter about though. After all, as she explained, 'My sister and I were identical twins, he was always getting us muddled up.'

Malcolm, Robert's partner at the accountancy firm, was sitting next to Miss Havisham, and was in full throttle talking about his prize catch from his last fishing expedition which everyone teased him about because the fish always got bigger and bigger with every retelling. Miss Havisham, being a lady with excellent manners, just did what any polite guest would do and looked truly impressed at his clear prowess as a fisherman.

Alice liked Malcolm and knew he had been through a rough time too. His wife Maud had done a Shirley Valentine on Malcolm four years ago and so, ever since, he had been a guest at Sue's every Christmas. Malcolm had been married for some years when Maud decided to go to Greece with a few old friends but, alas, had never returned. Malcolm told them all how he had received a rather short letter from Maud, he thought, considering their twenty-five years of married life. She had simply explained that she had met a man called Kostas who understood her every need and knew how to fulfil a woman.

Malcolm didn't seem too bothered about losing Maud because in recent years, as he explained to Alice, 'She had become very demanding in the bedroom department and he really didn't feel he had the energy any more, particularly after a day's fishing.' No, what had bothered Malcolm more was the clearing of their bank account, the ISAs in Maud's name and the disappearance of several of their investments. 'It's just a shame to have lost all that interest,' Malcolm lamented.

On the other side of the table sat Sue's mum Betty. She

always reminded Alice of Maureen Lipman from those BT ads years ago. No matter how bad a situation was, Betty would find the positives. So much like Sue, Alice thought. Betty was a woman who also loved her gin and could drink any person under the table and frequently did. Alice loved her feistiness, no one messed with Betty. Ben adored his nanna and was enjoying all the praise of how grown up he looked in his Chelsea kit and surely Lampard would be mad not to put this skilful young player in his junior squad.

Next to Alice was Miss Prendergast, Sue's next door and somewhat elderly and outspoken neighbour. She certainly always said it just how it was and never suffered fools gladly. She was a confirmed spinster who was never backward in coming forward about her distaste and dislike of men (well apart from Robert who she thought was the salt of the earth).

'No, Alice,' Miss Prendergast said in a very loud voice, 'you are better off without him, heed my words. These men come into your house, never wipe their shoes on the mat and always leave the toilet seat up.'

'Well, I don't know about that,' protested Malcolm, 'I always put the loo seat down.'

'Umm.' Miss Prendergast looked at Malcolm as if extremely doubtful of that particular claim.

Alice knew that some time ago Miss Prendergast had been involved with a man too but no one had ever broached the subject. Miss Prendergast had, despite her tough exterior, a kind of vulnerability about her and a sadness that belied her demeanour. Rumour had it that she had been involved with Terry from her local butchers in town but he and Miss Prendergast had fallen out over his sausages. Apparently, he had started giving her best friend, Julia, an extra free sausage or two as well.

On the other side of Miss Prendergast sat Ben. Well, he was kind of sitting at the table but he kept springing up in his brand-new Chelsea kit to add the next bit to his Lego batman empire or pretending he was scoring a goal like Pulisic.

And, there, of course, sat herself, the latest waif and stray to add to the collection.

The day continued with the ritual ceremony of lighting the Christmas pud, which, everyone declared they were far too full to eat, apart from Ben, of course, who proclaimed he was still so hungry he could eat a horse. The usual games of Charades ensued where Malcolm always forgot which hand signs were for what and just ended up making some dodgy hand movements.

'It's a *Play*,' he would say hopefully.

'No Malcolm that's the gesture for a bull, I think?' Robert shouted.

Miss Havisham did her usual rendition of '*Bed Knobs and Broomsticks*' much to the delight of all, particularly when she got to the knob bit.

The Monopoly board then came out which Ben always grew bored of, particularly as he lost his money so quickly. However, Malcolm was in his usual element. Yet again, as per usual, he won the game much to his great delight.

'Well, I do know a thing or two about money you know. In the blood as an accountant you know.'

Several hours passed. Then there was silence. All were asleep on the sofa, even Ben, who had snuggled in between his mum and dad with his poster of Frank Lampard on his lap and nodded off with a look of utter contentment on his face. Ben dreamt about how Frank was now the leading manager of the world, leading Chelsea to victory in every competition. Ben was his top striker and they went out to Big Al's every day to discuss tactics.

Evening came and, with everyone now refreshed, they went out for their usual stroll around the park. Malcolm had continued his discussion on fly fishing which Alice was now having to endure but he was such a nice guy, Alice didn't mind humouring him. Malcolm and Robert went back many years. They had been at school together, two academic years above Alice and Sue. Both Robert and Malcolm had ended up at Bristol doing a Maths degree and then had decided to go into Accountancy. They worked a while for Arnold Hill and Co, one of the best accountancy firms in London, before deciding to set up their own business.

Malcolm had been like a second brother to Alice and he was always full of very sensible and practical advice having handled her tax return for years. Malcom had always amused Alice. Here was a very decent man but one who was very preoccupied with himself. It was true he was a very pleasant looking man but he never knew quite how to handle his height of six feet five inches. His clothes never quite fitted him and the two true obsessions of his life, fishing and accountancy meant that any conversations would inevitably lead to fish or money or both.

'Financially, you are in a very good position Alice. Like Sue said, you can bide your time. Find something you really want to do or retire early and take up a hobby like fishing; a great sport to simply lose yourself in. There is nothing like the feeling of reeling in a big one. Did I tell you the story of the salmon I caught up in Lanarkshire?'

Alice keen to put this line of conversation to bed, tried to

71

alter the course of the conversation. 'Yes, Malcom, fab story but you were saying about my financial situation?'

'Ah yes, I can introduce you to some financial adviser friends of mine and they can take a closer look at some of those investments of yours. One of them, Paul, is a keen fisherman too. Caught a huge bream the other week…'

Alice could feel that the wine was now wearing off and she was now in need of another glass but maybe something stronger.

Robert looked over at Malcolm and Alice walking together and smiled at Sue. Sue immediately picked up on his meaning, responding, 'Don't even go there! Alice and Malcolm! No way!'

Robert just kept on smiling. He knew that Malcolm had always had a thing for Alice but she had only ever had eyes for Mark. Robert had never liked the man and he felt he was never good enough for her. Alice just couldn't seem to see past Mark for who he really was. Malcolm on the other hand was solid, reliable, had a good job and would really look after his little sister. Okay he had a big passion for fishing which could sometimes overtake everything else, and a little careful with his money, but Alice could sort all that out.

They continued their stroll and as Alice got to the stile, Malcolm was swift to help her over.

'Gosh Malcolm I know I have had one or two or maybe quite a bit more Prosecco than you but I don't believe I need that much support!' Alice thought Malcolm was forgetting how strong he was, he seemed to have a very tight hold of her indeed.

Malcolm smiled and continued to do up her scarf around her neck. 'There, that's better, you were letting all that cold air in.' He tried to give her a long hard stare in the eyes but it was completely lost on Alice who had spotted a rather good-looking jogger run by, smiling at her.

Later that evening, after their long walk, the turkey and baked potatoes were all on the table and the second feast started. Yet again, Alice had continued with the wine and the food was interrupted by the occasional karaoke renditions of '*500 miles*' by the *Proclaimers* and '*Merry Christmas*' by *Slade* with Alice and Ben on the microphone and Malcolm and Robert playing the drums on the turned over Christmas cake and biscuit tins.

Miss Havisham had made the Irish coffees which everyone said were absolutely marvellous, not wanting to point out that she had forgotten to put the whiskey in.

After a few games of *Articulate* and *Would I Lie To You*, most of the visitors left, apart from Malcolm who had fallen asleep on Alice's shoulder. On the other side was Ben who had also nodded off. Sue had retired some time earlier looking very pale indeed Alice thought and very unlike her to miss the evening fun and games but, well, they had gone for a very long walk. Robert came and lifted Ben up from the sofa.

'Time for bed little man.' Off they went.

Alice carefully lifted Malcolm's head off her shoulder. She headed for the Christmas tree and spotted an unopened present. Malcolm, disturbed by her leaving, sat down beside her on the floor. He picked the gift up and handed it to her.

'Here's mine,' he said.

'Oh Malcolm, that is so kind and thoughtful.' Alice was intrigued as to what this little box might hold. She quickly unwrapped the gold ribbon and paper.

Alice couldn't believe her eyes. Of all the presents he could have given her, 'Ah Malcolm, how lovely Tit-Tassels!'

'Yes, apparently they are all the rage at the moment. All you ladies are wearing them. These are the special deluxe ones with extra-long tassels.'

Alice felt she mustn't be ungrateful and gave Malcolm a kiss on the cheek but hadn't expected what came next. Malcolm suddenly took hold of her face, firmly between his hands, and kissed her on the lips.

Alice's eyes lit up like a Belisha beacon. What *was* going on with Malcolm today? To make matters worse, whilst he was in the thralls of this unwelcome passionate encounter, Ollie appeared at the living room door. Alice pulled herself away as quickly as she could.

'Not interrupting anything I hope?' Ollie's annoying grin had returned. Robert who had also appeared just behind Ollie, looking highly delighted.

'No, no certainly not,' Alice insisted as she bounced up as quick as she could from the floor. Malcolm also looking some-what flustered, returned to the sofa.

'Don't let us interrupt you!' Robert said. 'Come on Ollie, come into the conservatory and I'll give a you a taste of that Macclesfield Forest Gin I was telling you about.'

Alice's head, now reeling, made her excuses and hastily went to bed while Malcolm just nodded embarrassingly and retreated to the kitchen to join Robert and Ollie.

Well, what a day Alice thought to herself. Malcolm! What on earth had got into him? He just must have had too much to drink. So, unlike him! Alice tucked herself up in bed and was soon fast asleep.

7

Sit Down Next to Me

It was a couple of days after Christmas and Alice was getting ready to go out with the usual crowd of friends. They usually met every month for a girl's night out. Alice, though, had missed quite a few of these gatherings in recent months, preferring to stay in rather than have to answer kindly meant questions about her love life or rather lack of it. Sue had insisted she come along tonight as it would do her the world of good to get out.

Alice now needed something to wear and was in her bedroom sorting out her clothes. She had strewn them all over the bed and had sorted them into two piles: clothes that she no longer liked and the second pile clothes that simply didn't fit her anymore. The last one was the biggest pile. Alice was sure it wouldn't be long before she lost a bit of weight and would fit into them again. The clothes she hadn't been so keen on did at least fit her, so she decided to put the whole lot back in the wardrobe. Alice settled for a loose-fitting silk blouse.

'God, I have got to lose weight,' she moaned as she stuffed the remaining chocolate bar into her mouth followed by a gulp of her large G&T.

The doorbell rang.

Alice dragged herself off the bed and opened the door to

find Number 24 standing there. The usual vision of loveliness was even lovelier. There she stood with her long hair tied up in a messy but somehow elegant knot and her very tight dress hugged every curve. She really did have an hour glass figure and her shoes seemed to defy gravity.

'I am sorry to disturb you, but I have run out of milk. I wondered if I might trouble you for some,' asked Number 24 in a very well spoken, sexy and very-much-like-Joanna-Lumley style voice.

Alice was happy to oblige her new neighbour and went to get the milk thinking this might be an opportunity to get to know her a little more. The last time she had tried to acquaint herself with Number 24 it hadn't gone well.

Alice returned, only to find, however, a tall, dark and very handsome man had now appeared. He lifted Number 24 right off her feet declaring, 'We will worry about the milk later honey,' and he proceeded to carry her back down the corridor both laughing.

'Right, no milk today then?' Alice murmured. 'Yes, well any time, happy to be of service, no need to thank me!' But it was to no avail they were far too engrossed with each other to even notice her. Alice banged her own door shut and returned the milk to the fridge. There was nothing worse than feeling insignificant and neither of them had thanked her for her trouble.

'Manners - people just don't have any these days. Anyway, how does she manage it!' Alice shook her head in disbelief. She couldn't exactly remember the man who she had got into the Porsche with on Christmas Eve but this one, she was sure, looked different.

Young people just don't commit these days, Alice thought

to herself. Boyfriends that aren't boyfriends 'just friends' but clearly aren't 'just friends.' Having sex seemed to be just another pastime, a bit of fun.

She mused on this. Lucky devils she thought.

Alice finished getting herself ready but felt she really couldn't be bothered to go. On Sue arriving at the flat, she tried to make her excuses but Sue was having none of it.

'Your friends have missed you and they just want to make sure you're okay. Besides, when is the last time we all went out and had a real good laugh? Come on, we could all do with a fun night out.'

Alice thought back to the last one just after Mark had left her and remembered the umbrella and the policeman incident.

'Umm, well I guess it could be but it's just Lucy in particular, she's always in your face and wants to know every gaudy detail of everyone's life. I swear she thrives on other's misfortunes.'

'No, that's not fair, she is just,' Sue hesitated trying to find a kinder description 'she is well…'

'Bloomin' nosey!' Alice had no problem mincing her words.

'No, not nosey, just perhaps overly inquisitive and doesn't always think before she speaks but I am sure her heart is in the right place.' Sue felt happy with her character portrait of Lucy. 'And, what's more I have told all of them, there must be absolutely no Mark references or anything alluding to him, okay?' Sue looked hopeful that this would do the trick.

Alice looked doubtful. She was wary of Lucy who had really been more of a friend of Mark's at Uni than Alice's. Alice always wished Lucy had an off switch because she could be very loud and intrusive at times and never seemed to display much tact. However, Sue looked in one of those 'not taking any crap or no for an answer moods' so Alice acquiesced.

'Right, okay, I will go!' Alice knew Sue would not be happy until she agreed to the evening out. As annoying as her persistence was, she adored Sue's positivity in life and her conviction that all people were good at heart and that was a quality Alice loved in her. After all she could tolerate Lucy, providing it was in small doses. And, as Sue had promised, no one was going to mention Mark.

So, Alice made her way to Zizi's feeling confident that her silk blouse was covering all manner of sins and feeling that that Sue was right, a girl's night out would do her the power of good.

When they arrived, all her friends were already there and sat at their usual table. Lucy with mirror in hand and touching up her already-touched-up lipstick. Mary, Alice's old flat mate, and her girlfriend Cara were there. They had both been together now for some time. Then there was Simon looking incredible as usual; Sam, another close friend to Alice who had worked as her PA for a few months at Frobersham's to cover for Miss Havisham while an elderly aunt needed looking after. Finally, there was Nisha who Alice had got to know through Sue.

After all the usual hellos and how are yous Lucy launched straight in, 'So then, Alice, how is it going without Mark?' she enquired.

'Yes, what a bastard, that's what I say, I'd castrate the lot of them.' Cara announced.

'Castration just isn't enough,' said Mary.

Sam then joined the chorus of indignations. 'Fancy leaving you, just after your dad's funeral and all. What a bastard!'

Alice was lost for words and flashed a look at Sue who was rather sheepishly trying to find a non-existent item in her handbag.

Simon decided to change the subject by ordering the first round.

'Right then ladies, bottle of Prosecco or Cocktails to start or….?'

'Both,' they all retorted.

Alice tried to remember Sue's words and knew that most of them meant well. Alice looked around the table.

Both Mary and Cara were artists. They went on to set up their own studio selling their rather unique creations and running evening classes to make ends meet. Alice would often go to new exhibitions of theirs and would occasionally buy the odd piece of artwork, mainly out of loyalty rather than out of any desire to own a piece of their work. Their taste in art was never really to Alice's liking. Just after Mark had left, Cara had somehow managed to persuade Alice to buy one of her latest creations entitled '*Crucified Penis*.' However, it had been after drinking far too many glasses of champagne so she really couldn't remember much about the purchase at all. Except, of course, all the strange looks she had received on the tube journey home. Alice had displayed it for a while in her flat but then decided to put it away in the wardrobe after her cleaner had complained that all those nails kept catching and tearing her dusters.

The cocktails, prosecco and tapas all flowed. Nisha started the drinks mat challenge where you had to flip as many drinks mats as possible clean off the table and catch hold of them. Sue won that challenge. Next, Lucy was comparing who had the highest stiletto's which Lucy always won, being the only one who wore them.

Simon, gorgeous, handsome, tall and, as Alice always lamented, gay made sure the drinks were flowing. He had come to know Alice through some work he had done for them at Frobersham's. Alice felt her and Simon had a lot in common and what he didn't know about what gin should go with which tonic wasn't worth knowing. Simon, like Sue, was a salt of the earth person. Generous, kind and loving. If anyone needed cheering up and a good hug then Simon was your man. He didn't get to all of their gatherings as his job, as an employment lawyer for a top Manchester law firm, demanded long hours. This, coupled with his love of travelling, took him out of circulation more than Alice would have liked.

'Right then lady friends, got this new cocktail for you to try. It's called The *Last Word!* And it probably will be after you have drunk it! Got a kick like a mule!'

All the ladies gulped them back and agreed that it certainly could reach the parts other cocktails simply couldn't!

'Oh wow, yes it does pack a punch.' Alice looked in her element. 'Definitely one for the list Simon. What's in this one?'

'Well, when It's done properly, and you know how I like it done properly friends, it has ¾ fl oz gin with ¾ fl oz Green Chartreuse, ¾ fl oz Maraschino liqueur and ¾ fl oz lime juice over ice in a shaker. Shake and voila!' Simon was always up on the latest cocktails. He threw his arm around Alice and gave her shoulder a squeeze 'How have you been then girlfriend, come on give us the low down!'

Somehow the way Simon asked didn't seem intrusive. Alice knew he was genuinely interested and cared.

'Oh okay, nothing this cocktail can't cure!' Alice's eyes though said it all.

'Look, Alice, my advice to you is get straight back on the horse or even better find a stallion of a man and Mark will soon be history! I know you. You're hanging around waiting for him to come back. Sod him, get on with it and find someone else. Plenty of good men out there you know!'

'Yes, and plenty of shits too with bells on.' Alice had been so long with Mark, the thought of all that time getting to know someone else, all that investment, seemed too awful. 'When you have been with someone a long time you get to know each other's quirks. You create a life together built on similar foundations and you're heading in the same direction you both want similar things.'

Alice was adamant, no, she knew she couldn't face starting again. Those initial feelings of excitement would also be mixed with all those fears and anxiety as to whether the relationship would last. What did he mean when he said a certain thing and why didn't he text very much when he went away? Had he met someone else? Had he decided it was not going to work? No Alice had remembered those days as a woman in her early twenties only too well and didn't want to return to all that uncertainty. Mark and her went together like two peas in a pod and she had now known him for so long, they had created a life together that was just right; comfy, cosy, just all she had wanted.

'The thing is Simon if I give him time, give him space I think he will come back. It must have been harder for him than I thought. I think my Dad's death just reminded him of his own loss. Also, let's face it I was pretty miserable and stressed. I think I just took it out on him.'

Simon had only ever known Alice to put Mark first so

doubted this. Simon had only ever tolerated Mark. He, like so many of their circle of friends, never quite understood what Alice saw in him. True he was good looking, had a good job and could be very charming. But the charm always seemed skin deep to Simon. Mark always expected to be at the top of Alice's agenda and Simon thought he was too demanding of her. In addition, of course, Simon knew of Mark's recent antics and needed to try and persuade Alice that Mark returning was highly unlikely. Sue had persuaded all the group not to discuss Mark (but particularly the elephant in the corner) as she was going to find the right time, when she felt Alice was a bit stronger and able to cope with the news. So, Simon instead thought it prudent to persuade Alice to move on.

'Look, don't spend your life waiting, life is too short. Get on out there girlfriend and enjoy life. You've had a tough time recently and you need to think of this as a fresh start and a chance to meet someone new!' Simon paused to enjoy his cocktail. 'By the way, that bastard of an employer of yours, we could get him on unfair dismissal you know, just give me the nudge and the wink. Free to you of course!' Simon winked at Alice and gave her another squeeze.

'Oh God, no. I can't face that at the moment Simon. Besides, now that's one man I am convinced will have me back when he gives up on Tit-Tassels.' Alice finished her cocktail.

'Tit-Tassels! Oh, you haven't seen mine. I bought some the other day!' Sam exclaimed as she pulled them out of her hand-bag. 'Thought we might try a pair on!' Sam whipped them out of her handbag. Squeals of laughter roared out as she attached them to her dress.

'Simply, all the rage you know!'

Alice, swooning from the *Last Word* suddenly saw the comic element of these outrageous tassels and reached out to try them on. 'Well if you can't beat them, join them!'

Once everyone had tried them on and the laughter had died down, Lucy announced that it was her turn to host this New Year's Eve party and hoped all would be able to make it. Alice delighted to hear this and was keen to go as this was an opportunity of seeing Mark again and this would be an ideal time for them both to have a good talk, a heart to heart. However, when Lucy announced it, Alice thought it strange that everyone seemed so dead against a party.

Sue thought she would rather stay at home this year and play a few games with close family and friends which Alice thought seemed a bit odd. Sue always loved a good party. Simon announced that he would have to give it a miss as his recent boyfriend's family lived in Scotland and he would be heading up North to take part in as many Gay Gordon's as he possibly could.

'I can't miss Richard in a kilt and he has promised me a go with his large sporran! You can always come with me friends!'

Sam offered an alternative for them all to go away for a girl's weekend but Alice not wanting to miss out on the opportunity of seeing Mark again, protested.

'No. That is really kind of you Sam, no I am definitely going. Yes, one of us always hosts a party, let's keep up the tradition. Simon, why don't you bring Richard along with his kilt and well I am sure we would all like to see you in one too!' All the ladies sounded overjoyed at the prospect.

Sue, however, was quick to alter the course of the conversation and proclaimed that Steve, the resident DJ, was now getting ready to start up the music.

Steve was true to form and got them going with ABBA and, when everyone had warmed up, moved on to inviting his audience to do the usual karaoke turn. Alice was in her element. Everyone agreed she was the best entertainer with a great voice for belting them out and Steve was glad to see his old customer back. Alice did her usual rendition of *500 Miles* by the Proclaimers which got everyone jumping up and down and by the end of the evening got everyone into a circle to link arms and sing *New York, New York*. Finally, Alice always had to end the evening with *Sit Down* by *James* which involved everyone sitting on the floor waving their arms about. By this time all the customers had no choice but to join in and seemed to enjoy this as much as Alice. She loved this song, the words resonated with her more than ever in recent months.

They all said their goodbyes and hugs were plentiful. Sue was staying the night at Alice's and both walked home together still singing the song. They somehow managed to get back to the flat but Mr Hughes the resident nosey parker leaned out of his flat window and in his very slow and angry Welsh accent remonstrated with the ladies.

'Ladies, ladies as you full well know it is past twelve midnight and you will wake all the residents. You are fully aware, of course, of our Court's rules and regulations. Section A, paragraph 2 clearly states that any unnecessary noise beyond midnight will not be tolerated and will be dealt with promptly and swiftly by the Court's Committee Chairman which, as you full well know, Alice is me!'

Alice looked at Sue, Sue looked at Alice and both started to serenade Mr Hughes with a rendition of '*Strangers in the Night*' and Mr Hughes realising he was not going to get any joy out of the pair of them shut the window in a very marked manner whilst wagging his finger at them in a very disapproving way.

After they had both staggered up the staircase, which seemed to have become ever steeper and longer, Alice delved into every pocket in her coat, and then bag, to find the key. After a lengthy discussion on how inconvenient keys were and why hadn't someone invented something easier to open a door, they finally managed to get into the flat. Both talked about having another drink but soon fell asleep on the sofa.

Later that night Alice dreamt again.

Alice was back in the hotel room. She was sitting on an enormous sofa with Peter Kay and, there on her bed, was the band James. Everyone seemed so happy and she with Peter Kaye and the band just sang and sang Sit Down Next to me.

At the end of the song, Peter Kay turned to Alice,

'By heck you can belt it out Alice, what a great singer, don't you agree Tim and you lads?'

Every band member nodded. 'Yes, definitely.'

Peter continued, 'We need to release this one again lads, but, this time, with Alice. Are you up for it then Alice to be joint lead singer with Tim? Alice felt so chuffed and acknowledged that yes indeed, she knew every line off by heart, had a great voice and would, indeed, make a good addition to the team.

However, just at that very moment, Ollie came out from the shadows, singing the song.

Everyone turned to look at him in awe and wonder.

'Gosh what a talented singer.' Peter Kay got up from sitting next to Alice and went to on the other side of the room and stood by

Ollie, full of admiration. Alice couldn't believe her ears, why did they think he could sing? He sounded like a cat being strangled.

'Now that is a brilliant voice. That is a voice of an angel wouldn't you all agree lads?'

Yes, the band members did indeed and nodded profusely.

'Right then (turning to talk to the band) I think we have nailed it. Ollie's our man.' Peter looked delighted.

'But what about me?' Alice was astounded, 'I thought I was the woman for the job?'

'Sorry love,' Peter exclaimed 'Better with a man, you know. After all love, it is a man's band. Besides I really don't think we could choose someone who walks around wearing Tit-Tassels with a giant penis in her hand. Not a great image that now, is it?'

Alice looked down to discover an enormous pair of diamond encrusted Tit-Tassels hanging from her silk blouse and there, sitting on her lap, was the sculpture of The Crucified Penis. Ollie shook his head in great disapproval.

Alice didn't know what to say. She just sat staring at the enormous penis and started to cry.

'But I wanted to sing the song with you Peter! It's my turn to shine.'

'Ah,' said Ollie 'but are you ready yet?'

Alice was incredulous.

8

New Year's Eve

Alice spent the day getting ready for the party. The morning had been taken up flying from shop to shop to find an outfit. She ended up in John Lewis and decided upon a dress that fitted under the bust and then came down from there. This would disguise the lumps and bumps, and she admitted to herself that indeed it was actually very flattering. The red chiffon dress suited her colouring and looked very festive.

She spent the afternoon washing her hair, waxing her legs, shaping her eyebrows, applying a face pack and generally pampering herself. She was so excited! This would be the night when Mark would look at her and realise what he had been missing and they could start again. As she finished putting on her mascara, she started singing one of the songs she had heard earlier on the Radio 2 breakfast show, 'Blue eyes' by Elton John but she couldn't really remember the words so just kept repeating the same words *blue eyes* over and over again and then humming along to it before getting fed up and putting her playlist on.

Alice stood back from the mirror, 'You know what, girl, you're looking good! Not a natural beauty perhaps but a good-looking woman.' Yes, she thought she brushed up well.

'Right, shoes!' Alice had purchased a pair of high heels and had practised walking in them around the flat. Alice used to wear high heels but had got out of the habit in recent years and she did admit that the bit of extra height did add to the look and made her feel a bit more elegant and feminine and a bit sexier too. She put them on, yes, she thought! She was now ready to face the music and was delighted when the doorbell rang. Sue had promised to pick her up at 7.00 pm and they would go back to hers for a drink and collect Robert. Sue had told Alice she was happy to drive as she didn't want to drink much that night as Ben had a football match on New Year's Day, of all days, and it was her turn to drive anyway.

Alice answered the door with great excitement but the smile soon left her face when she discovered Ollie on the doorstep. Seeing her great disappointment and obvious irritation, Ollie was quick to explain that Sue had been delayed and he would take her to her house and they could all go on from there.

'Right, I see, well I will get my jacket and bag then, one mo...' Alice left Ollie on the doorstep. Ollie thought Alice brushed up well but wasn't very keen on the dress. It looked a bit like a tent on her and wasn't at all flattering. She had a good figure, why hide it? Alice returned and eyed Ollie up and down. He really did need someone to dress him, she thought, that shirt and those trousers. Definitely not!

They got to the car park and Alice saw Robert's car parked there.

'Oh, have they put you on the insurance too then?' Alice looked somewhat put out by her brother's car being driven by this man.

'Well, it helps to be insured if you are driving!' Ollie retorted.

Alice quietly simmered. Could this man not open his mouth

without being either sarcastic or plain rude. The car journey remained silent for the first five minutes. Ollie thought he ought to get the conversation going, to get to know her a bit better.

'It was very kind of Robert and Sue to invite me tonight. New Year's Eve can be a bit tricky one when you are single don't you think?' Ollie hoped this might start up some sort of conversation.

'Yes, I guess it must be quite difficult for you,' Alice answered. By her response, Ollie thought that she obviously didn't consider herself single, yet.

During the last ten minutes of the car journey, there were a series of polite exchanges but nothing more. Alice was relieved to get to Sue's. Ben was excited to see both of them and rushed out to meet the new arrivals but, to Alice's delight, he made a beeline towards her first.

'Coming to watch me tomorrow you two?' Ben reached out for Ollie's hand too, and both of them walked into the house. Robert appeared and ushered Ben straight upstairs.

'I am coming up in a minute to check your teeth and face, Ben.' Robert didn't hold out much hope that Ben would do a proper job of this but he was keen to play host.

Sue came over to Ollie and gave him a quick peck on the cheek.

'Hi Ollie, thank you so much for getting Alice. I fell to sleep on the sofa this afternoon and have been trying to catch my tail ever since.' Sue still looked very tired, Alice thought, but she was sure she would soon pick up as the evening went on.

Robert got the drinks but while they were all chatting, Alice thought Sue kept giving Robert funny looks and long hard stares as though she wasn't very happy with him or if prompting him to do or say something.

'You know what, well, Alice I was thinking about us just getting a takeaway or something tonight and us seeing in the New Year, just the four of us together. What do you think?' said Robert.

'Yes, sounds good to me, I don't mind that at all,' agreed Ollie.

Alice was not happy with this. She hadn't spent all day and all that effort to see Mark and then just abandon the idea and stay in and she certainly wasn't keen on the idea of staying in with Ollie. It suddenly occurred to her that her brother was mischief making and was probably trying to pair her and Ollie up. How brothers can get is so wrong, she thought to herself. No, she had to persuade them to go out.

Alice mustered up the most enthusiastic voice she could find, 'Come on, it will be fun tonight! Robert you know how much you like Lucy's wine collection. She would have put on a huge spread too, like she always does. It would be rude to bow out now. Besides your babysitter will be here in a mo.' Alice thought that would do the job.

Sue then chipped in, 'Oh I can still pay Julie, you know what teenagers are like, money for nothing is always a welcome treat and if we stayed in, I could rustle up some lovely titbits and then we could get going on the karaoke and watch Big Ben chime with all those fireworks at midnight.'

Alice was having none of this. 'Look if you lot want to stay in that is fine, really it is, but I fancy a night out.'

Sue looked at Robert. Robert looked at Sue. Ollie looked at both of them and also sensed something wasn't quite right but stayed silent. He really hoped the pair of them were not trying to match make him with the rottweiler.

'No that's okay, Alice, we will all go together.' Sue nodded at Robert as if she wanted a word with him in private. Both left the room making an even more awkward silence between Ollie and Alice who both sat down and picked up the nearest book to read.

Alice really didn't know what was up with the pair of them tonight. Robert then came back into the room and invited Ollie to come through with him into the dining room for a drink.

Odd thought Alice, why hasn't he asked me too? At this point Sue came in and sat next to Alice. She picked up her hand and pulled it towards her.

'Crikey, this feels a bit like a confession moment, Sue. What's wrong?' A thought suddenly occurred to Alice that Sue hadn't been looking too well and was probably coming down with something or other. She obviously wanted to bow out of the evening and thought Alice might be offended as having her friend there tonight of all nights would be important. Sue was about to speak when Julie arrived at the lounge door.

'Hope you don't mind me coming straight in Mrs Radcliffe but I have been knocking and didn't want to ring the bell in case Ben was in bed.' Julie went to sit on the other side of the room.

'Oh, that is so thoughtful of you Julie. Ben is upstairs, would you mind checking he is in bed?'

Alice got up. 'No, it is okay Julie, I promised Ben a quick five-minute story.' With that she left the room.

Sue wasn't too sure what to do and went to find Robert. Ollie noticed that she shook her head from side to side and

Robert's shoulders seemed to drop in earnest. Ollie thanked Robert for the drink and was very complementary of the malt whisky and, sensing Robert and Sue needed to talk, he left to get a glass of water from the kitchen.

Sue shut the door. 'I couldn't tell her, I tried but I just couldn't!' Sue felt her anxiety levels rising.

Robert took her hand, 'Look, I think it is unlikely *he* would have the nerve to show up, not tonight. I think you need to stop worrying and we will go and enjoy the evening.' Robert gave her a reassuring smile and Sue nodded in agreement.

Eventually, they all departed. A little bit later than Alice had wanted but parties often take time to get warmed up, Alice thought.

The drive seemed to take ages. Alice felt butterflies in her stomach and a real sense of excitement mixed with slight nausea. She hadn't seen Mark in what must have been about seven months now and she thought tonight would break the ice, the slight awkwardness of it all. A party atmosphere wouldn't place either of them under too much pressure. She just hoped and prayed he would be there. He was very friendly with Lucy and her husband. Yes, surely, he would be there.

She was not disappointed. As soon as she arrived at their apartment, she could see the back of Mark's head and he seemed in full flow with a group of people, laughing and joking. Lucy took their jackets and invited them to go over to the drinks cabinet to get a drink. Alice managed to sneak a peek at herself in the hallway mirror and adjusted her hair and plumped up her cheeks. It worked for Scarlet O'Hara she thought and it would do the trick for her too. Ollie thought it rather amusing how she puckered up her lips when looking in the mirror. He appeared behind her and mimicked her actions. Alice flashed a look of utter contempt and she hastened towards the bar while Ollie disappeared to the loo.

However, when she got to the drinks table, Alice noticed a kind of weird silence. Sue came and stood right beside her and Robert went to her other side. She turned round to see what had caused the silence and realised her friends were staring at her and then looking away. She slowly put the glass to her mouth and nervously sipped. Had she tucked her dress in her knickers she thought? She looked behind her to check. No. She then looked past Sam and Cara and saw Mark looking straight at her. She smiled a nervous but as warm a smile as she could muster and he smiled back. He smiled back! Alice looked into those gorgeous brown eyes of his. However, he soon dropped his glance at her. He just turned to look at the woman who was standing by him. She turned too to look at Alice. However, as she turned round Alice looked down to see this enormous bump on the woman and it was obvious she was very heavily pregnant. Mark then put his arm around her. He guided her towards Alice.

Alice looked somewhat bewildered. Who was this woman and why did he have his arm around a pregnant lady? This woman was pregnant? He had her arm around her? They were coming towards her?

'Hello Alice.' Mark nodded at Sue and went to shake Robert's hand who was having none of it. 'How are you all?' Mark moved forward and gave Alice a kiss on the cheek. Sue instinctively put her hand on Alice's arm. Alice was frozen to the spot. 'I'd like you to meet Charlotte,' he paused slightly, 'my fiancée.'

Alice looked at Charlotte and the huge bump. This didn't make any sense at all? She looked ready to give birth at any time. She was huge, so how... but it all too soon clicked into place. Alice felt sick. Mark carried on speaking but Alice couldn't hear the words, she was unable to hear or comprehend what was being said. She could feel her head spinning and her legs just seemed to give way from under her. Robert quickly moved forward and Sue grabbed hold of her arm tightly. All she could hear was Robert saying, 'I think you have said and done enough don't you Mark?' Mark did not seem perturbed at all and simply led Charlotte away.

Her friends were quick to gather around but nobody knew what to say apart from the usual inept and inappropriate comment from Lucy as she whispered, 'Yes, I have to say she looks ready to drop at any time!'

Alice was trying to hold back the tears. She looked at Sue who looked helplessly back at her friend. Alice turned again to face the wall trying to contain herself.

Sue got closer to Alice and started to try and explain, 'I did try, we both tried but somehow there was never the right moment and ...' Sue stopped. Alice looked at her straight in the eyes, 'So you knew? You both knew and you didn't tell me?' She turned around again to look at her friends who all dropped their eyes to the carpet.

None of them would look at her. None of them. Yes, of course, they all knew. Alice felt she was suffocating. She needed air, she needed to breathe. Everywhere was so hot, so stuffy. She started to walk towards the kitchen and Sue went to follow her but Alice held up her hand firmly, 'No, no leave me, please just leave me.' She continued towards the kitchen shutting the door firmly behind her.

Ollie had now finished in the loo to return to the living room to find a deathly silence. Sue had tears down her cheeks and Robert was looking furious.

'Bastard, fancy turning up here and with her.' Robert nodded towards a man and a heavily pregnant woman who had retreated to the corner of the far end of the room. Ollie knew who this must be and stood in stunned silence himself.

Ollie thought what a horrible shock for Alice this must have been and why had no one told her before tonight? He now realised why Sue had been so keen to stay home. But why had she not said anything to Alice before? What on earth had they been thinking of, bringing Alice here under these circumstances? Ollie felt they had been too overly protective. This had been a big mistake.

'Where's Alice?' Ollie enquired.

'She's in the kitchen.' Robert slammed his glass down on the table and turned to Sue, 'Come on we had better go home, I will go and get her,' but, at this point Robert saw Mark leave Charlotte and go into the kitchen himself. Robert's anger was now clearly visible and he started to move towards the kitchen door.

Ollie put his hand out to stop him, 'No, Robert. They need to talk, give them a few minutes.' Ollie was most insistent and Robert held back.

Sam came over, 'I had been texting you and trying to ring you Sue. They only just turned up before you arrived but I was hoping you would pick up so I could warn you.'

'Well, everyone, I think it is time to get this party started, don't you?' shouted an already drunk Lucy. She turned the music up and invited everyone to start on the food.

Alice stood in the kitchen. She simply couldn't take it all in. Her body starting shaking and tears welled up in her eyes. So, they all knew, they all knew. Why had nobody said anything, why had they let her come to the party? Her tears were now flowing.

The door opened.

Alice had her back to the door. 'Whoever it is, please just give me a few minutes.'

'It's me Alice.' Mark moved towards her as Alice turned around.

'Oh God!' Alice's head was now reeling. 'I just don't understand. What an earth is going on? To do this now, in front of all our friends. How many times did I say I wanted a family with you, you just kept telling me we were better off on our own, just the two of us, just the two of us Mark. Do you remember?' Alice felt her hands and legs tremble.

'Look, I hadn't planned it this way, well it just happened, these things do.' Mark went to move closer towards her and held out his arm ready to hold her.

'Don't you bloody dare, don't you dare touch me. What do you mean *it just happened*? How does a woman getting pregnant Mark, *just happen*? More to the point, you never told me.' Another realisation quickly flashed through Alice's mind, 'Oh God, you must have been seeing her while you were still with me?'

'Look your and my relationship had ended months before we split up, you know it had.' Mark continued to try to reach out for her but Alice was having none of it.

'No actually Mark I hadn't realised. You never ever said a

thing.'

Mark interrupted, 'Look you can't blame me, you were always so tied up with your dad, you never had any time for us. Things hadn't been right for a long time. You had started to get so bloody needy...' Mark wasn't given the chance to continue.

'What? You tell me *I* was needy. I can't believe you have just said that. My mum and dad had died within a very short time of each other Mark. Of course, I needed support. Just like all the support I gave you when you went through it all with your mum. Do you remember Mark? Do you remember all those evenings I sat and held you while you poured your heart out? Did it ever occur to you that it wasn't exactly a bed of roses for me too? But that is what people do Mark when they love each other. They stand by each other.'

'Look, things had run their course Alice. I met Charlotte on one of my conferences and I didn't mean it to happen but well you know what it's like, we just clicked and ...'

'You just clicked? It never occurred to you to be honest with me Mark, to tell me how you were feeling. To give me the chance to sort things out?'

Mark hesitated, 'You just weren't there for me anymore.' Mark turned away. 'It had run its course Alice, no more to be said.' He left the room and shut the door behind him.

Alice's head was reeling. His words *'No more to be said'* cut right through her. There was so much more to be said, so much more. She had so much wanted a baby but he had insisted life was just so much better with the two of them. How had he changed so much? Why had he done this to her?

Robert and Sue hung about outside the kitchen door, not knowing quite what to do. Robert glared at Mark as he exited the kitchen but Alice was still inside.

Alice felt the anger rage within her. And yes, as per bloody usual, Mark had the last word, he always did seem to get the last word. He must have been seeing Charlotte way before they split, when Charlotte got pregnant that must have been the prompt to end it all. Mark had been carrying on with Charlotte and she had never even suspected. All those business trips away at weekends, all those late nights at the office. She let out a scream in utter frustration. She just needed to get out. She just had to go. Alice left the kitchen, grabbed her coat and went straight for the door. Sue and Robert started to follow.

Alice couldn't even look at them, 'No, just leave it. I need some air, please just let me be for a while, I need to go on my own.'

'But, Alice…' Sue implored but Alice held up her hand to stop her following and quickly departed.

Sue didn't know what to do, 'It's dark out there, she's on her own, she can't go home on her own, Robert.' Sue was distraught. She had let Alice down and she knew it. There just never seemed to be the right time to talk to her. She was going to tell her but it just needed handling correctly. However, she could see now how this had been a big mistake.

'I'll go and find her.' Robert assured Sue. Ollie intervened

'Look, it seems to me right now, she needs a little space. I'll make sure she is safe but you need to let her go. She is too distressed at this point to talk to either of you.'

Ollie got his jacket and followed Alice at a safe distance. Alice walked and walked. She decided to cut through the park. It didn't matter how dark or late it was. She really didn't care. Her mind was whizzing and whirring. She replayed over and over again what Mark had said. She now could think of all the responses she could and should have said. Alice couldn't get the image of Charlotte out of her mind. How could he do this to her?

Alice started to run. She needed to get away. She needed to get home. Her high heels, however, got the better of her and she fell, feeling every ounce of life within her depart as she hit the ground. The contents of her bag emptied noisily all over the walkway. Tears fell down her face, she felt frozen to the spot. Every part of her was in pain. Ollie had now caught up and quickly bent down to pick up her things.

'And you can bloody sod off too!' she screamed. 'I suppose you knew too, didn't you? Is there anyone who didn't know apart from me?' Alice didn't allow Ollie the chance to respond. 'Come to gloat, Ollie, have you come to smirk and enjoy my misfortune?'

Ollie put his arm out to comfort her. She just retreated even more.

'Did you know too then Ollie? Was I the only bloody person who didn't know?' Alice started shivering.

Ollie took his jacket off to keep her warm but she was having none of it. 'Get lost, get bloody lost and go back to wherever it is you come from.' Alice walked on slowly but her ankle was killing her. Her walk quickly became a limp.

She managed to get to the end of the park but the pain was too much. Ollie followed from a distance. He felt so incredibly sorry for her and the anger welled up in Ollie too. He thought that Mark hadn't even the decency to call Alice to talk to her, to tell her what he had done. He must have known she would be at the party. He must have realised this was not the way for her find out.

Alice's limp grew worse so Ollie hailed a taxi and reluctantly Alice got in with him. When the taxi had reached the flat, she got out and slammed the door behind her. She walked off as quickly as she could. Ollie paid the taxi driver then continued to follow her.

Some people were coming out of the entrance to the apartments as Alice was going in. She, hastily took advantage of the open door and not even bothering to look behind her, slammed the door behind her leaving Ollie standing outside. She never looked back.

Well, Ollie thought to himself, he had at least got her home safely. It would be futile to try and get her to open the door now. He turned away and headed back to the party.

Alice walked slowly up the stairs. Every inch of her felt as if it was throbbing with pain. Her head felt dizzy. She struggled to her door and started to look for the keys. She searched every crevice of her handbag.

'Oh God, oh no, my keys!' Her mind flashed back to her fall. Everything had tumbled out of her bag. 'For goodness sake!'

Her back just slid slowly down her front door and she dropped to the floor. She started sobbing again, this couldn't be happening, surely this couldn't be real. Alice was completely oblivious to the arrival of Number 24 coming up the stairs. She gently bobbed down beside Alice.

'Are you okay? Please let me help you.' Number 24 put her hand out and rested it upon Alice's shoulder.

Alice just continued to sob and could barely utter the words that she had no keys. Number 24 looked inside Alice's bag but couldn't find them either.

'Right you must come with me, you are wet through and we need to get you warm.' Alice managed to stagger to her neighbour's apartment but the rest was a blur. The next thing she remembered was waking up in Number 24's bedroom with Sue sitting at the end of her bed. She started to cry. They both did.

9

A bit of a Spring clean

The next few days came and went. Alice remained in bed most of the time watching the odd movie from her laptop, listening to Radio 2, sleeping, crying or just watching the cobwebs on the ceiling. The cake and biscuit tin had been well and truly emptied and the fridge could not yield anything further to eat. With her cupboards bare she resorted to her usual takeaways of pizza and Indian meals. She had wanted to muster up enough energy to go and get some flowers to thank her neighbour but even that was too much of an effort.

A few weeks after New Year's Eve, Alice's friend, Simon, decided to pay her a visit. He had been contacted by one and all who were concerned that Alice was not picking up her phone; she wasn't answering the door and someone needed to do something. So, Simon, having, just returned from his latest travels to Scotland ventured round to see her. He appeared at her door and continued to keep knocking until she answered it.

An angry Alice begrudgingly left her bed and the comfort of her warm duvet and finally thrust the door open wanting to tell whoever it was to get the hell lost.

'Wouldn't you like to see what I have under my sporran then?' were Simon's first words putting on a deep Scottish accent and Alice, now overcome with emotion and the sight of

Simon in a kilt, threw her arms around him and they hugged. She cried. She sobbed. She wept. He held her.

'Right then Alice, tell me all about it then?' Simon led Alice to the sofa, plumped up the cushions and settled down to hear all her news.

Alice relayed the whole story managing to get through yet another box of tissues as well as Simon's own hanky. He listened very sympathetically and kept giving her reassuring hugs. When she had relayed everything to him, he sat and looked at her, taking her hands into his he offered the words that only Simon could have delivered.

'Yes, so he is a complete and utter bastard is the long and short of that one. Yes, we needed to tell you earlier but… well… friends don't always do what they ought to, do they?' Simon scanned the room and looking around he observed the unholy mess that had engulfed the flat.

'Right, come on you. You can't continue like this.' Simon looked clearly shocked at the state of the flat and Alice, knowing full well what Simon was about to say, sank even further into the sofa, put her head in her hands and groaned.

'I can't face it, I just can't. I stopped the cleaner coming because I couldn't be bothered to tidy up before she came.'

'None of this *can't face it lark*. You and I are going to sort this mess out now, then I will make the best hot chocolate you have ever tasted and then we will watch a movie my friend. I'll even let you choose it for a change, as long as it has Hugh Grant in it.'

Alice mustered up a smile and Simon started to beaver away. He stripped the bed and aired the room. Alice cleaned up all the takeaway food boxes, emptied the dishwasher and relieved the sink of all its dishes. Simon sprayed some of his aftershave around the room and declared that the place had never smelt or looked so good. Alice, reluctantly, relinquished the onesie and exchanged it for a top and jeans which she swore must have shrunk in the wash as she struggled to get the zip up, yet again.

They sat at the kitchen table and Simon pulled two hot chocolate mug kits from his overnight bag, a can of squirty cream, a bag of giant marshmallows and two chocolate stirring spoons.

'Your fave drink and if this doesn't cheer you up, girlfriend, I don't know what will!' Simon squirted the cream on top of the steaming, frothed up milk and they both sat stirring their chocolate spoons round and spooning up the cream.

'I can't believe *he* could do it to me? He was adamant he didn't want children, adamant. The worse thing of all is the deceit, he was seeing her whilst still living with me. Not only that my own friends all knew and nobody bloody told me.' Alice flashed an angry look at her friend.

Simon studied her. His friend had been poorly done by, that was true.

'Well, we didn't know he was seeing someone else until after he left you but yes as soon as we did find out about the baby, we should have told you. Lucy knew before anyone else but when she found out it wasn't long before we all knew. There is no excuse for not telling you, but you had been through so much with losing your dad, then Mark, then your job. Sue and the rest of us, well, we were just waiting for the right time. The problem is, it never seemed to come. It backfired though big time. We can't go back and put that right but we can only learn from our mistakes and move on.' Simon put his hand out and held Alice's hand. 'What I can promise you is that we are all here for you if you will let us. Don't push your friends away and don't let Mark win, Alice. He has behaved so badly and to be honest Alice, I have only ever tolerated him because of you.'

Alice looked surprised 'You never told me this before?'

'No, another error of judgement on my part. But who does ever tell their best friends they don't like their boyfriends? We saw how happy he made you and well who am I to judge what goes on behind closed doors?' Simon licked his chocolate spoon in a deliberately suggestive way, winking at her. This made Alice laugh.

'Oh, Simon I do love you!' They both smiled at each other.

Simon got up and walked over to the window. 'It's a lovely evening out there and you and me are going for a long walk. I have two more days of holiday left and I am spending them with you.'

So, they walked and talked and talked and walked. Life felt so much better with Simon around.

He cooked supper and they enjoyed the speciality of his prawn linguini which he had made the most divine tomato and chilli sauce with, all freshly cooked, real comfort food, just what she craved for.

Whilst they were eating Simon leaned over towards Alice as if telling her a secret, 'I tell you who I heard was the hero of the day at the New Year's Eve party that Ollie chap, the godson of Mario's.'

'Well, I would hardly call him a hero, but yes he did make sure I got home safely I guess.' Alice looked surprised she didn't really feel walking a girl home constituted being called a hero.

'Oh, hadn't you heard what Ollie did next?' Simon took the last sip of his wine and filled their glasses again. 'It turns out this

Ollie chap went back to the New Year's Eve party only to find Mark had returned to the party without Charlotte and was then flirting with Lucy! Ollie went over to have words apparently. No one quite heard what was said but the next thing was Mark made a swing at Ollie, so Ollie grabbed Mark's fist and was quick to restrain him pulling his arm tightly behind his back. Ollie then marched him out of the apartment!'

Alice couldn't quite believe what she had heard. She would have loved to have hit Mark around the face that night so she was glad to hear that someone had got the better of him, even if it was Ollie. Mark was tall and strong and not many a man would manage to arm wrestle him out the house.

Alice then sunk her head into her hands and groaned. She remembered how she had slammed the door in Ollie's face. As much as she didn't like him, it was a very rude thing to do considering he had followed her home to make sure she got home safely.

'I think, you owe Ollie a visit, don't you,' Simon raised his eyebrows, 'knight in shining armour and all that!'

Alice would never have described Ollie as a knight in shining armour, that was really going too far. 'That man is the most irritating, smug, conceited, self-satisfied person I have ever met.'

Simon raised his eyebrows even further, 'Oh, raises quite a few emotions then does he?'

'No, no not like that!' Alice protested. 'I mean he doesn't even have a proper job or home or well any redeeming features actually. Well apart from dealing with Mark that is.'

'And following you home to make sure you got home safely and paying your taxi fare! Yes, I see, you just keep convincing yourself of that.' Simon gave her an exaggerated giant wink.

Alice took a piece of her linguine and tossed it at him.

Alice did feel, however, that a trip to Mario's to acknowledge Ollie's kindness would be the decent thing to do.

'One job left girlfriend.' Simon pointed towards the bedroom and headed for the wardrobe. 'A spring-clean in here too, this'll do you the world of good too.' He took out one of Mark's suits. 'The only good thing about that man was his taste in suits.' He tried the Armani jacket on as Alice collapsed wearily on the bed. 'Umm, suits you sir!' Simon said giving himself an admiring look in the mirror.

'The thing is, well he might want to come back for them, come and explain.' Alice sighed and flung the duvet over her. What good would that do anyway she thought to herself. Simon took the jacket off and tucked himself under the duvet with her.

'Over my dead body is that man coming back here, girly. Are you mad, after the way he has treated you? Anyway, he will just have to buy more suits won't he? I am taking them round to the charity shop. It is not healthy you keep looking at them every time you pop into the cupboard to get dressed.'

Alice knew he was right but it just seemed a bit final. Her face, though, said it all. Simon put his arm around her and gave her another a big hug. There is something so comforting, Alice thought, about a man who gives a woman a hug without any expectations of anything else. Alice sunk into his arms and they both nodded off for what seemed like just forty winks but when she had awoken the suits, jackets and shirts were cleared.

'Right,' Simon appeared at the door with a mug of tea, 'Spring cleaning done, mission accomplished, time for a good movie.' Simon held up a dvd. 'Notting Hill? Time for a bit of

Hugh Grant don't you think?'

Yes, Alice thought, definitely.

10

Poldark

February was cold and the snow had arrived. The little boy from Number 2 was enjoying sledging down the slope at the side of the flats. Dad was dutifully at the bottom of the slope ensuring his little boy didn't go into the drive where cars, despite the 5mph sign whizzed round to get to the garages at the back of the flats.

Alice was at a bit of a loose end. She had scoured various on-line sites every day for a job but nothing had taken her fancy.

'Right,' she said to herself, 'need to get on.' Alice ambled into the bathroom. It really could do with a clean but instead she decided to get the weighing scales out of the cupboard. She duly placed them down on the floor and stepped on.

'Oh, for goodness sake!' Alice got off the scales. 'That can't be right?' She started to fiddle with the dial to make sure it was exactly on zero. She stepped back on again but her weight stayed the same. 'OMG, there must be something wrong with these scales, I can't be that heavy!' She popped the pair of scales back into the cupboard and reached for the electronic ones.

'This will be a bit more accurate,' she hoped.

She stepped on and looked down. 'Oh bugger, these scales aren't any better either, even worse.' Both scales went back in the cupboard and Alice placed some towels firmly over them. Alice was now not in the mood to clean the bathroom and decided to venture into the kitchen. She opened her mobile phone and looked at her to do list:

Job 1. Sort out clothes that don't fit.

Umm well she had already had a go at that job. Not today.

Job 2. Clean the car and empty the boot of all the rubbish.

God no, not that job, that would take far too long.

Job 3. Thank you letter to Aunt Agatha

No, she wasn't ready to write and thank Agatha for her Christmas gift. Aunt Agatha was a very dear old aunt who had been so kind through her Dad's illness. She was her dad's eldest, only surviving sister but, unfortunately, now at the age of 93, was very short sighted, practically blind.

Alice looked down at her aunt's gift of a book. Alice felt sure that her aunt had meant to buy Alice the autobiographical account of Richard Attenborough by his wife called 'Living with Dick.' Aunty Agatha had always been a big fan of his movies and his work as a director and often spoke to Alice about him. Agatha was obviously keen to share her love of him. However, I think her eyesight on this occasion had got the better of her. She had unfortunately bought Alice the self-help book entitled '*Living with a Dick in your life? How to get rid of them.*'

Alice wasn't too sure how to word the thank you letter for that one so would get round to that job another day.

Job No 4: Ollie???

Umm. Well it was the right thing to do and, as she really didn't want to crack on with the other jobs, she thought she ought to get on with thanking Ollie. After all, he had walked her home and she had been very rude to him. Besides she was dying with curiosity to know what Ollie had done or said to Mark for the two of them to have such an altercation.

She slipped on her new pair of jeans that had arrived earlier that morning. Had she really gone up another size? It was probably the make of jeans. Anyway, at least with putting on some weight her boobs had also acquiesced into growing bigger too.

'Umm,' she thought to herself, 'might need a larger size bra too. There really is a God up there.'

After Alice had done some shopping in town, she caught the tube and was horrified by all the Tit-Tassels still adorning the young girls. Some seemed to be dangling now from their ears too.

There, opposite the station, was Mario's. How she wished Mario was back. He was supposed to have been away for a few weeks but a few weeks had now turned into several months.

'Right keep calm.' she mumbled to herself. 'Don't let him rattle you, just do the decent thing and apologise.' She opened the café door, nodded to Henry who was glued to his usual spot and went up to the counter. However, out of the back of the café emerged a young, very handsome man. One of Mario's relatives? Everything seemed to go in slow motion from that moment on. He walked, no he seemed to glide, over to her. His thick, black Italian hair framed his face. His deep brown eyes were firmly fixed upon her and when he smiled, his strong white teeth came through. Alice felt she was having another Aidan Turner moment.

'Good afternoon,' the dark handsome Italian man said, 'what can I get you for?'

For a brief moment, Alice had completely forgotten why she had come into the café. The man ran his fingers through his thick dark wavy hair. She could see the well-toned muscles coming through his tightly fitted shirt. His dark brown eyes fixed firmly upon her. Alice felt herself go all a bit girly. Was this another of Mario's acquaintances? She definitely hoped so. At that moment she could hear Henry clearing his throat very loudly as if embarrassed by her obvious drooling over him. This brought her back to earth.

'Oh, I was looking for Ollie, just wondered if I might have a quick word with him?' Alice looked beyond the handsome stallion to the back of the café hoping Ollie would emerge.

'No, sorry, he in Italy. Mario needed him sorting things out, something to do with… with a, what you say, a horse's head I think.'

Alice felt somewhat alarmed by this statement. She remembered the movie *The Godfather* and an image of a horse's head in Mario's bed sent a shiver down her spine.

'Yes, Mario is helping my father, Abramo, to open new bar, The Horse's Head,' the young Italian confirmed.

Alice felt a sense of great relief. 'Oh, I see, right then. Do you know when he will be back?'

'Mario and Ollie back by end of month. Can I get drink for you?'

'Yes, that would be lovely, thank you,' but after Alice had seen Henry's disapproving look and eyebrows raised, Alice changed her mind, 'No, no it's fine. Thank you.'

Alice nodded at Henry and then left. She thought to herself

that at least Mario would soon be home.

Alice returned to the tube station. Whilst going back through the ticket barrier she caught a glimpse of her reflection. She really must lose some weight. Alice turned straight back around and decided not to take the tube. The walk would do her good. She only lived a few stops down from Mario's. Yes, she would walk.

Ollie had gone and though in a sense she felt a bit of relief that he wouldn't be hanging round Sue and Robert's all the time, she also felt guilty that she hadn't been a bit nicer to him. Oh well she probably wouldn't have to see him again. It didn't matter now.

She decided an early night was the thing. She slipped into her pj's and snuggled under the duvet. She so much wanted Mario to return. She missed him so much. Instead she decided to have a look at the book her aunt had bought her, may be this would have wise words. Her eyes, though, became gradually heavier and heavier and sleep came upon her at last.

Later that night, the same dream of Alice's returned.

As per usual, she was in a hotel room tied to a chair. Her hair was now her usual colour, sandy brown, shoulder length and shaped into a bob. The Tit-Tassels were still there but now they seemed even longer and her breasts looked fuller, giving her a deep cleavage. She was wearing a corset under a lace nighty that flowed to the ground.

Suddenly, a light went on over by the coffee making machine and there, out of the dark, emerged a man standing right in front of it. It was the man from the café! He turned around. Alice couldn't believe her eyes, no it wasn't the man from the café at all, it was Poldark! Poldark was standing right in front of her, right by the coffee machine. His smouldering eyes looked straight into her eyes. Gosh they were eyes to die for. She felt her body tingle all over. He was so tall and broad and even more handsome than on the TV. He had the most mischievous looking smile on his face and real come to bed eyes.

'Cappuccino or Latte?' Poldark asked.

'Oh, right, gosh, well a cappuccino please.'

'It will take but just one minute, my love,' and with that Poldark proceeded to take his shirt off. 'I always take my shirt off while making cappuccino.'

'Right,' whimpered Alice, 'yes, of course.'

Poldark frothed the milk whilst keeping a firm stare upon Alice. She was now completed entranced. 'When this is finished, I think it's time for me to put you back on the horse, don't you?'

'Indeed,' Alice said, not too sure what he was meaning by this but it sounded promising.

'But first,' Poldark walked over towards her and bent down to start to undo the rope tied around her, 'before we drink the cappuccino, I need to kiss you long and hard. Let me untie you my love.'

'Oh dear, I wouldn't do that if I were you,' a familiar voice piped up from behind the curtains.

Oh no Alice thought to herself. It can't be him, not again! Ollie was standing there, as bold as brass.

'In love with another man you know, never going to give that one up. Yes, tragic really, a bit like Scarlett O'Hara and Ashley!'

Poldark backed away from Alice. 'Another man you say? I thought I was the only man for you Alice?'

'Yes, yes you are.' Alice flashed a look of absolute hatred at Ollie. How dare he interrupt this perfect moment, yet again. How dare he interrupt this perfect moment of bliss.

'Sorry Alice. You see when I give my heart, I give it completely. You aren't ready for me yet. Are you Alice?' Poldark retreated back into the shadow 'I must go my love.' And with that he was gone.

'Oh God, no. Come back. Yes, I am completely ready for you.' Alice desperately tried to untie herself. 'Someone, anyone, please untie me!' Alice shouted.

Ollie, who was now on the bed, got up and walked over and studied the rope and knots. 'No can do I am afraid – those knots are done up far too tightly for me to release you.' In an instant he seemed to vanish into thin air.

Just as Alice thought things couldn't get any worse, she then heard a strange noise coming from the bed. She turned her head to find a horse was sleeping under the duvet.

Alice woke up with such a start. 'OMG! What on earth is going on?'

11

Malcolm

The beginning of March seemed as miserable as January had been. The snow had disappeared and had been replaced by rain, lots of it. It seemed unending. It was a Saturday, Alice was collecting Ben from football practice. She felt a very proud aunt indeed watching her nephew in his new kit. Ben seemed a natural at football and was playing in his favourite position of centre forward.

After the match, Alice was careful not to give him a big hug and embarrass him in front of all his friends, 'Hi, big fella, how are you diddling?' Alice instead gave Ben a huge beam of a smile which was duly returned.

'Brill! Scored two goals. You should have seen me Aunty Alice. Even Fred the Barnett only scored one!' Ben ran to the car.

'Did you now, well done you!' Alice went to help him take football boots off and Ben went through each goal detailing every manoeuvre. Alice made sure she sounded very impressed.

Ben then went very quiet. 'Aunty Alice?' enquired Ben, 'Mum got really angry with me last night, I mean REALLY angry.' Ben's eyes suddenly started to fill.

Alice studied Ben; he really did seem very upset. This was not like Sue. She was always very calm and very rarely lost her temper. 'So, Ben what had you been up to?'

'Nothing, honest NOTHING!' Ben could see the doubt in his Aunt's eyes. 'I simply asked Echo to play me *George Ezra's Under the Hot Sun* song and Mum came charging down the stairs and shouted at me.'

'Well, perhaps it was playing louder than you thought Ben. Perhaps Mum just wanted a bit of peace and quiet or perhaps she was having forty winks Ben and you may have woken her.' Alice continued to try and reassure Ben still tackling the very stubborn laces. Double knots, she dreaded them.

Ben continued, 'What at my teatime? AND dinner was *really* late. She was even grumpy with Dad when he got in from work. Dad just asked what was for tea and Mum shouted at him too.' A tear ran down Ben's cheek. 'I think she doesn't love me and Dad any more.'

Alice had finally managed to get the better of Ben's double knotted laces. 'Now, Ben, you are being silly. Your mum loves you so much you are the very centre of her life and being. You know that. She loves you to the moon and back.'

Ben still protested, 'She used to always help me with my homework and then we nearly always play a game but since Christmas, well she just doesn't want to. She is always leaving me to get on with my homework with Dad. Dad always gets irritable when I don't get my maths right. Mum explains it better too *and* they had a weekend away without me.' Ben looked very disgruntled indeed. He threw his dirty boots into his bag and let himself into the passenger seat banging the door a little bit too hard for Alice's liking. But in his present mood she decided to let it go.

Alice got into the car. 'Right, well Mum has a part time job to deal with Ben and Christmas is always hectic. She probably just needed a little break with Dad. It is important for mums and dads to get a little time on their own. It's not like they are always leaving you Ben. They very rarely take a break without you.' However, she could see this was not comforting Ben and decided to change the subject to Chelsea, asking him how their last match had gone. This did have the desired effect of gradually distracting him and Ben seemed happy to talk about this instead.

On arriving home, Malcolm was in the kitchen enjoying a cuppa and a natter with Sue. On seeing her, Alice could tell he was looking a bit sheepish. She gave him the usual hug and Malcolm seemed pleased that the Christmas incident had been forgotten. Malcolm quickly sloped off into the garden to have a kick around with Ben.

Sue came up to give Alice a big hug too. This took Alice by surprise as she hadn't even started to talk about her woes yet.

'Oh, thank you, that makes me feel cheerier already.' Alice beamed at Sue. 'How are you then?' she enquired thinking she might broach the subject of Ben's conversation.

Alice did think Sue looked a bit pale and down. 'Oh fine, just tired. I've been so busy at work and it's always difficult to fit a part time job into what really should be a full time one and, well, I have also felt a bit under the weather of late. Robert and I thought we might try and get away again this weekend. Robert has a work's conference thingy and I was thinking I might join him. I know we have just been away but...'

'Yes, of course, I would be delighted to look after Ben. You know it is never a problem but, well, I think we might have to sell it to Ben.' Alice wasn't too sure how it would go down after his little outburst in the car. Alice was about to broach the subject of her conversation with Ben, particularly as they were now planning on another weekend trip away. However, at that very moment, Malcolm and Ben reappeared.

'Just been mentioning about a fishing trip with Ben, he seems very excited Sue. I thought we might get away this weekend. What do you think Ben? And, of course, Alice you are very welcome too.'

Before Alice had the chance of heading Malcolm off at the pass Ben shouted, 'Cool, yes all three of use. Fantastic! Malcolm, we could be like that telly programme, you know that *Mortimer and Whitehouse Gone Fishing* programme. Dad and I watch it but Dad won't take me, he says he can't fish.'

'Anyone can fish,' said Malcolm, 'but you need patience and your father as you know can't sit for long.'

'Umm,' Alice thought. She could fully understand this. She, too, couldn't think of anything worse than sitting still near a cold river, hour upon hour, getting bitten by all the midges. However, Ben's power of persuasion with those eyes of his and the extra big hug, made her acquiesce.

'Yes, go on why not.' Alice said but every part of her body was willing her to say no, definitely not.

Malcolm could hear the doubt in her voice. He would just have to convince her that fishing with him was not such a bad option. He might even persuade her to enjoy it! Who wouldn't like fishing after giving it a go? He would take them to one of his favourite haunts the Grand Union Canal around Leighton Buzzard and give Ben a go at catching some bream. He had started fishing there as a young boy and he was sure Ben would enjoy it. He would take them both to enjoy all that fresh air, the peace and the tranquillity of it all. True it was early March and a little cold but they could just wrap up warm. He would bring a flask of tea and some sandwiches, after all it could be expensive at that local café.

The weekend came around all too quickly. Alice had stayed over at Sue's the night before the fishing trip and had suffered from very little sleep owing to Ben's insistence on climbing in with her during the night and talking incessantly about how he was going to catch the biggest fish ever.

'In fact, Aunty Alice, it will be so big that I might even get into the Guinness Book of Records Annual. I will be famous. So famous that I won't need to go back to school. I'll be too busy doing television interviews and appearing on *Mortimer and Whitehouse Gone Fishing*.'

Luckily, at some point he had drifted off. However, when he finally did get to sleep, Ben did his usual tossing and turning, taking up most of the bed. Alice woke to a very rude alarm call at 6.00 am with a creak in her neck and Ben's foot in her back.

Unfortunately, Malcolm had been most insistent to make the most of the day's fishing and wanted to get to the Canal as soon as possible so an early start was vital so up they got, ready to start the day.

The journey was an hour or so. Malcolm soon found the perfect spot to set up. He then proceeded to set about educating Ben about his favourite hobby.

'You know Ben, canals are really good habitats for fish of all shapes and sizes. Most canals are relatively shallow – only about four or five feet in the middle and perhaps two-foot-deep at the edge. There's plenty of food and lots of shelter from over hanging trees, shrubs or boats, particularly good for bream.'

'Oh, right yes. Can we fish now Uncle Malcolm?' said Ben who was doing his best to sound interested. 'I am going to catch the biggest salmon ever!'

'Well not in this canal Ben, bream, maybe, salmon no. You have to go elsewhere for salmon.' Malcolm could see the look of disappointment on Ben's face so added, 'You can get some pretty big Bream you know – the record so far is 4lb 12oz but well Ben you never know I bet you could catch a bigger one!' Malcolm winked at Alice.

Ben seemed delighted at this and was most insistent that they get on and get the rods set up. Malcolm dutifully did as he was told and started teaching Ben how to set the rod and bait up.

Alice at this point wished she owned a thermal vest and had put on some extra layers. She hoped Ben would pick this fishing lark up quickly and catch something. The quicker he did, the quicker they could all go home.

Luckily, Ben was a quick learner and Malcolm a great teacher. Alice had to acknowledge he was such a gentle, kind man and she thought what a shame it had been that he and Maud had never had any children but Maud always spouted on about how she didn't like them and thought that children were far too noisy, messy and restricted one's weekends. Alice thought of Mark. He was so adamant he didn't want children, so adamant. She wondered if she had got pregnant, Mark would have seen things differently, but then again, to have got pregnant when he had explicitly told her he didn't want children would have been dishonest, not a great start to family life.

Off Malcolm and Ben started, both sitting there, side by side nattering away.

Alice had spotted the café along the canal and thought it

would be a chance to warm up a bit announcing she would just pop off for a while.

'No need,' Malcolm said, 'I have bought flasks of tea. Plenty here. No point wasting money at that café, very expensive you know. They charge an extra fifty pence per cup.'

'Right,' said a very disappointed Alice. 'Lovely, a flask of tea it is then.'

Alice thought Ben would soon get bored and they could all go home. But, unfortunately, this was not the case. Ben was on a mission, he really did want that Guinness Book of records entry, that would really impress Fred the Barnett.

A couple of hours later, after several flasks of tea and a well and truly frozen Alice, Malcolm felt a nibble on the line and called Ben over to reel it in. Ben squealed with delight and together they skilfully reeled in Ben's first catch of the day. There were shouts of merriment and jumping up and down by all. Ben hugged Malcolm then Alice and then Malcolm in his excitement hugged Alice. Alice wondered how anyone could get excited over a fish that must have only measured a few inches long but I guess it was at least a catch!

Ben was a little worried about the idea of the hook in the fish's mouth but, once Malcolm had assured him it didn't hurt the fish, he whatsapped his achievement to Dad who duly replied with much praise and adulation. Ben put the fish back in the water and then promptly declared he was exhausted and wanted to go home.

Malcolm didn't seem to mind; he was so easy-going. After packing up all the gear, Malcolm brought out his ham and mustard sandwiches and, much to the relief of Alice, Ben insisted they made him gag and that he would much rather go for a burger. Alice was also pleased to hear this, so they made their way home, stopping along the way to eat.

'We must go again, soon, don't you think so Aunty Alice? Malcolm, brill day, thank you.' Ben was indeed very happy.

Alice got off the subject as quick as she could. She had only just started to feel her fingers and toes again and the midges had a field day on her legs, despite having sprayed herself with copious amounts of insect repellent. However, the day had kept her occupied and free from job hunting and all those jobs she kept avoiding.

The traffic had been pretty bad but they had managed to reach home by early evening and Ben enjoyed having all the attention and being the centre of it all. They played lots of his favourite card games and Ben and Alice were pleased with how they had managed to steer Malcolm away from the Monopoly, it took way too long and Malcolm always won anyway.

After some karaoke and Malcolm managing to hog the microphone for most of the evening, it was time for Ben's bedtime. Ben duly protested but Alice was having none of it. She argued how ten o'clock was way past his normal bed time and that no amount of persuasion would alter her mind. Ben realising when he had no more negotiation tactics left up his sleeve, resigned and departed to bed although he was very pleased with himself for managing to wheedle Aunty Alice into reading one of his Frank Lampard books.

Alice returned downstairs and was very grateful to flop down on the sofa. Malcolm handed her a large glass of her favourite red.

'This has never tasted so good! Thanks Malcolm.' Alice took a large swig and snuggled into the cushions behind her.

Malcolm came to join her and Alice showed him some of the pics she had taken from the day. Her eyes lit up when she talked about Ben. Malcolm enjoyed listening to her talk about the day. He had always loved those very deep blue eyes and amazing complexion. He was dying to kiss her but didn't want to make the same mistake again and frighten her away. He was sure she just needed a bit more time to get over Mark.

Malcolm knew he could look after Alice so much better than Mark ever did. Mark had taken her for granted and never truly appreciated how lovely and kind Alice was. He had been so selfish not wanting children and then going off like that with another woman. The affair had been such a cruel act of deceit and it had been so easy for Mark to change his mind, decide he did want to be a dad after all, and take up with a much younger woman. It would take her time to get over him. Malcolm decided he would wait, play the long game. Alice needed to see that he could be more than just a good friend, he could be far, far more. She had clearly enjoyed the fishing trip and Malcolm thought several more outings to Leighton Buzzard might just have the desired effect of wooing her into submission.

12

Getting back on the horse

It was now late March and Mario was finally coming home. Alice eagerly anticipated his arrival. There was something about Mario that everyone loved. He was a very generous, warm hearted man who would only ever see the good in people. He had been a close friend of Alice's dad, in fact more like a brother to him. Her dad had been a teenager when Mario had arrived from Italy had joined her dad's school and they soon became as thick as thieves, inseparable and would tell many a tale of their misadventures as young boys.

Alice and Robert had grown up with Mario being a constant guest in the house or the family visiting Mario's. Mario's dad was quite a wealthy man and had set up Mario to run a local café.

Whenever Alice had problems or just needed a chat, Mario had always been there. Through the usual troubled teenage years, Alice could go to Mario. She found him absolutely trustworthy, nothing she said would ever go back to her parents, she could rely on him to keep his silence. He was never judgemental. Always gave good advice and his café was always a welcome retreat from the world. Alice and Sue would often spend time after school at Mario's chattering or doing their homework. On a winter's day, Mario would make them tea cakes that oozed dribbling butter and a hot chocolate that could warm the soul.

This was the morning of Mario's return. Alice leaped out of bed and although it was really far too early to go to the airport Alice decided to leave anyway. It would be good to arrive in plenty of time. She might get stuck in traffic and she didn't want to risk keeping Mario waiting. He wasn't getting any younger and he would be tired from all the travelling.

Alice waited at Terminal 2 for his arrival. She watched the passengers gradually emerge through the doors, willing Mario to be the next one. There were young lovers, business men and women, tired children nagging their mums for one last treat at the café. Alice enjoyed studying them all, particularly the old couple with the man carrying far too many bags and his wife insisting he wasn't moving quickly enough. Finally, Mario emerged. Alice ran to him and gave him the biggest hug, much to Mario's delight.

'Hey, go gently with this old man,' Mario implored but his heart felt ready to burst. He was so thrilled to see her. Mario, now a widower, had been married for thirty long years but as much as they tried for a baby, it was not to be. Alice was like his own daughter.

Alice helped to take his bags. 'Mario, I can't believe you went without telling me!'

'Yes, yes, I know but everything happened so quickly. My brother would insist on upsetting the Mafia and well… you had enough on your plate. I really didn't think I would be away for so long.'

'Yes, sorry about your brother Mario.'

Mario waved his hand as if to dismiss the whole affair. He had never got on with him and seemed to spend his life cleaning up the messes Antonio always seemed to leave behind.

'Never mind all that now.' Mario gave Alice another hug. 'I am glad to be home. I need to catch up on all the news!'

'A lot has happened while you were away.'

It was a long walk to the car so Alice proceeded to tell Mario all about the recent events. Mario listened attentively and didn't seem at all surprised about Mark's behaviour. When they eventually got to the car, Alice put the luggage in the boot and Mario looked straight into her eyes, 'The arrogance of the man, how dare he treat you like that.' Mario was very quiet on the journey back to the café. Alice could sense his anger.

Over tea that night, Mario also broached the subject that he too had never liked Mark.

'Goodness, did no one like him?' Alice exclaimed. 'Could no one tell me? Not even you?'

'Look, I have made it a big rule in life not to interfere with other people's love lives. When you fall in love, you fall in love. Do you really think you would have listened? Do you really think that would have changed your feelings? In my experience there are none so deaf as those who are in love.'

Mario studied Alice. She hadn't deserved to be treated like this. 'You must now move on Alice, do not waste time grieving over a lost love. Futile. It is time to get back on the horse my friend, time to seek new love and adventure!'

'God, no. Never going there again Mario!'

'Has there not been anyone who has taken your fancy while I have been away?' Mario had a twinkle in his eye.

'Oh, you mean that dishy Italian man who was looking after your café while you were away?' Alice's eyes lit up.

'Although Ollie is my godson, he is not Italian! But, anyway, what do you think?'

'What?' Alice looked truly aghast at this thought. 'No, Mario, wasn't talking about Ollie, the one after Ollie.'

'Oh, you mean Angelico. Barking up the wrong tree there Alice – he is gay and one of Abramo's boys!'

Oh damn! Alice thought. Why are all the best one's gay? There was no justice in the world.

Mario continued, 'What about my godson Ollie? Now there's a goodun. The best of the best.'

'Really? Could have fooled me Mario. I found him to be a little too full of himself, personally.'

'Don't judge a book by its cover, you know that Alice. You should get to know him; he may be a wandering nomad but that gives a man great knowledge of the world and of people.'

Umm Alice thought. Ollie had obviously charmed his Uncle too. His sort always does.

'He is returning to help me out later in April. After all the goings on with Antonio, I need a break.' Mario looked very tired and Alice decided to take her leave and let him get an early night. There would be plenty of time to talk to Mario tomorrow.

'Hear what I say young lady, get back on that horse. I will ask my friend, André to call you. He runs a speedy bar.' Mario started looking through his address book.

'Don't you mean a speed dating bar, Mario?' Alice exclaimed with laughter.

'Well, whatever it is, you need to get on with your life and find a new man. We are not all bad you know.'

Alice got up and gave Mario a big kiss on the forehead and then a hug. 'Well you are certainly the best of the best Mario.

Right, well I will see. But these bars Mario can be very sleazy, lots of married men looking for a woman to spice up their love life.'

'No, no, this is a high-class establishment. André goes to a lot of trouble to get genuine people, looking for real friendship and hopefully love.'

Alice clearly wasn't convinced but she promised Mario she would at least think about it and with that Alice left to muse upon his words.

Alice got back to the flat quite late. She could hear laughter and giggling from Number 24. All had been very quiet on that front recently. Number 24 had clearly been away for some time now. Obviously, this was not a good time to try and knock again to thank her for her kindness. Her mobile rang, it was Sam.

'Oh, glad I have finally caught up with you.' Sam exclaimed.

Alice and Sam had also spent many an evening when Mark had been away or late home from the office, enjoying a large bowl of sweet and salty popcorn, drooling over the various leading men in their favourite movies. However, Sam's new job had kept her very busy of late, so it was time they had a natter and a catch up.

'How have you been Alice?'

'Oh, you know, surviving.' Alice couldn't muster up more than that.

They talked for a while about Mark and then Sam filled her in about her new job for a community magazine in the advertising department. When Sam thought the conversation was closing, Sam mustered up the courage to ask her a favour.

'Look, I have an idea. I have heard of this new speed dating bar up on Jackson Street near that expensive charity shop. Well I wondered if you fancied a lunch time drink there? Nothing serious of course, just a bit of fun!'

'Oh right, I see Mario wasn't slow at recruiting some extra help then was he? Just not sure Sam about meeting a load of strange people at a bar. It all seems a bit desperate to me. I know Mario knows the owner but, the thing is Sam, you often get a lot of weirdos and married men in places like that. Not my cup of tea at all. Besides I'm not sure I am ready yet, do you?'

Sam was not to be put off. 'Nonsense Alice. Thursday lunch-times are for the over forties, seeking new friends and possibly more, come on it might be a lot of fun. Let's give it a go. Let's have a laugh if nothing else.'

Alice really wasn't in the mood but didn't want to disappoint her friend. 'Look, I will have a think about it, *just* a think about it.' Alice could hear Sam's delight on the other end of the phone.

'Great, I'll ring you next week and we can have another chat.' Sam signed off and Alice decided to get to bed.

However, just at that moment, the doorbell rang. Alice looked at the clock it was now eleven. A bit late for callers at this time? She peered through the spy hole and saw Number 24 standing there. Alice opened the door.

'Sorry to bother you so late, but I believe a parcel was delivered here for me. I would have waited until the morning, but I am off early tomorrow for a few days.' Number 24 looked even more dazzling than usual.

'Oh yes, it came this morning. I completely forgot! I've been out most of the day.' Alice handed her the package. 'I had in fact meant to catch you before, just to say a big thank you for your kindness on New Year's Eve. I am sorry it has taken so long to speak to you. I hope I didn't spoil any plans or anything?' Alice felt sure that Number 24 would have had plans to venture out that night.

'No, don't be silly, nothing planned. I hate New Year's Eve. All that expectation and then you wake up the next morning and nothing has changed.'

Thankfully, Alice thought, Number 24 didn't seem bothered at all.

'Yes, I know what you mean. Well, thank you anyway, I don't normally end up on the doorstep without my keys in tears.'

'No, of course. How have you been, everything ok? I don't like to intrude but…'

'Oh gosh yes. You know the man I had been living with, well he decided it was time to get another woman, well not just get another woman but get her pregnant too.' Alice felt herself choking up a bit and decided to change the subject.

Number 24 put her hand on her arm. 'Men, can't live with them, can't live without them. You know you are a very attractive woman there are plenty more in the sea.'

Umm Alice thought. Maybe there were for a much younger, stunning girl.

Number 24 headed for the door.

'No, not quite ready but thanks for the compliment.' Alice went to open the door but just as she did, Number 24 stopped and looked her straight in the eye and smiled 'Look, women of your age are at the peak of their sexual prowess you know.'

Alice didn't quite know what to say to this. She was stunned into silence by the frankness and somewhat direct statement from this, well, to all intents and purposes, complete stranger.

Number 24 continued, 'Now is the time to use your freedom to meet new people, think about what you want and who YOU really are. Change the wardrobe, hairstyle whatever you want.' With this Number 24 asked Alice for a pen and paper. Alice was somewhat puzzled but obliged her neighbour. Number 24 started writing something on the paper and then handed it to her.

'This is a friend of mine; he is a well-known fashion guru. Trust me, he can change your life and attitude to it. He can transform a woman! He is great at making a woman feel good about themselves. When a man leaves it always leaves one feeling empty, less confident.'

Alice couldn't imagine any man leaving Number 24 but surmised that even the most beautiful women get hurt.

'Anyway, thanks for looking after my parcel. Give him a ring. I promise you, you won't be disappointed, mention my name, Isabella Armstrong. Isabella was now half way down the hall when the door to her flat opened. Yet another dishy man was standing there. Gosh Alice thought, how does she do it!

Alice looked down at the card, the name Gok Wan was written on it. Oh my goodness, she is a personal friend of Gok Wan's! She wandered into the bedroom as she carried on gripping the piece of paper in her hand. She looked in the mirror. 'None of my clothes fit me, my hair is starting to look a mess and well I have had the same style for years.'

Yes, Isabella was right, she thought, it was time for a change. However, a thought dawned upon her. It might be expensive though; it might mean going into one of her saving accounts? She hadn't earned anything in the last few months. But, then again, she had received the redundancy package! Sod it, she could afford it! Out with the old and in with the new!

Life suddenly seemed just that bit brighter. A makeover! Of course, why not? She had seen those programmes on TV where Gok had utterly transformed women. Women of all shapes and sizes. Women of all ages. Sod Mark, she would show him. He would regret leaving her for this younger woman. No, true, there was now too much water under the bridge for them ever go back but a part of her did want to make him suffer. She did want him to regret his decision. Maybe she had let herself go a bit, become too complacent.

Alice was not impressed with the mirror's reflection. Too many takeaways and glasses of gin. She went to the kitchen cupboards and headed for the snacks cupboard and promptly threw them in the bin. Then she headed for the gin cupboard. She picked up one of her many bottles and went to empty it down the kitchen sink. However, she soon hesitated. 'Hang on,' she thought. 'Maybe this was a step too far? Besides there might be an emergency. No, not a good idea, I'll keep the gin.'

She went back to the bedroom and stared at herself yet again in the mirror. Yes, she was going to survive without him. Yes, it may take a bit of time. Yes, it wasn't going to be easy. Yes, she did want him to regret his decision BIG TIME. But, more importantly, she wanted to feel the best she could be. Not for a man, not for anyone else. Just for her. Yes, it was a time for a change, out with the old, in with the new.

She pulled out her mobile and called her friend Sam back.

'Doing anything tomorrow Sam? I am going to treat us to a day out.'

13

Gok Wan

Alice sat waiting for Sam at Waterloo Station. Sam was running late. That girl just couldn't be on time for anything. Alice didn't mind really, Sam had always been such a supportive friend and trusted confident.

Sam, like herself, had been through many trials and tribulations. She was a similar age to Alice and had been single for some time now. Sam had been out with a guy for some ten years. They had finally bought their dream home. Three months later he had left declaring that he no longer loved her. All her friends were truly surprised. Alice wondered how men could do this? How could a man just switch his feelings off? Paul, her partner, had seemed like such a nice guy and they both seemed so well suited.

After Paul left, all the gang rallied round her and Sam gradually pieced her life back together again. But she had never mentioned wanting anyone else until now. Alice thought that any man would be lucky to have Sam. She was a very talented lady. She was a few years younger than Alice. Sam had originally trained as a dancer and, for some extra money, after Paul had left her, started dance lessons. All sorts of dance – Salsa, Swing, Jive, Tango, Waltz. You name it - Sam could teach it. Mark was never very keen and wouldn't go but Alice had gone and loved it. However, with all the recent events, Alice had refrained from going.

Whilst waiting, Alice was enjoying the buzz of everyone around her mulling about, some more purposeful than others but all moving along on whatever journey they were headed for. She wondered over to the newsagents and purchased a paper and settled down to her routine of completing the concise crossword puzzle. Alice was pondering over one of the clues when in the distance she spotted a person that resembled Mark. She blinked and tried to refocus. In fact, this man didn't just appear to be like Mark, she realised it was.

He was with his new woman and she was now pushing a pram. They seemed to be arguing about something because the woman was waving her arms and hands about in a very angry fashion. Alice knew they were heading her way so she quickly retreated to a safe vantage point where she was sure she wouldn't be seen. There he was as tall and broad and as good looking as she had always known him to be. He looked perhaps a little tired but that was only to be expected with a new baby.

Alice looked down towards the pram. There was a gorgeous, tiny baby with a blue bobble hat. So, he had a little baby boy. She felt her heart aching, this vision of a perfect family – this vision that she and Mark could have so easily had.

Mark stopped to tuck a blanket around the baby and at this point Alice could feel the tears and anger mounting. Her sense of loss was palpable. A loss of losing Mark and a loss for the mother she might have been. He had a new life, a new family.

She thought back to the time they were together. She remembered how he would meet her from work on a Friday evening and off they would go to some café or restaurant. She remembered how they would talk for hours about nothing at all really but it didn't matter, they were together. They were a unit. Alice's tears now ventured down her face.

Eventually, they moved on. She watched Mark disappear down towards the underground. Alice tried in vain to return to her paper and crossword but it was to no avail. Fortunately, Sam now appeared.

'Sorry I'm late! Just don't know where the time goes. Right so what's the plan?' Sam could see Alice had been crying. She was about to offer some sympathy but clearly Alice was now on a mission.

Alice recalled Isabella's words and she got up from her seat and spoke to Sam with real conviction. 'I'm going to have a makeover Sam, a complete transformation.' And with these words she strode on, taking Sam firmly by the arm.

Sam was left wondering what the next few hours would bring. After all, Alice had quite naturally been very up and down in her emotions recently. Was this the start of another break down? Alice had always been firmly entrenched in what she wore and how she had her hair. But, of course, nothing was now normal for Alice.

'I see, right then so a transformation it is then. But how exactly are we going to go about it then Alice?'

'Wait and see, wait and see.' Alice headed down to the tube and off they went. 'Gok Wan, here I come, ready or not Alice thought to herself.'

Soon they arrived at the address on Isabella's note. Alice rang the bell. No reply. Not to be deterred Alice rang the bell again. After what seemed like an eternity, a very well coiffured lady opened the door. She purveyed the two ladies on her door step, looking at them up and down. She raised her eyebrows in a very haughty and condescending manner as if to signal how utterly surprised she was to find these two on the doorstep. What could Gok possibly do to redeem these two?

Alice thought her rather rude but was not perturbed from her purpose. 'Gok Wan, please.'

'Is he expecting you?' The lady continued to eye these two rather dowdy ladies suspiciously.

'Ah, well no, not exactly. He has a friend who is an acquaintance of mine and well she gave me his name and told me to come and see him. Look I have this note from a friend of his.' Alice thrust it towards the haughty woman's face but this did nothing to persuade her to let these two women in.

'I'm sorry, he has a very special visitor today, a close friend, and really won't be able to see you. You really must make an appointment first, you know.' The lady then proceeded to shut the door.

In that very moment Alice felt an overwhelming sense of need. An overwhelming sense of entitlement to Gok. She hadn't ventured out to fall at the first hurdle. Much to Sam's embarrassment and protests, Alice put her foot firmly in the door.

The lady looked horrified. 'Excuse me, but as I said Gok is otherwise detained, please take your foot out of the door and I suggest you ring the office and make an appointment.'

Sam interjected, 'Alice didn't you make an appointment?'

'Well, no, not exactly. I couldn't get anyone to answer and well, I just wanted to get on with it.'

Sam rolled her eyes, not quite believing what she was hearing. The haughty lady seemed even more displeased at hearing this.

'Please remove your foot from the door right this minute or I will have to call security.' The woman clearly meant business but so did Alice.

'No,' Alice thought, 'I want to be a new woman and I want to be a new woman today.' She pushed past the lady. Sam, not wanting to be left behind, decided it was better to join her than be left without her on the pavement outside. Damage limitation would now be needed and Sam was not going to leave her friend in need.

'Really, I must protest, this is not acceptable!' But the woman's voice fell on deaf ears. Alice was in through the door and was on a mission to find Gok. He must be here somewhere. The whole building was full of glass doors and open plan studios. Surely it couldn't be that difficult to track him down. She ventured across the building. She scoured the surroundings and then heard the faint echo of his voice laughing. Alice headed towards the voice to find Gok standing there talking to Fern Britton who both looked somewhat puzzled and perplexed at the ladies' arrival.

The lady who answered the door, finally caught up with them, 'Gok I must apologise but this one (pointing to Alice) was most insistent and indeed rudely pushed her way in. Shall I call security?'

Gok looked at Alice. Alice looked at Gok. Gok wasn't too sure what to make of this one. 'I am very sorry ladies but you need to make an appointment, as you can see, I am with a friend and I really am fully booked for the next few months. Make an appointment with my secretary.' Gok turned away to carry on his conversation with Fern.

Alice's heart sank. For a brief moment she felt utterly

dejected and was about to turn back through the door but something inside her just ignited. She stopped and turned back. She walked straight towards Gok and tapped him on the shoulder firmly.

'Look you don't understand. All my life I have just trundled along being the same old Alice. I don't want to be her any more. My partner of years has left me for someone much, much younger. This, quite frankly, makes me feel not just rejected, utterly miserable, older and less attractive than I have ever felt but…' She couldn't find any more words. Once again, the tears starting rolling down her cheeks. Sam put her arm out to comfort her. Alice continued sobbing.

'He now has a baby that should have been ours and now is leading the perfect family life without me. But me, well I am just the same old me. Still just Alice. Good old Alice. Reliable, solid dowdy old me.'

Alice looked Fern up and down 'Besides Fern is already lovely, she really doesn't need a makeover.'

Sam's tears were now starting to well up in her eyes too.

Alice looked straight at Gok. 'Now it's my turn, now it's time for a new me that's all I want.' She turned around and headed for the door.

Fern looked at Gok. Gok looked at Fern.

'Hang on Alice,' Sam interjected putting her hand around her friend's shoulder, 'Neither of us are leaving not until… not until …,you have transformed us into the goddesses lurking beneath!'

Alice looked at Sam with total love in her eyes.

'I see ladies.' Gok studied them both, feeling quite over-whelmed by this lady's grief. He could see how upset Alice was.

He purveyed her some more. It simply wasn't in his nature to ignore a plea for help.

'Well we had better get those goddesses out of their shells then, hadn't we?' He beamed across at them and they both simultaneously went to hug him.

Fern smiled at the two ladies, 'I fancy being a bit of a goddess myself Gok!'

Gok was not slow to bring his ideas to fruition.

'So, then girlfriends, let us begin. Let's start with the undies ladies!'

How apt that at that precise moment Alice could hear Pretty Woman blasting through the sound system. She might not be a Julia Roberts but hey she knew this man could work wonders!

Out came the full range of Gok's underwear that seemed to truly cover up the lumps and bumps and wobbly bits, pull in the waist and accentuate the bust. Alice admired her new curves! She had always worn very loose tops over jeans to cover all the sins. However, with this underwear that transformed her body she was now ready to expose it!

'Now gorgeous ladies, we need to think about a revamp of that wardrobe of yours. Stop hiding those curves. Embrace that body. Be proud. Right, next on our list a shopping trip and I know exactly where to take you.' Fern's limo, which had been waiting outside, was summoned and off they went to Selfridges.

Alice hadn't been here in months. The store was so big and had so many clothes, it had always overwhelmed her. She always ended up not buying anything and leaving the store somewhat frustrated. However, she was now with the God of fashion and clothing and Gok seemed to know every nook and cranny of this store. Clothes, clothes and yet more clothes were brought to them and Gok just knew what would work and how to throw it all together. These clothes were so different to anything Alice had previously worn. Figure hugging clothes, wrap dresses, high heels, colours she would never have dreamt of wearing - colours that seemed to make her complexion and figure come alive. Alice bought them all - accessories too. Handbags, scarves, jewellery – the lot! Out with the old Alice she thought and in with the new.

Right my gorgeous ladies, Aunty Gok needs to finish this all off. A trip to the hair and beauty department. This man could open doors that no ordinary person off the street could do. He seemed to have the whole store under his control. All the ladies had their hair cut, make up applied and nails done.

Alice couldn't believe the new woman she now was. New hair, make up and clothes! What a difference a new wardrobe, high and low lights and being taught how to apply the make-up to enhance all those features made! She swore she looked ten years younger!

They all stood back admiring each other. 'I have to tell you ladies you all look absolutely gorgeous! Right, now you look like a million dollars don't forget to tell yourselves you are now capable of anything. No more hiding behind your clothes but show off your best with them.' Gok purveyed them all and, yes, he was very pleased with the results. He walked up to Alice and put his arm around her. Alice had the loveliest smile on her face and he could see and feel her happiness.

Alice couldn't believe her eyes. She didn't recognise this very striking lady and Gok could see the recognition of this was starting to show on her face too.

'Now listen to me, girlfriend, you are now ready to venture

back into the world a new woman! Start loving what you have. Be proud. You have a beautiful body, stop trying to hide it under all those baggy clothes. It is time for you to believe in yourself. Put the past behind you. I think it's time girly that you moved on!' Alice threw her arms around him and he warmly reciprocated. He felt this had been one of his most worthwhile transformations he had ever done.

It was now time for him to depart, his work was done. 'I'll send you my bill in the post ladies,' and winked at them all.

The three ladies ventured down Oxford Street and all heads turned to look at these striking ladies walking down the road. They felt like they were walking on air. Fern stopped to write autographs and everyone assumed the ladies with Fern must be famous too so Sam and Alice had a go at practising their autographs too. Eventually, a large limo pulled up and Fern's driver appeared.

'Can I take you anywhere Sam and Alice?' Fern enquired.

They both thanked Fern for being so generous to share Gok but declined the offer of a lift. Alice and Sam were now hungry and in need of refreshment so they both headed for The London Gin Club in Chapel Street. How amazing Gok had been and how kind of Fern to share him.

'Right, I think we are ready for a trip to that speed dating bar of yours Sam! 'What day did you say we should go?' They both had a giggle and guzzled back the gin. The new underwear would now allow for a few gins, Alice thought.

Later that evening, Alice and Sam went round to Sue's. Robert was talking over some business with Malcolm. When Alice appeared at the door, no one could believe their eyes. Robert took a double take and Malcolm seemed to lose the ability to speak. Sue had always known how Alice could brush up but this was brushing up with a difference!

'Hi, new Alice coming through the door. Out with the old, in with the new!'

'WOW! Lady in red. You look amazing!' Robert exclaimed.

Sue agreed, 'You look fantastic, you both look fantastic.'

Ben then appeared wanting to know what all the commotion was about.

'Hey big fella, you should be in bed, come on back we go.' Robert moved towards the door.

'I can't sleep with all that noise!' Ben looked at Alice and didn't quite know what to think, she all seemed a bit different. She had heels that went on for miles which made her look so tall. 'Wow, you look really lovely Aunty Alice!'

'Well, thank you Ben, now how about I carry on with that book of yours?'

Alice followed him back upstairs and they both snuggled up under the duvet. After a while, Ben placed his hand over the story book and pushed it away.

'I heard mum and dad talking about Mark the other night. I never liked him, Aunty Alice and I feel really bad I didn't tell you.'

Alice took him in her arms. 'Well it appears most of my friends didn't either Ben. Look it isn't your fault. It is really hard to tell people you love, things they don't or would rather not hear. You were thinking of my feelings because you are a lovely boy. I love you so much.' Alice kissed Ben on the forehead.

'Mum believes that you are well shot of him.' Ben snuggled into her arms.

'Does she now? Well I think your mum is right Ben, as

usual.' Alice hugged him tightly and read to him. It wasn't long before he had drifted to sleep.

She tiptoed out of the room and went to join the others. This time a bottle of champagne had been opened. 'Robert, popped out and came back with this!' Sue beamed a smile at her husband. 'Umm, Moet and Chandon! Very nice!

'Well, why not. You ladies looking so lovely and it will go well with the takeaway.' Malcolm poured Alice and Sam a large glass. Sam threw him a lovely smile and asked everyone to raise their glasses.

'To speedy dating and a new us!' toasted Alice.

Malcolm didn't much like the sound of that but well, if Alice was happier, then well that's all that really mattered.

14

Speedy dating

Today was the day.

'Speedy dating, as Mario would say, here I come.' Alice leapt out of bed with a real spring in her step. She phoned Sam just to check she was still up for it, which indeed she was and headed straight for the shower. Shampooed and defuzzed she felt ready to dress and peruse her new wardrobe of clothes.

'Right, I need sexy but stylish. It's at lunch time but you never know it might lead to an evening date so…' She scoured her new collection. 'Yes, this will be perfect.'

Alice decided to go with another one of her new fitted dresses. It was a gorgeous cream colour with large red flowers. The red high heels looked good with the outfit as did the large beaded necklace. Gok really did know how to utilise accessories to their best. Alice had spent a fortune but as her Aunt had always said, 'You can't take it with you, you know. God doesn't charge you a thing when you go through those pearly gates.'

Alice applied her makeup thinking about all the techniques she had learnt. She didn't quite look as good as the make-up artist at Selfridges had made her look but, after all, practice makes perfect. She stood back to admire herself in the hall mirror. Alice preferred this one to her bedroom mirror as the lighting in the bedroom always made her look a bit fatter and the wrinkles a bit more pronounced.

'Yes, pretty damn good – that underwear is a miracle worker. Bust looks bigger and my waist looks smaller.'

Alice could hear some laughter coming up the flat stairs. She was sure it was Isabella's voice and a second person. Alice was keen to show off how she looked but couldn't think of a reason to go out to meet her, particularly if she had a companion. Quickly, she removed one of her earrings and popped it'on the hall way stand. Opening the door, she started to pretend she was looking for a lost earing on the outer landing.

Isabella emerged at the top of the stairs 'Oh, Alice, how wonderful you look!' Isabella couldn't believe her eyes. 'Something tells me you have visited my friend?'

'Oh yes, he is marvellous isn't he. Thanks Isabella, a really good recommendation.' Alice returned to looking at the floor for her supposedly missing earing. 'Came in late last night, you know how it is, and I discovered this morning my earing had gone, just checking whether it is out here.'

Both started looking down at the floor for the missing earing. Alice felt a twinge of guilt for now getting Isabella to look for a non-existent earing. At this point more footsteps could be heard coming up the flat stairs. A tall, very broad blonde-haired man appeared.

'Sorry, just had to pop back to the car, forgot the wine.' There at the top of the stairs appeared a very Colin Firth look alike. Alice felt herself go a bit girly as he fixed his gaze upon her. Her body seemed to not quite know what it was about. Isabella turned to him, 'Alistair, I would like you to meet Alice, she's my next-door neighbour'

Alistair clearly looked pleased to be introduced to her and

moved forward to shake her hand.

'Hi Alice a real pleasure to meet you.' Alistair had even more come to bed eyes than Poldark she thought. He looked quite a bit older than Isabella, much closer to her age she thought. Isabella's father?

'Oh, yes, nice to meet you,' said Alice as she too moved forward to shake his hand. However, as she moved forward her heel had firmly trapped itself on the outside door mat in one of the holes. Alice moved forward but the shoe was most insistent on staying where it was. This caused her to lurch over and lose balance. Alistair was quick to support her arm, 'Oh mind how you go!' He held her firmly.

Although she felt embarrassed at not being quite as graceful as she had hoped she did at the same time feel a hot flush of something throughout her body as he firmly gripped her.

'Oh, thank you.' Alice felt her girly voice came from nowhere.

'My pleasure.' Alistair smiled and continued down the corridor to Isabella's. 'See you in a mo, Bella.' He disappeared through the door. Isabella turned to Alice, 'Well, you look like a million dollars, my friend. I could tell my brother thought so too.' Isabella winked at her.

What Alice really wanted to say at this point was how bloody fantastic he is your brother and not lover, and when is he coming round again and does he have a partner? However, she managed to restrain herself. 'Oh, your brother, how nice to have… (she couldn't quite think what to say) such a nice brother.' Alice continued to explain that she really must get on as she was having lunch with a friend of hers.

Isabella looked pleased 'Oh great, I hope you have a great time with him.'

Alice turned around to return to her flat. She thought how wonderful that Isabella would assume it was with a man and not a woman. The whole encounter had brightened up her day even more.

A little later Sam had arrived at Alice's. Sam too had brushed up very well and together they looked a pretty handsome pair.

Both ladies admired themselves in the hallway mirror. Alice couldn't help herself start singing *I feel pretty* from *West Side Story* and Sam wasn't slow to join in. Before long they were both competing to look at themselves in the mirror and were in full swing singing along.

After their musical rendition and a glass of wine or two for Dutch courage, they left the apartment in good time to get the tube. Alice was hoping to get another glimpse of Alistair but all she saw was his Audi TT parked in the guest parking space. Oh well, maybe another time. If they were both there later, Alice thought she could invite them in for a drink and some nibbles maybe but right now she was going to focus on meeting some new people, well hopefully, a man.

They arrived at André's speed dating bar and were greeted by the man himself and a glass of Prosecco. He was a tall, lythe man who walked with one arm on his hip and the other seemed to constantly gesticulate in the air.

'Come and sit down, lovely to meet you ladies. I have heard all about you from Mario.'

'All good I hope?' said Sam

'Positively not ladies!' André winked at them both and made the usual polite conversation.

Alice couldn't quite make out André's accent. She had never heard anything like it before. Was it Russian? Hungarian?

Something Eastern European? What's more every time before he spoke, he had developed the habit of swaying his head in order to move his very long fringe back from his eyes. Was that all his hair Alice wondered?

Alice looked around. No men. Just as she had thought. 'So, no luck with attracting any men along today, André?'

André raised his eyebrows. 'Now, now ladies, as eager as you are. You need to have a little more patience! The men are in the lounge next door. Time for all to calm the nerves with a drink first don't you think? Besides we all like a bit of anticipation, adds to the excitement you know.'

When Alice had got her head around his strange accent and all the head swinging, Alice had to admit that, yes, he had a good point.

She started to feel a bit more nervous so took another large swig of the Prosecco and sat down on one of the enormous leather Chesterfield sofas. 'Wouldn't it be fab if Alistair or an Alistair look alike turned up,' Alice thought.

Sam started to introduce herself to another group of ladies sitting opposite. They looked a bit older, later fifties perhaps, very sophisticated and good-looking women. Definite competition.

The Prosecco continued to flow. Gradually more women started to arrive and all of them started to relax and enjoy the ambience of the lounge and watching the bar tender mixing up the cocktails. Laughter could be heard from the men in the lounge next door and, it was true, there was an air of anticipation mixed with hope that a man, maybe Mr Right, would walk through the door.

After about an hour, the door adjoining the two rooms

opened and the men came through. Alice was surprised to see a fair number, not enough to go around all the women but not a bad show. They were all shapes and sizes: some short, some tall and one who had combed his hair over his bald patch. Never a good idea Alice thought because any gust of wind would reveal it and just made a man look silly.

André introduced everybody.

'Now we are all acquainted, time to start the ball rolling! Now ladies and gents, in a minute I will take you through to the dining room. The tables and chairs are arranged for two and there are numbers on each of the tables. At first, you will get five minutes with each partner. You will know when the five minutes is up because a bell will ring. Ladies you stay where you are and gentlemen if you have started at table three for example you will then move to table four. Everyone clear?'

A couple of the women weren't. Always someone who doesn't listen thought Alice and we have the easiest job we just sit at the same table. André repeated the instructions again.

'Right ladies and gents through you go!' André ushered them into the dining room. 'Now at the end of everyone having the chance to meet, you will be invited to mingle again back in the lounge for some drinks and snacks. You will then be given a card and you will write down the names of those people you would like to see again; hand it to me and then I can arrange a further meeting if both party's consent, of course.'

Sam winked at Alice, 'Here goes, lift off!'

Everyone shuffled through to the dining room. The tables were small and round and seated a decent distance apart, making it more difficult to eavesdrop on your neighbour's conversations. Alice sat down and one of the shortest men she had ever seen came to sit opposite her. He looked a bit like Ronnie Corbett extremely short in stature but with a very friendly, smiley face.

'Hello I'm Bertie, lovely to meet you.' He held out both hands and gave Alice a very enthusiastic, firm and lingering handshake. Alice wondered when he was going to let go of her hand as it was now starting to lose its circulation.

'Shall we sit down?' Alice asked.

The bell rang. Let's hope this would be a quick five minutes Alice thought.

'I thought I recognised you, you are one of my customers.' Bertie stated.

Alice looked long and hard but no one came to mind. Bertie looked somewhat put out.

'The extra sausage in the bag?' Bertie said most indignantly.

It suddenly came to Alice like a lightning bolt. 'Gosh, yes of course. Please forgive me, you're from Mr Bertie Bigg's Butchers, yes, sorry I didn't recognise you. Out of your usual overalls Mr Bigg.' Alice couldn't help being amused at the name considering this man was so short. Bertie clearly looked offended at Alice not recognising him and his smile speedily disappeared from his face. Alice thought she better make amends quickly, after all he was the only butcher on the high street and his bacon and sausages were to die for, 'By the way, your sausages are lovely, really good, never tasted anything better.'

Bertie's face now turned back into a smile. He now looked very pleased with himself. 'Well it's all about the meat and herbs you know. It's ensuring just that right combination to make that perfect sausage.'

'Right, well that is…' Alice tried to find the right words, in fact, any words, 'Very… interesting.' But perhaps these words, showing too much interest in his sausages, was not, she soon reflected, a good idea.

Bertie proceeded to use their five minutes to tell her all about the sausage recipe in copious detail. Despite assuring her that he could never reveal his most well-kept secret he seemed to be giving away quite a lot. Alice kept willing the bell to ring, surely it must be five minutes by now? After what seemed like an hour, the bell rang.

Bertie got up, somewhat reluctantly and clearly irritated that he was unable to continue educating her on how the perfect sausage was made, and went to shake Alice's hand. As her hand was still recovering from its last encounter, she was quick to direct him to the next numbered table.

Chap no 2 arrived. Tall, about her age, smart suit and not bad looking. Alice lent forward to show her interest and played a little with her hair (she had learnt this from a dating website). Sadly though, throughout the whole of his five minutes whilst talking to her, he was clearly looking at another woman on the table behind her. He rambled on about himself and didn't seem the least interested in what Alice had to say. When the bell went, he leapt up from his chair and jumped quickly to the next lady sitting behind her without even saying goodbye. How rude Alice thought. Definitely not her type anyway.

Man no 3 arrived.

'Harry's the name. Keen birdwatcher well, as in the feathery type of course!' His high-pitched nervous laugh filled the room as he swayed back and forth in his seat in an almost rhythmic motion every time he spoke.

'Of course,' Alice replied. What else could you be with a peak cap and tweed jacket she thought.

Harry proceeded to tell Alice all about the different species of birds you could find in the neck of the woods where she lived. Again, he seemed to have little interest in what Alice said and only asked one question, 'So, do you think this might be a hobby you would like to get involved with?'

'Well, I can see how some people would love it but…' thankfully the bell rang, 'Oh dear, time has run out, never mind, see you later.' Alice sank back into her chair feeling this may have not have been such a good idea.

She was thankfully left alone for the next five minutes as there weren't enough men. André offered her another drink and brought her a magazine to read. The magazine proved to be the best company as yet and she drooled over an article on Colin Firth. Yes, Alistair really did look like him. Maybe he would still be there when she got back. If Sam stayed with her, she would have a bit more confidence to invite them both in for a gin. Alice turned round to see where Sam was. She was with birdman and the glazed expression on her face said it all.

Throughout the next hour, there were a few pleasant men to talk to who seemed genuinely interested in who Alice was and what she had to say but the problem was she just didn't fancy any of them. She really didn't mind the man with the huge buck teeth who couldn't pronounce his 'r's but, unfortunately, his main interests appeared to be wugby, wunning and wally wacing.

All in all, she just hadn't felt that all important spark come alight inside with any of the men she met.

When the final bell had rung, both Alice and Sam were

eager to get back to the lounge and collect their coats. André tried to persuade them to stay, protesting that they hadn't filled their card out, registering who they were interested in but it was to no avail. Alice thanked him profusely but both were determined to get out of the door as soon as they could.

'Well that was an … well it was an experience!' said Sam.

Both burst into laughter.

'Fancy coming back to mine for a drink then love?' Alice enquired.

'That is the best offer I have had all day.' Sam beamed her a smile and off they headed home.

Early that evening, Mario phoned Alice to ask her all about her day. Alice filled him in and Mario apologised that it hadn't been more successful.

'No need Mario, it was good for the experience but whether I will get another free sausage now is debateable.' Alice sat back in her armchair and hugged the cushion.

Mario filled Alice in on his day and then reminded her that he would soon be going away again for a short break to have a well-earned holiday. 'Ollie will be coming to take care of things, I told him if he needed any help to ring you, I hope that is ok?'

Alice was glad he was coming back for a short while, at least she would be able to thank him.

Mario signed off and Sam filled Alice's glass again, 'Oh, well, you never know until you try these things I suppose. I might try one of those dating apps next time. Probably easier!'

'Yes, indeed, though it was worth a try.' Alice took a sip of her drink and then asked Sam if she would like to meet Isabella, her next-door neighbour. 'I have some snacks and plenty of tonic left.'

'Yes, that would be nice, I am intrigued by this Number 24 woman, Isabella, you keep telling everyone about and how kind she was to give us Gok's details.'

Alice checked her make-up and lipstick and then off she trotted to Number 24. She rang the doorbell and was delighted when Alistair answered. Alice's body went all funny again and that strange girly voice seemed to leave her mouth.

'Oh, I didn't realise you were still here, sorry for bothering you, I just wondered if Isabella was in?' Alice felt another tinge of guilt for lying having already spotted Alistair's Audi TT was still parked outside.

Alice continued, 'We, my girlfriend Sam, well not my girlfriend as in girlfriend, just girlie friend Samantha, we wondered if Bella and you wanted to pop over for a drink?'

'Yes, how lovely, that would be great. Bella and I have been twiddling our thumbs a bit in the last hour or so.' Alistair's, Colin Firth eyes, were firmly fixed upon her and this made Alice's insides all swoon. Things were definitely looking up.

Isabella came to the door. 'Yes, sounds great, we will be over in five.

When everyone was seated in Alice's living room, Sam handed around the snacks and various gins were offered. Alistair chose Alice's favourite.

'Ah, *Bombay Sapphire*, always a great gin and hard to beat.' Alistair clearly enjoyed his first swig and started telling them all about another favourite of his, *Shed No 1*, a gin distillery in Ulverston in Cumbria. He seemed to know a great deal about lots of different gins and they all enjoyed talking about their favourites and the types of tonics that went well with them.

Alistair went on to discuss his recent business travels to

Southern Spain, his love of cuisine from the Basque region, particularly San Sebastian which he felt had some of the finest restaurants in the world. Alice listened intently thinking that it would make a great holiday destination in the Summer particularly if Alistair was with her!

Sam could clearly see Alice was enamoured by him and he did seem a really nice guy. He wasn't overly charming or smarmy like Mark just really pleasant to listen to and he seemed to be genuinely interested in finding out about them both.

After a few hours, Alistair and Isabella thanked Alice for her hospitality, saying they must do this again sometime soon. Alice readily agreed and walked them both to the door. She watched him disappear down the hall.

She shut the door and stood in the hall way, 'Wow, is he gorgeous or what! Well, what do you think?' Alice went to hug a cushion on the sofa, 'Who needs speedy dating with men like that on the door step!'

'Yes, indeed, I can see you are quite smitten by him.' Sam came over to join the cushion hugging. 'Not my type but, yes, I can see what you see in him.'

Alice returned to the sofa. 'I think it is time for another gin, don't you think? And a bit of Pride and Prejudice? I have the box set of the original series.'

'Definitely, nobody can beat Colin Firth as Darcy.'

'Certainly not!'

The evening was full of chatting, drinks, a take away and lots of drooling over Colin Firth.

Having drunk a little more than Alice had originally intended, her bed now seemed to beckon her. It wasn't long before she was fast asleep and as soon as she looked around her, there she was in Pemberley.

The massive mansion and grounds stretched out around her. She was still sitting on a chair, all tied-up, but at least she was no longer in the hotel room and was now in the fresh air, in front of an enormous lake. There in the lake Darcy was swimming. His strong arms and streamlined body glided through the water.

He stopped as soon as he noticed her and invited her in. Strange, Alice thought, he should be getting out of the water and then notice me? After all, he was in Pride and Prejudice, he should know this? But Alice didn't want to turn down this exciting offer.

'Yes, what a splendid idea. The only thing is, is that I seem to be a bit tied up. You need to come and set me free Darcy.'

Just at that moment, Ollie appeared and sat down beside her. 'I thought you only got your 10m swimming badge? I think diving into a deep lake with just a 10m swimming badge to your name, is a bit foolish really. Don't you?'

'Look, I can swim like a fish, thank you very much,' Alice said most indignantly, annoyed that this man, yet again, was meddling where he shouldn't. However, she had to admit to herself that it was true, she really wasn't a great swimmer.

At this point, Darcy had got out of the Lake. Alice could see his broad, manly chest through his wet shirt. His breeches were revealing a well-endowed man, she thought, considering he had been swimming in a cold lake.

He walked with great purpose towards her. His eyes were fixed most ardently upon hers. He reached the chair but instead of bending down to untie the rope he just looked down upon her, in what Alice considered to be a rather haughty manner.

'No, I think Ollie is probably right, the water is far too deep

and with just a 10m badge to your name, it would hardly be a good idea now would it?'

'Well, I will have you to hold me Darcy, to keep me safe in the water.' Alice implored.

'No. Another day, I think.' With those last words he walked off. Alice tried in vain to call after him. She looked around for Ollie but he too had now disappeared. Alice was left feeling helpless yet again on the chair.

'Why is it that no one releases me? It's ridiculous!

15

La comida del amor

April arrived. Alice took Mario to the airport and bid him farewell.

Mario was off to Innsbruck, one of his favourite holiday destinations. They gave each other a big hug and Mario took Alice's face gently into his hands.

'Now, in three weeks I will return, you promise to keep the job search up, it is not good for you to be sitting at home and twiddling your thumbs for too long. It is good to have a purpose in life and a new job can bring new and interesting challenges and unexpected friendships. Make sure Ollie is all right, won't you? He is doing me an enormous favour; I am very grateful to him.'

'Yes, yes, I promise to keep the job search up and you must promise to look after yourself. I will keep an eye on the café and Ollie and I will make sure all is well when you return.'

They both waved goodbye and Alice watched Mario disappear through the gates and wondered slowly back through the airport lounge. It was still quite early and she started to feel peckish. She stopped at Costa and looked longingly at the last pain au raisin sitting in the basket looking rather forlorn and inviting her, in fact pleading with her, to eat it. No, she thought, she would be good. No more bad carbohydrates for her. She was going to watch her figure. She was going to get slim again. There would then be less need for the underwear to cover the expanding waistline. Besides, Alistair had talked about doing another gin evening very soon and she wanted to look her best. No, she definitely wasn't going to have that last croissant.

She ordered her usual medium, skinny single shot cappuccino and ignored the pastry. No, she would not look at it.

The man behind the counter was swift at producing her drink, adding 'Anything with that, a pastry or croissant or....'

Alice now faltered, she looked back at the pastry. It seemed a shame to leave the last one in the basket, 'Oh, yes go on.' And the immediate feeling of guilt and realisation that she still had zero willpower overcame her. Well she thought, I deserve a treat. I have been up since the crack of dawn. She would diet in May – not many days away now. Yes, she would diet in May.

The pastry tasted as good as it always did, and she left Costa to go the carpark walking quickly to work off some of those calories. As she passed WH Smith's, however, a large poster caught Alice's eye. She came to a complete halt to read it.

Do you want to be irresistible to everyone you meet?
Do you want to learn how to
get what you want and when you want it?
Then you need Daphne D'Armour's latest book:

'Learning the art of SEDUCTION and become that
TEMPTRESS you know is lurking inside.'

It didn't take Alice too many seconds to decide to purchase the book and with that she strode off back to her car, keen to get home to read it. A little help and a few tips on how to seduce Alistair would do no harm at all. After all, she was a bit out of practice on that score.

That evening she decided to have an early night and she tucked herself up in bed with her new book. She studied it in great detail pouring over and reflecting on each page. Alice wrote down the main points from each chapter, writing her thoughts beside each one.

1. **Use your smile to seduce him** *(better practise it in the mirror to get just the right look).*

2. **Aim your belly button at him** *(gosh not sure about this one? Do I lift my top up and expose it to him?).*

3. **Touch Him. But not too much** *(the book doesn't say where? His arm? His leg?).*

4. Avoid crossing your arms you must **Seduce with Your Body** *(yes, I do a lot of folding my arms, I don't want to create any barriers).*

5. **Use a Power Pose to Improve Seductive Body Language** *(what does a power pose look like? Again, one to practise in hall mirror).*

6. **Lock Eyes with His**…Then Lower Your Eyelids *(How long for? Do I fully shut them?)*

7. **Make the Most of Your Lips** *(right, lipstick, red? pucker them up – how much? Both probably).*

8. **Dishevel hair slightly** *(need to grow hair even longer to achieve this properly).*

Alice went over to the mirror to practise. She puckered up her lips to make them fuller and stared long and hard at herself whilst slightly messing up her hair, then she fluttered her eyelashes.

'Oh for goodness sake, my contact lens! It's now moved and now I can't see what I am doing? Oh bugger that was painful.'

Alice went back to bed and soon nodded off content that with a new wardrobe, new look and now some new seduction techniques in the bag, Alistair simply wouldn't be able to resist her.

She curled up and went to sleep.

There she was again, in the usual chair, but this time it was on the beach. There was a signpost saying San Sebastian: el lugar donde los amentes se encuentran y pueden probar la comida del amor.

Miraculously she was now able to understand Spanish. 'The place where lovers meet and can taste the food of love.'

Alice could see the feisty waves and hear the breeze whistle pass her ears. There along the golden sandy beach, walking barefoot in the sand, was Colin Firth. No wait a minute was its Alistair? She couldn't quite tell. No, as he came nearer it was definitely Colin Firth. He sat down beside her. Strange she thought, can't he see I am all tied up? Why doesn't he untie me? He turned towards her.

'It is time for us to taste the food of love,' Colin stated in a very dark, alluring voice.

There in front of them appeared a picnic blanket with lots of food. Colin starting tucking in and was obviously enjoying the food, 'Umm this speciality of grilled chistorra is perfect. The spices are perfectly combined and the meat is so succulent.'

Alice looked down, 'Yes the sausages do look very good indeed.

But with my hands tied up Colin, I can't…'

Colin, however, was quick to interrupt her. Entranced by the food, he picked up another dish. 'Ah! My goodness the pimientos de piquillo are perfect. Did you know they are cultivated in and around the village of Lodosa in the Navarre region of Spain? After picking, the small bright red peppers are roasted over smoking embers giving them a subtle yet rich smoky flavour.' Colin was now licking his lips very slowly and extremely seductively.

Alice longing to try, instinctively licked her lips too, 'No, I didn't know that. The thing is Colin, I wondered if you would just quickly untie me?' Alice continued to try to loosen herself from the grip of the ropes.

'And this my love, you must try this Torrija. There's something so comforting about baked egg custard, especially when it's been soaked into buttery brioche with the added bonus of a crunchy caramelised crust to crunch through…'

Alice looked at the magnificent spread of food and was most desirous of just a quick bite. 'Yes, absolutely, my love, but as you can see, my hands are…' Alice, yet again, was unable to finish her sentence as Colin was determined to continue.

'… or what about the Pastel Vasco. It is a traditional pastry made up of a rich, moist and dense cake crust encapsulating a soft creamy interior of crème patissière and kirsch-soaked cherries. Did you know each patisserie has their own recipe so there are hundreds of variations of this truly unique Basque dessert? Some are crunchy on the outside while others have a cakier exterior. Either way, the texture of creamy crème patisserie combined with the outer shell makes Pastel Vasco a pastry masterpiece.'

'I am sure it is a masterpiece but the thing is, Colin, I would absolutely love to come and eat with you, I really would Alistair,

I mean Colin, but you would need to untie me first, I can't eat with my hands all tied-up, now can I?' She felt herself now getting a tad impatient.

'Hang on, did you just call me Alistair?' Colin seemed greatly perturbed by this.

'Uh, well yes, sorry, I mean Colin, Alistair is Number 24's brother.'

Alice could see damage limitation was needed but, alas, it was to no avail, Colin's face said it all.

'Are you seeing a man called Alistair? Are you Alice? Have you been cheating on me?' Colin stood up in a most indignant fashion.

Then another voice seemed to come from nowhere.

'Alistair is it now? First its James Bond then Poldark and now Alistair. Goodness me, you do know how to get through them.'

Alice turned her face to find Ollie standing under a palm tree. 'What? What an earth are you talking about you stupid man!'

Colin was furious.

'I can't believe I have just prepared this picnic just for you. I have been cooking all day long, for hours on end, and then I find out you have been carrying on with all these other men.' Colin turned his back on her and walked away up the beach.

'No, wait, you don't understand, it's you, you're the one I want!' But her words fell on deaf ears. He was gone.

Ollie tutted, 'I really think it is time you made up your mind who and what you want. Poor guy, and all that cooking. I don't know? But, well, we really shouldn't let it go to waste, should we?' Ollie sat down and started to tuck in.

Alice was flabbergasted and, in her efforts to untie herself, she swung the chair so vehemently that it fell back into the sand leaving her legs now dangling up in the air.

'For goodness sake would you bloody untie me and NOW'

But all the screaming and yelling was to no avail. There she was, feeling most bereft, hungry and looking up at the sky when a bell started ringing in the distance.

She came to, and soon came to the realisation that the front door bell was beckoning her. She looked at the clock 6.00 am? Who could it be at this unearthly hour she wondered?

Willing herself out of bed, she went to the door and looked through the spy hole.

'Oh, for goodness sake it's Ollie!' This bloomin' man she thought is always in the wrong place at the most inconvenient of times and very begrudgingly she opened the door.

16

Shaken and definitely stirred

'For goodness sake, do you know what time it is?' Alice shouted as she opened the door, highly irritated that this man was not only happy at ruining her dreams but was now interrupting her beauty sleep. However, she was soon overcome when she saw the state he was in. 'Goodness what on earth has happened to you?'

Ollie had a bruised eye and a grazed chin. Ollie apologised for disturbing her but started to explain. He had been out the previous night with Robert at his local. They had spotted a very drunk man getting quite argumentative and abusive to the woman he was with. Both Ollie and Robert had decided to intervene and the man, after much arm waving and shouting, eventually seemed to have simmered down and went off to the toilets. Ollie finished his last drink and said goodnight to Robert who decided to stay to see the last ten minutes of the Chelsea match. However, unbeknown to Robert and Ollie, the angry man and one other had followed him out and when Ollie had turned down a rather dark and narrow lane to take the shortcut to the flat above the café, the two men attacked him.

'They got my wallet, mobile and keys, though goodness knows what good the keys will do them, there is nothing to link the shop or Mario's flat to them.'

Alice beckoned him in and she got him to sit on one of the bar stools in the kitchen. 'Look your hands are bruised and bleeding, Ollie, let me take a look.' Alice retrieved some antiseptic wipes from her first aid box and started to tidy his face and hands up. 'Did you phone the police?'

'Yes, yes, I have reported the incident and have been at the police station until the early hours of this morning. It took ages until someone came and wrote a report. They mentioned looking at whatever CCTV footage they can find but they are not hopeful. They dropped me off here. I am sorry for not calling you first but without my phone it was impossible and I need the spare set of café keys. Mario says you and Robert always keep a set, just in case. I could have gone to Robert and Sue's but I was worried disturbing them and with Ben and then Sue ...' Ollie was keen to explain but Alice felt no explanation was necessary.

'No, no it is no problem. You were right to come here.' Alice looked at Ollie's hands, 'By the look of things, they must have come off pretty badly too.'

'Well, I tried to defend myself but two versus one is not great odds.' Ollie winced in pain, he put his hand on the left side of his ribs. They were clearly giving him trouble.

'There is no way in this state you can open up the café Ollie. I have nothing on today, let me go. The delivery of the croissants and pastries will be due soon so I will go and sort all of that out. You stay here for a while and have a rest. In fact, I think you could do with a soak in the bath.' Alice headed to the bathroom again to collect some towels and she found some of Mark's toiletries lurking in the back of the cupboard.

Ollie was very grateful and somewhat taken back at her

kindness. When she returned, she started to apply some more antiseptic wipes. She was very gentle and caring, the rottweiler had disappeared. In fact, he found her quite cute in her rabbit pj's.

Ollie sat back and enjoyed the moment. When Alice was content that he had been patched up as best she could, she headed for the bedroom and hastily got dressed. No time to put together an outfit, she just reached for the jeans and a top.

When she returned to the kitchen, she could see Ollie was still very shaky.

'You stay here and rest and I will sort the café out,' Alice insisted. 'Help yourself to tea, coffee it's all in this cupboard and milk in fridge. Just help yourself.'

Ollie started to try and protest and was keen to get back to the cafe but Alice was adamant he was in no fit state to be working today. Alice retrieved the spare set of keys and left strict instructions that Ollie was to take a bath and go to bed for a while. She made up the bed in the spare room and departed.

Poor Ollie, she thought. I guess the men wanted to teach him a lesson for interfering? Anyway, it was a brave and admirable thing for Ollie to step in. He didn't know this woman after all.

Alice got to the café and opened it up. The deliveries soon arrived and she checked them all off. She knew the morning shift was Mario's busiest, with all the commuters popping in for breakfast or to collect their takeaway coffees, teas and bacon baps, so she headed straight to the kitchen to turn on all the ovens and proceeded to start the bacon. She phoned Sam, who lived near to the café, to see if she could spare a few hours, which indeed she could. Together they were able to hold the fort and muster up some half decent butties. The only complaint they got was from the resident old boy, Henry, who only ever bought one coffee and managed to make it last most of the morning to read the free papers. Apparently, Mario made his coffee just the way he liked it, strong, dark and not too milky. Where was Mario he had enquired? The coffee was far too milky and not nearly strong enough. Alice tried to rectify the situation and make him another but he also managed to grumble about that one too.

'Of course, you can always take your custom elsewhere.' Sam declared

Henry muttered under his breath, 'Really indeed, after all the business I have given Mario? No manners at all.'

During a quiet moment, Alice phoned Robert to fill him on the previous night's incident and both he and Sue turned up at lunchtime to offer some help. Sam was very grateful as it would give her a bit of time to sort some shopping out before she started work and Alice could get on and prepare some more sandwiches.

The afternoon was as busy as the morning. Five thirty arrived and they all were grateful to finally sit down and enjoy the peace and quiet and a cup of Mario's special blend.

Robert said he would pop round with Alice to see Ollie. He felt guilty that he hadn't noticed the two men following Ollie when he left the pub but he was so engrossed in catching the last bit of the Chelsea match he just hadn't been aware.

'You weren't to know, honey,' Sue said. 'Luckily, Ollie is fine and we can help look after him at mine for a bit.'

Alice said there was no need and she was best suited at the present time to help him.

Robert looked around the café, 'Well, at least we have been of some help today. Gosh, I don't know how Mario does this every day, it is quite full on at times and he is no spring chicken.'

'He runs this business like a well-oiled machine, you know how he moans when anyone tries to help. It can never be done as well as he feels it should be.' Alice starting reminiscing at all the times her and Sue had earned a bit of extra pocket money in their teens by helping Mario after school and sometimes on a Saturday, but he only ever let them take the money, clean the tables or sweep the floor. He really didn't like them meddling, as he called it, in anything else.

Alice looked at Sue, 'You look so tired Sue, you both need to be thinking about getting Ben from football practice you know how he hates you being late. He will be threatening social services on you again! I have a few jobs to do and then I will lock up, off you go.' Alice thanked them both and hastened them away. She did a bit of prep for tomorrow's breakfast run, grabbed the last unsold BLT sandwiches to have for her and Ollie's tea and headed for home eager to see how he had been.

On entering the flat, Alice was met by the most wonderful smell that filled the whole flat. To her great surprise and wonder, Ollie was in the kitchen cooking.

'Gosh, that smells amazing Ollie, what is it?' Alice enquired as she perched on a kitchen stool, grabbed a spoon and proceeded to taste the creation. 'OMG, that is so good, Ollie.'

'Thanks.' Ollie looked very pleased to be complimented, 'I hope you don't mind I just used up a few bits from the fridge and raided the cupboards for some herbs, spices. You also have a great selection of tins of all sorts. Just the right combination of ingredients to rustle up something.'

'All I have are some BLT sandwiches! This is a much better

offer, thank you.' Alice studied Ollie's face. 'You look so much better, Ollie. Did you manage to sleep?' Alice headed for the booze cupboard to see what she could offer him.

'Yes, I had a long bath and then slept solid for quite a few hours.'

Alice poured them both a glass of red. 'I am not sure about this one, Robert is the one who knows all about wine. He bought me over some bottles the other week. I hope this is okay, unless you would prefer white?'

'No, this is perfect.' Ollie took a mouthful and looked as though he was enjoying it.

Alice laid the table and Ollie served the food. Alice thought this as good a time as any to broach the subject about New Year's Eve.

'Look, Ollie I was a bit all over the place on New Year's and I was, well I was…' Alice was unable to get the words and then Ollie interrupted

'No problem, Alice. I quite understood. How have you been?' Ollie seemed genuinely concerned and interested.

'Oh, ok. I need to get on with my life now. I saw him the other day with the baby and he… he looked fine. I still feel very, angry, upset and betrayed. I thought I could have talked him round about having a baby and then as time went by… well no point going on about, all too late now.' Alice reached for the glass of wine; she needed another drink. 'But as Sue says there is no point dwelling on the past. I need to move on, but it is never as easy as it sounds…' Alice's voice wavered and Ollie could see some tears appearing in her eyes. 'Goodness, I am so sorry, look at me. I am just tired, it's been a long day.'

Ollie looked across at her, he felt an overwhelming desire

just to hold her for a bit. It must have been so hard to see Mark with his new girlfriend and what's more with a baby. Mark had been a complete and utter dick but, by all accounts from Robert, Sue and Malcom, she was well rid of him but he knew how hard it is to get over long term relationships. He resisted going round the table and holding her, besides that was the last thing she needed right now.

Ollie took his glass and gestured a toast. 'To new adventures! Let there be many!'

Alice felt uplifted by his sentiment and clinked his glass, 'Yes to new adventures.' Alice thought of Alistair and a smile returned to her face.

At this point, Ollie detected her cheeks flush a bit and her eyes seemed to sparkle. She really was a very good-looking woman but he wasn't going there again, too complicated.

Both enjoyed the evening, chatting away. Like Alistair, Ollie was well travelled and to her surprise she started to enjoy hearing all about his various escapades. She could see why he had got the travelling bug but she did think he should have outgrown the wondering nomad bit.

Ollie enjoyed Alice's company. She seemed a very honest and forthright person and he enjoyed hearing about all her misgivings of people like him. It gave him a chance to defend his lifestyle choice.

'So, what's wrong with a holiday once or twice a year then?' Alice enquired. The practical side of Alice was obviously wondering how an earth people like him have enough money to live off.

'The problem with that is you can only go when work dictates you can go, it is very restricting and my kind of travelling involves having to get to know people quickly, I need to work but I am free to choose where I work and, to some extent, who I work with.' Ollie filled both glasses again.

'Where will you live when you need to retire and are too old to work Ollie? I mean not to have a place to call your own? I can see the glamour of it all but it isn't very practical in reality, is it?'

'Well yes, there is that side of things but wherever I have been, wherever I have travelled to, I always meet people willing to help. I do odd jobs and can earn a meal or a bed for the night. You can't always worry about tomorrow you need to live for today. I decided a long time ago not to get trapped in to the next highest paid job and bigger house. My Mum never seemed satisfied with what she had, always on at Dad for a better lifestyle.'

Alice wasn't convinced. It all sounded like he was afraid to embrace the realities of life. His lifestyle felt all too risky, a bit haphazard; dependent on others. No, it wouldn't suit her at all.

The evening and conversations flew by. Both were surprised at how they had enjoyed each other's company. Alice offered for Ollie to stay to give him another day of rest but he was most insistent on getting back to Mario's flat above the café. He thanked her again and Alice followed Ollie to the front door. He turned and something came over him, to his surprise before he could stop himself, he was asking her if she would like to do this again one evening. Alice looked genuinely pleased to be asked but as he opened the door, Alistair was there on the door step ready to knock.

'Oh, hi Alice.' Alistair looked a little put out at this man standing beside her.

'Bella thinks the postman has left a package with you?' Alistair eyed Ollie up and down, 'Sorry I didn't mean to interrupt you or…' Alistair was unable to finish the sentence. Alice was keen to jump right in, she was panicking about what Alistair would be thinking. She didn't want him to think she was with Ollie in any shape or form.

'Gosh, no! You are not interrupting anything at all Alistair, no, no nothing. Absolutely nothing. It's just Ollie.' Alice waved a dismissive hand towards Ollie who seemed slightly put out by her hasty dismissal of him and complete disregard for the evening they had just spent together.

Ollie looked at this rather good-looking man and wondered how long Alice and Alistair had been acquainted? Ollie then remembered the delivery of a parcel earlier during the day and retrieved it from the hall table and handed it to Alistair. 'Yes, it came earlier today.'

Ollie, to Alice's annoyance, lingered in the doorway.

'Thanks, Ollie. Glad you are better now, I was glad to help out, like you said, you want to get back to Mario's tonight.'

Ollie though didn't move. He was transfixed by Alice's sudden change of behaviour. Alice was definitely behaving strangely around Alistair. She was fixing a firm stare upon Alistair and was now playing with her hair, kind of messing it up in front of him. What a shame Ollie thought it had looked quite good earlier on. Alice was also pouting her lips at Alistair except it just exaggerated the little wrinkles above her top lip.

Alice was now getting increasingly agitated by Ollie's presence.

'Yes, well goodnight Ollie, thank you…' She was about to say 'for the dinner' but thought the better of it. She certainly didn't want Alistair thinking anything at all was going on. She continued, 'Thank you for doing that… that thing… that job… for me.'

Ollie smiled his mischievous grin and he felt his wicked sense of humour get the better of him. He grabbed Alice towards him and held her tightly in his arms, 'Goodnight darling, fab night, thank you.' On saying this, he promptly kissed her on the lips.

Alistair's eyebrows were now fully raised, not too sure where to look or what to do, 'Thanks for the parcel, I will be seeing you around, no doubt.' Alistair left and proceeded to walk back to Isabella's.

Alice drew away as quickly as she could. She was flabbergasted. Furious. Utterly speechless. The Cheshire grin continued to grow even broader on Ollie's face. This was like a red rag to a bull to Alice.

'What an earth… how dare you… what do you think you were playing at!' The whites of Alice eyes were clearly visible.

'Oh, sorry I just don't know what overcame me, sorry about that. Never mind I am sure your sultry looks and gestures didn't go unnoticed and I am sure a man like Alistair will like the thrill of the chase don't you think?' With that, Ollie winked at Alice and left.

Alice slammed the door behind him. 'The bloody cheek and nerve of that man. To think I have just wasted an evening of my valuable time, to think I have just given up a day trying to help him. Never again, never again!' And with that, she hastily cleared the dinner into the dishwasher and threw the remains in the bin. What would Alistair think now? How was she going to explain the kiss?

17

Hugh Grant

'Well what a cheek. I mean the nerve of the man.' Alice attempted to slurp back her coffee but being so distracted by the previous night's capers ended spilling most of it down her blouse, yet again. 'Oh, for goodness sake!' Alice shouted as she hastened over to the sink and grabbed a cloth to wipe herself down.

'I can see Ollie has stirred quite a few emotions, but by all accounts, up until he kissed you, you had a very pleasant evening with him it would seem?' observed Sue as she continued to bake her courgette and lime cake.

'To think he would treat me like that when I have gone out of my way to look after him. The utter nerve of the man!' Alice continued to wipe her top down, muttering under her breath about how expensive this top was and how typical it would be if *HE* had ruined this as well.

'So, talk me through what happened again. I can't understand why he just grabbed and kissed you like that - very *Rhett Butler* and *Gone with the Wind* don't you think?'

'Alas, Sue, Ollie is no Clarke Gable.' Alice started to think back to the previous evening. 'Alistair was at the door and I simply didn't want him to think Ollie and I were an item so I just thanked Ollie for doing a thing for me… well a job… that's all.'

Sue stopped mixing the ingredients.

'Right, so Ollie cooks you a meal, which you have already admitted was a really good meal. A meal which you were very impressed he had put together, probably not feeling a hundred percent after the previous evening encounter with those two men. You then spend a pleasant time talking and sharing your film and music interests with each other and then all you can do is thank him for doing *"a job"*.' Sue waved her fingers in the air as if creating inverted commas around her words.

Alice begrudgingly reflected upon Sue's words but, still feeling sore about the whole thing, decided she really didn't want to give him any more thought and moved the conversation on.

'Anyway, I am here to see if you want to do a bit of clothes shopping with me today?'

'What about the job hunting?' Sue enquired as she grated the lime into the ingredients.

Alice knew she really ought to be getting on with the job hunting but couldn't face it today so avoided answering the question. 'I thought I could treat us to some new clothes and then go for a coffee and a natter in that new place that has opened, just off Oxford Street.'

'Well, you have become the big spender! Gosh here is a woman who would never spend anything on herself but rather invest it, who always worried about breaking into the monthly saving routine and now here you are wanting to go and spend, spend, spend.' Sue was glad, however, that her friend had definitely turned a corner over the last few weeks. The clothes shopping did sound good and Ben was fast outgrowing his current jeans so it would be useful to have a trip into town. Besides, after Alice's recent makeover, she was keen to get a few tips.

'Right, go on then, but I will need to put this cake in the oven first – it will take about forty minutes so I will get ready whilst it's cooking. Let me just set the timer.'

Alice was delighted, particularly when Sue left her to lick the spoon and scrape the remaining cake mixture up. It was delicious she thought but she wasn't sure about the courgette bits. Maybe it would taste better when cooked.

Cake baked, off the two ladies went up to Oxford Street to peruse the latest fashions and try the odd garment on. Both enjoyed going in and out of the clothes shops, nattering away and Alice enjoyed hearing about Ben's latest letters to Frank Lampard. He had been writing to persuade Frank to take him and Fred the Barnett, on in the junior squad. He hadn't been successful, of course, but Frank had sent him a signed post card of himself which Ben now insisted was probably worth millions.

Sue took on some of Alice's tips for colours and accessories and after making their way gradually up Oxford Street, they headed up towards Bond Street Station and in the direction of where a new coffee shop had opened. Along route, however, Alice spotted a poster in the window of Waterstones Book Shop. It was a gigantic poster with a picture of Hugh Grant. She stopped immediately.

'Gosh he still looks amazing! Look at those eyes. Look at that hair of his!' Alice read the poster:

'Here for just one day, come and join Hugh Grant on the second floor, signing his latest book:

'Coping with being Hugh and Huge,
an open account of my life as a celebrity.'

'OMG, Hugh's here!' Alice could hardly believe her eyes. 'He is right here, on the second floor!' All her dreams seemed to have been answered in just one instant. Sue rolled her eyes, she had never been a fan, she thought him a great actor but could never see why Alice drooled over him so much.

'What about our coffee and cake? Anyway, what about Alistair? Sue, however, was not hopeful in distracting her friend and much to her great reluctance and protests, was hastened into the store.

Meanwhile, on the second floor, Hugh was happily signing copies of his new book. There was a big queue and. although Hugh was very pleased to have a brief chat with each of his fans whilst signing his book, he needed a loo break. He gave his apologies, explaining he would only be a few minutes and made his way to the toilet, closely followed by his body guard.

'No sign, Mr Grant, of that stalker and all seems to be going well, don't you think?'

'Indeed.' Hugh looked relieved. 'One can never be too careful, it was a big decision to come here and expose myself today, if you get my drift!' The security man didn't seem to get the joke looking somewhat bemused. Did Mr Grant not realise the seriousness of the situation he thought?

'Of course, we mustn't be complacent, sir, a woman who can write so many increasingly threatening letters and, judging by the content of some of them, clearly seems a bit deranged, may never be far away.'

'Yes, indeed, I realise I must be aware of any strange behaviour.'

'Yes, sir, always wise to be on the alert. But, don't worry Mr Grant, I am right here.'

Hugh looked reassured and, after popping to the loo, got back to the signing, enjoying all the adulation of his fans.

Eventually, Sue and Sam had reached the second floor by the escalator. Both looked at the long queue and Sue moaned at Alice. She really didn't want to waste so much time queueing, just to get Hugh's autograph and, realistically a very few, brief words. Alice, however, was not to be deterred from her mission.

'Look we are talking about *THE* Hugh Grant, for goodness sake. God, he looks amazing!'

Alice's eyes were growing larger and it was clear to Sue that her friend was not to be headed off course on her mission. She was definitely not to be deterred. Alice spotted the bookshop's coffee lounge and headed straight over and grabbed a table. She would appease Sue by getting her a coffee.

'Look, you sit here, I won't be long.'

Sue rolled her eyes and reluctantly sat down.

Alice got Sue a latté whilst she studied the queue. Gosh it was long, she thought to herself and now, even more women were taking a book from the shelf ready to join the queue. She hastened back to Sue with her drink. Alice had one of her lightbulb moments.

'Of course, I know what to do. There can't be that many of the books left on the shelf, I am going to stop any more women buying it and purchase them all myself.' Alice looked very chuffed with her idea.

'What!' Sue retorted. 'You must be mad, there are loads of books over there, it will cost you a fortune. They probably have more in stock anyway.'

'Look, the more books he has to sign with me then the more time I get with him. It will stop any more women joining the queue if they can't get a book for him to sign. Hugh will be delighted that I have bought so many and it will give me time to have a longer chat with him, you never know…'

'For goodness sake, I have heard of some pea-brained ideas but this takes the biscuit!' Sue exclaimed. 'He's a celebrity, he mingles with celebrities. Do you really think for one second he is going to ask Miss Ordinary off the street out with him? He's dated Liz Hurley for goodness sake!'

Sue's words however were wasted and falling on deaf and very distracted ears. Sue started to get up but Alice placing her hand firmly on Sue's shoulder, pushed her back down into her seat.

'Look, you sit here and I will quickly scoop up the rest of the books!' Alice was not to be perturbed by her mission. She grabbed a trolley that had been abandoned by the escalator and hurriedly went to collect the remaining copies. Five minutes later she was back with Sue who had now finished her coffee and couldn't quite believe how quickly Alice could empty a whole shelf of books.

'What an earth will you do with them all?' Sue couldn't believe her eyes,

'Alice this is ridiculous!'

'No, it isn't, it's a brilliant plan, I will give them as Christmas presents.'

'What are you mad! All fifty books? You don't have that many friends or relatives.' Sue frowned at her but her words were not being heeded.

'It will also mean that I will get longer at the stand with him! You do know he is single again, don't you?' Alice was not to be

181

diverted from her plan of action.

Sue groaned, 'What about Alistair! I thought he was the new love of your life?'

Alice raised her eyebrows, 'Look as lovely as Alistair is, who could beat Hugh!'

Sue rolled her eyes, again.

Alice, not even allowing Sue to finished her drink, ushered her over to the cashier to get her to help unload the books.

'So, you want ALL fifty copies Madam?' The girl on the checkout couldn't quite take it all in.

'Indeed. Christmas presents.' Alice was too busy to notice the look of utter bewilderment on the girl's face as she had her eyes firmly fixed upon the queue and Hugh. What Alice hadn't realised though was that the bodyguard had now clocked Alice at the till with a trolley filled to the brim of Hugh's books.

This, the bodyguard thought, was very strange indeed, who could possibly want all those copies of Mr Grant's book? Yes, definitely strange. He went over to the cashier just to see if he could eave's drop a little.

Alice kept hastening the cashier who seemed to be taking forever to count all the books and process them through the till. She looked over at Hugh and, to her great disappointment, he seemed to be apologising to the ladies in the queue that it was now lunch time and he would be stopping for some refreshment. 'However, ladies, I promise to return straight after lunch and very much look forward to meeting you all then.'

Alice couldn't believe her ears. This would never do; she was most put out. Besides, she thought, Sue would never wait that long to get her books signed.

'Quick, Sue, we can't let him get away!' Alice shouted in a

very loud voice and with that she turned the trolley quickly towards the book signing stall and started running towards Hugh.

The bodyguard immediately responded and spoke into his microphone 'Security, security, I think we have a red alert, repeat red alert. The stalker is here in the store... assistance required immediately on floor 2!'

Alice was oblivious to the bodyguard who now was in quick pursuit of her. Alice was clearly on a mission, in full flow with her trolley as she hurtled towards Hugh.

Hugh looked up to see a rather frantic lady, screaming his name, charging down the aisle, straight towards him with a large trolley in tow.

'Hugh, Hugh, just a minute!' Alice shouted.

Hugh froze. 'Oh my God, it's her, it's the stalker!'

Alice was getting closer and closer, but what she hadn't factored in was the downward slope of the aisle and the insistence of a trolley, now full of books, not to slow down. It was now getting the better of her.

The bodyguard swiftly moved Hugh out of the way by diving and rugby tackling him to the floor. Two of the store's security guards seemed to appear from nowhere and were in hot pursuit. As Alice's trolley lurched towards the stand, the queue of ladies quickly dispersed with screams and protests. Alice also ended up being herself rugby tackled to the floor by one of the security guards.

Sue, meanwhile, froze to the spot in utter amazement and complete disbelief at what she had just witnessed.

'Get your hands off me!' Alice protested. 'How dare you manhandle me like this!' She turned towards Hugh, 'I just have a few copies of the book for you to sign, Hugh.'

However, Hugh was already running towards the lift with his bodyguard safely by his side. Popping into the lift Hugh took out his hankie and mopped his brow, 'Goodness, that was a close shave, thank you so much. Trying to mow me down with a trolley, the woman is clearly insane.'

Alice was not happy as she tried to reason with the security men.

'Look, I just want Hugh to sign my books that's all. I didn't want to wait until after lunch, my friend here...' Alice turned round to find Sue but she seemed to have mysteriously vanished, 'Well my friend was here...'

The security guards hastened Alice to the back of the store and promptly phoned the police who arrived in no time at all.

Alice insisted she be allowed a phone call and rang Sue on her mobile. Sue thought it best to stop hiding in the loo and go and support her friend.

'Look, you have got it all wrong officer, I was buying Christmas presents that's all. I just lost control of the trolley, it's as simple as that.' Alice was most indignant that not only has she been humiliated by a public arrest but had now lost any chance at all of meeting Hugh and having her books signed.

Sue finally emerged and, much to Sue's embarrassment, was able to corroborate her friend's story.

The police officer, in charge, was not convinced by their tale.

'We have reason to believe madam that you are the woman who has been stalking Mr Grant for some time now. His liberty and peace of mind has been seriously curtailed by your actions, madam.'

'What a load of nonsense. Me a stalker? How preposterous!

I demand I phone my lawyer immediately.'

Sue lent over to whisper in Alice's ear, 'Do you have a lawyer?'

'No,' Alice mouthed back, 'we can't let the police officer know that though can we? The threat of a lawyer will be enough to ensure my release'.

'I see,' the Police Officer replied. 'Please feel free to ring him or her.'

Alice was not expecting that response, 'Right. Good. Just as well.' She turned to her friend, 'Sue, please phone my lawyer, immediately.'

'UHH, right yes, right I will call him now then. Yes indeed right now.'

Sue left the room and immediately phoned Robert in the hope he might know someone.

After many hours of questioning back at the police station and many written statements, Alice was released. Robert had phoned a local solicitor who was very proficient in clearing the matter up. Having taken hand writing samples from Alice it was very clear that her handwriting did not match that of the stalker's. Alice was cautioned about her behaviour and went home with Robert and Sue and fifty copies of Hugh's book, unsigned.

'Well, I am glad that has been cleared up. A stalker indeed, who would have thought that? Preposterous, don't you think?' Alice clearly wanted some reassurance but Sue, still speechless and seething about the whole incident, remained silent throughout the whole journey back to Alice's flat.

As Alice got out of the car, she now felt a bit sheepish that she had probably ruined Sue's day. 'Well,' she said hopefully, 'at least it was a bit of an adventure, don't you think?'

Sue remained silent but her face said it all.

Luckily Robert saw the funny side of it and knew how Alice's great passion for Hugh had obviously got the better of her.

'Yes, Alice I'm sure it was, for you, but perhaps next time, just the one copy of his book will suffice. Oh, and Alice please don't give *me* a copy of that book for Christmas, will you?'

18

Job hunting

May had arrived. Everyone thought it was definitely time Alice got a job. She had one phone call after the other from all her very well-meaning friends urging her to get a job but what they were really telling her was, basically, to get a life.

Alice scoured the papers, searched the internet, but couldn't find anything remotely suitable. She had worked for so long at Frobersham's. She knew her clientele and they clearly had great respect for her judging by the cards she received stating how sad they were that she had retired.

'Retired, indeed, you jammy old devil, Frobersham.' Alice was most put out. 'Anything but a scandal for his beloved company.' However, the deal she had finally allowed Simon to negotiate was a good one, and she had received a very generous settlement. She had managed to buy out Mark from the flat which was now well and truly her own. But she knew the remaining money was soon going to dwindle and she really didn't want to go into her pension investments. Malcolm would not have approved of that.

She decided to take herself and memory stick off to Mario's. An employment agency was nearby and she would pop in and have a chat about what might be available. She had managed to muster up a C.V. but having not done one in years, it had taken her much longer than she had imagined. It was remembering all those dates of what she had done before Frobersham's. Digging out certificates from school and Uni had proven tricky enough. Basically, the only real experience she had was in sales. Button sales. There was no hard sell as such. Clients often came to Frobersham's with their designs and it was Alice who brought them to fruition. Besides, she felt that a new Alice required a complete change from who she had been. A new direction. Something different. But what?

She dressed herself to look smart and business like. Alice, satisfied that she looked the part, set off to Mario's where she was hoping to use his printer as her one had now decided to depart the world. She thought it was no doubt fed up with the constant printing out of unfinished CV's and the occasional slam she had given the printer when it refused to connect to her laptop.

The only problem with using Mario's printer was seeing Ollie. She still hadn't forgiven him for his last caper and really didn't want to engage with any sort of conversation with the man. However, needs must. She couldn't go to the agency without the CV and it wouldn't look good asking them to print it out.

Having once again fought with the ticket barrier, which seemed reluctant this time to take her ticket, she proceeded to have an argument with a member of the station staff, insisting that ticket barriers needed to work or there was no point to them. She finally emerged onto the High Street and walked across to Mario's. It was a gloomy day and the month of May was living up to April's reputation of plenty of showers. Alice was now armed with her latest acquisition of a giant golf umbrella, not wanting her hair to get the slightest bit damp and frizzy.

She walked past the café's huge front window to get to the door but she wasn't expecting to encounter what she next witnessed. Robert was sitting in the café with a woman. Alice hadn't seen her before. She would have dismissed the woman as a client of Robert's but there was something about their body language. They were both leaning in towards each other as if having a rather intimate conversation. Alice hesitated and decided not to go in. She decided to walk on past the café. However, she had only gone a few metres when she stopped and decided to retrace her steps. Once again, she looked through the window but, this time, the woman now had her hand on Robert's arm and both still looked deep in conversation.

Alice thought the most likely scenario was that this woman must surely be a client. But how strange to be so intimate with each other? It couldn't be anyone from the office as Miss Havisham had taken up the position of office manager and was looking after Robert and Malcolm's admin requirements.

Alice knew Miss Havisham had tried both her brother's and Malcolm's patience in the last few weeks. Robert could never find where Miss Havisham had filed his documents and neither could she. Malcolm was having to get used to having sugar in his tea, in spite of the fact he had never taken any before. Whereas Robert who always did, now had to get used to no sugar at all. However, they did both agree that Miss Havisham had a lovely phone manner even though she did sometimes get a little muddled with some of their clients names. Robert had grumbled that one of his oldest client's Mr Fasiski kept being called Mr Frisky.

So, yes, it was true, Miss Havisham had been trying both of their patience but Robert would never get rid of Miss Havisham. Not without telling Alice and Sue hadn't mentioned any new employees. It had always just been Robert and Malcolm.

Alice continued to stare through the window when a face suddenly emerged staring straight back at her through the same pane of glass. It was Ollie, giving one of his nauseous smiles. Having been discovered there was nothing more to do than go into the café. Ollie had already opened the door and gestured her in with a bow. Ignoring his obvious sarcastic greeting, she went straight towards Robert who, having spotted her, immediately jumped up from the table and gave her a warm but, she thought, somehow furtive smile.

'Ah Alice, lovely to see you,' and with this Robert kissed her on the cheek. 'Let me introduce you to ...' Robert hesitated a bit too long, Alice thought 'to Lynn, one of my...' again he hesitated but the lady quickly interjected.

'Clients, one of Robert's clients.' The lady stretched out her hand to greet Alice.

Alice really didn't know what to make of this tentative encounter. There was something definitely not right. This chance meeting had clearly left them all surprised. Robert was avoiding eye contact with her and Alice knowing her brother too well felt that something was up. The thought did enter her mind that Robert was having an affair. Surely not. She had to dismiss this. Not in Mario's café, surely? Far too exposed and besides, he would never do that to Sue, he loved her. No, he would never cheat on Sue. Her mind, though, was now in a whirl. Would he? After all, she had never thought Mark capable of such behaviour. But the way Robert was behaving? Let alone Lynn? She was getting deeply suspicious. What on earth was going on?

Robert and Lynn got up and seemed keen to leave. 'Well time to be heading back to the office, see you later perhaps Alice. Sue mentioned she would call you later to see if you are free?' Robert was already heading for the door as he spoke and obviously wanted to make a hasty exit. Lynn was not far behind. They both departed.

At this point, Ollie came over and handed her a cappuccino. 'Just the way you like it, I believe.'

Alice thought Ollie looked shifty too as if he knew something she didn't. She followed him as he disappeared into Mario's office.

'That's strange, I didn't know Robert entertained his clientele here?' Alice looked Ollie straight in the eyes.

Ollie's eyes now moved to stare at the ground beneath him. He shuffled from one foot to the other. 'Well, I am not sure. I haven't been here long enough, have I? I really couldn't tell you. But it's good to get out of the office and get a change of scenery. Why not? He is free to entertain his clients where he wants, is he not?'

Alice was sure by Ollie's demeanour that he knew something she didn't. This rankled her even more but she wasn't going to discuss the matter any further with this man.

'I've come to use the printer, Ollie so if you don't mind, I need to get on.' Alice turned her back to him and proceeded with her task of printing out her C.V. Ollie hovered for a while which irritated her. She flashed him one of Sue's Paddington Bear stares which seemed to do the job. Her head was now reeling. She would have to talk to Robert directly about the matter but now she had to get on with the present task in hand. Looking for a job.

Once the document. was all printed, she headed straight for *ASAP Staffing Services* where she was greeted by a Mr Justin Case.

'Quite a handy surname, *just in case* isn't it!' She paused and repeated it, he obviously hadn't heard this before. '*Just.... in... case* handy in your line of work don't you think?' Alice clearly wasn't getting anywhere with this and decided to just smile instead.

Mr Case, having heard this a thousand times before, couldn't even muster up the faintest hint of a smile. He would simply ignore her remark, 'Please do take a seat.' Mr Case gestured to Alice to sit on the seat opposite his desk.

Alice sat down and started to tell him all about her work experience. She handed over her C.V. which he seemed to scan rather too quickly for her liking.

'So, tell me,' Mr Case enquired, 'what exactly are you looking for?'

'Well, I'm not too sure, really. I have no idea of what is out there and feel a bit daunted by the whole change of job thing.'

'I see.' Mr Case, tapped away at his computer. 'Well let's have a look.' Mr Case continued to tap away, making the occasional utterances.

'Umm no, ah no, not that one. No not than one. No definitely not!' Mr Case gave a rather loud chuckle.

What was even more disquieting, was the way he kept looking at the screen, then Alice, then back again. What exactly was he deciding she wasn't suited for?

Alice didn't like his demeanour and dismissive looks.

However, she had spent so much time doing the wretched C.V., she didn't want to give up at the first hurdle. No, the new Alice was stronger and more determined than that. She decided to persevere.

'I am happy to give something new a try. I am not expecting to go back into the same industry. In fact, a change would be great.' Alice felt it necessary to reassure Mr Case that she was flexible on her requirements.

'I see…well… I just don't think I have the right opening at the moment but leave your C.V. with me and I will see what we can do for you.'

Alice felt that somehow her C.V. was going to end up at the bottom of the big pile he already had on his desk. She pursued her line of enquiry.

'Mr Case, what exactly do you have on your books at the present time?' Alice was eager to ensure he wasn't passing her over for an opportunity she might be able to have a go at. Besides, she wanted to show she was a determined woman, not easily dissuaded. Those were qualities he would surely admire.

'Right, well, as I explained, nothing in at present.' Mr Case went to stand up ready to usher her out the door.

Alice, however, was now somewhat irritated and stayed firmly rooted to her seat. Mr Case could do nothing more than sit back down again.

'Well you obviously have something on that computer screen, so why not run them past me?' Alice was pleased with her confident and obviously self-assured approach. Mr Case would be impressed with this.

Mr Case sat down wondering how the hell he could get rid of her. This woman had little experience other than the button industry and a degree in something he had never heard of. To make matters worse the woman had listed 'drinking gin' as a hobby. He also sensed this was a woman with attitude. Not a great start. He didn't think she would be an attractive prospect for any company.

'As I have already said, nothing in at the moment. However, I now have your details and we will get back to you as soon as something suitable gets in.'

Mr Case got up once again from his seat and went to shake her hand, hoping to guide her out of the door. What Mr Case hadn't yet realised was that Alice was on a mission to succeed and was not going to be fobbed off by his procrastinations.

Alice sat firmly rooted to her seat. Mr Case sat down, yet again.

'Like I said Mr Case, what exactly do you have on your books? You never know I might just like the sound of one of them.' Alice was sure that this confident sounding woman would surely impress.

Mr Case, let out a big puff of air from his chest and sat back down again. He clearly wasn't going to get rid of her so he would print off some jobs that she certainly wouldn't be suited for and that would surely get rid of the woman.

Alice starting scanning them all.

1. *Masseur required: Heavenly Touch Parlour - no experience required. Min Statutory pay applies.*

2. *Dog groomer. A love of dogs preferable but not essential. Min Statutory pay.*

3. *Mr Bigg's Butchers. Apprentice butcher required. A generous package for the right candidate, including a free weekly*

variety pack of meat. Meat lovers preferred but vegetarians will be considered.

4. *Apprentice office window cleaner. Must like heights and be willing to clean the odd window.*

'Right, I see.' Alice was now getting the message loud and clear. No suitable jobs. 'Well thank you for your time.' She tried to muster up a fake smile. 'I won't waste any more of it.'

As she left, she saw Mr Case put her C.V. firmly to the bottom of the pile. So that was that then. No jobs today. Feeling somewhat dejected she headed home and decided that maybe it was best to leave job hunting to another day.

19

The mystery woman

Sue rang as promised asking her if she could collect Ben from his new karate club. She said she was coming down with something or other and would Alice mind, which, of course she didn't.

The afterschool club finished at 4.30 pm which would give Alice enough time to drop off her details to some agencies in town. So many had admin roles but nothing she thought quite fitted her requirements and some of the more senior roles, she just didn't have the right experience for. However, one of the ladies at Reed's, called Kate, gave her some good advice about how to spruce up her C.V. and to make more of her experience to show off what a diverse skillset Alice actually had.

Kate was so warm and friendly and made Alice feel better about her prospects. 'It might be that you have to start on a slightly less ambitious salary, gain more experience with a company and then you never know what might happen! Perhaps you could have another look at your interests perhaps you could change 'gin drinking' to a 'love of discovering new wines and gins through your local wine tasting club', this suggests how sociable you are and you are keen to increase and widen your current knowledge.'

Alice couldn't really see how belonging to a club would do

this, after all, she kept enough bottles on her own shelf and ordered anything new that she fancied on line. Surely joining a club would mean having to pay and contribute to everyone's else's love of the stuff. However, although she was sick of the sight of her C.V., and really didn't want to revisit it, she knew she had received some good and well-intentioned advice.

She headed off to Ben's school and enjoyed watching him learn his new found hobby. He looked so sweet in his gear but Alice felt it wouldn't be long before he might be practising his moves on her.

They did their usual trip to Big Al's. Alice was about to order their Knickerbocker Glory's when Ben protested.

'No, I mustn't eat those any more. Karate is a martial art, Aunty Alice, and it is important I look after my mind *and* body.

'Right, I see?' So, what would you suggest we have instead then, in what is after all an ice cream parlour Ben?'

Ben pondered and looked at the menu.

'I think two hot chocolates would be fine.'

'Ok, two hot chocolates it is.' Alice pointed to the one's on the menu and was about to order but Ben was quick to interject.

'No, not those one's Aunty Alice, these one's.' Ben pointed to picture of the two luxury hot chocolates. They looked massive with lots of whipped cream, enormous marshmallows and gigantic chocolate buttons and a large chocolate flake.

'Right, I see. I think these hot chocolates Ben would look after the mind rather than the body?'

Alice duly ordered them thinking they probably had double the calories but didn't want to pursue that line of argument. Meanwhile, Ben proceeded to tell her all about Mr Li his Karate

Master. Ben explained that it was important she didn't mix him up with *the* Mr Jet Li. Alice was still oblivious much to Ben's disbelief.

'*Mr Jet Li*, the famous martial artist. He was the same age as me when he started and he won five gold medals at the Chinese Championships. You know him Aunty Alice, he was the one we watched the other day in The Black Mask.'

'Oh yes, that one.' Alice remembered having watched some sort of martial arts film with Ben but had fallen asleep half way through. There were only so many fight sequences she could watch, each one as predictable as the next. In fact, they were so predictable, Alice was not surprised to see Mr Li win them all.

After Ben had told her the history of Karate, and they had guzzled down what was truly the best hot chocolate Alice had ever tasted, they headed for home.

Much to Alice's delight Robert was already there in the living room. Ben rushed over to give his dad a big hug and his dad warmly responded. This would now give Alice the chance, she thought, to mention this morning.

Robert put Ben down. 'Now, Ben, I need you to be a really good boy and go upstairs quietly and change. Mum is trying to have a sleep at the moment.'

'Not again! Can't I just give her a quick hug? I won't be long.'

'No, that's a good boy just leave Mum for now.' Robert went to pour himself a drink.

Ben though had some exciting news about his day and wasn't going to give up that easily.

'Just a quick word with Mum, I want to show her....' but Ben never got to finish his sentence. Robert was quick to respond and started shouting at him, 'For goodness sake do you NEVER listen. Leave your mother alone and stop being such a spoilt brat for a change, will you?'

Ben's eyes filled up and he ran past Alice and shot up the stairs, banging his bedroom door behind him.

'Hey, that was totally uncalled for, Robert, what an earth has got into you?' Alice walked towards Robert who had now retreated to his sofa with his head in his hands.

Alice sat down next to him. Robert could sometimes be quick to temper but rarely had he lost it to this degree with Ben.

'Robert, what *is* going on?' Alice did not get a response. The incident at the café sprang to mind and now seemed as good a time as any to bring it up 'Robert, has this anything to do with that woman I saw you with earlier?'

Still silence. Robert slowly lifted his head up. He was avoiding looking her in the eye.

Alice decided to keep going, 'Robert are you... are you having an affair...' but before Alice could say anymore. Robert sprang to his feet.

'What? What on earth do you mean? What are you on about? Goodness, we all know you have had a hard time recently, but now you are going from the sublime to the ridiculous! I could never, I would never...' Robert just shook his head in disbelief at his sister's words.

'It's just that today in the café with, what's her name, Lynn. You and her just seemed, well you seemed deep in conversation and then she held your arm.'

Robert stood up and flashed her an angry and bewildered look. 'I can't believe you. It isn't always about you, you know. Has it ever occurred to you that other people might not be going through the best of times at the moment? You sit there going on at me. What kind of sister, what kind of friend are you? Are you completely blind as to what is going on right in front of your eyes, are you?' But Robert was unable to finish his sentence. Sue appeared at the bottom of the stairs.

'That's enough Robert, that isn't fair.' Sue held her hand out to Robert who simply sank back down on the chair with his head in his hands.

Alice walked over to Sue.

'Would someone please tell me what's going on between you two? Something is clearly not right between you both?'

Sue rested her head against the wooden stair rail. 'I'm not very well Alice.'

Alice sat down beside her; her legs seemed to lose the will to stand.

'I can't go into everything now, not with little ears to hear but well, yes, I'm having treatment at the moment, it makes me very tired …' Sue's eyes filled up.

'Sue…' but the words wouldn't come out. Alice threw her arms around her. They both hugged. The tears welled up in Alice's eyes. 'Why didn't you tell me? For goodness sake, why didn't you talk to me?'

Sue smiled her usual gentle smile and held Alice's hands. 'You have had the toughest time recently, all you needed was me adding to your worries.'

'That is ridiculous Sue. My worries? Well they are just so insignificant compared to yours Sue. I should have known something was wrong.' Alice felt a huge wave of guilt come over her. She had been so preoccupied with her own worries; it really hadn't entered her head that anyone else's problems could possibly surmount her own.

Sue went over to Robert and bent down and held him.

Alice followed too. They all started to hold each other. Complete silence engulfed them all. After a while, the only words Alice could eventually muster up from anywhere did not really suffice, 'I'm sorry Sue… Robert, I'm so sorry.'

Ben made a loud entrance. He stomped down the stairs and flashed his dad the most hurt and angry looks he could summon up but on seeing the tears start to run down his dad's face, Ben's anger quickly fizzled out to an anxious, hesitant demeanour. He went over to his dad, 'It doesn't matter you said those mean things, it is alright, I still love you.' Ben reached out to hold his dad's hand.

'Oh Ben, come here.' Sue beckoned him over and placed him on her knee. Sue held him very tightly. 'Dad didn't mean to shout like that Ben, Mum is just not feeling herself at the moment, Dad is just feeling out of sorts too. We all are. I am feeling a bit under the weather and a bit down, I just needed to rest and Dad was trying to look after Mum.'

Ben brightened a little, 'I can do tea tonight Mum, don't worry. We can have peanut butter soldiers, Dad's favourite. I'll make them.'

Sue beamed him a smile. 'Well that would be amazing, thank you.'

'Couldn't think of a better tea, splendid idea.' Robert came to sit down too.

It didn't take long for Ben's eyes to light up. 'First I want to show you what I made at school. It's just for you Mum, it was really for *Mother's Day* but I couldn't get it ready in time.' Ben got down off his mum's knee and rushed up the stairs.

Sue turned to Alice. 'Look, I am under the care of the

hospital. Robert saw a counsellor earlier, we were both due to, but, well, I just felt so tired. Robert saw her this morning. Lynn usually comes here but well you know the rest. She has been brilliant, she is going to support us throughout.'

Alice couldn't take it all in and had a thousand questions but didn't feel this was the right time. 'I wish you had told me Sue; I feel so bad at how I have been so wrapped up in myself, I am so sorry.'

'Look, you weren't to know. None of us did. I've only recently had the diagnosis. The hospital is deciding on the best way forward. I wish I had gone earlier now but you know what it's like. Life is always so busy. Robert persuaded me to get checked out. I didn't think much of it. Anyway, I was sent for some tests and it turns out, well you know the rest.'

Alice hugged Sue even tighter. Ben reappeared with a large brown paper bag.

'I did this in woodwork today with Mr Finch.' Ben very proudly handed his mum the packet which she hastily opened.

Sue and Alice looked at it. Both simultaneously looked at each other knowing exactly what each other was thinking. There in front of them Ben had placed a very phallic looking object with two nails coming out of it. 'Ben this is… this is simply amazing.' Mum replied.

'Ah yes, well this is definitely splendid… yes it's a really good…' Alice wasn't too sure what it was?

'It's a key holder, Aunty Alice, can't you see?' It seemed blatantly obvious to Ben.

Both Alice and Sue tried to restrain themselves from laughing.

'Yes, Ben, of course it is,' Sue looked at the phallic object with only the pride a mother could have in a piece of wood with two nails in it. 'Fancy Aunty Alice not knowing what this is!'

Alice and Robert were both trying to hold back a smile, let alone laughter. Robert leaned over and whispered in Alice's ear, 'Even better than the original Crucified Penis don't you think?'

The image of the sculpture was firmly in Alice's mind though, in fact, this one was perhaps truer to form.

'We're going to get through this, all of us, we are going to get through this.' Robert smiled at Alice and then grabbed Ben to tickle him who responded with much laughter and merriment. All seemed forgiven. The key holder took pride of place near the front door and Ben told his dad that there was no need to ever lose his keys again. Peanut butter soldiers were flowing and Ben told Dad all about his amazing hot chocolate.

20

Definitely stirred

It was now late May and Ben's half term holiday was shortly to begin. Sue was shortly to attend hospital for an operation and Robert and Ollie decided to join forces to cook a meal for family and close friends. Alice and Sam, meanwhile, were busy keeping on top of the house, cleaning and tidying and generally trying to make themselves useful.

During the morning, they all stopped to sample Ollie's chocolate brownies which Alice had to admit were absolutely gorgeous. Just the right amount of gooiness and so chocolatey. Alice could not argue that the man was a good cook.

As they sat sampling brownies, Sue was expressing concerns about Ben and the holidays. They were used to spending time with Sue's mum, in Anglesey and thought it best for Ben to go there for his usual half term holiday break. However, quite naturally Sue's mum, Betty, was equally as anxious to be with her daughter and wanted to come and stay with Robert and Sue. This was not really what Robert had in mind hoping that Ben could still go and get a holiday and generally be distracted from what was going on at home. It then would mean Robert could go back and forth to the hospital without worrying unduly about Ben.

Alice understood Betty's point of view. She understood how

Betty must be feeling and thought a good compromise was to have Betty stay with her.

'Look, I am closer to the hospital than you. Betty can stay with me and that means she can also visit when she wants.' Alice was keen to do her bit and it would be no trouble at all to have Betty come and stay.

Robert perked up a bit. 'That could work.' He wasn't quite as keen on Betty as Alice was, thinking her a real fuss pot, who never stopped tidying the house. It was bad enough that he could no longer find anything at work owing to Miss Havisham's curious filing system and didn't want the stress of the same situation at home. Betty staying at Alice's was a good idea. Robert brightened up a bit.

Sue however, wasn't as keen, 'But, look, if Ben doesn't go to mum's and mum isn't coming here to look after Ben what exactly Robert are we going to do with Ben? Alice's flat is too small to have Mum and Ben and besides I don't want Ben going to and from the hospital, he is already getting anxious about the whole thing of me going away! I want him to be distracted from it all.'

At this point, Sam interceded, 'Well why don't I have Ben for a few days, we can go away.' However, it wasn't long before Sam remembered that her boss had categorically stated no one was to go away over their busiest period. So, they all agreed that wouldn't work either.

Ollie then interceded. 'Look, I have a friend, Varjak, who has a holiday cottage near Ulverston up in Cumbria. Why don't I see if I can get the cottage for a few days? I would be more than happy to look after him. We get on well, Ben and I. He might be open to this.

However, Alice was quick to try and squash this idea. 'Well, I am not so sure. That is very kind of you Ollie but I think, at a time like this, Ben needs to be with family.' Yes, Alice thought, they had all got to know Ollie much better and, yes, he was Mario's godson but at the end of the day, she wasn't happy with Ollie looking after Ben.

Robert and Sue however, seemed to think this could work.

'That is so kind Ollie, Ben loves spending time with you and he has been so impressed with your martial arts knowledge and he is so chuffed with how you have brought his football skills along.'

Alice started to bristle at this. She decided to end this before it got out of hand.

'Yes, but at a time like this, he needs to be with someone, well people who are really close to him. If he gets upset, let's face it, it is me he comes to when you two aren't around. So, I think we really need to think of an alternative.' Alice was sure this would now put the idea firmly to bed.

Ollie however, was not put off by Alice's protestations, 'Well, we could both go and take Ollie away. There is plenty of room at the cottage.'

Alice was clearly shocked at the idea of having to go away with this man, even for Ben's or Sue's sake. No, it seemed a ludicrous idea and she was about to put paid to the whole thing when Robert and Sue interrupted.

'Of course, what a splendid idea!' Robert exclaimed.

Sue then added her full approval, 'Yes, gosh, Ben would love it. He loves the pair of you! Of course, why didn't I think of that? Betty can then stay at yours Alice and have the place to herself and you and Ollie can enjoy a few days with Ben.'

Ollie knew full well Alice wasn't keen on the idea but was pleased Robert and Sue clearly held him in such high regard.

Alice was about to protest again when Sam chipped in. 'Yes, perfect solution. Robert, you won't have to worry about Ben or Betty. Ben gets a holiday. Problem solved.'

Everyone, apart from Alice, raised their coffee cups up and Robert hi-fived Ollie.

Alice was quietly seething, how could her closest and dearest friends and family expect her to spend a day with this man, let alone a week.

'But what about me?' Alice protested. 'I will need to visit you Sue at the hospital. I mean you will need me there too. Surely?'

Sue put her cup down and put her arm around Alice, 'Yes of course, but I think Ben has the greater need, don't you at the moment?'

Alice couldn't disagree with that. Ollie continued to flash that sickening smile at her. That man could be so irritating.

The meal came and went and everyone, even Alice, had to admit that Ollie had really done a good job on the food. When he wasn't being annoying, he could be quite entertaining and was quite similar to Mario in the way he could tell a good tale. He really had travelled such a lot and had lots of all-round knowledge of so many different places to visit.

Ben was now really excited about going away with his two favourite people in the whole wide world. He had planned lots of Jet Li movies as well as wanting to show Ollie his Chelsea video on Chelsea's greatest matches. On being put to bed later that evening, Ben was keen to share his thoughts and this great idea he had.

'I think Aunty Alice should marry Ollie, don't you think so

Mum and Dad?' Ben was eager for them both to agree.

Robert and Sue were in the middle of packing Ben's bag for his holiday. The comment was enough to stop Robert in his tracks and Robert was keen to put the whole idea to bed.

'No Ben, that wouldn't be a good idea, at all. They are very different and lead different lives. Besides, Aunty Alice needs a very solid and reliable…'

'Like Malcolm?' Sue interrupted. 'Oh Robert, Malcolm is like a big, older brother to Alice. It wouldn't work at all.'

'Oh, I don't know, I think Malcolm would be very good for Alice.' Robert was surprised at his wife's quick dismissal of the idea.

'You know what a romantic Alice is. Malcolm could never fulfil that side of things. Malcolm is far too… well far too…'

Ben interrupted, 'He is nice Dad but a bit boring.'

'No Ben, not boring at all.' Sue liked Malcolm and didn't feel this was a fair judgement. 'No, he is just a bit, well set in his ways'.

'Yes, boring.' Ben repeated.

'But, I think your Dad is right Ben, Ollie is not the settling down type, he loves travelling too much. He is known as the wandering nomad in Mario's family. He wouldn't settle anywhere for long. Though, I have to admit, he is a great guy. I am glad he has come into our lives. I can't believe we have heard about him so many times and never actually met him until now'.

Sue continued packing Ben's favourite Chelsea pj's and Robert was swift to agree.

'Aunty Alice will meet someone Ben but these things happen in their own good time.'

Ben wasn't happy with that. He was adamant he was going to get the two of them together and the next few days would be perfect for doing that.

Meanwhile, Alice was back at her flat also getting packed up but with less of a spring in her step than Ben. Sam was helping her get the spare room ready for Betty but was unfortunately getting the full blast of Alice's anger and frustration.

'I mean how would anyone in their wildest dreams think that I would like to spend a few days with *HIM*. What an earth were you doing agreeing with them all?'

Sam started to reply but it was futile when Alice was in full swing.

'What's more, it can't be good for Ben to have this man wheedle his way into his affections and then just disappear again. The man has a habit of coming and going.'

'The thing is Alice...' but Sam was yet again interrupted.

'And another thing, if he thinks we are just going to spend the whole time talking about karate and Jet Ski or whatever he is called, they have both got another thing coming.'

Sam decided to let her friend have her rant. After all, she did feel a bit guilty being so ready to support the whole idea.

Alice was in full flow when the doorbell rang. Alice looked at her watch, 'A bit early for Betty?' She headed for the door and was pleasantly surprised to see Alistair there. Gosh, she thought, he really is gorgeous. He wore a suit so well. It made him look even taller.

'Hi Alice, sorry to interrupt but Isabella said she left a key with you and she's still out. I wondered if I might grab it, I seem to have left mine at home.' Alice thought what a great idea it has been of Isabella's to look after each other's spare front door key.

'Yes of course, Alistair, do come in. I will just get it for you.' Alice went to the coffee cupboard to retrieve the key she had hidden in the old biscuit caddy. 'Let me get you a cup of coffee, it is so nice to see you.' Alice beckoned Alistair to follow her into the kitchen.

Sam couldn't help notice how quickly her friend's mood had changed. All smiles and laugher were now emerging. Well at least this man's arrival had stopped all her moaning and ranting.

'Hi Sam, nice to meet you again.' Alistair also flashed Sam a smile that Sam was all too ready to respond to.

Both of the ladies were now doing their utmost to make him feel welcome.

Alistair noticed the suitcases in the living room. 'I see you are going away?'

'Oh yes, just a few days, back before you know it.' Alice was keen to give Alistair the idea that she would soon be available again should he and Isabella want to return the invite of another gin evening.

Alice handed him the key but Alistair hadn't quite got hold of it and dropped it. They both went down to pick it up but unfortunately on the way back up, Alice headbutted Alistair in the nose.

'Oh no, I am so sorry Alistair.'

Alistair winced in pain and grabbed his nose. 'No problem, really, no problem.' However, his face said it all, the man was clearly in pain. Alice insisted he sat down.

'Alistair, I am so sorry, how clumsy of me.'

'Please don't worry, I have suffered worse.'

Sam made the coffee and both women hustled and bustled

over the poor injured man.

Keen to stop all the fussing, Alistair enquired where Alice was off to. Alice however was so mortified at injuring the man she was lost for words so Sam took over the conversation.

'Yes, Alice is going to Cumbria with Ben and Ollie.'

Alice couldn't believe her ears. What on earth was her friend telling him that for?

'Well, when Sam says I am going to Cumbria with Ben and Ollie what Sam really means is that I am taking Ben to Cumbria and Ollie has decided to tag along too.' Alice flashed Sam a most disapproving look.

'But the cottage belongs to Ollie's friend Max, so it is really Ollie taking you and Ben really, isn't he?' Sam seemed completely oblivious to Alice's imploring stares of disapproval inviting her to shut the hell up.

'Oh, I see, it was just that Bella and I were going to spend a few days in the Lake's ourselves and Bella wondered if you would like to join us. There are a number of us going, she just thought you might be free. There is a great gin distillery which is very close to Ulverston, you know the one I told you about the Shed 1 distillery.

Alice couldn't believe her ears. This man was inviting her away with him. The rest of his words were lost on her. How could she be missing this trip of a lifetime?

Sam however was quick to step in, 'Oh what a shame, Alice you are away now yourself. Oh well, never mind, these things always come up to coincide with each other. Always the way.'

Alice was still sitting there reeling. OMG she thought. I can't believe that I am giving up several days away with Alistair to have to spend it with Ollie. Life simply wasn't fair. It could be so, so cruel.

'Well, there will be other times, I am sure of it.' Alistair went on to discuss the time he had spent in Cumbria and what a great place it was but Alice was truly in melt down. Every word was lost. She just sat and stared at this gorgeous man and couldn't believe that she now had to miss the holiday of her dreams. This could have been it! This could have been the moment that her life completely changed. Alistair and her walking hand in hand. Sharing an ice-cream and laughing and drinking and laughing and … sex, yes, the most fantastic sex she would probably ever have had.

After a few minutes of polite exchanges between them all, Alistair, got up to go.

Alice followed him like a lost sheep to the door, 'I hope your nose gets better Alistair, I'm so sorry.'

Alistair gave her such a warm smile, 'Look no problem, I hope you have a good holiday with Ben and…

'Ollie,' Sam shouted from the top of the hall way.

'Yes, of course, Ollie. I think I met him before?'

Alice blushed and winced at the thought, remembering Ollie's kiss.

'Look, Alistair, when I get back and you get back, well I wondered if you and Isabella would like to pop around again for another evening. I could get that gin you mentioned from Ulverston and we could share our thoughts and ideas on it. I still have the Macclesfield Forest Gin and maybe we could do a gin tasting?' Alice started tussling with her hair again.

Alistair thought it such a shame when she did this, it was messing up her blonde curls that framed her face so nicely.

'Absolutely,' agreed Alistair. 'We will make it a date then.'

And with that he wondered back up the hall to Isabella's flat watched by Alice's adoring eyes. Alistair couldn't help wonder about this Ollie chap? What exactly was their relationship? Mind you, he thought, a woman as attractive as that was bound to have plenty of admirers. He would just have to bide his time.

An hour or so later, Betty arrived and, after a light supper, both felt tired and decided an early night would be beneficial. Alice was keen to forget about the lost opportunity of getting to know Alistair and felt anxious over what was to come. She was glad to retreat under the duvet and was soon off to sleep but it wasn't long before she was dreaming, yet again.

This time there was no rope or chair in sight. She was walking along the beach with Alistair. There was a perfect sunset in the evening sky. The waves blew her hair gently into her face and Alistair carefully and gently pushed her hair out of her eyes. He held her face between his hands and kissed her, a long slow passionate kiss. After this, they both continued to walk up the beach, giggling and laughing, laughing and giggling. Alistair stopped and pulled her down to the sand. He started to admire her Tit-Tassels and Alice agreed that Chanel had done a great job of turning the tit tassel into a piece of art rather than just an ordinary accessory. Alistair popped open a bottle of champagne and they kept staring into each other's eyes. Everything was perfect. Perfect simply perfect. Alistair whispered in her ear, 'I can't wait to make love to you, but, first let's get a knickerbocker glory.'

'A knickerbocker glory, darling? Why yes that would be perfect.' An ice-cream van seemed to appear from nowhere.

Ollie appeared from under the counter. 'So sorry the ice cream machine isn't working I'm afraid. However, I could teach you

Karate instead?'

'What? I don't think so!' Alice turned to Alistair who surprisingly looked very enthusiastic about the idea.

'Gosh yes, that would be great, never learnt Karate at school, always wanted to learn, yes great.'

'Right, good.' Ollie jumped over the counter and landed on the sand beside them both.

'Let's get to it, a few simple moves to show you...' Ollie was already kicking his legs up into the air.

Alice interrupted, 'But darling, we are going to bed soon. Let's go now.'

'What! Bed, now? Oh honey, not now. Not now we have the Grand Master to show us how to do Karate. No darling, now is not the time for bed. I want to karate like Jet Ski'

Alice was astounded, 'But... Alistair, Alistair...' Alice watched Alistair and Ollie go off together into the sunset. Alistair turned round, 'You go and get a cup of tea, darling, I won't be long.'

Alice heard this strange knocking. Slowly came round from her sleep, disturbed by Betty tapping on the bedroom door. 'I've made a nice cuppa for you dear.'

'Right, great Betty, thanks for that.' So close she thought and yet so far. Story of her life.

21

The cottage

Alice reluctantly put her suitcase in the car, moaning and groaning to herself about how this was possibly going to be the worst week of her life. Alistair's car was still in the guest parking space and all she could do was stare at it, lamenting and sighing over what could have been.

The journey took longer than usual to get to Sue's. First, she had to steer as carefully as she could out of her carparking space. Why did Number 27 always have to park as close as he possible could to her car? He never parked down the middle of his space, oh no, he obviously had to make life as hard as he possibly could for her. She swore he did it deliberately. Then to make matters worse, someone, not being able to find a car parking space, had managed to park not far behind her making reversing even trickier.

Whilst trying to manoeuvre herself out, old nosey neighbour from Number 18, Mr Hughes, appeared offering his penny's worth, uninvited. He had a thick welsh accent, deliberating over the end of every sentence.

'NO! I wouldn't do it that way if I were you! I think you should try… Oh goodness no, don't do that… I can show you if you like?'

After about 20 minutes of her neighbour huffing and puffing

over her efforts, she had managed to get going but now, to make matters worse, every traffic light she approached had decided to turn red and every madman that could be out driving was now out on the roads.

The only thing that cheered her up was arriving at Sue's and seeing Ben run out of the door, rushing out to greet her with great excitement.

'I've got it all planned out, Aunty Alice, see I have written a timetable.'

'Have you indeed!' Alice studied it with due consideration but adamant in her mind that none of Ben's ideas of watching a series of Jet Li movies and scheduling in Karate lessons with Ollie were coming to fruition. No, this would be a weekend of fresh air, exercise and spending as little time indoors with Ollie as possible.

Ben handed Alice a large tin and she was delighted on investigation to see Sue's Viennese swirls and shortbread filling it to the brim. Things were looking up Alice thought. However, this brief moment of happiness was soon brought to a halt by Ollie's appearance at the door, carrying the bags.

'Ben, take this, will you, just while I...?' Ollie handed Ben's bag to him but as he proceeded to open the boot of Alice's car, his eyes were met by an already jam-packed boot. 'Goodness! Planning to be away some time are we?' Ollie purveyed the collection of bags large and small, wondering how any person could possibly need so much luggage for a mere four days of holiday. 'Well, it's a good job you and I, Ben, travel so light!' Ollie commented as he squeezed their bags on top of Alice's.

Alice was about to give him a mouthful when Sue interjected. 'Thank you so much, *both* of you. It really means a great deal that you are doing this for Ben - and for me.' Sue went over and put her arm around Alice.

At this, Alice mellowed. Yes, after all, Alice thought, this was all for Ben and Sue. She could manage a few days away with this irritating man for the two people she loved more than anything in the world. Alice gave Sue a big hug, but was now interrupted by Ben keen to get going and protesting at all this girly nonsense of hugging all the time.

Robert then emerged and shook Ollie's hand, thanking him for arranging the few days away. He picked Ben up in his arms.

'Right you, behave yourself and no going to bed too late and no trying out your latest moves on Aunty Alice, she needs to come back in one piece.'

Ben smiled and promised, whilst having his fingers crossed behind his back and winking at Ollie.

They all got in the car. The sun started to shine as they left the driveway. Ben waved at his mum and dad all the way to the end of the road. However, they hadn't even reached the edge of the town centre, before Ben was already asking how much longer the journey would take. Ollie explained that Cumbria was quite a way off and it would be a few hours yet and tried to distract him with a game of eye spy. However, Ben soon got bored of this and repeated his usual mantra of 'Is it much further yet?' or 'Haven't we got there yet?'

Thankfully after about an hour of constant enquiries, Ben nodded off to sleep having been far too excited the night before to entertain the idea of closing his eyes with so much to plan. Although the silence at first was gratefully received it soon turned to an awkward silence. The conversation had now dried up completely. Ollie felt he ought to make polite conversation but his attempts did not get him very far as his words were met with frosty one-word responses.

Ollie reconsidered his tactics. Maybe a bit of music would lighten things up a bit. He wasn't hopeful of his driving companion's taste in music but was pleasantly surprised to find some of his old favourites hiding in her glove compartment. Alice meanwhile, thought it very rude of him to root through her things without asking but relented when he had chosen one of her favourite CD's. This might just shut him up too.

'Ah, ELO's greatest hits. Nice one.' It wasn't long before Alice had forgotten her woes and was singing and humming along to 'Mr Blue Sky.'

They stopped along the way for a toilet stop and some lunch. Ben wanted a McDonalds, insisting that he could eat a Big Mac, extra-large fries followed by a donut without making him feel the slightest big sick. Alice reluctantly acquiesced, realising protests were futile, when Ollie also announced there was nothing better than a Big Mac with Fries.

Um she thought, well *HE* can clear up the mess when Ben succumbs to travel sickness. Ben wasn't the greatest of travellers at the best of times and this long journey, she was sure, would not be the exception.

After they all ate, Ben decided it was time to put part of his plan of matchmaking into action.

Whilst downing his coke, Ben exclaimed, 'Ollie you don't have a girlfriend, do you?' Ollie was most surprised at the question but answered that he hadn't.

'Aunty Alice, you certainly don't have a boyfriend, do you?' Ben was hoping it would now occur to the both of them that as they were both free and single, they would see the sense in being boyfriend and girlfriend.

Alice and Ollie quickly realising where this was heading promptly got up and insisted it was time to get going.

The next leg of the journey took a bit longer than expected. There was a lot of traffic on the motorway and they had to stop several times for Ben to go to the toilet and for Ollie to clear up the back seat of the car when Ben had managed to projectile vomit over the back of both of the front seats as well as himself.

After many, very weary hours of travel, they arrived. Ollie collected the key from a neighbour whilst Alice and Ben admired the cottage. Alice had to admit it was so much better than she had expected to find. It was quite a large stone cottage with pink clematis plants shooting up the walls and a climbing rose adorning the front door entrance. Alice thought that it must have been a nineteenth century cottage and had a charm that only houses of this age can have.

Once inside, Ben quickly set about investigating all the rooms and was delighted to find a pool and table tennis table in the Games Room. The only disappointment was the lack of a television set but Alice was relieved about this as she would not have to negotiate the number of Jet Li films they would have to watch. They all ventured out into a fairly large back garden, filled with roses, apple trees and rhododendron bushes. Ollie proudly pointed over to the brick barbecue saying how he had built this for his friend. Indeed, Alice thought it was a good, sturdy piece of workmanship and the thought of a barbecue excited Ben.

Alice thought things were looking decidedly better. Around the barbecue area there were iron chairs and a small round table inlaid with some beautiful stained glass. If the warm weather continued, she was looking forward to catching up on some reading, whilst catching the early morning sun.

Ollie nipped out to the local grocery store, which also housed a delicatessen, and set about cooking Alice and Ben some Pasta Carbonara. Ben was keen to eat outside and Alice retrieved a bottle of gin and made herself and Ollie an aperitif or as Ben liked to call it 'a pair of teeth.'

After several gins and a few glasses of wine, Alice had definitely mellowed and Ollie who, after all, had cooked a delicious meal now seemed less annoying. In fact, she had to admit she had enjoyed learning about his travels in Austria and how he had learnt cooking from his very good friend Florian. Ben, on growing tired of the grown-ups relentless talking, soon took himself off and occupied himself on the pool table.

Alice decided this was a good time to broach the subject of Mark again. She never did find out exactly what happened on New Year's Eve.

'Ollie, look I heard you were a bit of a knight in shining armour on New Year's Eve.'

Ollie protested but said he was glad to have helped and asked her how things had been.

'Yes, I am fine, all water under the bridge now. It obviously wasn't to be and honestly it was better to have happened now than further down the line. I guess the thing I am most hurt about is the fact he was so adamant he didn't want to have children whereas I…, well I think I would have enjoyed being a mum.'

Ollie had witnessed the great relationship she had with Ben and he felt for her. He thought that this must have been a particularly hard hurdle to get over.

'Well there is always adoption, I guess?'

Alice was taken aback by this. 'God no, well I mean, I have never really thought about it, probably all too late now.' Alice dropped her eye contact.

'Anyway you never know what is around the corner…'

'Well that's certainly true.' Alice laughed. 'Amen to that!' She lifted her glass and they both clinked glasses.

Alice was still eager to find out more about that night with Mark, after she had left the party.

'A little bird tells me that you had a bit of an altercation with Mark?' Alice looked earnestly at Ollie who realised she was obviously keen to find out more.

'Ah, yes, well… yes, it is true. Just thought he was behaving like a real dickhead…' Ollie suddenly stopped, feeling that maybe insulting the man she was probably still in love with, was not a great idea considering their friendship and had not got off to a great start.

'Well, yes he was a dickhead, I will drink to that!' Alice raised her glass again.

Ollie relieved and became less cautious of relating the night's events. He proceeded to explain what had happened when he got back to the party and how appalled he had been at Mark's treatment of her and his outrageous flirting with another woman whilst his girlfriend, who he had previously taken home, was heavily pregnant. Ollie was keen to point out that it wasn't the way he usually behaved but something just flipped that night. He explained how Mark had been so flippant about it all and completely blind to his unacceptable behaviour and when Mark had turned his back on Ollie to continue flirting, quite inappropriately, with another woman and, indeed, right in front of Sue and Robert he just flipped.

'Well, Ollie, it seems that everyone had got the measure of him, apart from me. How blind love can obviously be. I am glad you hit him! Goodness I would have loved to have witnessed that. It's not many who get the better of Mark. I believe you gave him a black eye!'

Ollie gave one of his mischievous grins, 'Yes indeed and I think I gave him more than a black eye. I feel certain my knee to his groin would have put paid to any amorous advances he had in mind that night too.'

Alice picturing the scene, suddenly roared with laughter, delighting in the thought of Ollie having kneed Mark out of his manhood. This, in turn, set Ollie off who could now see the humour in it all.

Ben appeared in the garden, pleased that these two were obviously enjoying each other's company and that his plan to get them together was surely going to be successful. 'Right you two, I think it is time for a game of pool. Ollie you can play first and Aunty Alice would you mind making the hot chocolate while you are waiting?'

'Sounds like a plan Ben.' Ollie was keen to get his hands on the pool table as it had been many years since he had last played.

That night much fun was had by all. Alice thought that maybe she had been a bit hasty in her opinion of Ollie and Ollie thought using the word rottweiler had been a bit strong, perhaps more of a Staffordshire bull terrier was a better description.

22

Such a Perfect Day

Alice woke up to the sound of table tennis balls clicking and got out of bed to find Ben with Ollie.

'Breakfast?' Alice enquired.

'Oh yes, please Aunty Alice. Can I have my scrambled eggs but the way mum does them please?'

Alice cooked a full English breakfast and they all enjoyed eating it in the garden whilst admiring the skilfulness of a squirrel negotiating the washing line to get to the bird feeder. Ben was eager to know what they were going to do. Ollie had been busy the night before perusing through leaflets he had found on the hallway table on things to do in Cumbria, particularly for children, and started to run through the possibilities with them both.

Alice and Ben liked the sound of visiting Lingholm Estate in Keswick to see the alpacas and then a boat ride around Lake Windermere. Alice looked through the box of groceries she had brought from home and set about preparing a picnic. She had been delighted to find a large picnic basket in the under stair's cupboard and was soon assisted by Ben who was adamant he could make his own peanut butter sandwiches claiming he *always* did his own at home.

'Do you know what, Aunty Alice? I think this is going to

be the best day of my life!' Ben was enjoying the freedom of sandwich-making telling his Aunt how he was looking forward to meeting a real alpaca and maybe even milking one. His mate Fred the Barnett had boasted that he had milked goats whilst on holiday in France. Surely an alpaca would top that!

'Goodness Ben! Well, we will have to see about that but I am glad you are excited about our day.' Alice, was now mindful at how surreptitiously Ben managed to keep sweeping spoonfuls of peanut butter into his mouth while thinking no one was watching him.

They packed up the basket with sandwiches, a few sausage rolls, crisps and some of Sue's baking. Perfect Alice thought. That would keep the wolf from the door or at least keep Ben off the subject of food until tea.

They journeyed to Lingholm Estate and all were delighted to meet the alpacas. The keeper imparted her considerable knowledge, 'Yes, they are prized as both pets and cattle around the world. They are related to llamas which are domesticated versions of another wild Andean ruminant the guanaco. While llamas are used for pack animals, alpacas are used for their soft wool....'

Ben declared that he no longer wanted a rabbit for his birthday but now an alpaca. He could keep it in the garden shed as Dad would no longer need his mower for keeping the grass cut. In fact, dad would be really pleased not to have to mow *that wretched lawn* again.

Alice had to admit they were gorgeous and their fur was so soft. The baby alpaca was probably the sweetest baby animal she had ever seen. Ollie too seemed impressed and was surprised to learn how they don't have teeth at the top front of their mouths.

Ben asked to borrow Aunty Alice's phone and was quick to check *You Tube* to see how to milk an Alpaca.

'Look here Aunty Alice, it is quite easy you know!' Keen to distract Ben from this idea she took him off to the shop where Ben was delighted to be bought his own alpaca toy which fitted perfectly in his adventure back pack.

After a brief visit to get a coffee, or in Ben and Alice's case a large hot chocolate and cake, they set off to Windermere. Along the way and after having got slightly lost, Ben spotted a crazy golf course and Ollie and Ben felt they did a sterling job of persuading Ben's somewhat reluctant aunt to stop off for a short while to partake in a game or two.

Much to her surprise, as well as the others, Alice turned out to be a dab hand at golf although she did almost knock Ollie out at the third hole with a somewhat overly zealous swing. Ben declared that she was probably the best mini-golfer in Cumbria or probably the world. Ollie readily agreed with Ben, despite his sore chin, and this praise, readily accepted by Alice, assured them both of a second round of the golf course.

Lake Windermere was stunning and even though they had to queue for well over an hour for the boat, the ride did not disappoint. When on board, Alice got the picnic hamper out and all readily tucked in to a rather late lunch. Ollie commented on the prowess of Ben's mum as a baker and Alice was pleased with the delicious sausage rolls, she had previously acquired from Mr Bigg's butcher. Keen to impress Alice, he had given her two extra sausage rolls at no charge at all whilst enquiring whether she had received a card from André yet about their next date. Alice, admitted, she indeed had not. She then had to endure (yet again) a long conversation on the merits of using only the best sausage meat, but, on tasting the sausage rolls, she did feel the time had been worth it. Ben said they all had to pretend that the pink lemonade was really champagne. He then proudly displayed his alpaca to the elderly couple on the seat behind his, telling them all about his plans to get one for his birthday and how easy they were to milk.

The sun shone in the sky and the gentle breeze on the lake kept them all cool. There was only the odd interruption to the tranquillity of it all with the break out of hysteria from Aunty Alice when she spotted a wasp near Ben which then involved everyone nearby trying to kill it.

When the boat ride had finished, Ben declared he was tired and hungry so they set off home listening to Ben's timetable of activities that he had planned for the evening which mainly consisted of pool, table tennis and a game of '*Slippery Mary*' or '*Hairy Mary*' as his dad called it. Ollie said he would cook tea again but Alice insisted she was going to so Ben settled it by saying they both could do it together. Ben was delighted when they agreed and thought to himself this would surely make them girlfriend and boyfriend if they cooked together.

Alice stopped off at the grocery store to pick up a few items whilst Ben was telling Ollie about his plan to get an alpaca and how he might need to get Ollie to persuade his dad too, 'It's really quite simple Ollie, I will tell dad about the grass they eat and how mum can knit lots of jumpers from their wool and you can tell them all about the advantages of breeding them to make babies and then make money selling them. I think Dad would see it as a good investment as our Malcolm often says.'

'Right, I see.' Ollie didn't seem as keen as Ben on the idea. 'Well I think Mum and Dad have got a lot going on at the moment Ben, so let's not mention it just yet.'

'Ollie, are you going to ask Aunty Alice tonight then?' Ben decided to change the subject, he would use his super powers of persuasion for later.

'Ask Alice what, exactly Ben?' Ollie was now distracted by a man across the road wrestling with his next-door neighbour's dog to let go of his gardening gloves.

'To be your girlfriend of course!' Ben now had Ollie's full attention.

'The thing is Ben, me and your Aunty Alice. Well, I mean I am a bit busy at the moment to be having a girlfriend and I think Aunty Alice's affections lie elsewhere anyway Ben.'

Ben was not having any of this. 'No, she hasn't got a boyfriend at all, she would have told me first.'

'Ah, well the thing is Ben…' but luckily, to the relief of Ollie, Alice had returned at this point and the conversation could be steered elsewhere.

'Got a Cartmel sticky toffee pudding Ben and some custard. Thought we could treat ourselves tonight.'

Ben eyes lit up as big as saucers but, then out of loyalty to his mum, was quick to remind his aunt that it could never be as good as his mum's but he would try it just to make sure.

Alice and Ollie set about cooking as soon as they got home. Ollie helped with the chopping and Alice ended up doing most of the cursing when she managed to chop her own finger instead of the carrots. With blood quickly emerging from the wound, Ollie was swift to act, very gently cleaning up her finger.

'Goodness, it is deeper than I thought, here, elevate it while I find a plaster.' Ollie rooted through cupboards until eventually he found the first aid box. 'That could be a bit sore for a bit.'

Alice was taken aback at how this big man could be so gentle. He blew on her finger to dry the area and it was at this point that they both caught each other's eye. Ollie thought Alice really did have the most gorgeous blue eyes and when she smiled it lit up her whole face. Alice was equally as admiring of Ollie's twinkly eyes and there was something about the way he blew on her finger that made her feel a bit strange inside. Both stopped and just stared at each other.

At this point, Ben emerged. 'Gosh I am starving, Aunty Alice is the tea ready yet?' Ben spotted Aunty Alice's finger firmly in Ollie's hand, 'Ah, so are you two now...'

Alice was swift to intervene knowing full well what was coming next, 'Go and put these mats Ben on the table and then come and get some knives and forks.'

Ben, thankfully, was distracted by this and the cooking resumed but this time in silence. Everyone was busy with their thoughts. Alice and Ollie pondered over the brief encounter and Ben was planning the wedding. He would insist on walking his Aunty down the aisle in his Chelsea kit.

The evening came and went. Ollie enjoyed the card game of Slippery Mary and Alice agreed that Ben could have just one more game of pool with Ollie whilst she cleared up. Both were pleased to have escaped the washing up and Ben decided this would be the game when he would beat Ollie. Clearing up achieved and game played, Ben was ushered up to bed by Ollie. Ben kept protesting at such an early night at *just* nine o'clock because Dad let him stay up sometimes until *at least* midnight in the holidays. Both adults, who were now exhausted, were adamant not to budge on the subject and Ben soon realised he would have to settle for having a few pages of his David Walliam's books *Slime* read to him and he liked Ollie, for a change, reading to him.

When Ben had settled, Ollie ventured down the stairs to help with the rest of the clearing up but Alice had been very efficient and had completed it. She was now curled up on the sofa, asleep. Ollie got one of the rugs out of the basket near the fireplace and gently placed it over her. She seemed to smile in her sleep and she had snuggled deeply into the cushions. Ollie sat down opposite her and reminisced over the day. He could see what Florian meant there was something lovely about coming home after a day out, sharing a meal as family and just enjoying each other's company.

He went over to Max's cd and old LP collection and started to rummage through. He found Lou Reed's Transformer album and put it on. Yes, he had to agree with Lou that the day had been just perfect.

23

Milking the alpacas.

Whilst Alice was snuggled up on the sofa, she drifted off to sleep.

*She was at the farm surrounded by alpacas and Ben was complaining about all the milking that had to be done and why couldn't **she** learn to do it? Alice reminded him that she had the job of shearing the alpacas which he was far too small to do. Ben complained that his hands were hurting and if only she had bought him a rabbit instead, life could have been so much better. With his frustration reaching boiling point, he kicked the pale of milk over and stormed off.*

Alice went to pick up the pale but as she reached for the handle another hand got there first and a voice said, 'Here let me senorita.' Alice looked up to find Alistair standing there, dressed as Zorro. He had a sword in his hand and quickly flashed the sword around his body making full sweeps with the blade before thrusting the sword down in front of her eyes and cutting her corset open and with another quick swipe of the sword swiping her Tit-Tassels off. He threw the sword into the ground and grabbing her, he masterfully swept her back into his arms, kissing her long and hard. Alice felt every part of her body pulsating as Alistair held her tightly. This was heaven. No, this was paradise!

Just then, however, Alistair felt a tap on his shoulder. 'Excuse me.' came another man's voice from behind. They both tried to ignore the man but he was becoming most persistent.

'Excuse me, Mr Bigg the butcher here. I think you will find this lady is already spoken for.' Mr Bigg looked most indignant and looking at Alice saying 'I have to say, having given you my last two sausage rolls, I am very disappointed to see you carrying on with this man, have you no shame?'

Alistair let go of Alice and she fell back on the hay, 'Is this true, Alice? Has this man given you **two** sausage rolls?' Alistair looked aghast and deeply hurt at this blatant betrayal of his trust.

'Well, yes but…' Alice was struggling to find the words 'but… the thing is…they are just sausage rolls, Alistair, I certainly didn't promise anything else, honestly.'

Mr Bigg tutted loudly, 'Well, I never, and to think I put extra spices in the meat!'

Alistair looked long and hard into her eyes 'Look if a man gives you not just one sausage roll but indeed two sausage rolls, you must surely know this is more than just an empty gesture or a mere flight of whimsy, this is a gesture of true love.'

Alice just couldn't quite get what Alistair was going on about. She got up and reached out to hold him but Alistair pushed her away.

'No, my love you belong to this man, I can see that now.'

'What? What on earth do you mean? I'm not in love with Mr Bigg, Alistair! I love you.' Alice went to try and hold him again but Alistair was having none of it and stormed out of the door.

At this point, Ollie walked in holding an alpaca.

'This alpaca hasn't been milked yet, if you are going to keep these animals you really must look after them properly, you know.'

Ollie looked somewhat disgruntled as he stroked the alpaca's head. Ben had now returned and was complaining that tea hadn't been cooked and what on earth was she wearing?

Alice looked down and saw her tightly corseted dress had disappeared and had now become an alpaca onesie. She rushed over to the window and watched Alistair as he strode off into the distance. This couldn't be happening. She ran out the door, shouting his name and chasing after him but it was all to no avail she could never, quite reach him.

'Aunty Alice, who's Alistair? Aunty Alice, Aunty Alice wake up, who is Alistair?' Ben was standing over her and looked most puzzled.

Ollie having nodded off to sleep himself on the sofa opposite, quickly got up and took Ben by the hand, 'Come on you back to bed.' Ollie picked up Ben and took him back upstairs

Alice could feel her face start to flush. Oh Lord, she thought, what had she been saying?

After about 10 minutes Ollie re-emerged smiling from ear to ear. 'Well that must have been some dream?'

Alice's face was now as crimson as the cushion. 'Oh, was it? I really can't remember. Some strange dream about alpacas.'

'Indeed! An alpaca called Alistair, interesting?'

'Alistair? Really, no I don't really recall.' Alice decided it was time to get herself to bed and proceeded to climb the stairs, followed by Ollie.

They got to the top when Alice turned round to say goodnight, Ollie still had that annoying look on his face and was first to wish her goodnight and 'Pleasant dreams.' But as she really couldn't think of how to respond, she turned her back on him, tutted, and went through the bedroom door as quick as she could. What was it Scarlett O'Hara used to say, she thought to herself. Ah yes *'tomorrow is another day...'*

24

My Boy Lollipop

Alice was woken by the smell of bacon wafting up the stairs and Ben's foot pressed firmly against her back. At some point in the night, unbeknown to her, Ben had managed to climb into bed with her and had taken up his favourite position of lying horizontally across the bed. She covered up his bare leg with the duvet cover and watched him sleep. She looked at this handsome little boy with curly blonde hair and the most enormous long lashes. She thought how completely wasted they were on a boy. She started to reminisce about the day he was born, everyone crowding around the hospital bed looking at this beautiful little miracle. Sue and Robert just looked overwhelmed and everyone declared how he had his mother's eyes and his father's nose. Mark, however, had just sat in the corner of the room reading his paper looking singularly unimpressed, clock watching and fidgeting in his seat. Alice had laughed it off at the time but looking back, she could see how selfish he had been on that day, not even wanting to acknowledge how special this event had been for Robert and Sue.

She looked at the clock. About four hours until Sue's operation and she decided that after breakfast it would be a good idea to ring Sue before she was admitted. Her stomach started to churn. She had this feeling of dread that just maybe it was all going to be worse than everyone thought. She pulled Ben towards her and put her arm around him but the movement made him stir and he snuggled his head under her arm.

'Aunty Alice, I had a nightmare last night, I couldn't find Mum and Dad anywhere. They kept hiding from me and I didn't like it.'

'Ah Ben, it was just a dream, it's all gone now.' Alice stroked his curly locks and tigged his nose. 'I think it's time for some more adventures today don't you?' However, Ben remained still and silent.

Alice sensing the anxiety in him too thought it best that she kept him busier than ever today. 'Right, well that bacon seems to be calling to us to go and eat it! Let's get a bacon sandwich and then we can plan our day. Perhaps you could do another one of your timetables, Ben? That will make sure we don't waste any time.' But Ben just shrugged his shoulders.

After washing and dressing, they both headed downstairs. Ollie had laid the table and a plate of bacon awaited them. Ben didn't want any and no amount of cajoling or offers of cereals, toast or eggs could persuade him to eat. After a while, Ben got down from the table.

'I think I would like to go home now please Aunty Alice. I think mum will be missing me too much.' A tear started to emerge in Ben's eye. Alice felt herself about to cry too.

Ollie was swift to respond, 'Gosh, mate, we have got far too much to do today. I was planning a barbecue and need a Head Chef. I really couldn't manage it on my own, Ben, what do you say?'

Silence. Ben just shook his head from side to side. Ollie continued, 'And of course then there will be the trip to South

Lakes Safari Zoo and maybe a train ride on Ravensdale and Eksdale Railway.'

Ben lifted his head up, his eyes lit up 'Well, I suppose Mum and Dad could spare me another day? What do you think Aunty Alice?' Ben looked at his aunt for reassurance.

'Definitely Ben, but I tell you what why don't we give Mum a quick ring and then you can tell her all about your day yesterday and how you won the world championship pool contest.' Alice reached for her mobile and the call was made.

Ben brightened up considerably and whilst he was talking to his parents, Alice thanked Ollie for his kindness. 'You really are good with him and you have gone to so much effort…'

'Nonsense, I have really enjoyed our time together. He is a lovely boy, Sue and Robert have done a good job there.' Ollie sensing Alice's anxiety too, placed his hand on Alice's arm, 'It will be fine.' This kind gesture brought another tear to her eyes and she decided she had best get on and clear up. She needed to keep busy too. Ollie headed off to the local butcher to buy some meat and veg for the barbecue.

Alice watched him as he went up the garden path. When he wasn't being smug and annoying, he could actually be a really nice guy. He had gone out of his way to spend his time and play with Ben and he had so much patience. Mark never really gelled with Ben. Whenever Alice took Ben out or there were family gatherings, Mark always seemed to have an excuse for not going.

Ben had finished on the phone and handed her mobile back for his aunt to have a word too.

'Hi, Sue how are you doing?' Alice enquired, feeling a bit overwhelmed herself about the day her friend now faced.

'Bit nervous, you know but… well.' Alice could hear Sue's voice waver but she managed to continue, 'Ben seems to be having a good time. He is looking forward to the zoo and apparently he is in charge of the barbecue tonight.'

'Indeed. Ollie is doing a sterling job on the entertainment front, and the busy itinerary is managing to keep them both out of mischief. Anyway, Ben is fine and we have another fun day ahead of us. More importantly, you take care today Sue, I will be thinking of you, get Robert to ring me later will you? Just for an update.'

Sue agreed, they both sent each other their love and with that they said adieu. Both of them needing to end the conversation before either one of them got too emotional.

Ollie was soon back and they both set about planning the car journey making sure there were regular stops along in case Ben needed either the loo or to be sick or both.

The zoo didn't disappoint. Ben decided as well as an alpaca for a pet and he would also like a penguin. Ben got a chance to feed them and was delighted when Aunty Alice told him about the opportunity of adopting one. Although he was sad he couldn't take it home, he loved the idea of receiving a certificate of ownership. Alice enjoyed the giraffes and Ollie the lemurs, doing his Madagascar impression much to the delight of them all. Ollie bought everyone an ice cream and Alice and Ben readily tucked into a whippy ice cream with a double chocolate flake. Ollie set them a challenge to eat the ice cream in the manner of different types of animals. Ben decided he would be a monkey and to much amazement he was somehow able to do a rolly poly on the ground while managing to keep his ice-cream intact even if it did now have the added flavour of grass to enhance its taste.

The café didn't disappoint either and Ben was delighted to find chicken nuggets on the menu. Ollie had a glass of wine with his roast and Alice enjoyed the ginger beer with her tuna salad. The gift shop also beckoned and Ben spent some of his own pocket money on a bouncy ball which managed to last about five minutes before Ollie and Ben managed to bounce it up onto the café roof. Alice ended up buying another one but was most insistent this time it went straight into his adventure back pack much to Ben and Ollie's disappointment.

The steam train ride at Ravenglass and Eskdale didn't disappoint either. Ben was completely absorbed, declaring, once again, that this was the best day of his life. They walked from Dalegarth station up to the Eskdale Mill and Ben was delighted to stop off at the Brookhouse Inn for a very weak shandy. Ben took his notebook out of his bag and starting to draw up a timetable for the evening putting the barbecue first with him as Head Chef. He would be in charge of the burgers and Ollie could do the tuna as he didn't like the smell of it.

While they were busy planning, Alice looked at her watch. Sue would be out of surgery now and, not wanting to wait for Robert to call her, she decided to call Betty. Betty informed her that Sue was now in the recovery room after her operation and the surgeon had been very pleased with the outcome. All would be well.

Alice went back to Ben and Ollie excited to tell them the news, Ben flung his arms around Alice and then put his hand out to Ollie to pull him in for a group hug. Ollie seemed overcome too by the moment, a tear also appeared in his eye and Alice without thinking just seemed to naturally put her hand up to his face to comfort him. Ollie instinctively put his hand on hers and, in that split second, the world seemed to stop and as they stared into each other eye's both had a strange feeling they couldn't explain. The tender moment though was short lived being interrupted by Ben declaring that that another shandy and packet of crisps was a really good way to celebrate. No one disagreed.

The evening came all too quickly, bringing much merriment with Ollie doing his John Torode impersonation but, failing to keep an eye on the situation, managed to set fire to the steaks - well and truly cremating them. Everyone though enjoyed the burgers declaring Ben had done a top job. Alice was most insistent no one ate the chicken legs as they looked decidedly pink in the middle proclaiming that Ollie should now put them in the oven, just to make sure they were cooked.

After Ben had finished some of the sticky toffee pudding left over from yesterday, Ben declared he was very tired and wanted to go to bed, insisting that both Ollie and Alice take him. Each took a turn to read a page of his *Slime* book and it wasn't long before Ben succumbed to sleep and Ollie and Alice tiptoed out of the room and down the stairs.

Alice was keen to investigate the record collection, finding a single by Millie, *My Boy Lollipop*.

'Gosh I remember my mum used to sing this to Robert and me when we were little.' She played the record, singing along.

Ollie meanwhile dug out '*The Legend of Xanadu.*'

'Gosh this brings me back. Good old Dave Dee, Dozy, Beaky, Mick and Tich, what amazing names.' Ollie recalled how he had seen some old footage of the band on television with a whip as the lead singer slashed it across the stage. In fact, he had been so impressed he remembered turning his sister's skipping rope into a whip, pretending he was one of the band members on stage!

'Umm, very kinky!' Alice announced remembering her dream with Alistair and feeling herself flush a little.

'Yes, I suppose it was!' Ollie said as he delved into the records for his next choice.

Alice got there first, 'Oh, we must play this, this is a given.' Alice found another oldie and goldie a copy of *Where do you Go to My Lovely* by Sarstedt. 'Sue and I used to play this over and over again at Uni.' Alice swiftly put the single on the turntable.

Ollie held out his arms 'Fancy a dance then love?'

Alice laughed as Ollie started to waltz her around the living room. 'Gosh they make it look a lot easier on *Strictly* don't they!' Alice declared.

'Umm, I don't think we are doing too badly though'. Ollie swirled Alice around a little too quickly and they both ended up tripping over each other, landing on the sofa with Alice sprawled on top of Ollie. Alice starting laughing. She had one of those infection laughs and Ollie couldn't help but join in too. Both had got a bit giddy with laughter and Alice then lost her balance and tumbled off Ollie from the sofa to the floor, this time with Ollie on top. More laughter ensued. Then some more. Something inside at that very moment caused him to stop laughing. Alice stared back. There was now silence. The record had finished playing. Just silence. Ollie felt this overwhelming desire to kiss her and gave her a short kiss on the lips. Alice responded and the short kiss then turned into a much longer kiss. Both were now clearly enjoying the moment.

Alice was overcome by what a great kisser this man was and it wasn't before long they were passionately enthralled in each other's arms, pulling off each other's clothes. Alice however, thinking she heard a movement from upstairs, suddenly stopped.

'Ben! Look, we mustn't wake Ben, suppose he comes down the stairs?'

Ollie got up, pulling her up too. 'Well then, I think it's time for bed, don't you?' He seemed to effortlessly pick her up in his arms and headed up the stairs.

'Ollie, suppose he comes to look for me in the night?' Alice now started to feel anxious about Ben discovering them together. It wouldn't be appropriate.

'I've got a lock on the door, he can't come through a locked door, now, can he?'

'Yes, but….' Alice wasn't given the chance to protest as Ollie kissed her yet again, even more firmly than before. She felt her body melt into his arms as he continued to lift her up the stairs.

'Gosh, you are heavier than you look,' Ollie grinned at her. 'Glad it's only a short set of stairs.'

'Well, you cheeky….'

But he didn't give her the chance to respond and Alice, somewhat overwhelmed by a very Gone with the Wind moment, thought she would let him get away with this, just this time…

25

The stuck door

Alice was awoken by Ben calling her name. He had gone into her bedroom but couldn't find her there so had run downstairs hoping to find her in the kitchen. He had then proceeded to the garden feeling sure she would be reading her book outside but all his searches were to no avail. Alice could now hear him running back up the stairs heading straight for Ollie's room.

'Ollie, Ollie, I can't find Aunty Alice?' Ben struggled with the door.

Alice and Ollie dashed up and out of bed. 'OMG, OMG, quickly Ollie get some clothes on.' Alice was now in a state of panic. She really didn't want Ben getting the wrong idea, well the right idea.

'Aunty Alice, I can hear your voice in here too, I can't open the door, it's stuck?'

'Ah, yes, yes, the door has got a bit stuck Ben and I am just helping Ollie try to get it open.' Alice got dressed as quickly as she could and Ollie in his rush to get his trousers stubbed his toe on the bedroom fireplace hearth.

'Oh F...k.' Ollie shouted far too loudly and much to the disapproval of Alice who had him fixed firmly with her Paddington Bear stare.

'Gosh this door is tricky, isn't it Ollie?' Alice pulled at the door handle as if trying to get out. Ollie came over to help.

'Gosh, yes this is tricky, think it might need some brute force here.' And with that Ollie made a loud banging noise with one of his shoes while disguising the sound of the key turning in the lock. The door miraculously opened.

'Ah Ben, good morning, so lovely to see you darling.' exclaimed Aunty Alice. 'Goodness you're up early!' Alice stated looking at her imaginary watch.

'Not really Aunty Alice it is quarter past nine?!' Ben was most bewildered, his aunt was nearly always up before this time.

'Ah, right, well then, time for breakfast.' Ollie interjected as they all headed off downstairs, Ben leading, followed by Alice and then Ollie who playfully slapped Alice's bottom as she descended.

They all headed for the kitchen and Ollie put the kettle on.

Ben had that puzzled expression on his face, the one Alice knew was going to lead to questions, quite a few more questions.

'So, what was wrong with the door, Aunty Alice, it was okay yesterday?' Ben enquired.

'Ah, well you know these old houses, Ben, doors often get stuck.' Alice felt a tinge of guilt as she realised more explanations and outright lying may be needed before the Spanish Inquisition finished.

Ben was silent for a while obviously mulling this over but then not quite content with the answer continued.

'So, you could get *in* to the bedroom Aunty Alice but *not out* of the bedroom?' Ben was clearly giving this point careful consideration.

Alice knew this would have to be a good one to get her

out of this. 'Yes, well, Ollie needed some…' She had to think quickly what he might need but thankfully Ollie was quick to help her out

'Towels, Ben, I needed some towels.' Ollie poured the coffee not being able to look at either of them in the face, lest it set him off.

'Yes, towels Ben. Ollie needed some towels. So, I went to give him some towels from the cupboard in the landing and on coming back into the bedroom, the door just seemed to shut behind me. Well, you know the rest.' Alice thought this would knock the matter on the head.

'But, Aunty Alice, why didn't Ollie just get himself some towels from the airing cupboard on the landing?'

Alice and Ollie looked at each other for help.

Ollie decided that distraction tactics were best to get off the subject.

'Right well, today, if you remember I am visiting some friends over in Broughton the ones I met on my travels in Mexico and you and Aunty Alice are going to have the day together.

Alice felt her heart sink a bit. She had forgotten about this arrangement and had rather hoped they would have all spent the day together. Couldn't he cancel considering the previous night? However, the more she thought about it and what had happened the previous night she started to feel her cheeks flush again and decided that, actually, it was a good idea for them to have a bit of time apart. She needed to do some thinking.

Ollie was disappointed that he had made prior arrangements for today as he didn't want to leave them all. Besides, what would Alice think of him clearing off like this, after last night?

However, the more he thought about it the more he agreed with himself that a bit of separation time, a bit of mulling over what last night actually was or had meant to Alice, indeed to both of them, was probably a good thing. She had been hurt before and would not want to rush into anything and then there was Alistair.

Ollie looked at her while Ben came to sit on her knee. She looked so lovely this morning and he thought back to how they had made love the previous night. The night had been amazing and he hadn't felt so connected with someone in such a long time. However, knowing her past history with Mark, and now Alistair, this could get complicated. She did seem to be over Mark. Then, of course, there was Alistair. Only the other night she had clearly been dreaming about him. What had exactly happened between them already? He needed time to think and so did she. He would go ahead with his plans.

'Are you sure it is okay to borrow the car today? I can always get Varjak and Julia to pick me up?' Ollie really didn't want her to think he was taking advantage of the car.

'No, no of course, you must take it. No problem. I hope you have a great time.' But inside Alice was wishing he wasn't going. She felt the need to talk to him, to try and make sense of it all though with Ben around there wouldn't be much chance of this until later anyway.

Ollie departed. The day, however, seemed a bit flat without Ollie and Ben grew bored at his aunt's poor attempts to play pool. Her table tennis was better but he got frustrated that he couldn't return the ball very often. As Ollie now had the car, Alice took Ben on the bus into Ulverston town to visit the Laurel and Hardy museum.

Alice enjoyed telling Ben how Laurel and Hardy had been a part of her childhood and how she had watched the old movies on telly with his dad on Sunday afternoons. Ben's dad was a particular fan of the comic duo liking the slapstick humour. Alice explained that although Hardy had been born in the USA, Laurel was a native of Ulverston, hence the museum. She sensed Ben wasn't quite as enthralled but when he got to the museum, he seemed to perk up a bit and enjoyed finding out all about the duo.

For lunch they headed off to get some sandwiches, crisps and cake to enjoy so they could have a picnic in the garden.

Ben insisted on getting out the picnic basket, even though they were just travelling from the kitchen to the garden explaining to his aunt that he wanted to do it *properly.'* Alice made Ben some very weak shandy and they both enjoyed watching the squirrels play in the trees. After lunch, Ben decided he would build a den under the oak tree and Alice got out some of the old rugs from her car as well as some of the ones she found in the understairs cupboard. Ben spent hours building and playing in it and Alice collected twigs around the garden to make a pretend fire.

Alice thought back to the previous night. It had been so special, magical even. However, thinking about it, Ollie had been pretty keen to get away today. Of course, he had been. Being a man, of course, he probably wouldn't be even sparing her a thought today, enjoying the company of his friends. He hadn't even thought of inviting her and Ben. But, well, maybe this would have been tricky. He seemed to have made love to her with such passion but it had probably all been in the heat of the moment and that was that. After all, this was a man who probably had a girl in every port. Anyway, they weren't right for each other. He seemed a man who just lived from day to day, not getting bogged down with the realities of life. No, that would never suit Alice. He clearly had felt it was all a mistake otherwise he would have stayed today. There was no point dwelling on it. Yes, it was just a fling and that was that. Besides, Alistair was awaiting her return and there was a man who was far more suited to her. She had far more in common with Alistair than Ollie. Her and Ollie, well it just wouldn't work, would it?

Ben disturbed her from her thoughts and asked her if he could have some of his mum's biscuits to put in the den. Alice made a flask of hot chocolate and they both sat there enjoying the drink and snacks.

Ben didn't go to bed until quite late that evening hoping to see Ollie and tell him all about his day. However, it became clear at ten o'clock that he couldn't escape bed any longer. They both got changed into their pj's and they both curled up under the duvet while Alice read to him. She kept straining to hear if the car was coming into the driveway but, every time she thought it was him, it turned out to be just a car passing by. After about thirty minutes of reading, Alice turned the light off and they both chatted for a while until both nodded off to sleep.

When she awoke it was about eleven o'clock but there was still no sign of Ollie. He clearly wanted to stay away as long as he could so as to avoid her. Oh well, she thought, just as well. She really didn't want any awkward conversations of them both having to explain to each other what a mistake the previous night had been. She snuggled up with Ben and went to sleep.

26

Barking up the wrong tree

Ollie was worried. Not only had he gone out for the day but now also the whole evening. He really hadn't expected Varjak and Julia to have gone to so much trouble to entertain him. Not only had they made lunch but they insisted on taking him out for dinner too. He had tried to make his excuses but to no avail. They were adamant as arrangements had been made. Any other time this would have been great but not today of all days. Ollie had not managed to get home until midnight, having lost his way coming into Ulverston; getting caught up in the one-way system meant it had taken him longer to get back to the cottage than he had originally envisaged. He had hoped that Alice might have stayed up to see him but everything was quiet in the cottage on his return.

Ollie was restless that night, hoping he might hear Alice get up to go to the toilet or go downstairs for a glass of water. No such luck. All was still and silent. He felt bad for being away the whole day *and* evening. It hadn't been great timing.

He decided to get up early that day and make a special breakfast. He pulled out all the stops, buying croissants and pastries from the local baker, bacon from the deli and some more fresh coffee, the one Alice liked. After breakfast, he would simply explain how he had got held up longer than he had anticipated and once he had explained this it would be fine. And he had gone to all this to get breakfast, this would definitely show how sincere he was in his efforts to make amends. He hurried about the kitchen. He felt excited at the thought of seeing Alice again that morning and how pleased they would both be at the sight of this extra special breakfast. As he prepared the feast, he hoped the smells would waft upstairs and wake them both. However, in his rush to get the butter from the fridge he accidentally knocked a jar of jam on the floor and the glass seemed to go everywhere. Having thought he had cleared it all up, he managed to tread on a tiny shaft of glass which lodged itself firmly into his toe.

Alice and Ben stirred to the noise of Ollie swearing loudly in the kitchen. Alice was angry. Did the man have to keep swearing and, if he did, did he have to swear so loudly? Ben was very adept at learning new words, particularly the ones he shouldn't. Alice got up to investigate, closely followed by Ben. Ben, being delighted to see Ollie, and the amazing spread of food, ran to give him a hug. Alice, however, kept her distance. Not only did he go to such lengths to obviously avoid her yesterday but now he was, well now he was... Well she wasn't sure what to think? She felt hurt and angry and decided to give Ollie the frostiest look she could muster, chastising him for making such a racket and bleeding over the kitchen floor.

'I hope you have managed to clear up all the glass because you haven't done a great job of cleaning up all the blood every-where! I really don't want Ben treading on any.' Why could men never properly clean up after themselves she thought?

Ollie was somewhat put out by this. Could she not see his foot had been injured? Could she not see the tremendous amount of effort he had gone to get her breakfast? What was wrong with the woman?

'Oh wow, pastries, look Aunty Alice.' Ben rushed to the table and sat down. 'Chocolate croissants, umm, they smell amazing'. Ben's eyes were now as large as saucers.

Alice went to sit down next to Ben, requesting that he stopped putting the fourth croissant on his plate and eat one at a time. Ben looked up at his aunt. It was clear to him she had woken up in one of her moods.

Ollie put a plaster over the bleeding toe, hoping Alice might have helped but she sat firmly in her seat. She purveyed the table. Yes, she surmised, this was some sort of an olive branch to ensure that there were no hard feelings. After all it was clear that he wanted to spend as much time away from her as possible. It had just been a one-night fling as far as he was concerned and he was obviously feeling bad about the whole affair. Well that was fine with her.

Despite Ollie's many attempts to talk to her over breakfast, she seemed very indifferent to anything he said and Ollie thought her very cold in her response.

Right he thought, she clearly regrets the other night. She obviously isn't in the right place for a relationship yet and well this is her telling me to keep my distance. Fine, no problem.

Ben was oblivious. He was just enjoying his third croissant. Alice feeling churned up, didn't feel like eating and left to get herself dressed and sorted.

Ollie, not feeling hungry either, decided to challenge Ben to a game of pool and all Alice could then hear was laughter coming from the Game's Room. This made her even more grumpy. Right well two can play at that game she thought.

She would be perfectly friendly and civil; she would show him how he really didn't bother her. After all, Alistair was far more suited and she almost felt ashamed she had allowed herself to have been carried away by the moment. She would continue in her efforts to get to know Alistair and for now the best thing was to stay friends with Ollie, after all they had to be in the cottage together for another two days. There was Ben to think about. This was the reason why they were here.

Ollie, meanwhile, was also distracted and Ben could see his mind clearly wasn't on the game because he was winning the Championship far too easily. Ollie was deep in thought. He decided he would display his normal, calm exterior. He had obviously been just a distraction to the woman and it was clear her affections lay elsewhere. He had been foolish to think he might have given this a go. His notions of settling down were not very realistic anyway. He liked his freedom and his travels. Anyway, she clearly wasn't ready for a relationship. This he accepted. It was better for all concerned that they just stay friends after all they were going to be together for another few days yet and it wouldn't be right to spoil the holiday for Ben.

So, the next few days, came and went. Both were civil to each other and Ben continued to enjoy making his timetables and spending time with them both. Surely, Ben thought, it wouldn't be long before Ollie would be going out with Aunty Alice?

27

Much Ado About Something

The holiday now over, they all duly returned home. Sue was recovering well from her operation but Robert reminded Ben that Mum had to have complete rest and that he would have to be patient with Mum over the next few weeks. Robert was glad to see Alice as it gave them both a chance to catch up on Sue and all the news. He had a bit of a moan about Betty who had tidied and cleaned the house twice a day with Robert declaring it was like being at the office with Miss Havisham - never being able to find a bloody thing.

'Oh, she means well, Robert. I am looking forward to seeing my flat – gosh if it is half as clean as this, I will be happy!' Alice looked around the living room, it was spotless. All of Robert's novels had been neatly placed in the previously empty bookcase that Robert had bought to store his many books but had never got round to actually using. Everywhere was thoroughly dusted and hoovered and the kitchen floor had never sparkled so much. Alice couldn't understand Robert's irritation with Betty or as she liked to call her 'Aunt' Betty.

With Sue and Alice having been firm friends since primary school they had virtually lived at each other's houses during the holidays. Alice's mum and Betty had also got on very well, establishing a firm friendship. As time had progressed, Alice had grown very fond of her and somehow, though she couldn't remember when Betty became Aunt Betty and it had stuck.

Robert acquiesced. 'Yes, yes I know. I sound ungrateful. I just want to get things back to normal, back to my own family, our own trio. Anyway, how was your week away? Ben clearly enjoyed it and it sounds as if you packed a lot in.'

Alice thought back to the fateful night, 'Umm well yes, you could say that.' She watched Ben kicking the ball around in the garden shouting with glee at every goal he scored. Alice and Robert chatted some more, she briefly went up to see Sue but she was fast asleep. She decided to set off home and giving her brother a big hug, she departed.

On returning to the flat, she was delighted to find it sparkling too.

'Aunt Betty this is amazing, thank you so much.' Alice threw her arms around her and Alice told her all the news of the holiday, well not all of it but most of it.

However, Betty seemed distracted and all of a sudden started to cry.

'Oh Betty, what's wrong?' Alice sat her down on the sofa.

'Oh, it's just me being silly, I have just found the last days so difficult. I just kept thinking of the worst all the time. Thinking there were going to be serious complications after the surgery.'

Alice headed for the kitchen to make Betty a cup of tea. Betty always said things were better after a cuppa and she thought that probably she could now do with some looking after. Over their cuppas Alice had an idea.

'Look Aunt Betty, why don't you stay for a few more days? I bet we could both do with the company, don't you? Let me look after you, it's the least I can do for all you have done for

Sue and Robert and it's always a bit flat when you go home on your own. Besides, I would appreciate the company. What do you say?'

Betty cheered up, 'Oh that would be lovely dear. To tell you the truth I have been dreading going back to my house but I really don't want to get in the way, are you sure?'

'No, don't be silly and yes, of course you must stay.' Alice and Betty went back to Betty's car to get her bags out as Betty, being so efficient, had already packed her bags away ready to depart. They both ventured downstairs and on the way down Alistair and Isabella appeared. Alistair's eyes lit up on seeing Alice and Alice's clear joy at seeing him was also evident. They all briefly shook hands and kissed on the cheeks. Except when Alistair went to kiss Alice, she felt him hold on to her hand a bit longer and he looked directly in her eyes, fixing upon them.

Alice, once again, felt her legs turning a bit like jelly and introduced Betty to them both and for a few minutes they all chatted about their time away. Betty noticed how Alice was clearly very taken with Alistair and the feeling seemed to be mutual. After Betty had explained all about her daughter's operation and how Alice had kindly invited her to stay a few more days, they say their goodbyes and Alice and Betty headed for the car.

'Well, what a nice young man that Alistair is, very handsome too.' Betty raised her eyebrows and she could see Alice starting to blush.

'Yes, yes, he is a very nice guy, Betty but I haven't known him long, we are just acquaintances really through Isabella.'

'He seems very taken with you dear.' Betty shot Alice a knowing smile and Alice felt herself blushing again. She was delighted that someone else had noted Alistair's interest in her and it wasn't just a figment of her imagination.

Betty was glad that they maybe some sort of development on the love front. What an improvement she thought this man was over Mark. A definite improvement. Alistair seemed to have a sincere charm about him unlike that loathsome Mark, all charm and no depth. It hadn't surprised her in the least when Mark had gone off with a younger girl that would definitely have boosted his already, over-blown ego.

Betty was about to enquire some more when Mr Nosey Neighbour appeared.

'Lovely day ladies, lovely. I hope you are keeping well? And this is ….' Mr Hughes was now flashing a large smile at Betty.

'Oh yes, this is Betty, Betty this is…' but before Alice was given a chance to introduce Mr Hughes, he had already waded in.

'Mr Hughes, Mr Dylan Hughes, pleased to meet you Betty.' Mr Hughes held out his hand and shook Betty's hand.

Alice was about to walk on but Mr Hughes, however, was clearly not finished yet. 'Now ladies, I don't like to be a kill joy and all that, but I did just want to clarify a few car parking rules. Now Betty, I see you have parked in the guest car parking space. That is your vehicle is it not, the white one parked in the guest bay?' Mr Hughes was starting to sound like some detective.

Betty and Alice nodded to the affirmative. 'Ah, well yes ladies, as I said, I really don't like to be a kill joy or one of those difficult neighbours, no that would never do *but* I would like to remind you that the guest parking space is just for short visits only.'

'Yes.' Betty responded 'I am just a visitor and will only be staying for a short while Mr Hughes.'

Mr Hughes felt the lady clearly hadn't fully understood and didn't let this deter him, 'Ah but Betty I think you will find you have been parked there for nearly a week now. Is that not correct?'

Betty seemed a bit confused as to why the man was stating the obvious. 'Yes, that is correct but I forgot to check with Alice what number her car parking space was so thought it best to park in the guest space. I am sure you would agree that this would be preferable to parking in the wrong space, don't you agree Mr Hughes?' Betty was not a woman to be trifled with.

'Ah, well the problem is you see, Betty, according to regulation number 6 under section A, paragraph number 2 under chapter 3 of Howarth's Court Rules and Regulations, this simply isn't the procedure, so Betty I think it would be a good time to move it, your vehicle that is!' said Mr Hughes feeling it was his duty to ensure the lady understood that he had the true weight of the law behind him.

Alice and Betty were both somewhat speechless. Mr Hughes thinking he hadn't made clear the gravity of the situation to the two ladies thought it best to clarify the point a bit further 'Also ladies it is mentioned under regulation number 2, section A, paragraph 2a under chapter 3 of the same regulations that the guest parking space may only be used for the duration of no more than 24 hours.' Yes, Mr Hughes thought to himself this was now very clear.

Betty, eyed the man up and down, giving this some thought, 'Well Mr Hughes, I tell you what, I can understand how Rules and Regulations would be very important to a man, well to a man like yourself (Mr Hughes smiled thinking this was a compliment) but I think it is only right and proper that you take Howarth Court's Rules and Regulations and stick them up your bottom, good day to you Sir.' Betty took Alice firmly by the arm and proceeded to walk straight for the car.

Alice was still speechless and somewhat in awe of Betty who simply added in as loud a voice as she could muster 'That is the only way of dealing with men like that dear.'

Mr Hughes was now feeling very put out indeed. There was nothing for it he decided but to take the matter up at the next Howarth Court Committee meeting for which he was Chair. Well, as he often lamented, not only Chair, in fact he was Treasurer and Secretary too. If only he could muster up more members, he thought, other than himself and Mrs Goddard from No 32, who, let's face it, was now 98 and very deaf and virtually blind.

The next week came and went, Ben was glad that Nanna Betty had decided to stay at Aunty Alice's a bit longer, as he particularly enjoyed her most amazing Bakewell tart. His mum was now able to get up for a brief while and Robert was clearly happy watching the occasional TV programme with the three of them back together again, just like it had always been. Dad sitting on one side of Ben and Mum on the other.

Life was getting back to normal. In fact, Robert was in such good spirits he decided it was time for another small dinner party. It would be the least he could do to thank Betty before she departed home and thank Ollie for Ben's holiday at the cottage. It would also give Malcolm the chance of spending a bit of time with Alice. After all, he had spent a great deal of time enquiring how Alice's holiday with Ollie and Ben had gone.

Everyone knew he clearly had a thing for Alice and, besides, Robert could think of no better match for his sister. Malcolm was an honest, caring and all round decent human being. Alice deserved some happiness. Robert also decided to invite Miss Havisham as it was shortly going to be her birthday.

Betty offered to make the pudding, a Bakewell tart, and Alice brought a bottle of Shed No 1, a gin she had acquired while in Ulverston for them all to sample. Malcolm brought the wine and Miss Havisham was going to bring the starter but, unfortunately, she had left it on the No. 34 bus.

Alice was a little uncomfortable with Ollie's presence but both were very civil and managed some polite conversation. Betty, however was clearly enjoying Ollie's company as she enjoyed hearing about his time in Paris, where Betty and her late husband had enjoyed many a break. Ben had managed to persuade his mum and dad to let him stay up for just the first part of the evening provided he promised to go straight to bed at nine o'clock. Malcolm was delighted to be sat next to Alice, giving her is undivided attention and complimenting her on how lovely she looked in her new dress.

All were in good spirits as Sue was now clearly on the mend and all were enjoying Robert's Paella. Everyone had a tale to tell and were particularly amused at Miss Havisham's story of how she had ordered a curtain pole but, whilst she was out, the delivery man, who was obviously keen not to return, had attempted to post it through the letter box, pinning her poor poodle, Rufus, to the wall where he had been truly and well stuck until she had got home that evening.

Ben at this point wanted to add his own story, 'Aunty Alice got stuck in the bedroom with Ollie, didn't you Aunty Alice?'

Ben continued to eat his dinner unaware that everyone now had ceased eating and Malcolm who had just swallowed a glass of wine had now sprayed it all over the table. Alice's cheeks started to feel warm again. Ollie looked at Alice. Alice looked at Ollie. Robert looked at Sue, Sue looked at Robert. Betty looked at Miss Havisham and Miss Havisham, completely oblivious didn't look at anyone. Malcolm was now trying to mop up the unholy mess of red wine on the white tablecloth.

Not too sure where the conversation might lead to, Sue decided it was time for Ben's bedtime.

'Right Ben, well I think it is time for bed now, don't you?' Sue took Ben firmly by the hand indicating that Robert should follow. Eventually after much obvious winking and gesturing, Robert got up to assist.

'Say goodnight now Ben,' which Ben duly did a little disappointed that his attempts to stay up gone nine o'clock had not worked.

Miss Havisham thought it all too silent around the table and thought she would rescue the situation with a joke that Ben had told her earlier in the evening. Meanwhile Sue and Robert got Ben ready for bed.

When finally upstairs, Sue was keen to find out a little more.

'So then, Ben, how long do you think Ollie and Alice were stuck for in this bedroom?'

'I don't know mum; it was when I woke up and I was looking for them everywhere and then I discovered Aunty Alice was in Ollie's bedroom. Aunty Alice had gone in to give Ollie a towel and the door got stuck behind her. The thing is mum, the airing cupboard with the towels was just outside Ollie's bedroom so he could have just got one himself, couldn't have he?'

'Umm.' considered Robert. 'Well maybe Ollie didn't know that the towels were just next to his bedroom Ben. You know how helpful your Aunty Alice is.' Robert stared at Sue, who stared right back.

'Well, yes that must be it! Of course.' Sue was keen to reaffirm her husband's account. 'It sounds as if you all had a great holiday Ben and I am sure Ollie and Aunty Alice get on well, then?'

'Oh yes, they are practically girlfriend and boyfriend.'

'Really? What makes you say that Ben?' Robert enquired trying to sound disinterested but clearly wanting to know more.

'One evening, when I had gone to bed, I heard them both singing, dancing and giggling and when I got out of bed to find out what all the noise was about, I saw them both from the top of the stairs and Ollie was dancing with Aunty Alice around the lounge floor. Ollie fell over and Aunty Alice was on top.'

'Oh my goodness!' Sue exclaimed worried about what Ben might have witnessed at such a tender age.

'Don't worry Mum, no one got hurt, they were only getting really silly and giggly. I went back to bed because I thought it best to leave them to it, I was too tired to be bothered to go down and tell them to be quiet.'

Robert and Sue looked at each other feeling somewhat relieved that Ben had not witnessed anything he shouldn't and on leaving the bedroom Robert seemed very bemused by it all.

'Well I never!' I didn't think those two were that bothered about each other. I mean Alice is so rude about the man and to his face too! Let's face it she has been completely indifferent to the man this evening!'

Sue gave an exasperating sigh, 'Oh Robert, you men can be

so blind! The fact Alice spends so much time acting disinterested and going to such lengths to dislike him clearly means that of course she likes him.'

'Right?' said a puzzled Robert, 'Goodness, you women are so bloody complicated!'

With that Sue playfully punched him in the arm and then took his hand to go back downstairs.

Miss Havisham was still trying to remember the end of one of the jokes she had been trying to entertain them all with.

'No, no I remember now it's not *you're under a shirt* no, no hang on a tick, no its *you're under a vest!*' Miss Havisham gave out a loud laugh accompanied by silence by the rest of the guests who didn't seem to be on the same wavelength at all after hearing at least six attempts at the punch line.

'Oh great, I like a good joke what was the first line again?' enquired Robert as they returned to the table. Miss Havisham repeated it once again, hoping these two might get it.

'What did the policeman say to his belly button?'

'Ah, good one.' smiled Robert, 'Yes I get it, one of Ben's favourites.'

Alice had now lost the will to live and downed another glass of wine, closely followed by Ollie and then Malcolm.

Sue turned to Ollie, 'So, Ollie I hear your time at Mario's will soon be over. What are your plans now?'

Alice looked at Ollie. Her heart seemed to sink a bit. Of course, he was moving on she thought to herself. That's what he always did. That is why it would never have worked.

Malcolm was relieved to hear the news. Maybe they had just got temporarily stuck in the bedroom, these old cottages can be so damp. Stranger things have happened. He thought Ollie was a decent chap but not at all suited to Alice.

Ollie was hesitant in his answer. 'Well, not sure really, I had been thinking of maybe staying a bit longer but what I had planned hasn't turned out as expected so, now I am not sure.' Ollie looked straight at Alice. Her eyes dropped from him to the glass of wine. Why did he make her feel like this? Why did she feel so bothered and churned up about him going? It was just a fling. Alistair was the one for her, she knew it.

Ollie continued, 'I have had an offer to go to New York for a few months, so thought I might go there. A friend of mine owns an art gallery and is keen to expand the business and open a second one. He has asked me to help set it up and run it for a while.'

'Well, glad to hear it,' said Malcolm. 'Splendid opportunity, wish you all the best with that.' A few thousand miles would be a good distance he thought.

Sue, however, was genuinely put out by the news.

'Oh Ollie! We have so enjoyed getting to know you. I can't believe all these years have gone by and we haven't had to the opportunity of meeting you properly until now. You could always stay you know Ollie; Mario is getting too old to run the café and he is going to need help managing it.'

Malcolm not pleased that Sue was trying to persuade Ollie to stay protested. 'No, no, gosh plenty of life left in the old dog yet. Mario is as fit as a fiddle.' stated Malcolm. 'You make the most of the opportunity Ollie, I would if I were you.'

Ollie looked at Alice. 'So, what do you think Alice, do you think I should make the most of New York or help Mario?'

How dare he, she thought, he obviously wants his ego flattered and for me to tell him to stay. Well not from me. 'It really doesn't bother me whether you stay or go Ollie, you have to do what suits *you* best,' then pausing slightly added, 'like *you* normally do.'

Silence again around the table. Alice continued

'After all, we all know how you like life to be one big adventure. So much easier not having to commit to anything, just move on when it pleases you.'

Still an awkward silence.

Ollie nodded slowly and gave a strange smile but this time Alice thought in not his usual self-satisfied smuggish sort of way. He almost seemed if he was slightly disappointed at her response. It was as if he had hoped for something else. With this he raised his glass at her and drank some more. He fixed her completely within his glare.

'I see, Alice, and of course this comes from a woman who has no idea or inkling of what new adventures can bring, you would rather just stay in that cocoon you have built for yourself. Much safer there, after all.'

Ollie raised his glass again at her, taking another sip of wine but this time flashed his usual self-satisfied grin.

At this point, Sue and Robert seeing red in Alice's eyes quickly got up from the table, closely followed by Betty and Malcolm who all became very busy at clearing every item from the table and quickly disappeared into the kitchen. Miss Havisham, however, who hadn't picked up on the vibes, was a little puzzled at the sudden departure of them all. She stayed firmly put.

'Well,' said Miss Havisham 'there are merits in travelling and merits in not travelling, I can see that both have their advantages. My Uncle Dickie liked to travel but Aunty Melissa preferred to stay at home looking after her guinea-pigs'.

Her comments though fell on deaf ears.

Alice wasn't letting him get away with that, 'Well the thing is Ollie, you call it a cocoon I call it a warm wrap. A warm wrap of friendship and family, something you just wouldn't understand. I *willingly* have responsibilities, the responsibility that family and good friendship often demands.' Put that in your pipe and smoke it, Alice thought.

Miss Havisham joined in, 'Ah yes, friends, we can't live with them, we can't live without them… Or is that family? Come to think of poodles would fit nicely into that saying too.'

Ollie again fixed Alice with his eyes, those very menacing eyes. 'Ah, so you are talking about loyalty to the friends who couldn't even tell you the truth when you most needed it, could they?' But as soon as Ollie said this, he had regretted it. This was not a good moment to allude to the fact that Alice had been let down by most of the people around her. No one had told her the truth about Mark.

Alice was now seething.

This was a good time thought all of those listening in through the open kitchen door to return, something was needed to break up the atmosphere and no one was confident Miss Havisham was up to the job.

'Well, Ollie, that red you bought was jolly good,' said Robert as he walked in whilst opening it with a corkscrew. 'Really good bottle, very generous of you.' Robert poured everyone another glass.

Alice put her hand over hers as Robert went to pour. 'The thing is Ollie, we all have friends who can let us down but sometimes it is done for the very best of reasons, because they genuinely feel they are doing the best for you, gunning for you at every port but, sadly, there are those friendships that can so quickly form with such seemingly genuine affection and trust but are cast aside by the other at a mere whim.'

Miss Havisham thought it best to intercede with some of her words of wisdom, 'Yes friends are a bit like borrowing books you know from a library, enjoyable to spend time but you can always pop them back on the shelf to enjoy for another day.'

No one knew quite what to say to that but Ollie decided it was best to go.

He duly thanked all around the table and Alice watched him head off into the night. She couldn't explain how she felt. Why did he always seem to wrench up such different emotions in her? She felt so frustrated with the man.

All sat quietly in the living room. Alice realised she had probably put a bit of a spoiler on the evening thought it best to make amends quickly.

'Anyone for a game of Charades?' Alice asked hopefully.

'I think we have had quite a bit of charades already this evening, don't you?' Sue frowned at Alice

'Look, I just find the man so annoying, he just maddens me!'

Silence once again.

'Well, he is just one of those men who can be so… well so… I don't know he just can. I mean he keeps turning up and then has these crazy ideas and then that self-satisfied smug grin of his. He clearly thinks he is oh so clever and witty and well he isn't, is he?'

No one knew what to say to that apart from Miss Havisham 'I thought he was a very nice man you know, dear. Very good looking with those dark eyes of his.'

'Well' protested Malcolm, I wouldn't go that far.'

'Yes, but you're not a woman, dear are you.' said Betty

Alice said, 'Look, I am sorry but he just annoys me. Not only is he satisfied with riling me during the day, he also now riles me in my dreams.' Alice suddenly stopped realising what she had just said. 'Well, when I say dreams, I meant nightmares of course, really bad nightmares.'

'I see.' said Betty

'Right.' said Robert

'OK?' said Sue

'How awful to have him in your nightmares!' said Malcolm.

'Personally, I like a good nightmare, it can shake away the old cobwebs you know,' advised Miss Havisham.

Alice, realising she was just digging a big hole, suggested to Betty that it was a good time to go home and everyone agreed. Sue came to give her friend a big hug as she approached the door to leave,

'I think you and I need a bit of a chat, tomorrow don't you?'

Alice gave a resigning nod and they all left.

Having dropped Malcolm and Miss Havisham home, Betty thought it time to have a bit of a heart to heart with Alice too. The time to do it was now, whilst still in the car with no exit routes.

'Well, I think perhaps your holiday at the cottage might have turned out to be more than just a holiday?' Betty kept her eyes firmly stuck on the road ahead.

'Well, yes, I think things did briefly get out of hand, just in the moment of it all, that's all.' Alice started to look through her handbag to look for her keys.

'Um, well to what extent does 'get out of hand' exactly mean, dear?'

'Well, we… we had a bit of a one-night stand that's all. Nothing in it. I mean the next day he went off to see his friends and couldn't be bothered to stick around. He is the sort of man, Betty, that likes to keep things simple. Mario calls him the travelling nomad for good reason.' Alice looked out of the window at the drops of rain now making their way down the glass.

'It strikes me Alice that he is quite taken with you. When you were deep in conversation with Malcolm or Sue and Robert, he couldn't keep his eyes off you.'

'Nonsense!' Alice waved her hand at Betty as if to dismiss the idea but then thought the better of it, 'Really, was he really staring at me so much?'

'Couldn't keep his eyes off you dear and that wasn't the only one either!'

'What Malcolm?'

'Well I wasn't talking about Miss Havisham dear!'

'Oh goodness, Malcolm is such a sweety, he really is but we go back years and I just feel he is more like a brother, Betty.'

'And then of course there is the lovely, charming Alistair, too.' Betty turned her head briefly from the road ahead and raised her eyebrows.

Alice laughed. 'Now that is a man, I am happy to talk about, there is a man I wouldn't mind having a liaison with!'

'Indeed! You know dear, men are like buses. None on the horizon and then three turn up all at once! Lucky you! Well it strikes me as if you have your heart set on Alistair?'

'Oh Betty. I haven't even been out on a date yet; chance would be a fine thing.'

Alice searched for her lipstick and then proceeded to touch

up her lips. Talking of Alistair had reminded her that she needed to look her best in case of another chance encounter.

When they got back to the flats, Alice was delighted to see Alistair's car now parked in the guest parking space. Let's hope, she thought, that it would be for more than the 24-hour allowance!

Unfortunately, no chance encounter occurred and Alice and Betty decided to watch one of Betty's favourite movies, Titanic, sharing a box of hankies and a large bowl of popcorn.

28

Alistair, I'm flying!

Alice had gone to bed thinking that Titanic may not have been a good idea after an already tumultuous night of mixed feelings. Betty had gone through two boxes of tissues and now Alice had to suffice with the loo roll by her pillow. She must insist next time on a happy-go-feel movie. She didn't mind how much misery there is in the middle of a film as long as the end turns out not just fine but has a feel-good factor. A film that leaves you feeling life is worth living and yes, the boy gets the girl or you are left with the definite impression the boy *will* get the girl. In Titanic, she felt, Jack dies and Rose is left with her memories. Umm as great as the film is, the ending just didn't do it for her. Why couldn't the rescue boat get both of them? He could have got poorly and nearly died but then, through Rosie's tender care, miraculously recovered. They could have got married and had many children. Yes, that would have been a better ending. Whilst Alice mulled this over, eventually she fell to sleep.

Alice dreamt she was in her own car park. Mr Hughes appeared, waving his arms about and complaining about how The Titanic was now in the Guest Parking Space.

'People have no respect these days, I mean look at the thing! I

certainly hope it won't be here longer than twenty-four hours you know or I am going to have to call the police to deal with it.' Mr Hughes was clearly not a happy man.

Alice was about to talk to him but suddenly she found herself on board the ship. She ran around all the decks but she didn't really know why or what she was looking for? Then she found herself on the top deck. She felt the wind blowing through her hair and her dress was clinging tightly to her body. There, in front of her, was Alistair. He was standing at the bow, looking down at the waves below. She went up to him and, as she called his name, he turned around and smiled. He stood there so tall and manly, broad shoulders, with a thick set of blonde, wavy hair. His muscles could clearly be seen through his flimsy shirt. Alistair held out his arm and pulled her towards him, lifting her onto the bow railings. Alice looked down and saw dolphins dancing in the water or, hang on, were they sharks? She couldn't quite tell. In the distance, there was a brilliant sunset of pinks, oranges and purples. The wind continued to blow through her long hair which flowed around her shoulders. Alistair held on to her, his hands firmly around her waist. Alice outstretched her own arms 'I'm flying, Alistair, I'm flying!'

They both laughed and Alice turned her head around to face Alistair and he kissed her, long and hard.

'Excuse me, excuse me,' an angry voice called from behind.

'How long do you intend to park your ship here for. I mean, look at the size of it!' Mr Hughes seemed most put out. 'I have to warn you that there are strict regulations to follow at Howarth Court you know, you can't just park your ship here.'

With that Alistair released Alice and punched Mr Hughes straight on the nose and then kneed him. He turned around to continue to kiss Alice but when she opened her eyes, Alistair had gone. It was Ollie! Ollie was now kissing her. Alice pulled away.

'How dare you!' she went to slap Ollie around the face but his hand came up to stop her. 'Where is he? What have you done with Alistair?'

'Alistair, who is Alistair?' Ollie looked most put out.

She started to run around the deck calling for Alistair. Then, out of the corner of her eye, she saw him. Alistair was now sitting down on a deck chair, chatting away to Malcolm who seemed to be advising him on taxation and how he was paying far too much tax.

'Alistair, there you are, thank God you are ok!' Alice went to put her arms around him but he held his hand up.

'Not now darling, please, can't you see I am right in the middle of my tax return?'

Alice then found herself back in the car park. It was pitch black and all she could hear was a strange sound coming from the bushes. She went to investigate and there sitting right in the middle was Rufus, Miss Havisham's poodle. His collar was stuck on the end of a curtain pole.

29

More than just an accountant

Malcolm had just finished seeing Mr Papadopoulos about his company's annual return and was going to ask Miss Havisham to file some of the key documents but thought the better of it and instead asked her to get Mr Papadopoulos's coat and umbrella.

Malcolm sat down at his desk pondering over the previous night. Robert had assured him that when she had gone away with Ollie it was just an arrangement that would help Sue and Robert. There was nothing in it. They were just good friends, well not even that. After the events of the previous evening, Malcolm who, at first, was sure nothing was going on, now had the distinct impression something was or, indeed, had definitely gone on. That business of being locked in a bedroom together rang alarm bells.

He got up from his office chair and wondered over to the window watching his client getting into his car. He pondered some more. He really could be so much more than just an accountant if only he could get her to see it. Maybe she needed to see him in a different light. He thought back to the fishing trip. Maybe that hadn't been the best first date. After all, he probably hadn't given Alice the right start to how exciting fishing could be. She had been more preoccupied with Ben.

Perhaps Alice did see him as being like a big brother to her but somehow, he had to change this. It was true she had only ever really known Malcolm as her big brother's close friend and colleague. However, there was so much more to him than that. He really could do more than just her tax return.

Malcolm thought it was time to go on the offensive. Robert had often commented on what a great romantic Alice was at heart so he thought he could easily buy the odd bouquet of flowers and box of chocolates.

He thought it best to strike while the iron was hot. He would pop round to see her this evening with flowers and chocolates in hand. He would offer to take her out to dinner or she may suggest eating in. He didn't mind. He would then tell her how he felt and ask her to at least give it a go. After all, he was single and so was she. If they spent time getting to know each other than he was sure love would eventually blossom. He wouldn't even mind watching one of those Richard Curtis movies she liked so much though he would put his foot down about *Love Actually*. It was ridiculous making Hugh Grant Prime Minister, that was just going too far. Although he had to admit he had made a splendid Jeremy Thorpe.

Miss Havisham entered the office. 'I have Mr Ratarse on the line Malcolm are you free?' Malcolm had to think for a moment. He couldn't remember a client called *Ratarse*? Anyway, it could be potentially a new client so he asked her to put him through.

'Hello, Mr Ratarse, Malcolm Foulds here, how can I help?'

However, this was clearly not his name.

'Ah, so sorry Mr Stratarsé the line is very bad, I think my secretary misheard you. I do apologise.' Malcolm realised he should have thought better than to rely on Miss Havisham for a correct client name. After all, she frequently got them wrong.

Miss Havisham shut the door and found Robert was busy trying to find a client's folder.

'The problem is Robert that people do mumble these days. They need to speak up and pronounce their letters with clear diction.'

'Yes, well either that Miss Havisham or perhaps, well I was just wondering if you might benefit from a hearing aid?'

'Nonsense, Robert, my hearing is as sharp as a meerkat's. I could hear a brick fall.'

Robert thought about this 'Don't you mean a pin?'

'Don't be silly Robert, no one can hear a pin fall!' Miss Havisham thought the idea most ridiculous.

'Well, yes I suppose so, I just think that perhaps...' But Robert never got to finish. Malcolm appeared

'Miss Havisham, I was just wondering if perhaps it would be a good idea if you got your hearing tested? It's just that...'

The phone rang again. Both Malcolm and Robert rushed to answer it but Miss Havisham was far too quick off the mark.

'Hello, Mr Stropodopolous, yes, yes .... ah yes so you did. Yes, I have your umbrella safely here. I will ask Robert to drop it off on his way home tonight. Thank you. Good bye.'

Robert and Malcolm decided to tackle the matter of her hearing another day.

Malcolm left the office promptly at five. He popped into Thrift and Thrive's budget store and picked up the last bouquet of roses. They were starting to wilt a bit but he decided they would soon pick up with some of that rose plant food that was stuck to the stems. He picked up the largest box of chocolates he could find. He thought they did look a bit pricey but court-ship was never cheap. Besides, if it didn't work out, he could always keep the receipts and put them down as a 'Business Gift'. After all, HMRC will allow a business gift worth up to £50 to any one person in any one tax year and Alice was, after all, a client of his.

Meanwhile, Alice had attempted, once again, to clear out some of her old clothes, pondering on why she had ever worn dresses and blouses that made her look as a big as a tent or clothes that seemed to have shrunk in the wash. She laid the items out on the bed and remembered that programme she had seen the other morning *'Spring-clean with Moira the Mindfulness Guru.'*

Alice recalled that you needed to lay each item of clothing out on the bed and stroke it gently several times listening to Moira's Meditative Music. As you touched each item of cloth-ing, if you get feelings of joy and happiness, keep the item. However, if you didn't feel any warm fuzzy feelings, ditch it. Alice diligently stroked each item but wasn't getting any vibes from any of her clothes. Surely, she couldn't throw them all away?

Whilst putting her clothes back into the wardrobe, the door-bell rang.

Alistair, it might be Alistair! She rushed over to the mirror, plumped up her cheeks, put some lipstick on and brushed her hair. Going to the front door she kicked off her old slippers and hastily put on her heels. She then slowed down, breathed in and opened the door. Her excitement and anticipation of seeing Alistair was short lived. No Alistair just Malcolm.

'Oh Malcolm, how... well how nice to see you?' She tried

to muster up as much excitement in her voice as she could but deep down felt a pang of disappointment.

Malcolm handed Alice the wilting flowers and chocolates.

'Gosh Malcolm, how very, yes, well, very thoughtful of you.' Alice looked at the fading flowers and the enormous box of Thrift and Thrive's Continental Delights. All those calm feelings from Moira the Mindfulness Guru had disappeared. Malcolm had never bought her flowers or chocolates before? She just got the one birthday and Christmas gift and that was it.

'Yes, well I think you deserve a treat, every now and again.' Malcolm went to give Alice a kiss on the lips but Alice hastily turned her cheek. 'I thought we could spend a bit of time together this evening. I…'

Alice could now only feel vibes of panic.

'The thing is Malcolm, Betty left this morning and I was going to have a long soak in the bath and watch a movie tonight and well…'

'Splendid,' said Malcolm smiling from ear to ear. Excellent idea he thought to himself. A perfect night in. 'I tell you what, while you have a nice long soak in the bath, I can rustle us up something nice to eat.' Malcolm looked at Alice who didn't seem too keen. Right he thought to himself he would have to try a different tack on this one. 'Well, a takeaway. Indian? Chinese? Italian?' but none of these suggestions seemed to be hitting the mark either.

Alice looked at Malcolm worrying how she could get rid of him without hurting his feelings. This was the first night alone without Betty and she felt sure Alistair would have noticed Betty's car now missing from the car park and he might just venture over at some point in the evening. Or, failing this, she might just muster up the courage to go and ask if they both wanted to pop over. She really wanted Alistair to try the new gin she had purchased in Ulverston.

'The thing is Malcolm, I have just had Betty stay for over a week now and although I have genuinely enjoyed her company I was hoping for a night, well a night just to myself.' Alice looked hopeful this would do the job.

'Ah, I see, well yes of course.' Malcolm really didn't know what to say.

Alice could see the disappointment in his face and she could see he was clearly embarrassed. She thought how very lonely he must be since his wife had left him. He really didn't seem to have much of a social life apart from evenings with Sue and Robert and being a member of his fishing club. Alice felt a twinge of guilt. He was so good to her and always did her annual tax return free of charge. Robert had told her how he had done a sterling job of looking after the office in his absence at their busiest time of the year. He had even managed to get the filing system back to the way it had been before Miss Havisham's arrival.

Alice relented, 'Well, I tell you what. Why don't I order the takeaway now, we can have an early tea and then I can have my bath later. How about that?' Alice thought this was a good compromise.

Malcolm was thrilled, this was an excellent idea. Perhaps he might extend the evening by suggesting a movie she would like to watch? Yes, this was a good start indeed.

They both agreed on Chinese for tea and Malcolm phoned The Lucky Dragon as he thought this might be a good omen for the evening. After one very long hour, that Alice thought seemed to last an eternity, the order thankfully arrived. Malcolm had made a point of telling her all about the recent changes in the law and how this would affect her next Tax Return. After going through every new statute in minute detail, Alice thought that Malcolm would have been a splendid addition to Howarth Court's Resident's Committee. In fact, it was a shame Mr Hughes was a man and not a woman because it was possibly a match made in heaven.

They both enjoyed the Chinese. Malcolm talked about his last fishing trip up to Scotland where he had done some salmon fishing and then he asked Alice how the job hunting was going and Alice related her recent experiences. She explained how she was now going to tweak her C.V. and hoped this might just do the trick. Malcolm offered to help her with it but as time was now ticking on, Alice thought it best to manoeuvre the conversation towards him going.

Seeing Alice start to clear up the dishes, Malcolm thought this was now the perfect time to broach the subject of them going out with each other.

'The thing is Alice, well I thought that I might just suggest something to you.' Malcolm took a swig of wine for Dutch courage. 'Yes, the thing is I think it is about time that you and I, well I think the time is right for you and I to give it a go and perhaps go out on a few dates and then well, see how it goes?'

Alice now took her own swig of wine. Goodness, she thought that after the last encounter he would have got the message. She now had to put the matter firmly to bed. 'Look Malcolm, you know how fond I am of you … you are like family to me.'

Malcolm interrupted, 'You see that is just the problem. I believe we can be more than just family. We are both adults you know, both single people looking for love and a fresh start. I think it is time you stopped thinking of me as family but more as, well more as a lover.'

Alice took another even larger swig of wine. The word 'lover' was not a word she would every associate with Malcolm. However, he had now put his cards firmly on the table and she would now have to put the matter firmly to bed.

'Look, Malcolm...' however, she never got the chance to finish her sentence. The doorbell went. Alice now was dreading who she thought it might be and went to open the door to find her fears realised. Alistair was on the doorstep.

'Hi Alice, I was wondering if you would like to pop over for a drink this evening?' Alistair stood there still looking like some ancient Greek God.

Alice's heart raced but then it was soon overtaken by an overwhelming feeling of disappointment. Why was every opportunity to be with Alistair always curtailed by visitors? Malcolm at this point on hearing a strange male voice had got up to investigate. Oh Lord, Alice thought, another man to explain to Alistair.

'Good evening,' Malcolm said as he went to shake Alistair's hand. Malcolm looked Alistair up and down and was distinctly curious who this man was. Maybe he just needed to borrow some coffee or sugar, hopefully for his wife and six children.

Alice reluctantly felt it was now necessary to do the introductions and duly did.

Alistair was introduced as her neighbour Isabella's brother. Malcolm needed to find out more. 'And your wife, is she....'

Alistair was quick to interject 'No, no wife.'

Malcolm was now somewhat perturbed. 'And you are here

because?' Malcolm eyebrows were now meeting in the middle displaying a mixture of annoyance, curiosity and angst.

Alice invited Alistair in feeling that the Spanish Inquisition had gone on long enough.

'Please Alistair do come in and join us. We are enjoying a glass of wine, let me get you one.' Alice knew this was now going to get tricky. She had told Malcolm she wanted an early night so how was she going to get rid of Malcolm but also ensure that Alistair stayed?

Alistair and Malcolm were now eyeing each other up. Alistair was just as curious to know who Malcolm was. This was now another man in her flat. Not bad looking but the cardigan made him look a bit dowdy he thought. Not really Alice's type but who was he to judge? Alice clearly had some male acquaintances who may be more than just 'friends'.

Malcolm was not happy about Alice's offer of a glass of wine. He hadn't spent an extra two pounds on a bottle of wine to have to now share it with, well whoever this man was. Alistair could see the look of disapproval on Malcolm's face and thought it best to decline the offer.

Alice tried to make polite conversation. As soon as Malcolm found out that Alistair owned his own company, he proceeded to tell him that *he* ran a very successful Accountancy firm, one of great standing in the town. Not wanting to miss out on a business opportunity, Malcolm handed Alistair his business card. However, Alistair was not forthcoming with his own.

Alice, clearly embarrassed at Malcolm's blatant sale of his company to her visitor, tried to steer Malcolm towards leaving. 'Yes, well Malcolm is just about to go now, aren't you Malcolm?'

'Am I? Well I thought we might finish the wine first and then you were going to have a bath and I thought…?'

Alice couldn't believe her ears and gave a nervous laugh, 'Well Malcolm the bath was planned for after you had left.' Alice's heart sank.

Malcolm didn't seem very happy about leaving before drinking the rest of his wine and he certainly wasn't leaving these two together. He thought Alistair had the sort of eyes that just couldn't be trusted. Alistair realising Malcolm was going to be here for some time and was obviously interrupting something, though he wasn't sure what, felt it was best to come back another evening. He made his excuses and departed, leaving Alice feeling, yet again, bereft of her chance to spend some time with him. For goodness sake, why did she always have to have bloody visitors!

Malcolm feeling delighted that this man had now gone and could continue with their cosy soirée, was now seated on the living room sofa. He decided to make himself a bit comfier and arranged the cushions to rest his head on whilst looking through Alice's collection of DVD's.

'Goodness are there any movies here that don't have Hugh Grant in them?'

Alice sat down on the opposite sofa now feeling more desperate than ever to get rid of him, 'Look Malcolm, as I was saying, I am very fond of you but...'

Malcolm now moved over to sit next to her and took her hand, 'I know you see me, well you see me as a big brother - or maybe even just your accountant but, don't you see, we are the perfect match. Both single and free. I think you and I will rub along together very well indeed. Don't you?'

Alice stood up, enough was enough.

'No Malcolm, that is not going to happen. I don't want to just 'rub along' with anyone. Malcolm, I just don't have those kinds of feelings for you and never will.' Alice got up from the sofa and headed for the kitchen. Malcolm duly followed.

'Well when I said 'rub along' together, perhaps that was a bad choice of words. What I mean to say is that I know I could make you happy. You just need to give us a chance. There is so much more to me than just being your brother's friend and workmate, being an accountant and fisherman. There are other things too you know.' Malcolm couldn't think of anything else at that precise moment so continued with, 'Well, lots of things.'

'Malcolm there is no *us,* or ever will be an *us.* I just want us to stay friends.' Alice looked at Malcolm who now looked like some little lost boy who had lost his favourite conker. She knew she had hurt him but she just had to be honest.

'I will never have those sorts of feelings for you Malcolm, it just isn't going to happen, but what I do know Malcolm is that you are a wonderful, kind and caring man. I know that someone out there is just perfect for you but it isn't me Malcolm and never will be.'

Malcolm shuffled from one foot to the other. 'Right, I see. Well, that is that then. No hard feelings of course. I mean I am very happy to do the tax returns and all that, if you still want me to of course?' He looked hopefully at her.

'Oh Malcolm, you are one of my most trusted friends. I could never think of anyone else I would rather have do my tax return, honestly. After all, you are considered to be one of the, if not, *the* best accountant in town.'

Malcolm seemed to cheer up at this and decided that perhaps it was best to leave things for now. He knew from his experience of fishing that to hook a fish can take a considerable amount of time and, after all, there were always more fish in the sea. He said his goodbyes and Alice, finally, got her bath.

Alistair would have to wait yet another day. Alice sighed as she grabbed the bath bubbles and proceeded to pour the whole bottle in. All she needed now were rose petals and, of course, Alistair. Hey ho!

30

A heart to heart

A lice had spruced up her CV and decided to take it back around a few of the agencies. She had planned the day to pop in on Sue first, then into a few of the job agencies and finally catch up with Mario. Mario invited her around for dinner and she was looking forward to telling him all about the latest news and, of course, Alistair. Mario would be pleased that she had decided to get *back on the horse!*

She decided to leave the car at home and walk. It was a sunny bright day and, at last, it had stopped raining. Anyhow, there was no point trying to get it out of her parking space. Someone, again, had parked right behind her own one, and she really didn't want to risk another encounter with Mr Hughes so she decided to walk to the tube station and make her way round to Sue's.

Sue had put the deck chairs out in the garden and was looking forward to catching up with her friend's latest news. She had baked some scones and had some clotted cream left over from the previous day and her mum had left some delicious homemade strawberry jam. Alice was delighted to see Sue continuing to look well and bright. She had more colour in her cheeks and seemed a bit more sprightly. They both sat and enjoyed the garden, the scones and a pot of Sue's favourite

Empress Grey tea. After a bit of a natter about Ben, it didn't take Sue long to broach the subject of the holiday at the cottage.

'So, you got *'accidentally'* locked in the bedroom together did you?' Sue took another big bite of her scone and licked the jam in a suggestive way off her lips.

Alice laughed, 'Oh, look, it was just a fling, one of those nights where we had both had a bit too much to drink and well one thing led to another.'

'Did it indeed? So, you did actually sleep together then?' Sue put down her scone and cup of tea. 'I knew it, I just knew it!'

'It really was just a one-night thing, really there isn't much to say.' Alice tried to look as disinterested in the conversation as she could and tried to change it. 'Mr Bigg has started making some amazing Cornish Pasties, I must bring you some.'

However, Sue wasn't going to let her get off that lightly. 'I always thought he fancied you. So, go on then, tell me about this night of passion.'

Sue picked up her second scone and Alice was about to pick up hers but Sue whisked the plate away, 'Oh no, answer the question first – then you can have your scone.'

Alice knew exactly where Ben got his persistence and quest for every last detail.

'Well it was very, it was very, well, pleasant.'

Sue laughed. 'Pleasant. So, it was just pleasant then?'

Alice thought back, in fact that wasn't really how she would have described it. The sex had been fantastic. It all seemed to happen so effortlessly.

'Well, no okay, it was great but the next day he couldn't get out of the house quick enough and quite frankly I was relieved. Besides, Ollie isn't the only man you know in my life. Now, can I have another scone please or are you going to deny this poor little spinster any of the few pleasures she has left in life?'

'Ah you poor old thing – here have another one.' Sue relented and passed her the plate. 'So Malcolm then is in the running? I heard all about it from Robert. Malcolm asked Robert to the pub last night for a heart to heart and it all came out.'

Alice gave a deep sigh, 'Oh goodness what an evening. What on earth had got into the man! I hope Robert hasn't been encouraging him?'

Sue did explain to Alice that Robert had always thought the two of them might be a good match. Alice couldn't believe her ears, 'On what planet is that brother of mine living on?'

'I know, men just don't have a clue at times. He meant it kindly though Alice. Robert never did like the way Mark treated you and Malcolm, well he would never carry on like Mark did. He might be a bit, well a bit...

'Boring.' Alice finished the sentence.

'No not at all. I wouldn't say that, he is a good man who is just, well, a bit set in his ways, perhaps.'

'Yes, as I said, boring. But yes, he is a lovely man and he has a good heart, this is true.' Alice knew Sue would be keen to support a long-standing friend of her husband's and indeed the family.

'So, if it isn't Malcolm then?' Sue passed another scone over in exchange for a bit more information.

Alice's eyes lit up, 'Ah yes, the God of all Men – Alistair. He is absolutely gorgeous: tall, broad and blonde with a bit of grey that makes him look very distinguished and gives him a touch of sexiness.'

'OOOH, Alice, tell me more but first let's get the kettle on again and you can give me the whole low down. Don't miss anything out!'

Alice got up to make another cuppa whilst telling Sue all about her brief, but sadly fruitless, encounters with Alistair. Sue could tell by how animated Alice's face became when she talked about this new man and how completely captivated she was with him. However, she did feel a little disappointed that Ollie and Alice hadn't hit it off. She liked Ollie and thought Alice and him would have made a good match but thought it best not to broach the subject.

They continued chatting away for quite some time until Alice realised the time and explained how she needed to chase up some of the agencies she had emailed her C.V.'s. Sue invited her back for tea but Alice declined and explained she was seeing Mario that evening.

'Have a great time, send Mario my love.' Sue gave her friend a squeeze as they walked to the front door.

'Yes, well let's hope Ollie is out, then it should be!' Alice didn't feel ready to face him again.

'Oh no don't worry, Ollie left this morning for New York.'

'New York? Goodness that was sudden.' Alice looked shocked.

'Well, he did say he was thinking of going and well Mario is now back and it's not as if there's anything to keep him here, Alice, is there? Sue gave Alice a wink.

'No, absolutely, nothing at all. Well that's a relief!' Alice however wasn't feeling relieved but she couldn't quite sum up how she felt. Anyway, no time to dwell on that now she thought. He was gone and that was that.

Alice headed off into the city and popped into some

employment agencies, thinking it better to go in person. However, she got a familiar response that there wasn't anything at the moment but they would keep in touch.

She wandered up to Selfridges and decided to give herself a little treat. She spotted some jeans and jumpers which she felt sure Gok would approve of and headed up Oxford Street to have a cuppa in John Lewis's. She would have normally gone to Waterstones but after that incident with Hugh she thought it best not to venture in there.

Whilst sipping her coffee she decided to make a plan of action. Alistair's car was no longer in the car park and she really didn't know when she might get the opportunity of seeing him again. Perhaps it was time to take matters into her own hands? Yes, she would have to jot down her options. Make a plan. She took out her notebook and started to doodle. She wrote his name in large letters A L I S T A I R. She wrote it again but this time in much fancier writing A L I S T A I R. She then wrote a huge question mark under his name but couldn't think what else to write. This wasn't a great plan of action she thought but well she enjoyed writing his name anyway.

Her eyes started to wonder around the café. There were the usual people of all ages, shapes and sizes. One couple were obviously having an argument, both waving and gesticulating at each other. Another couple had probably just had an argument and clearly weren't talking and trying to face the other way as much as they possibly could to avoid any conversation at all. But then she spotted an elderly couple, probably in their late seventies who were sitting and holding hands. This gave Alice a warm fuzzy feeling inside. How lovely she thought. How great after all those years of marriage to be wanting to still hold hands. She could picture her and Alistair doing this in years to come. She went back to her doodling and this time drew a big heart around his name. However, she still didn't have any ideas of how to get things moving along a bit quicker so she put her notebook away. She would just have to wait until another day. He would surely be back soon.

She picked up her bags and headed down the escalator and out of the store. It was time to head to Mario's. She couldn't wait to spend some time with him. He might have some good ideas on how to get things moving a bit quicker with Alistair!

The journey took a bit longer than usual as she had now hit peak commuter time. She stood most of the way on the tube journey, with the only blessing being the fact she could no longer observe any more Tit-Tassels. Having been sandwiched like a sardine for around an hour she finally got to Mario's.

The flat was looking remarkably clear and tidy. 'Oh Mario, your flat looks as if it has had the Betty treatment!' Alice looked at his desk which was normally covered in heaps of paperwork that usually overflowed into the rest of the flat.

'No, no just the Ollie treatment! He is such a good man, all my paperwork has been filed, there was months of the stuff. What's more I can actually find the documents when I need them!' Mario made them both a coffee and they sat down together. Alice had to admit, Ollie had done an excellent job.

She asked Mario for all the news and Mario set about explaining what he had been doing during his most recent trip to Italy. Mario had spent much of his time helping Abramo set up his new bar The Horse's Head or as Mario called it *Testa di Cavallo* which sounded so much better than the English translation. After due consideration, Abramo had decided that being gay was not for him anymore and had made the decision to go out with one of the local village ladies.

'She keeps a herd of goats and apparently makes the best goat's cheese in the area, giving Abramo a regular supply of cheese for his new bar. Although I think Abramo is very happy with his new woman, he did complain about her favourite goat always being allowed in the house. In fact, not just the house, their bedroom too. However, I explained to Abramo that this was probably no different than keeping a pet dog.'

'Right?' said Alice musing over how Mario could possibly compare the two as being similar.

Mario, having related all his news, was keen to find out how Alice had been getting on. Alice excitedly relayed her news about Alistair and Mario listened very attentively. It was clear Alice was very taken with the man and was hoping for more than just friendship. Mario though, like Sue, was disappointed nothing more had happened with his godson. He really had wanted Ollie to settle down now. Travelling had its merits but now it was time he stopped all that gallivanting.

Mario had spent a great deal of time over the last few months learning more and more about his godson. He liked the man and felt he would be a good match for Alice so he would often try and put in a good word about her now and then. At first, it was clear that Ollie had got the wrong impression of Alice. Mario was keen to relate how wonderful this woman was and what a great match she would make for any man lucky enough to go out with her. Mario had told Ollie that he had never liked Mark and had spent much time relating to Ollie how useless he was and how she deserved so much better. But Mario's saddest lament was that Alice would have made a great mother but it was not to be. Mario had been furious at Mark for wasting her time and then getting another woman pregnant. This was simply the last straw! In fact, if he had been on better terms with Abramo's family he might have arranged for Mark's manhood to be cut short.

As Mario got to know his godson the relationship had developed into one of good friendship and of mutual respect and trust. Ollie had confided in Mario about the evening at the cottage and Mario felt it was about time to have a heart to heart with Alice before she rushed into a relationship with this new man, Alistair.

'I hear you and Ollie went to a cottage in the Lake District with Ben. I know he had a great time there and I heard about *everything*.' Mario looked at Alice in a very knowing way. Alice was surprised that Ollie had told him and felt somewhat embarrassed.

Alice though was not in the mood to talk about Ollie and wanted to talk about Alistair. 'The thing is Mario, Ollie is probably used to one-night stands and is keen to protect his status as a single and fancy-free guy. However, Alistair…'

Mario interrupted. 'I know he regretted leaving you the next day. I think he was foolish. It is not wise to make love with a woman and then depart. However, Alice, knowing Ollie I am convinced this was down to the fact that he is a very loyal man. If he says he is going to do something then he does it. He felt obliged to see his friends. He is not a man to make arrangements and then cancel. Ollie is a man of principle.'

Alice thought about this. She did agree that it would have been hard for him to have cancelled at such late notice but then he might have texted her several times or rang during the day. *And* he had got home so late. Was there really a need to get home so late?

'Look Mario, Ollie is the kind of man who probably has lots of flings – you know the type – a girl in every port but Alistair he is a man who is settled; he travels when he has business to see to but that is that. He has a lovely sister, though quite a bit younger, who I get on well with and Alistair has a secure job. Aunt Betty likes him too. She told me what a nice man he was and how he was very charming.' Alice thought this might assuage Mario.

'Charming, charming! Well you had a charming man before if you remember and look where that got you!' Mario was not going to let this go.

'But Mario, I hardly think a travelling nomad who takes advantage of people's hospitality and who basically, let's be honest, is a bit of a free wheeler dealer earning a living here and there is exactly a good match for me. Do you?' Alice thought that surely Mario would see this.

'Well, I think you have the wrong impression. True the man likes his travels and with that lifestyle the man needs to earn a living but saying he is a 'wheeler dealer' is not fair. You do realise I let him have this apartment in return for some wages whilst he ran my café and when he left this morning to go to New York, on the table was six months' rent. Now I never asked for that. That says something about the man, wouldn't you say so?'

Alice thought about this, yes it was true she thought

'But, Mario…'

However, Mario was in full throttle

'This is a man who gives up his time to go to the trouble

to take Ben away and help Sue and Robert. A man who gives up his Christmas Day to help a friend to cook food for the homeless and goes out of his way to deal with that no good ex-boyfriend of yours. I would say this was a man of honour, wouldn't you?'

Alice felt a little like a young girl again being told off for having misbehaved. However, Mario had succeeded in making her feel a bit guilty, perhaps she might have been a bit unfair in her summing up of the man. Perhaps she should have been kinder to Ollie, more understanding. The problem was she had been messed about by Mark and she just wasn't going to be the doormat anymore. How was she to know all of this, if Ollie or no one else had told her? Why wouldn't anybody tell her things?

Alice got up from the table and started to clear the dishes. No more could be said on the matter and Mario clearly didn't want to talk about Alistair. She would just have to let the two of them get to know each other. Mario would love him in time, he just had to get to know him.

31

Taking the bull by the horns

The next morning Alice awoke to the sound of the flat's lawns being mowed and Mr Hughes's voice resonating around the whole Court. She got up and wondered over to the window and opened it to see what was going on. Mr Hughes was in full throttle pointing out where the gardener had missed bits much to the obvious annoyance and frustration of the poor man.

Another few minutes passed, Mr Hughes's patience seemed to be running out.

'You see I think you need to do it more methodically. When you turn around to come back down the lawn you need to be very precise as to where you start again, and you need to move in very straight lines. Here man, let me show you.' Mr Hughes firmly took the mower from the somewhat surprised gardener and started to demonstrate exactly how he thought it should be done.

The man, now resigned to the fact that it was futile to object, simply shrugged his shoulders and went to sit on one of the lawn's benches and watched Mr Hughes. Unfortunately, the large mower was not as easy to handle as Mr Hughes had, initially, assumed. The man, realising the demonstration from Mr Hughes might take some time, decided to sit back on the bench and proceeded to get his flask of tea out and poured himself a cuppa.

'Silly old sod!' muttered Alice and now feeling a bit more awake decided to make herself a cup of tea and some toast. When done, she placed them on a tray and wandered back to bed and snuggled down under the duvet ready to read her paper. Not working had its definite advantages she thought: leisurely mornings, a cleaner and tidier flat - well most of the time *and* most importantly the occasional meeting with Alistair.

Alice pondered over the last few months, it was now July, so much had happened in such a short space of time but that is how life can often be she thought. A new image, a brief fling, no partner - but the prospect of one soon she hoped! Life seemed better, settled again. Simon was due to spend next weekend with her and she was looking forward to dinner with the usual gang, well apart from Lucy who she hoped would not make an appearance. On the other hand, though, when she thought about this again, there was a part of her that would quite like Lucy to be there. She would surely relate back to Mark how well she was now doing. The new image, the more self-assured woman. Alice would be sure to drop the name Alistair into the conversation as often as she could. Knowing Lucy's thirst for gossip, she would surely relate it all back to Mark who would get the definite message that she was doing well and getting on with her life even better than before.

Alice was just about to settle into reading her paper when the phone rang. Miss Havisham was on the other line.

'Something dreadful has happened Alice, it's Mr Frobersham!' Alice immediately thought the old boy had finally kicked the bucket. Miss Bond had probably worn the old man out by now. 'You need to get over to his office as quick as you can, he is, well he is…'

'Oh God, he's dead, isn't he?' Although Alice had been angry at the old fool she had known him now for so long and they had once been a team. She wouldn't have wished anything bad to happen to him.

'No, he isn't dead, he's sitting on the rooftop of the office building and threatening to jump off! He is insisting on seeing you, something about wanting to make amends before he meets his maker!'

'Oh goodness!' Alice couldn't believe her ears. Mr Frobersham, jump off a rooftop? He had such a high opinion of himself and was incredibly vain, surely not Mr Frobersham? Anyhow, he would never want to get one of his beloved Simpsons of Piccadilly hand tailored suits ruined by jumping off a building. Very messy indeed.

'Right, so he wants to speak to me?' Alice couldn't take it all in. Even if the man was about to jump off a roof, surely, he didn't want to spend his last minutes in conversation with the woman he fired. Anyway, where was Miss Bond?

'Yes, they have one of those trained police officers there, keeping him talking.' Miss Havisham sounded truly alarmed and upset.

'I know he hasn't treated you very well Alice, but you will go, won't you? The police are sending a car for you now.'

Alice had suspected that Miss Havisham had always had strong feelings for Mr Frobersham and that her loyalty to him was owing to this.

'Oh gosh, well, yes, of course!' Alice leaped out of bed and threw a pair of jeans and a top on. She gulped down the rest of her tea and ate the now cold toast. It wasn't before long the police car had arrived. She ran down the stairs and ventured as quick as she could to the car. However, Mr Hughes had managed to get to the police car first.

'Not something serious, I hope? You haven't been up to your old tricks again with that umbrella of yours, have you?' Mr Hughes had a very supercilious smile on his face, pleased that he had managed to get one over her after the last rude encounter with herself and Betty.

'No actually, Mr Hughes if you *must* know I have been asked to attend a very serious incident - suicide attempt, now if you don't mind, I need to get in the car!'

Mr Hughes's face changed somewhat. 'Oh, I see, I am very sorry. Look, I could go with you.'

'What? What an earth are you talking about Mr Hughes?' Alice started to get into the car. Mr Hughes hurried around to the driver's seat to speak to the police officer.

'Look, I think you should know I am a trained *Safetalk First Aider*, I may be of assistance officer. I did the course last year when it had occurred to me that living in a block of flats, well you never know who might decide they have had enough. Let me get my Certificate.' Mr Hughes however was stopped in his tracks.

'No, sir, thank you sir, that won't be necessary, we have our own specially trained police officer to respond to situations like these.'

Mr Hughes looked rather disappointed but thought it best not to get into a disagreement with the police so decided to go back to his mowing.

The journey was quicker than Alice had ever known to get

into town. The police car sped to the offices and Alice was greeted by a plain clothed officer who proceeded to give her advice on what she could and shouldn't say. The lifts, of course, were once again out of action so he led her up the outside fire exit attached to the building. It was a large wrought iron staircase that that went up eight flights. Alice wondered how the old boy hadn't killed himself just climbing the stairs, enough to give anyone a heart attack.

Alice finally got to the top of the roof, completely breathless, and saw Mr Frobersham sitting with his legs dangled over the roof and a man trying to talk to him. Mr Frobersham just kept shaking his head from side to side.

'No, no it's too late officer I am resigned to my fate, it's what I deserve.'

Alice looked at the utterly forlorn and very dejected looking man. He was unshaven and bedraggled looking, so unlike the Mr Frobersham she knew, with his crisp suits and highly polished shoes.

Alice approached cautiously and spoke to him in as quiet and as calm a voice as she could muster 'Hi, Charles, Mr Frobersham. It's Alice.'

Mr Frobersham turned his head and seemed relieved to see her. 'Oh Alice I just wanted to talk to you before, well before I depart this world.'

'OK, Charles, but you will have to come back a bit from the edge of the roof because I can't talk to you while you are there.' Alice really didn't want to sit next to the man, after all she didn't like heights and didn't want to be accidentally pulled to her death with him.

'I just wanted to tell you, before I jump, that I am very

sorry how I treated you and, of course, Miss Havisham too. I have been a silly old fool, I can see that now, will you ever forgive me?'

Alice felt like giving him a mouthful but decided this wasn't perhaps the best time.

'She left me you know. Babs left me.' A tear appeared in Mr Frobersham's eyes.

'Miss Bond?' Alice enquired.

'Yes, the firm is ruined. Completely and utterly ruined. Nothing left. Over a hundred years of Frobersham and Sons and nothing left. She took everything.'

'Oh Mr Frobersham, Charles, that's awful! What on earth happened?'

'First there were all the demands for the fancy handbags, shoes, clothes, the trips to Liberty, Harrods and Fortnum and Mason. That was bad enough to endure but then it all started going wrong when her brother moved into the house. Things started to go missing - antiques, paintings. Then there was the business of her brother's own business struggling and Babs said they needed just a few loans to tide them over. Just to help her brother's business get back on its feet. Well, I kept forking out but to no avail. The business always seemed to need more. Anyway, it turned out that this brother of hers was actually not her brother but her boyfriend and well gradually they drained me of everything. Then Tit-Tassels plummeted in sales. Accentuise stopped ordering and that was that. None of my old friends want to talk to me. My old clients won't even take calls from me. Everyone has shunned me.'

'I told you, you silly old goat, it would just be a fad, why didn't you listen to me, how could you let her do that to the business?' Alice was furious but a frosty look from the trained officer made her think she may not have said the right thing to a man whose legs were dangling over the edge of a roof.

Mr Frobersham looked at her, 'You're right, you're right, it's over now, everything gone.' He made a move forward, everyone gasped.

'Just one thing though, before I jump, I wanted to thank you for all your years loyal service and dedication.' Mr Frobersham leaned forward even further and everyone gasped again.

Alice reached out to touch his shoulder, the pavement looked a very long way down and she started to feel somewhat dizzy.

'Look, Mr Frobersham, wait a minute! Remember the depression back in 2008, well we came through that didn't we? Look, we have built up some of the best clientele a firm could have. We did it once – we can do it again. Frobersham & Sons aren't beat, not yet, not ever.'

Mr Frobersham lifted his head and lent back again. 'Yes, yes, it is true, we have been a good team you and I but there is nothing left, I mean just think about the office – I can't even afford the rent. No, it's too late. What was it Hamlet said *All that lives must die, passing through nature to eternity* and of course then there was Macbeth, *Out, out, brief candle! Life's but a walking shadow, a poor player that struts and frets his hour upon the stage and then is heard no more: it is a tale told by an idiot, full of sound and fury, signifying nothing.*'

For a very brief moment Alice felt it might be preferable to let Mr Frobersham jump than hear any more Shakespeare but, nevertheless, she thought she ought to try one more time.

'Look Mr Frobersham, life is not over yet. You have so much ahead of you. We have so much ahead of *us*. Where's the fighting spirit gone? Eh? Every day you used to say *let's take the bull by its horns* and that is what we did! Look, we will ride through this, I promise you. I have some savings and then there is the redundancy money, we can use that, we can get through this I promise. I can afford the rental for a while and you can go and take some of our ex-clients out to lunch and woo them back again. You have done it before; you can do it again!' Alice looked straight into Mr Frobersham's eyes and there she saw a flicker of light appear.

'You would do that for me?' Mr Frobersham wiped the non-existent tears from his eyes.

'Yes, you silly old sod now come back from the edge of the building and we can talk about it, will you?' Alice smiled at him and he smiled back. 'There is nothing so bad Charles that you and I and Miss Havisham can't sort, together as a team.'

With that, Mr Frobersham carefully shuffled back away from the edge of the rooftop and, to the relief of all, he made his way to the top of the iron staircase.

'You know my dear, there is another saying from Richard III *True hope is swift and flies with swallow's wings; Kings it makes gods, and meaner creatures kings'*

'Right, Mr Frobersham, we have still got to get down this very old iron staircase in one piece and preferably alive so let's leave Shakespeare until later, can we?' Alice had had enough. Two silly sods, she thought, in one day was just too much. She needed a large gin and tonic.

32

The other woman?

Alice woke up eager to face the day. There was much to do and organise and she didn't want to waste any time. She had rung the management company to see about leasing the office again but on finding out the cost and realising that there was no guarantee of wooing back her previous clientele, she decided the best course of action was to rent more modest accommodation. Alice did consider them working together from her flat but this had its own complications and she really didn't want to add any more confusion as to her single status where Alistair was concerned.

She set about looking for something closer and more affordable, finding a small but perfectly suitable office just up the road near her brother's office. It was set in lovely grounds and would be suitable to receive any clients. She rang Robert to find out how soon they could release Miss Havisham and, to her surprise, they seemed very quick to oblige saying he could release her today, in fact that very hour.

With all the balls set in motion, Alice then concentrated on her weekend. Simon would be arriving the next day and she wanted to spruce up the flat and get some treats in for them both. When that was ticked off her list, she decided a new outfit for Saturday would be the order of the day. She also arranged for her hair and makeup to be done by the new lady who had opened up a salon just up the road from her flat called *OOOh Girl Who did Your Hair?* She would go in for a trial later that day.

Alistair's car still wasn't parked in the car park but she hoped to see him this weekend, particularly as she would be dressed up to the nines and hopefully look like a million dollars with her hair and makeup all done. She would have liked to have bumped into Isabella to try and find out about his next visit but Alice hadn't seen her either.

Alice set off and headed to find a new outfit. Something that would send out a message to all that she was back! Yes, back and on form! Back to rule not just the working world but all of it. She didn't need Mark any more, she had survived without him and new adventures lay ahead. However, she really hoped Mark had regretted losing her. She had daydreamed on many an occasion that he would roll up to her door, swearing undying love, telling her what a big mistake he had made and then she would have the great satisfaction of telling him where to go.

Whilst she was shopping, she remembered Gok's words, 'Look girlfriend, don't you keep hiding those great legs of yours. Get them out there!' After many hours of searching she eventually found the perfect wrap dress. Cut just above the knees and fitted at the waist. Lovely creams and blues. She purchased the shoes and handbag to go with it and set off to the make-up salon where the owner, Laura, did a great job. The make-up looked natural but emphasised her blue eyes and made her cheekbones look more prominent. Laura swept Alice's bob back into a very sophisticated French pleat. All in all, Alice was delighted. Having swapped many stories on family, love and the many shortcomings of men, Alice emerged feeling like a million dollars. Yes, she would definitely re-book Laura for Saturday. Laura was equally delighted to have a new client, well her only client, and such a satisfied customer. She needed her new business to succeed and Alice would, surely, tell her friends hopefully where to come.

Alice popped into Thrift and Thrive to get some of the fudge Simon loved and was very surprised to meet one of her old school friends Minnie, who, as soon as she saw Alice, complimented her on how great she looked. They chatted away for a while and then Minnie mentioned Mark. 'I am so sorry to have heard you split up; I hear he left for a younger woman. I don't know, men and their mid-life crises. Well, if it is of any comfort, you are better off without him.'

Alice waved her hand as if it really didn't matter. 'Oh, well water under the bridge now.'

'Yes, indeed. I hear his new relationship is now on the rocks too!' Minnie leaned forward and started to whisper, 'I believe he is finding having a baby quite difficult, you know, and then there are all the arguments and talk of this other woman too.'

Alice thought Minnie had got her facts mixed up. 'Other woman? No, surely not, I mean they have hardly been together all that long?'

'Well, I have heard he knew her for about two years before she got pregnant and then.' Minnie suddenly stopped realising how inappropriate her comment was.

Alice was taken aback she knew he had been deceiving her but she had never actually asked Mark for just how long?

Minnie feeling awkward thought it best to wrap up the whole conversation. 'Well, I must be getting on, so much to do. Tony will have cooked tea by now.'

She put her hand out and held Alice's arm.

'You really do look amazing! Love to Sue and Robert.' And with those words Minnie made a hasty retreat.

Alice retrieved the fudge from the shelf and placed it on the conveyor belt. As it moved along, she remembered the time Mark had come home late one evening. She had gone to kiss him but he had quickly turned around and retreated into the kitchen making the excuse that he was desperate for a drink and then bed. He had muttered on about such a long day he'd had, so very tired. He would have to work again at the weekend with business being so fraught. What a fool she had been not to have seen the signs. So, trusting but then why shouldn't she have been? Isn't that what relationships are all about. Trust? And then what had Minnie meant by this other woman? Surely, he couldn't have tired already of, let's face it, the mother of his child? Alice paid for the fudge and forgetting it was for Simon, she promptly opened the bag and dug in.

Back at the flat, she finished arranging the gin cupboard placing her new purchases at the front. Plenty of gin, tonic and wine she thought and then she went to place the last piece of fudge next to the rest of the nibbles but changed her mind. It looked mean just one piece left for Simon, no, she had better eat that too.

The phone rang. Miss Havisham sounded very happy, 'Well I knew we would get the old team back together again. What wonderful news! Your brother and Malcolm were so kind to let me go at such short notice. They insisted I didn't need to finish my filing before going. So kind. I think they will miss me you know.'

They chatted for a while and Alice said she would meet Miss Havisham the following Monday to arrange for her to see the new offices. She would leave Miss Havisham the job of making sure Charles didn't spend too much money on furnishing the office and to ring round some of their established button manufacturers and contacts, not forgetting, Kate, their freelance designer to see if she was interested in coming back to work for them.

Alice went to bed feeling optimistic. So, what if Mark had moved onto yet another woman. Good riddance. She was well rid of him. She snuggled under the duvet and read her novel and before she knew it, she was asleep.

33

Brief encounter

Friday finally arrived. The flat was looking tidy, clean and ready for her visitor. Alice bathed, defuzzed, and set off to meet Simon from the station. Still no car in the carpark, still no Isabella. Well, plenty of time left she thought, the weekend is but young!

The day was sunny and bright, there was a gentle, refreshing breeze and even the sound of Mr Hughes arguing with No 2 for leaving his muddy bicycle in the lobby could not bother Alice, at least not today. No, she was happy. She walked up to the station and, on the way, she popped in on Laura to check she was still okay for her appointment later, which indeed she confirmed she was.

While Alice was waiting for the train to arrive, she sat on one of the station benches. Five minutes and Simon should be here. Five minutes to the start of a great weekend. She looked around her and saw the usual mums with their prams, teenagers ready for their next adventures and an old man sat on the next bench obviously pondering on life too. She looked up at the notice board, no delays. Well that's a change she thought to herself, this one was always late. Three minutes and Simon would be here. She wondered over to the book stand and perused the latest novels and skimmed the blurbs. Whilst she was looking a familiar voice came from behind and spoke quietly in her ear,

'Looking for a thriller or a romance?'

Alice turned around to see Alistair standing right there. Alice could feel herself again feeling quite light headed and overcome with a strange mix of nerves and yet excitement. God he was gorgeous! He stood there with that warm, friendly smile and those come to bed eyes of his that seemed to embrace her whole body with just one stare.

'Both actually.' Alice blushed slightly but was just so grateful that she had managed to compose herself and reply with a fairly suitable response.

'Aren't we all?' Alistair raised his eyebrows fixing upon her with his self-assured eyes and picked up the novel from out of her hands. 'Ah, an Alliott fan I see.'

'Yes, I like her books. Always funny and uplifting.'

Alistair smiled. He popped the book back on the shelf.

'So, are you off somewhere?' he enquired.

'Oh no, in all weekend Alistair, just waiting for a good friend, yes a gay good friend of mine. Yes, he is very much gay and coming down from Manchester and you?'

Alistair smiled, 'Just waiting for Bella, I am hoping she is on this train too. However, she is rarely on time.'

Alice felt overwhelmed with even more excitement. The weekend couldn't get any better! Alistair was obviously picking his sister up and taking her back to the flat. She probably had loads of luggage; Isabella never travelled lightly.

Unfortunately, Alice spotted the train approach the platform.

'Oh bugger it!' Then, realising she had actually said this out loud she felt she had to explain herself. 'Just when I need the train to be late, so I can choose my novel. Typical!'

Alice quickly paid for the book and they both walked together along the platform looking for their arrivals. Alice soon spotted Simon. He seemed to have a great deal of luggage with him for a weekend she thought? Simon soon spotted Alice as she ran towards him with great excitement. Alice always felt overcome when she saw him, and rushed to give a him a big hug. Alistair looked on with an admiring smile. She was so affectionate and caring.

Simon whirled Alice around in his arms and it was at this point Alice spotted Isabella too.

Isabella gestured towards Simon, 'This very charming man has helped me with my luggage.'

Simon handed Isabella her bags. 'It was a pleasure to help, it was a treat to have such lovely company.' Simon flashed another warm smile at Isabella who, as many women did, seemed quite taken with him.

Alistair joined them and the four continued chatting for a while. Simon had spotted Isabella trying to wrestle with her bags to get them on the overhead luggage rack and Simon had kindly intervened. They then discovered they were booked on seats right opposite each other! More chat followed along the lines of what a small world it is and what were the chances of meeting someone with mutual acquaintances.

Simon kept looking at Alice. Now realising who this Alistair man was and, seeing Alice's obvious delight in her eyes every time she looked at the man, decided to help things along a bit. Simon suggested Alistair and Isabella join them all for drinks tomorrow night at the Flying Scotsman bar. Alice beamed a warm and grateful smile at Simon. She could have hugged him to death at that precise moment. What an absolute hero!

Isabella and Alistair also thought this a splendid idea. Alistair offered them both a lift back to the flats which they gratefully accepted. He managed to park in the guest parking space under the watchful eye of Mr Hughes who pointedly looked at his watch and wrote something down in his notebook.

Once in the flat and out of earshot, Alice gave out a little scream of delight and hugged Simon again. 'You absolute star. I do love you so much!'

'Yes, I know, the saviour of the day, yet again! Well I can see why you are taken with him, I am quite overwhelmed by him too, my friend, he is definitely a walking God on legs. Wouldn't mind a bit of him myself!'

They chattered away with all their latest news and decided on their plans for the rest of the day. Robert and Sue were joining them for dinner and after this they had planned on a late-night movie watching *Bridget Jones's Diary* or may be *Love Actually*. They would decide later, depending on their fancy.

Alice filled Simon in on all the news about Mr Frobersham and as she did so, Simon could clearly see the change in her. She seemed so much happier and self-assured. Her whole complexion looked brighter and her hair was growing to a much longer bob. It suited her. Yes, this was a huge change to the last woman he had encountered, very broken and unsure. She still had that touch of vulnerability about her but, then again, she always had. He was so relieved that life had moved on for her.

'Well, friend, tell me what happened with Ollie then? I hear you had a bit of a fling?'

'Gosh is nothing sacred! Oh, well that was nothing. Really nothing. Not to be. Some men, you know, just can't take the pressure of being in a relationship. He's in the States now, doing something or other for a friend in some art gallery. It really doesn't matter, anyway I don't want to think about that now. Far bigger fish to fry!'

'I see?' Simon hesitated for a moment, 'So, he wasn't any good in bed then?'

Alice blushed.

'You are so naughty. No, he was actually very…' She stopped herself.

Simon spotted an air of doubt. He took Alice's hand. 'Some people go through life single because they just haven't met the right person. Few of us actually want to go through life without a partner, a soul mate. It is easy to convince yourself that you are happier that way, what other options are there? You look around and some partners seem blissfully happy, some seem to muddle along and some just don't work and we have both witnessed the heartache that bring. Relationships take a great deal of investment and with that comes risk. When that person does turn up, it can take a while to trust your judgement; to trust that all that expenditure of time, worry and anxiousness of *will it* or *won't it* work, will be worth it. The protective barrier and all that…'

Alice looked at Simon. He had been in and out of relationships for a long while now and she knew that he, like her, wanted a soul mate. She put her arm around him and gave him a big kiss on the cheek.

'Let's have a gin. I have some new ones for you to try.' Alice started to raid the gin cupboard.

They both enjoyed sampling them. Simon enjoyed cooking and Alice said she would be the assistant chef for the evening and help with the chopping or whatever needed doing. So, they cooked together, laughed together and exchanged many tales of misadventures from younger days.

It was soon early evening and Robert and Sue arrived and there was much merriment over hearing Ben's recent decision to pack school in and concentrate on his football career and becoming an alpaca farmer.

Alice looked around the table at her friends. She was blessed to have such a great family as well as friends but soon she hoped there might be an extra place set at the table. She imagined Alistair sitting there, chatting away. He was such good company. He would fit in like a glove.

When the world was finally put to rights by all four of them and movies watched Alice's bed soon beckoned. It wasn't long before she disappeared under the duvet and fell fast asleep.

Alice soon found herself back in the train station. It looked like the one in the film at Carnforth in Brief Encounter. Everything appeared as if it was in black and white. Alice looked down at her rather old fashioned 1940's dress and when she caught a glimpse of herself in the window's reflection, she now thought she looked rather like Celia Johnson.

There, in front of her was a pot of tea and the café looked a bit dowdy. The door opened and who should come in through the door but Trevor Howard, no wait a minute it was it Trevor or Alistair? He asked if he could join her as there were no other seats. Alice looked around, somewhat puzzled as the café was completely empty. However she was happy to oblige.

They started a polite conversation about how he had just arrived to catch the 5.40 down and she had arrived to catch the 5.42 up but Alice hadn't a clue what either of them were talking about.

Alice noticed how posh both their accents had become. Alistair, yes it was definitely Alistair, complimented her on her choice of Bath bun. She started crying and he held her hand.

'I really didn't want the Bath bun; I wanted the large chocolate éclair but Mr Hughes always gets there first.'

Alistair now took both her hands, 'My darling, is it so very bad to have a Bath bun rather than a chocolate éclair?' Alistair gripped her fingers even more tightly, 'I know what this really means, darling, of course I do. You are unhappy with us keep meeting like this. It's the guilt isn't it?'

Alice was confused, they had only just met. What did they have to feel guilty about? She did like him holding her hands though.

'Well yes, I guess so?'

'I can't bear the thought of you not being in my life, we just must meet one more time, do you promise darling, just one more time?'

Alice felt a sense of desperation now, why just one more time? They had only just met? This wasn't making any sense.

The café door opened and Ollie came through it dressed in a very smart suit indeed. Alistair quickly withdrew his hands from Alice's as if he didn't want to be seen with her. Ollie walked over to an elderly woman serving at the bar.

'Have you seen my wife? She is short and blonde with lovely blue eyes and eats Bath buns.'

The woman pointed towards Alice. 'She's over there with Trevor Howard.'

Alice looked up, Alistair had gone and Trevor Howard was now sitting opposite her talking about the weather. She looked around. Where had Alistair gone? Why was she now married? When did she get married? She didn't remember getting married?

Mr Hughes and Ollie came over. Mr Hughes gestured to the

spare chair and, without being asked, promptly sat down. They both talked about how good the chocolate eclairs were.

Ollie turned to her. 'Darling don't you think it is time you were getting home to cook my tea?'

Alice felt the anger welling up inside her.

'Cook your tea? Why don't you cook your own bloody tea!'

Mr Hughes tutted.

'Difficult wife there I see, and I think it is only right you should know that she keeps eating all the Bath buns as well!'

Alice put her head in her hands and all she could hear was someone in the distance talking.

She awoke to the sound of Simon's voice, 'Here, brought you a cuppa, Alice, and what on earth was all that muttering about Bath buns and Trevor Howard?'

Alice was going to explain her dream but then thought the better of it. She really didn't want Simon thinking she was dreaming about Ollie. He might get the wrong idea completely.

34

Murder in mind

Alice and Simon decided to go to Mario's for breakfast. Alice for the third time this week had decided that today was the day to restart her diet. She was definitely not going to have the full English like Simon. No, she would settle for an egg on toast instead. However, after spotting the very lonely looking pain au chocolat sitting on the plate she decided that just a few more calories would do no harm, particularly as she had been so good just having an egg and the croissant did look small. After, much to Simon's amusement, she bought the last two apricot and almond slices stating she had nothing in for pudding after lunch and it was Saturday after all.

'You have to have pudding on a Saturday, Simon!' Alice announced.

Simon laughed.

'Well Alice, no interesting conversation ever started with *today I had a great salad* or *I have lost a pound or two.*'

Mario looked a bit pale Alice thought as he joined them for a brief while, eager to catch up on Alice's latest news of joining the working world again. Mario mentioned that Ollie was doing well in New York and the gallery had got off to a good start. Simon enquired whether Mario knew if Ollie had plans for coming back to London. Alice was keen to shift the conversation away from Ollie and mentioned that her friends Carla and Mary were soon to launch their new art exhibition called '*The Power of the Vagina*' which, much to Carla's and Mary's annoyance, seemed to attract a large number of men.

Simon laughed. 'Well, I am relieved they have moved away from penises. After all there are only so many penises with nails in that one can look at!'

Alice flashed Simon a disapproving stare for making fun of them but couldn't help but laugh herself. Mario looked completely confused and Alice didn't feel she had the time to explain. There was still much to be done before this evening. She wanted Simon to look at her new dress as she now wasn't so sure about the shoes, they had even higher heels than her last pair and she was keen to get a bit more practise wearing them. She quickly hurried Simon out of the café and they headed for home.

The sun was still shining and there wasn't a cloud in view. On the way home Simon mentioned the same man again, Richard, who he had spent New Year's Eve with. He had joined Simon's firm not long before Christmas working in the legal department of Construction and Engineering. Richard shared the same interests and their friendship had grown into something much more. Alice insisted that Simon brought Richard over to meet her but Simon, as always, seemed reluctant. 'Well yes of course, out of all my friends you will meet him first but let's see how things develop. Anyway, never mind me, let's get you sorted first! I have a funny feeling that tonight may just be the start of something!'

'Oh Simon, I do hope so! I just have such a good feeling about him.' Alice couldn't help smiling. Her face just couldn't manage one grimace. Not one. Tonight, surely, would be the night!

Her dress and shoes approved by Simon, her make up professionally applied and her hair put in a French pleat, Alice was very happy with the results. This girl looked a million dollars she thought and Simon wasn't backward in coming forward with all the right compliments too. Everything felt right, Alice felt positive and very excited.

The evening was soon upon them. Simon and Alice went to Bella's for a drink first and then they all headed off to the Flying Scotsman. Lucy, and Nisha were already there and, much to everyone's relief, had acquired a few tables as the pub was always very busy on a Saturday night. Sue arrived soon after with Sam who she had picked up along the way in a taxi. All were delighted to meet Alistair and Lucy wasn't slow to do her usual flirting with this new and rather good-looking man. However, much to Alice's relief and satisfaction, Alistair was very unresponsive to her. In fact, Alice got the impression he didn't care for her much at all.

Sue and Sam kept smiling at Alice in a very telling way, raising their eyebrows and whispering the odd comment to her about how amazing she looked and why had she gone to so much trouble, particularly tonight? Alice was not going to rise to all the teasing and batted off any comments as quick as they came her way.

Alistair was very much at the centre of attention all evening with Alice's friends all eager to get to know him. Alice was so glad; she really did want all her friends to like and get on with him.

At about nine, they all decided to head to the local Italian and Simon was glad to sit next to Alistair to find out a bit more about the man. Alice noted how they were soon engrossed in conversation. Much to Alice's surprise and delight, Mario turned up and everyone squeezed around the table even closer to accommodate an extra chair. Mario made a bee-line straight for Alistair.

Lucy's attempts to flirt with Alistair were still going nowhere and it was clear that she was now starting to get a little bored. Typical, Alice thought, she always had to be the centre of everything. Back at Uni she just wasn't happy unless she had the men swarming around her like some queen bee. Alice could never understand the attraction. Yes, she was very pretty, that much was true, but there was no substance to her. No redeeming features. She just always came across as a very vain and selfish person.

Lucy turned her attention to Alice, 'Well, I see you have bagged yourself a very good-looking man!' Lucy flashed her eyes towards Alistair. Alice was very embarrassed and was praying Alistair hadn't heard. Lucy continued, 'Let's hope this one lasts longer than the last!'

Alice felt the anger raise within her. How dare she talk to her like that. Sue, however, was quick to intervene. 'How is David, Lucy? You know, the man you are married to?'

Alice was very puzzled by this. Sue was never short with her friends, let alone sarcastic in such a cutting way. Lucy and David had been married since shortly after Uni. Both as vain and as flirtatious as each other but despite this their marriage had always seemed solid. David was very wealthy and their lifestyle suited Lucy who always had to have the latest fashions and accessories, the next big house and car. They had been together for years. But the way Sue had spoken made it sound as if Sue knew something wasn't right between them. Whatever it was, Lucy was now very quiet and didn't respond. In fact, about twenty minutes later, Lucy announced she needed to go and made her excuses.

Alice went to sit next to Sue. 'So what was that all about then, that comment you made to Lucy?'

Sue and Sam leaned forward. Sam started, 'Well apparently, according to Robert, they are no longer living together. Lucy moved out a few weeks ago. Robert thinks it is another married man, he thinks, but hasn't found out who yet.'

Sue interjected, 'Yes, but we are all on a mission to find out!'

Alice really couldn't care less. Lucy was not worth any expenditure of time or effort over. As much as she wasn't keen on David, she thought it a lucky escape for him. She thought back to the conversation she had with Minnie but soon dismissed the thought. Mark and Lucy? No, surely not.

The food arrived and everyone was busy complimenting everyone else's choices. Bella was finding out all about Carla and Mary's new art exhibition and promised to call in much to their delight.

Alice felt she needed to try and get to sit next to Bella and get to know her a bit better. Bella always seemed quite aloof and she really did want the two of them to get on. Alistair was obviously very close to her and the age difference meant that Alistair was also probably a bit of a father figure to her.

Luckily, Simon announced that before pudding, they should all move around and sit with different people. Alice was delighted to find herself now sitting between Alistair and Bella. However, Mario still insisted on sitting next to Alistair on the other side and Alice had never seen someone being given the Spanish Inquisition with such vigour. There wasn't a stone Mario was leaving unturned.

Alice, realising she couldn't get a word in, turned to Bella to compliment her on her beautiful hair. Her thick, long brown hair was looking stunning. Bella wasn't slow in returning the compliments either.

'You look amazing Alice. I love the shoes and dress and your hair transforms you!'

The two talked about Bella's job and, of course, Alistair. It was obvious Bella was very close to him and spoke of him with very high regard indeed. Alice broached the subject of whether Bella had anyone special in her life at the moment to which Bella was quick to say no. 'I find commitment hard, I just like men too much, I guess. I really don't want to get tied down. Not yet anyway. Alistair keeps saying that when I meet that special one etcetera, etcetera but well, it hasn't happened yet. I like the expectations of a new relationship very much but I guess not the reality of it.'

Alice pondered on her words. A part of her envied the clear independence and inner confidence Bella had. She wished she had half the confidence at Bella's age. Alice had always needed the security, the confidence of knowing that one special person was hers, a soul mate.

Alistair turned to her and spoke quietly in her ear, 'You have lovely friends, Alice, I am glad I have had the opportunity to get to know them. They obviously care about and love you very much.'

Alice smiled back at him, 'Well thank you for joining us, it so nice we can all get to know each other. Bella is a lovely neighbour to have.'

Alistair poured everyone another glass of wine. 'So, tell me about you Alice. Bella told me you have recently split up from a long-standing partner, that must have been difficult.'

Alice explained what had happened and Alistair attentively listened. As Alice talked, he became impressed with her frankness and honesty. She didn't mention anyone else in her life at the present time, so Alistair hoped that the two other men he had seen her with now history.

Alice asked about Alistair, 'I think Bella is very lucky to have an older brother to look after her. I know I have always appreciated having Robert.'

Alistair explained about how his parents had married very young and had indeed split up for quite a while, shortly after Alistair was born. However, after many years, his mother and father had decided to get back together again and Bella had been a welcome surprise.

They continued to talk and Alice found herself feeling more and more attracted to the man. He loved his work as a PR Consultant, doing lots of freelance consultancy which took him to many different places. More recently, he had stuck to clientele in the London area but was always open to offers elsewhere. It seemed, from what Alice could gather, he had not been involved in any serious relationships before now but Alice knew that some people were not ready to settle until later in life. They talked about everything from gin, wine, latest travels. Alistair was so knowledgeable. He would get on well with Robert, Alice thought. In fact, Alistair was the sort of man who would get on with anyone. He just had that persona about him.

Alice studied his face. He did have very blue eyes that seemed to engulf one with every word. His mouth was perfect too with very pearly white perfectly shaped teeth. She imagined him kissing her.

Simon was about to order another bottle of wine but the waitress announced it was soon closing. Everyone was surprised at how late it was. Sue, Sam and Nisha ordered a taxi declaring they had drunk far too much and what a very soporific effect it had; their bed was calling. Carla and Mary were going to be at the gallery the next day and were keen to get moving too. Everyone hugged and said their goodbyes and talked about how wonderful it was to meet Alistair and Bella and that they should all meet up again soon.

Alistair organised a taxi for the remaining four of them and Alice was delighted when Simon insisted on sitting next to Bella to catch up on the news. This now meant of course that she could carry on her conversations with Alistair. All were now busily chattering away and they were soon back at the apartments. Simon was quick to help Bella out of the taxi and they walked on up the stairs.

When Alice reached the foot of the stairs, Alistair held his hand out and gently pulled her arm and body towards him.

'I have had a great evening, Alice. Perhaps we can meet up during the week?' Alice suddenly felt her insides churning with butterflies. She felt sure he was now going to kiss her. He moved in towards her and pulled her in even closer. Alice instinctively shut her eyes. However, the kiss she had planned didn't happen because walking through the entrance door at that very moment was Mr Hughes.

'Ah, hope I am not interrupting anything,' Mr Hughes said with a slightly nervous smile. 'I just wondered if this was a good time to catch you both?' However, as per usual, Mr Hughes didn't wait for an answer he waded straight in. 'The thing is, I was wanting to discuss your car, in the guest car parking space.' Mr Hughes was now looking at Alistair.

Alice couldn't believe her ears. It was so late, did the man not sleep? This bloody man was obsessed with the guest car parking space. Why on earth did it matter so much? Mr Hughes never seemed to have any visitors so why did it affect him? This was all getting ridiculous.

Alistair seemed very bemused but very much kept his cool and very calmly said, 'Well, Mr...?'

'Mr Hughes, Mr Dylan Hughes,' came the reply.

'Well Mr Hughes, I think the issue of the guest parking space is one to be resolved but, perhaps, tomorrow? And not at midnight. I think we will all benefit from giving this our full attention and consideration. Don't you? It is after all an important matter to resolve?'

Mr Hughes seemed delighted to finally meet a man who not only had a great deal of common sense but who also understood the gravitas off the situation, a man who clearly understood the importance of rules and regulations.

'Yes, you know you are right, absolutely, perhaps we should meet tomorrow, yes, right well I will let you two get to bed. It is late after all and some of us need our beauty sleep more than others, hey Alice!' Mr Hughes winked at Alice who failed to see the humour in the comment at all.

The moment of a potential passionate enthral, the two of them knew, had passed. A potential long, lingering kiss was now not on the cards. Alice wondered up the stairs thinking of several things she would have liked to have done or said to

Mr Hughes, most of them involving murder.

Simon was busy chattering away with Bella outside the apartment and were making arrangements to visit the gallery the next day asking if Alistair and Alice would like to go too which, indeed, they said they would.

They said their goodnights and off they departed to their respective homes.

'Gosh that bloomin Mr Hughes, I could kill him. In fact, I swear, I will and dispose of the body underneath the bloody guest parking space. Let's face it, no one would miss the man!'

Simon laughed, 'Umm well divulging this to a man in the legal profession is perhaps not the best plan of action.'

Alice kicked off her shoes and collapsed on the sofa. 'I swear if Alistair doesn't take me in his arms very soon and kiss me, I will simply burst.'

Simon sat on the other end of the sofa and Alice rested her legs upon him and he gently massaged her feet.

'Oh gosh Simon you would make the most brilliant partner, I swear!'

Simon discussed how he liked Bella, 'And Alistair seems a very nice chap indeed, I wonder what dark secrets he keeps in his cupboard!'

'Nonsense! There is the cynic in you again. He is perfect, I won't have a bad word said against him!'

'Well, we all have parts of us that could do with either getting rid of or working on, missy, each and every one of us!' Simon stopped massaging her feet and started to look for some music to play through his phone.

Alice went over to the window and looked down at the carpark at Alistair's car. 'There is something very reassuring about an Audi TT, don't you think so, Simon?'

Simon walked over to the window, 'Well yes, he has money you mean?'

'No, no not that!' Alice looked aghast at the thought that Simon thought it was about the money.

'I see, so if he drove an old clapped out Ford Fiesta, he would still have the same appeal, would he?' Simon said, raising his eyebrows in disbelief.

'Simon, Simon, you are such a cynical old thing. I mean Ollie didn't even own a car and did I let that influence me? No, I did not!' No Alice thought to herself, she wasn't like that.

'Ah I see, your disapproval of him had nothing to do with the fact he didn't run a successful business and lives from job to job, place to place living on a shoe string?'

'No of course, not. He was simply an annoying man. Well, I mean he could have got a decent job and stopped being homeless. That is not good financial common sense, particularly as you get older, now is it?' Alice kept admiring the Audi TT, maybe it was time for her to get a new car as well. Her VW did look a bit warn out.

'Umm well I heard he helped the homeless too and has done many a good deed by all accounts.'

'Oh, you seem very well informed on a man you have never met Simon?'

'Well Mario and Sue talk very highly of him; you can often get a measure of a person by the way others talk about them you know.'

Alice really didn't want to spend time dwelling over Ollie, she wanted her thoughts firmly on Alistair.

'Exhibition tomorrow!'

Simon laughed. 'Yes, well thank goodness Carla and Mary are no longer working in the medium of sculpture, just paint! I hope it's not too pornographic. I don't think Bella and Alistair would be too impressed!'

Alice pondered upon these words, 'Oh gosh, I hadn't thought about that! Well now they have got to know them both a bit, I think Alistair will realise that the both of them are a bit eccentric and well, slightly mad but, as Sue would say, their heart is the right place.'

Both decided it was time to turn in for the night and Alice went to bed feeling confident that tomorrow would bring much joy indeed.

35

The Exhibition

The gallery Carla and Mary had hired was on the second floor above a boutique just around the corner from Marylebone station.

Mario had also decided to pop along, intrigued by the conversations he had overheard the previous night.

When in the gallery, they all studied the paintings not quite knowing what to make of them.

'So, Carla,' Alice enquired, 'explain this one again, would you?'

'Ah yes, well this painting is called *Fertility.* It catches the essence of a strong, independent woman, don't you think?'

'Right, yes definitely.' Both Alice and Simon, took a long, thoughtful, look at the picture. All Alice could see was a painting that looked like two pieces of celery flopped over in opposite directions. 'So, tell me what you are seeing here Carla?' Alice was pleased with her attempts not to simply say 'What the hell is this?'

Mary now took over. 'Well if you look closely you will see these lines here are the fallopian tubes, see, just here…' Mary and Carla both went over to their painting to point this out. Mary continued, 'The fallopian tubes are the ultimate sign of womanhood even more than a vagina. A vagina gives birth but the fallopian tubes transports the all-important egg to the uterus so it is really a powerful symbol of creation at its best, don't you think?'

'Oh yes, definitely.' Alice and Simon responded almost in unison.

Carla continued, 'This is probably our masterpiece, the best yet. The ultimate painting to show not just creation but a woman's power to say yes or no.'

Simon and Alice tilted their heads in opposite directions. 'Right, yes, of course,' they both replied nodding quite emphatically but both not having a clue what they were on about.

'I see,' said Simon 'but yes or no to what exactly?'

Carla looked very surprised and almost disappointed that Simon had not realised the answer, 'Well whether she chooses to have a baby or not, of course.'

'Yes, of course, how dense of me.' Simon winked at Alice who quickly jabbed him the side in case his sarcasm was picked up by either of the two artists.

Carla and Mary went over to a prospective client leaving Simon and Alice still musing over the painting.

Mario came over and rather loudly said, 'I don't understand what celery sticks have got to do with fallopian tubes?'

Alistair and Simon couldn't help sniggering but Alice insisted Mario keep his voice down lest he offend Carla and Mary.

They all studied the other paintings and Alice was relieved that none of the actual paintings with the word vagina in them actually resembled vaginas at all. Well, perhaps there was just the one entitled '*The soul in my vagina*' but again Mario thought it just looked like an avocado cut in half.

Alice did her usual thing of buying one of the art pieces and settled on the painting that resembled many hairy caterpillars sitting on a tomato. She thought this would not offend her reinstated cleaner or indeed any of her visitors.

Bella bought the celery picture as a gift for a friend but although Alice wondered what sort of friend would appreciate this, she was very pleased that Carla and Mary had managed to sell another picture and one of their most expensive ones too.

Having viewed and perused all the paintings, they made their excuses and left. Alistair said he knew of a good wine bar in the vicinity that did some light bar snacks and off they went. Once fed and watered Simon headed back to the flat accompanied by Bella but Alistair, Alice and Mario remained. Alice had hoped Mario might have left the two of them alone but no such luck. He was firmly entrenched in his seat and was telling Alistair all about his trip to Sicily and the unfortunate business with the Mafia. Why he needed to tell Alistair all about this, Alice hadn't a clue. She really didn't want Alistair to think Mario had any dealings with such people.

After lunch, Alistair declared that he had to head off home as he needed to be on an early flight to Glasgow the next day. Alice was disappointed but Alistair was quick to make arrangements to take Alice out later in the week. He thought they could do a movie or show followed by dinner. Alice was delighted. Alistair gave her a lingering kiss on the cheek and departed, leaving Alice smiling into her glass of wine.

'Ah, well he seems a nice enough guy,' Mario retorted. 'But, well…' Mario struggled at first to find the words. He mused some more. Alice raised her eyebrows waiting in expectation.

'Well…?'

Mario continued, 'He is pleasant enough, I suppose, but

if you like Alistair why not Ollie? From what I have heard Alistair and Ollie seem to have quite a lot in common. Both well-travelled, amusing tales to tell one. One has money and a very good job the other doesn't. However, Ollie has had many jobs to add to his rich tapestry of life. One has acquired business contacts the other friends for life and I wonder who is the better man for it?' Mario looked hopefully at Alice that she might see what she was missing.

'Look Mario, I know you wanted Ollie and I to get together, I realise that but it just simply isn't going to happen, not now, not ever. So, please just be happy for me, will you? Alistair is the one. I just know it. It's just the feeling I get inside.'

'Well, carra lagazz, dear girl. I must go. So tired and not feeling quite myself today.' Mario slowly got up and kissed Alice on the forehead. 'If he makes you happy then so be it, you have my blessing of course.'

Alice could see the disappointment in Mario's eyes but she knew that once he really got to know Alistair, he would see what she saw and love him. She gave him a big hug and off Mario departed. Alice finished her wine and headed off back to the apartment to spend the evening with Simon. Tomorrow, she thought, was a big day for her. The working world beckoned at last! Life really couldn't get any better.

36

The Working World

Alice was pleased to get back to work. She would now have far more say and control over the firm and was keen to get it established again in all the right quarters. Mr Frobersham soon arrived after Alice but as Alice noted with Miss Havisham. She felt he had needed a little looking after and so she had invited him to stay a few days. Alice thought the old boy looked back to his old self and even had a bit of a spring in his step.

Alice was worried Charles would not be keen on how modern these offices were, compared to the Victorian building he had been used to with the very high, decorated ceilings. These offices were not in the fashionable centre of town. However, thankfully, this was not the case at all. He complimented Alice on the rooms and furniture and headed straight to the largest office, much to Alice's amusement.

Alice had contacted the designer and they all sat together thinking about some new designs that might interest their old clientele but Alice also phoned around to get some appointments in the diary. She was relieved that Mr Chanterelle from Chanel sounded delighted to hear from her and announced how pleased he was that she had decided to return from retirement. He had felt the firm had gone in the wrong direction with Tit-Tassels and did not want his company associated with such a *'common fad'* as he called it. Mr Chanterelle told her about some new fashion designs he had in the pipe line and he would send over some drawings, giving the company the opportunity of quoting for the work.

Miss Havisham set about rearranging one of the office rooms to turn it into a suitable reception area but would stop, every now and again, to make everyone a cup of tea. Mr Frobersham kept complimenting Miss Havisham over the biscuits she had made, declaring no biscuits had ever tasted so good. Miss Havisham was delighted but confessed to Alice that she had actually intended them to be chocolate brownie cakes, not biscuits, but if Charles liked them, well, what did it matter?

Alice knew how Miss Havisham had always had a thing for Charles but the old fool had been completely blind to it. However, Alice could now see that recent events had impacted upon the man. Perhaps now he could see the qualities of this very devoted woman, a woman who had a very good and kind heart. So, Alice was chuffed that the two old birds were smiling and flirting with each other at every opportunity. Love can blossom at any age she thought and the later in life it happens it becomes somehow even more cherished and of substance.

Robert, Malcolm and Sue popped over to find out how everything was going. Sue said she would pop into Mario's for lunch and offered to bring everyone back some sandwiches. Everyone made their orders and Alice, who was watching her figure, gave strict instructions on egg mayo but without too much mayo and absolutely no cake, unless of course Mario had ordered that amazing carrot cake.

Sam also popped by with some flowers and a good luck card. Mr Frobersham complimented Miss Havisham on how wonderfully she had arranged them in the vase, claiming she had enhanced each flower to its full potential. However, Mr Frobersham being Mr Frobersham, had to go that extra mile, 'Luscious woodbine, with sweet musk-roses and with eglantine: There sleeps Titania sometime of the night, Lull'd in these flowers with dances and delight.'

Sam and Alice tried to hold back their obvious amusement of comparing Miss Havisham with Titania but it was to no avail, they both started to giggle in a somewhat schoolgirlish manner thought Mr Frobersham. Miss Havisham, seeing his obvious embarrassment was quick to respond.

'Ah, Charles, my favourite Shakespeare play!'

Mr Frobersham beamed a smile of delight thinking to himself that yes of course this well-educated woman, and a woman of such obvious taste, would know and understand.

Robert started to look at his watch, declaring that Sue was taking her time getting their lunch and moaned that it wouldn't be long before they would need to leave to pick up Ben from school. Robert decided to ring her to find out what the delay was. After some attempts, he was finally able to get through. Alice couldn't quite make out what was going on but it was obvious from Robert's expression that something was very wrong indeed. Robert eventually put the phone down.

'It's Mario. Sue went round to find the café was shut. She went round to the back entrance and on entering the office she found Mario, he wasn't moving or responding. An ambulance has taken him to the hospital.'

On hearing these words, Alice dropped everything. She grabbed her jacket to find her car keys but Robert, knowing the state she was in, insisted he drive and take her. The tears were welling up.

'Oh God, yes he did look so tired yesterday, why didn't I go back with him, it's just I had Simon waiting back at the flat but I should have got him home.' The tears started to stream and Robert who instinctively wanted to console her found himself lost for words.

By the sound of things, Robert thought the ambulance would not be of any help. Sue had said Mario was completely lifeless. She was sure nothing could be done. Robert just couldn't relate this right now to Alice. Sue may have been wrong, there may have been some hope.

Miss Havisham drove the rest of them as they followed Alice and Robert to the hospital. Alice rushed in to the A&E department hardly being able to find the words to find out about Mario. They were eventually ushered into the relative's room and it was there Alice discovered that indeed, Mario, had had a heart attack and despite their efforts were unable to resuscitate him.

Everyone fell silent. No words were forthcoming. Sue went over to put her arm around Alice and they both just sobbed. Malcolm went over to comfort Sam. No one could quite take it in.

37

Time to reminisce

Robert did most of the arrangements for the funeral. Mario only had nephews in Italy and most of them really hadn't had much contact with Mario for some time now, particularly as he had been estranged from his brother for so long during his lifetime. No one knew exactly what had caused the fall out. It was way before Antonio had announced he was gay and left his wife but something had occurred and he never talked about it. Alice knew that Mario had made several attempts to reunite with his brother but nothing had ever come of it.

Sue phoned Ollie to tell him the news and he asked her to let him know when the funeral was and he would make sure he came back for it. Sue could hear the shock and sadness in Ollie's voice. Like Alice, Mario had been more of a father figure to Ollie in his life and he had always been so grateful for the way Mario had supported him. Ollie's dad had once been very friendly with Mario, hence him being Ollie's godfather. However, Mario had never been very impressed with their parenting skills and Ollie was often left to fend for himself.

Alice, took some days at home to try and take stock of it all and Simon who had been doing some business in London cancelled his arrangement to stay with Richard and came back to be with Alice. Simon called on Bella to ask her to contact

Alistair to cancel Thursday evening and Bella was quick to offer any help she could.

Alice stayed huddled up in bed most of the time and Simon cooked the meals and generally took care of her. He was unable to distract her with her favourite movies or tempt her out for a walk so he just sat and hugged her whenever she needed it.

Robert had been able to arrange the funeral for the end of the month. Knowing that Mario had been greatly loved in his community, Sue posted details of the funeral in the café shop window just in case anyone wanted to pay their last respects.

What everyone hadn't anticipated was the huge turnout at St Robert's Church in Farringdon for the funeral Mass. This man had obviously been greatly loved and admired. Alice had been asked if she wanted to do the eulogy but she really didn't think she could hold it together to do this. Ollie kindly offered and everyone agreed it was apt that Mario's godson should say a few words.

It was the first time Alice had seen Ollie in a suit and he brushed up very well indeed. She could see how difficult this was going to be for him so, as he got up to speak to the congregation, she squeezed his hand and he gratefully smiled and nodded in appreciation.

'Thank you to everyone who is here today. The kind messages that have been received have been truly overwhelming. Seeing how packed the church is today, shows how Mario was a greatly respected and well-loved man. I don't think there is anyone here in the Church today who hasn't at some point had the benefit of wisdom or kindness, or indeed both, that Mario bestowed on all he met. He accepted people for who they were and would always encourage one not to dwell on the past but to look to the future, to make the most of the opportunity's life has to offer. Mario would often say that whenever someone new comes into your life, don't ever pass the opportunity of getting to know them, spend time with them, for every person has hidden treasures. Finding the very best in people was a fundamental part of who he was. Mario was an immensely loyal person, once he befriended you, then there was no chance he would ever forget you or decide to move on to other friendships. Mario was a great believer in people and in loyalty.'

At this point, Ollie hesitated, he was clearly struggling to continue and he lowered his head trying to summon up the courage to continue. Alice instinctively got up and went to stand beside him. She continued, 'Yes everyone's life was truly the richer for knowing him.'

Ollie was clearly overwhelmed that Alice had come to stand beside him and as she continued to talk, he could understand the great love and respect Mario had for her.

After the Mass, everyone, without exception, complimented them both on a great eulogy stating that Mario would have been very pleased and proud of them both.

Only a few went on to the actual burial service. Alice looked around and studied the people. Aunt Betty was there with Robert and Sue. Malcolm nodded across at her and winked, mustering up a smile to reassure her. Alice noted how he had put his hand on Sam's shoulder during the funeral to offer her comfort too. Sue reached out to hold Ollie's arm. They all paid their last respects and left for the wake which was to be held in a nearby venue around the corner from St Robert's.

Again, there was a great turnout. Alice, Ollie and Sue had done their best to get around to say their thankyous to all who had attended. Alice was pleased to finally meet Abramo and his girlfriend.

'Yes I very grateful to Mario for all he did for me. Very sad business about his brother. I be amazed he gave me so much time, considering… well considering everything.'

Yes, Alice thought, considering you were partly responsible for Mario's brother's demise and then Mario being dragged into it all. However, this was not a time for unkind words. Mario would not have approved. Abramo's girlfriend couldn't speak much English so trying to have a conversation with her was very difficult. Nonetheless Alice endeavoured to try.

'How long are you planning to stay for?' Alice enquired

'Until I find goat.'

Alice thought she must have misheard the woman; she must have meant coat?

'Excuse me?'

'Goat. I need goat. English goat very good.'

'Ah, I see, yes, of course. I didn't realise English goats were so, well so sought after?'

'Yes, English goat give plenty milk and very friendly.'

'Right well that is good.' Alice was wondering how she was going to get the goat past quarantine but she thought it best not to pursue that line of enquiry.

Even Henry had turned up. 'Lovely man, knew how to make a proper cup of coffee. One of the very few who did you know.'

'Indeed,' said Alice.

'He knew just how much to froth the milk and put on just the right amount of chocolate sprinkles. Yes, he will be greatly missed indeed. So, do you know who will take the café over now?'

Alice, feeling slightly irritated that the only thing Henry

was worried about was his cappuccino, made her excuses and decided she needed to find a quiet space. The venue had some gardens out the back and Alice wondered around following a path that led to a pagoda adorned with clematis.

'I see you needed some time out too then.' A voice came from behind her. Alice turned around.

'Ollie, lovely to see you, please come and sit down.' Alice patted the seat beside her and Ollie duly sat down. Silence ensued and then they both started to speak at once. Smiling they invited each other to continue. Alice went first.

'Thank you so much for such a lovely speech Ollie. Mario would have been so delighted.' Alice put her hand out again to touch his hand.

'Well I had a bit of a wobble at the end, thanks for coming up to join me, that was a very kind and thoughtful thing to do.'

They looked into each other's eyes and, at that moment, Alice felt that same connection as she had done that night at the cottage. He gave her that strange feeling in the pit of her stomach that she just couldn't explain.

Ollie studied those very blue eyes of hers and gently squeezed her hand too. He regretted not heeding Mario's words of advice but had now heard all about Alistair from Sue and Robert and knew where her affections truly lay. He made his excuses that it was time to get back to the guests and duly left. Alice really didn't know what to make of the encounter. Everything was now such a muddle. He had only come back for the funeral and then he would be gone again.

Later that evening, back at Sue and Robert's, they all reminisced about Mario. Robert put on one of Mario's favourite songs sung by Mary Hopkins and they all sang along to *Those*

Were the Days.

Next, people started to recount their many tales of Mario. Aunty Betty had remembered how kind Mario had been when her husband died. Sue and Alice remembered how cross Mario would get when they bunked off school to avoid handing in any unfinished homework and how they would go and hide in Mario's café. He would always insist they got their homework done, getting very cross with them chastising them. He told them a good education was the sure key to success in life but, whilst getting angry and moaning, he always plied them with hot chocolate and pastries.

Ollie talked about all the contacts Mario had and that whenever Ollie needed a job, Mario would always seem to know someone in every nook and cranny of the world that could give Ollie some paid work or put him up for the night.

After several bottles of wine and the world was put to rights, slowly one by one, everyone said their goodbyes leaving just Alice, Ollie, Sue and Robert to chat. Ollie was staying the night at Sue's and Alice had agreed to stay on the guest bed in Ben's room. After Sue and Robert cleared up the pizza boxes and kitchen and put Ben back to bed for the fourth time that evening, they said their goodnights and Alice and Ollie were left to finish the wine.

'So how is America then?' Alice enquired

'Well there are certainly people there who have a great deal of money and then there are those who have none. No real welfare system for the poor and no healthcare unless you are over sixty-five so a country of many extremes indeed and a strange one too.' Ollie went over to the book case and started studying its contents.

'America is a country I have never been to. I have always fancied going there for New Year but have never got around to it. I've always loved the old Sinatra song *New York, New York* and wanted to visit there and wake up after New Year's Eve having discovered its magic the night before. I agree with you though, I wouldn't want to live there. So, you are not planning staying long term then?'

'No, my job to set the gallery up and get it going is coming to an end but I will go back there to finish what I started and then who knows where life will take me next.'

Alice smiled, remembering Mario's words of Ollie being the great wandering nomad. No, he would never change, that was for sure.

'Well, wherever you end up Ollie, I hope we can always be friends.'

'Absolutely.' Ollie felt deep down this was not going to happen. He had too many feelings for her. It would all be too complicated.

Alice found herself saying the words but deep down herself wasn't sure it was a sensible thing to say. Somehow, she knew that being friends with Ollie was never going to be that simple.

Alice got up to go to bed but having had too much to drink, was a bit unsteady and knocked over her glass. It shattered on the floor and having previously kicked off her heels to feel more comfortable, she promptly cut her foot as soon as she got up to retrieve the broken glass.

'Damn, that is so painful!' She sat back down again and Ollie made his way over to help pick the glass up. Spotting the blood now coming out of her foot, he stopped and grabbed his hankie out of his pocket and placed it on her cut foot. As he held her foot, she felt again this strange sensation. He looked up into her eyes and just at that very moment he too felt overwhelmed. Both having had too much to drink threw caution to the wind and they leaned forward and another kiss happened.

Every part of her seemed to completely want to give herself to this man. His kiss seemed to completely devour her and they held each other so tightly. For several minutes they seem lost in the sheer bliss of the situation. However, it was Ollie who decided it was best to end the kiss. He knew this was just complicating matters. Again, this was not the right time, she was overwhelmed by grief, it was not a good time to be caught in something that obviously meant no more than a casual fling to her. Alistair came to mind and he held back.

Alice looked in Ollie's eyes. He would soon be gone again. He would never settle. She would only get hurt, once again. He would never commit.

They both simultaneously got up from the sofa. They resumed picking up the last fragments of the glass and Alice retreated to bed leaving Ollie with his glass of wine and feelings of complete and utter frustration. He was too late, he knew it.

38

Walk Away

Alice once again returned to the working world. She needed to keep looking forward, that is what Mario would have said, that is what Mario would have told her. That is what Mario would have done. She must move on, get the business back on its feet.

On returning, she was delighted to hear the news that Mr Frobersham had been in contact with some of his old friends from 'The Club' as he called it and some more orders were soon on their way. Alice was particularly pleased with the order from Liberty's; this was definitely a triumph to be back on the books of this renowned and established business of many years. To have them was a great coup and would do wonders for their marketing of the company.

Alice was also pleased to see how Mr Frobersham was now regularly arriving with Miss Havisham of a morning. Alice had never seen Miss Havisham positively glowing and as happy as she was. Mr Frobersham was very attentive and Alice loved the way he always opened the car door for Miss Havisham and how Miss Havisham would then straighten his already perfectly straightened tie for him. She wondered why it had taken the old fool so long to realise the love and high regard Miss Havisham had always had for him. Men can be so blind she thought!

Ben was due to visit her new offices straight after school today and he would be a very welcome distraction for her. She knew she just had to keep herself busy. Every now and again, though, she would think about her kiss with Ollie. She really must curb the amount of alcohol she had around the man. She felt a bit guilty as she thought of Alistair but, well, they weren't actually going out as a couple yet. It wasn't as if she had cheated on him. Alistair had sent her the loveliest card and flowers with the note '*Thinking of you. xx*' She had kept touching the flowers and smelling them, taking them into the bedroom of an evening to look at them before she went to sleep. It really was an enormous bouquet! Even Mr Hughes had commented on them as she set off for work. He had nearly frightened her to death as he seemed to appear from nowhere from behind the rhododendron bush, now growing profusely in front of her carparking space

'Well, now, that is the fanciest bouquet I think I have ever seen, must have cost a fortune. Camellias you know are very pricey indeed, mind you there were only four of those.'

Alice, as angry as she tried to be, somehow couldn't be. Gosh this man spotted everything, literally everything but there was a part of herself that was glad the bouquet had been noticed.

Later that day, at around four o'clock, Robert had dropped Ben off. It didn't take long for Ben to find his way to Mr Frobersham's large leather swivel chair. As he was testing it out and swivelling at high speed, he decided it was a good chance to talk to his aunt about a very serious matter. 'So then Aunty Alice are you going to marry him or not?' Ben put his hands up in the air as if he was just simply exasperated by his aunt.

'Well I think it is early days in our relationship to tell that yet Ben, don't you?'

'No, not at all. I mean you have known him for months and months. He has everything a girl could want. He is an amazing footballer, a great cook, almost as good as mum, he plays air guitar like a true pro and his karate moves are simply the best. Don't you agree? And he knows how to milk an alpaca!'

Alice soon, of course, realised Ben was not talking about Alistair but Ollie, yet again.

'Look Ben, Ollie and I are good friends and that is all, absolutely and completely that is all there is to it. Okay? And I am not sure about the alpaca Ben?'

Ben stopped swivelling. 'Mum says you should never look a gift horse in the mouth.'

'Right, well as wise and as clever as your mum is Ben, Ollie and I are just friends, that is all.'

Ben raised his eyebrows in great disapproval, 'Women, so complicated.'

Alice smiled, she knew exactly where he had heard that statement from and would need to have words with her brother later.

'Now here is a diary I meant to give you, it's a freebie from one of the local companies, I thought you might like to keep it and record the best events of the day. What do you think?' Alice handed Ben the diary and a pen. He seemed quite enthusiastic and the diary, thankfully, did the job of distracting him from any more talk of Ollie.

Miss Havisham made Ben a hot chocolate and soon after he was persuaded to get on with his homework whilst Alice made a few more phone calls. It wasn't long before Sue then turned up to take him home.

'Are you coming for tea tonight Alice? Miss Havisham you are very welcome too?'

'Ah, thank you dear, no Mr Frobersham is taking me out for dinner tonight,' beamed Miss Havisham.

Sue and Alice winked at each other in a very suggestive manner and Miss Havisham tutted at them both but was clearly enjoying the moment.

Alice declined the offer much to Ben's disappointment. 'No, I can't tonight, I really must get down to this paperwork and file it before…before I forget.'

Sue raised her eyebrows, 'You don't need to worry about Ollie. He is only with us briefly this evening before going back to stay with Florian tonight and then back to the States tomorrow. You are not trying to avoid him again are you?'

'Gosh no I wouldn't be doing that, no, just really busy Sue.'

'Uhm I see, well the offer is open if you decide to change your mind and come over later, I can always keep some for you in the oven. Think about it.' Sue continued. 'Ollie has been a real help sorting out the café with Robert and contacting the solicitor and everything.'

Alice felt guilty she had not helped with any of this but she just couldn't face it.

'That is really good of Ollie, Sue, thank him for me, will you?'

'Or,' Sue held out her hand to hold Alice's, 'you can thank him yourself?'

'Yes, well maybe I will pop over later, let me see how things go.'

However, Sue knew Alice wouldn't. Something had occurred between them, yet again, she could just sense it and Ollie wouldn't be drawn into any conversations about Alice at all either with her or Robert. Sue couldn't make up her mind about Ollie and Alice. She just had a gut feeling that Ollie would settle and make a go of things if the two of them got together. Sue liked Alistair, she really did, but she had far more of a soft spot for Ollie. He could so do with being a little looked after instead of always looking after everyone else. He was so like Mario; it was a shame that Alice and him had got off to such a bad start.

Sue and Ben then departed to leave Alice to her thoughts.

Alice returned to her hot chocolate and biscuit or was it cake? Miss Havisham had been baking again.

No, she wouldn't call in tonight. She would write to him and thank him. Yes, that is what she would do. Besides, Bella had mentioned Alistair might call in one evening this week and she really didn't want to be out when he called.

39

Florian

Ollie was also very unsettled. Why did she evoke such feelings in him? Why did it always have to be so hard? She clearly had something going on with Alistair. He noticed how her eyes lit up when his name was mentioned. Besides, could he really compete with a man with his Audi TT and top PR consultancy job. Those were things that Alice obviously thought were important, that she obviously judged a man by. A woman like that just wouldn't be right for him.

He sat on Florian's balcony and looked out at the various hues of oranges that were lighting up the evening sky. Florian sensed something wasn't quite right with his friend. He had been so quiet and not his usual self at all. Well, he had just lost his godfather and he knew how much closer Ollie had become to Mario in recent months. He went out to join him on the balcony to see if he might like to talk.

'Well this is certainly a beautiful evening,' Florian said.

'Indeed, and a beautiful view Florian, you have a fantastic apartment.' Ollie continued to watch the evening sunset.

'How are Robert and Sue?' Florian asked. 'I know Sue in particular was very close to Mario and I believe, what is her name, the rottweiler you called her? She was too.'

Ollie smiled.

Florian continued, 'Now that is the first smile I have seen today, Ollie. So how is the rottweiler then?'

Well, she is fine, Alice is good. She was hit hard by Mario's death but I know she will be fine. She is a survivor and she has many people around her to support her. Yes, she will be fine.' Ollie drank his wine and everything fell silent again. Florian decided just to sit with his friend. Words may come he thought. A few minutes passed. His patience was rewarded.

'The problem is Florian, just when I thought that, well, maybe I might settle here in London, well now I think the moment has passed.' Ollie looked at Florian who nodded. A few more minutes silence ensued.

'I mean it's not as if I didn't try with her, I really did but well circumstances and events and...' Ollie paused and drank some more wine.

'I see, so tell me my friend, a little more. I need to try and understand the story, the events, you need to tell me some more.'

So, Ollie related to his friend the whole story from the very first encounter with Alice. Florian sat and listened in earnest.

'I see. Well if I was to put myself in her shoes, I can understand maybe some of her thinking, maybe not all her actions but yes some of her thoughts maybe?'

Ollie looked at Florian, 'Really? Well please enlighten me Florian because I find her all very hard to understand indeed and somewhat, well, quite frankly frustrating. Just too much like hard work.'

'Well, I think you may be a little harsh Ollie. Look at it from her point of view. She sees a man who is known to the family as the travelling nomad, the man who regular travels around,

349

doesn't want to settle down, doesn't want the usual trappings of life. She had just lost a soul mate. Someone she thought she would happily spend the rest of her life with. Some people, Ollie, need security that special someone. Your lifestyle would not have reassured her of this now, would it?'

Ollie pondered some more.

Florian continued, 'You are clearly attracted to each other, that is for certain. I think you got off to the wrong start that is all. I think had circumstances been different and Mario hadn't needed to go to Sicily then maybe things would be different but then again, Ollie, you wouldn't have taken over the café. Everything happens for a reason.'

Ollie pondered some more. 'The thing is, what about this Alistair guy? She obviously has feelings for him. I mean here is a guy who has it all, the lifestyle she wants, everything.' Ollie went to pour some more wine out of the bottle.

Florian considered this. 'Now you cannot say this with real conviction or knowledge. She has her own independent means by the sound of things. From what you tell me, and from what Mario told you about her, it doesn't sound as if she is shallow enough to just want a man for what he can offer her in way of money and all that brings. Alistair is there, regularly there and available, that is the attraction. A car and a great job may help Ollie but there are far more important things in life.' Florian was joined by Emily. They sat together and held hands.

Florian continued, 'But from what you say, it is only in its early stages so what have you got to lose, my friend, by being straight with her. Tell her your feelings but make sure Ollie you really are ready to settle. Make sure you can make that commitment. Otherwise, maybe it is best you keep travelling my friend. All I can tell you is how happy I have been since I met Emily.' Florian put his arm around her and they both gave each other a warm smile, 'You really don't know what you are missing my friend!'

Florian got up. 'But make your decision Ollie because you have your flight tomorrow and if you leave her again, then yes I think Alistair will be a strong contender for her affections.' They both wondered back into the apartment leaving Ollie to muse over his words.

Ollie continued to look at the evening sky. When he thought of her, he really didn't want her to be with someone else. He really did want to make a go of it. Yes, Florian was probably right. She did need the security and needed to know that he would be dependant, reliable, steadfast. He could be all that, he just needed to tell her, to reassure her. He grabbed his jacket and much to the delight of Florian and Emily, he left.

40

A matter of urgency.

Alice wondered over to the flowers. The camellias were now in full bloom. She touched the flower gently with her hand and bent over to smell the wonderful perfume.

Mr Hughes had been knocking on all the flat doors trying to drum up some membership for his beloved Howarth Court Committee. Alice reluctantly opened the door and politely took the leaflet and pretended to read it in front of him while he talked *at* her.

'I always provide tea and biscuits at the meetings but if you have any allergies you will need to bring your own. Next Tuesday's meeting, as do all the Howarth Court meetings, start promptly at 7.00 pm. I am strict about no chitter chatter as I like to get straight down to business. Meetings never last more than two hours.'

Two hours! Alice couldn't imagine what possibly needed to be discussed to fill two whole hours! But, then again, Mr Hughes did like the sound of his own voice.

'Thank you, Mr Hughes, well I will give it some very careful consideration.' As she shut the door, she promptly threw the leaflet in the bin.

Alice looked out of the flat window up to the evening sky. It looked so beautiful and the birds were chirping away in the trees. Alice was delighted to see Alistair's car parked in its usual space and very much hoped he would pop in to see her.

She had changed into something casual but very feminine she thought, yes and sexy too. She refreshed her make-up, sprayed herself with perfume and then perused her cd collection. She decided on some Rolling Stones and snuggled into her chair and cushions and started to read her book.

It wasn't long before the doorbell went and she was delighted to find Alistair there with yet even more flowers.

She invited him in. 'Alistair that is so kind, even more flowers!' Alice went to get a vase.

'I hope I am not intruding or interrupting anything. Just thought I would see how you are?' Alistair stepped in but both were unaware he had not fully closed the door behind him.

Alice offered Alistair a drink and he accepted coffee. On making the drinks they wondered over to the sofa and sat and chatted a while. Alistair enquired about the funeral. He hoped it had all gone well and told her how much he had enjoyed talking to Mario when he met him.

'He clearly thought very highly of you Alice. I think he was very protective of you, gave me a real grilling he did!'

'Oh, yes that was Mario. He really did treat me like one of his own. I couldn't have been luckier to have someone who would always look out for me. I loved him so much, I really did.' Alice's voice faltered and she felt the tears come to her eyes.

Alistair was quick to respond and took out his hanky and sat next to her. He gently wiped the tears away and squeezed her hand. 'It is always so difficult at first, I know, but things will get better. You have had a rough ride recently but I promise you, it will get better.'

Alice wiped her nose and now worried about her make-up. 'Silly me, gosh I bet I look like a panda now, make-up smudged and everything.'

Alistair laughed 'Well only a bit like a panda!' He winked at her.

Alice laughed.

'No, Alice, you look stunning, you always do.' Alistair leaned forward.

Alice knew it, this was the moment, this was the moment she had been waiting for. Finally, Alistair was going to kiss her, it was just meant to be! Her stomach felt the usual butterflies and she closed her eyes as Alistair kissed her. He took her in his arms and yes, he was kissing her!

However, unbeknown to the pair of them, at this very same moment, Ollie seeing the door open had come in knocking quietly on the door but it had fallen on deaf ears. He bobbed his head around the hallway door and looked into the living room. There was Alice kissing Alistair! Well, that was that he thought. Too late. It clearly wasn't to be and Ollie left and headed down the stairs. He would get that flight. That was now a certainty. It just wasn't to be.

On the way out he passed Mr Hughes who was standing outside number 2's flat waiting for the door to be opened.

Mr Hughes turned to acknowledge him, 'Ah and you are…?'

Ollie didn't reply and just walked straight past him. Mr Hughes recognised the man but couldn't quite place him. He noticed how very forlorn the man looked but it was clear to Mr Hughes, the man did not want to engage with him. Ollie left.

Alice completely unaware of her visitor had now been kissed by Alistair but what happened next came as a complete surprise.

Strange, she thought, why didn't she feel more elated? This man of her dreams, literally her dreams, had just kissed her. Alice looked in Alistair's eyes. Something didn't feel quite right.

'Alistair, I need you to kiss me again. Would you kiss me again?'

Alistair smiled and was very pleased to oblige. Alice thought one more kiss, yes that was all that was needed. She would then feel what she was supposed to feel. Alistair kissed her again.

Alice felt confused. This didn't feel like it was supposed to feel? The kiss, the moment, didn't feel the way she thought it would. This couldn't be right? What was wrong? Alistair sensing something, stopped the kiss.

'Alice?'

'Alistair, I think I must be tired, that's all. I just think I need to rest.'

Alice got up from the sofa. She really didn't know what to think and neither did Alistair.

Alistair decided it best to leave, to give her some space. The last few weeks would have been very hard for her. 'Well, Bella is waiting for me, I really must go.'

Alice walked Alistair to the door. She turned to Alistair. 'Alistair, I'm sorry. I am really sorry but…' She didn't need to finish her sentence.

'No, no that is fine, please don't worry.'

Alice couldn't believe the words that came out of her mouth but they did, 'No, I am sorry, this just isn't for me.' She couldn't explain it. She really couldn't. She had waited so long for this moment and now it had arrived, it wasn't what she thought it would be.

Alistair smiled and took her hand, 'That is fine, Alice, don't worry,' and with those words he left.

Alice shut the door. She really didn't know what to say or what to feel. She felt in more turmoil than she had ever felt.

Alice went into the bedroom and hurled herself on the bed.

'Oh Lord, I can't believe I have just turned down Alistair, of all men, Alistair?' She sank her head into the pillow and cried. The kiss, the long-awaited kiss and she felt nothing. Nothing inside at all. What was wrong with her?

Alice sobbed herself to sleep. She awoke the next day and decided to get into the office early. She needed to keep busy, really busy.

When Miss Havisham and Mr Frobersham arrived it soon became very clear that something clearly wasn't right with Alice. Miss Havisham went to go and make her a cup of tea and Alice started to sob. Mr Frobersham, not knowing quite what to do, retreated back to his office to let Miss Havisham sort it all out.

'Right, now Alice, this is never going to do is it?' Miss Havisham reached for the box of tissues and gently wiped Alice's tears away.

'I can't believe it Miss Havisham, the one man I have waited a life time for and I have told him to go away. I can't understand it.'

'Ah, this is Ollie I presume?'

Alice looked most surprised, 'No, Alistair, of course!'

'Umm well it seems to me dear you were always barking up the wrong tree there. As lovely as your Alistair was or is rather, he clearly is not the one for you.'

Alice looked surprised, 'Barking up the wrong tree? What do you mean?' Alice finished wiping her nose.

'Yes dear, falling in love with the wrong man,' Miss Havisham continued, 'Look I think you need to go home and have a good think. It seems clear to everyone that perhaps the man you really should be with is Ollie.'

'Oh, not you too Miss Havisham. I know that yes when he kisses me I do feel kind of strange all over and yes I do know I keep dreaming about him. Yes, I do dream about him and everyone says he is the salt of the earth kind of guy, just like Mario and okay yes he does have those amazing eyes and he is tall and he really can kiss a woman but...'

Alice stopped. She took in a deep breath. 'But the thing is, well the thing is he will never settle down and, besides, he keeps leaving me!'

'Ah well, sometimes a man needs a little nudge in the right direction dear. A little persuading that life is far better with you in it than without you. That life has much to offer with that one special soul mate. And you dear, are just right for that man. We all agree. All of us.'

'All of you?'

'Yes, indeed, all of us.' Miss Havisham was not to be swayed. 'That man has more substance in his little finger, more heart, more, well more of everything than any man I have had the pleasure of encountering. Now go home and have a think about it. Take the day off and life will seem better tomorrow I promise you!'

Alice heeded her words and set off home. She parked in the car park. Unfortunately, Mr Hughes was there again and came over to tell her that she needed to straighten her car up a bit. At this moment, Alice saw red.

'Mr Hughes, will you please stop telling me how to park or unpark my car, it really isn't any help at all you know and frankly…' but Alice didn't get to finish her words.

Mr Hughes was in full throttle and anything she was saying was clearly falling on deaf ears, yet again.

'I now remember who that man was from yesterday evening. It has finally come to me!'

'What man, what are you talking about Mr Hughes?' Alice really didn't have time to mess about and wanted to get into a hot bath and forget about life.

'That nice man who brought you home that night. You know that night when he took you home in a taxi?'

'You mean Ollie, Mr Hughes?'

'Yes, that's the chap the one that brought you the flowers and left them on your doorstep.'

'You mean Alistair, Mr Hughes?' Alice thought the old fool had got them muddled up.

'No, no,' laughed Mr Hughes, 'I know Alistair. I mean he uses the guest car parking space enough doesn't he? No, I know who Alistair is! No, no the other tall chap, good looking but a bit dishevelled at times. What did you say his name was? Ollie, yes that is right, Ollie. He gave you that lovely huge bouquet of flowers. He was here yesterday evening too; he had been up to your flat.'

Alice remembered the card '*Thinking of you xxx*' Gosh! It wasn't Alistair at all.

Alice turned away as if to walk back to the flat but then something inside of her made her stop. 'Oh Lord, he was here, here at the flat last night! Alice remembered the door that was ajar. He would have seen me and Alistair together!'

Deep down in the pit of her stomach she could feel the panic rise within her. She remembered back to when Ollie had kissed her that second time. The way he had held her. The way she had wanted him to continue. Her eyes lit up.

'Ollie, oh goodness, why have I been such a fool!' Alice started to sob again.

Mr Hughes didn't quite know what to do with this sobbing woman, other than give her his handkerchief. 'Here, now, now, there, there, take this,' but on seeing how much tears and other stuff was now coming out of her nose he thought it best to add a proviso, 'However, it would be nice if you would give it a bit of a wash, before returning it, please.'

Alice started to shake. She remembered Ollie was leaving today. Leaving to go to the airport. This time he might not bother coming back particularly if he thought she was with Alistair.

She started to look for her car keys. She had only just had them. Where on earth were they? Mr Hughes was now very concerned about this somewhat distraught lady wanting to get back into the car.

'I am sorry Mr Hughes I need to go. I need to get to the airport. I think I have made the most dreadful mistake.'

Mr Hughes, seeing the state she was in thought it his duty to protest. 'Now, young lady, there is no way you can drive in the state you are in! You will get yourself arrested again, that is what will happen and I don't think we need any more scandals here in Howarth Court do you? Might lower the price of the neighbourhood you see.' Mr Hughes looked most concerned.

Alice cried out, 'Mr Hughes I must get to the airport, it is an emergency! He is leaving!'

'Who is leaving?' Mr Hughes thought she was now well and truly hysterical.

'The man I love, Ollie of course.'

Mr Hughes, always loving a crisis, swiftly took the car keys from her hand.

'Right, well, I had better drive then. Much more sensible. It means I can park the car and you can go straight into the terminal. You can pay me for the parking later.'

They both hurried around to their respective seats and off Mr Hughes went.

'So what time is the plane leaving then?'

Alice realised she didn't know and made a speedy call to Sue. It seemed to take forever for Sue to answer her mobile.

'Come on Sue, answer, come on!'

Finally, a voice at the other end, 'Hello?' Sue had been enjoying a cuppa with Sam both having been just lamenting on the fact that Ollie was leaving and what a shame it was.

'Sue, Sue it's Alice what time does Ollie's plane leave?'

'Twelve, midday, I think. Yes, twelve that's right. Florian should be taking him to the airport as we speak.'

Alice looked at the time. 10.00 am already.

'Sue get to the airport now, you are nearer than me, get there I will meet you. Don't let him get on the plane. Whatever you do, don't let him on the plane.' Sue duly and happily responded to her friend's urgent request and leapt out of her seat and rushed to the staircase.

'Robert, Ben, quick we are going up to the airport.' Sue shouted up the stairs. Robert and Ben emerged at the top and Sam came out of the kitchen.

'What an earth are we going to the airport for? I thought Florian was taking Ollie?'

'Yes, yes, but quick no time to explain now, I can do that

in the car.'

'I'll come too.' Sam was just as curious to find out what this was all about.

Robert grabbed his car keys, 'Right, well I will drive.'

So now Mr Hughes was driving Alice and Robert was driving Sue, Ben and Sam. Everyone was heading to Heathrow.

Sue explained their mission was to stop Ollie getting on the plane.

'So, why does Alice want to stop Ollie getting on the plane?' asked Robert, confused by all the rush.

They all looked at each other 'Well, it is obvious isn't it?' Both ladies tutted at Robert. Ben was so excited, 'Yes Dad, it is obvious, really it is. Dad don't you know anything?'

Robert still looked confused.

'Dad, Aunty Alice doesn't want Ollie to leave, of course.' Ben just shook his head in disbelief that his Dad just not getting it.

'Right, I see,' said Robert 'But what about Alistair?'

Everyone just tutted again and nodded their heads in disbelief.

Meanwhile, Mr Hughes announced how pleased he was that he had done his advanced driving test. 'Yes, I knew it would come in handy. I am far more qualified to be driving in an emergency you know, than you, young lady. After all, it imperative to be the safest driver one can be you know, roads can be a dangerous place. Let's face it people like you are on the roads.'

Alice, let that comment go. After all, he was giving up his time to take her. 'Yes, yes Mr Hughes, you are an excellent driver but you need to put your foot down! We will miss him!'

'Now, now Alice. We must observe the speed limits you know. It is the law.'

Alice blasphemed at every set of traffic lights. The minutes seemed to go by just too quickly. She was never going to get there! If he had to go through security an hour before departure, she needed to get there fast.

'Mr Hughes if you don't put your foot your bloody foot down, I am going to stop this car right now and drive myself, is that clear?'

Mr Hughes worried about being driven by an hysterical woman, decided the best course of action was to increase his speed but be vigilant for any police cars.

Meanwhile, Florian and Ollie had got to the airport somewhat flustered. Ollie had left his passport at Florian's having put it in his jacket which was still sitting in one of the wardrobes. Realising this half way there, they had to turn back to get it.

Ollie had not spoken to Florian about what had happened the previous night, but Florian knew from Ollie's arrival back home, things had not gone to plan. Ollie just felt the urgent need to get on the plane. To leave and get on with his life.

They arrived at security somewhat flustered, Florian put his hand on Ollie's shoulder, 'Well my friend, don't forget you always will have a bed at ours. I hope the gallery continues to be a success.'

An announcement came over the Tannoy.

'Last call for Virgin Atlantic flight VS4031, passengers please make their way through security.'

Ollie hugged his friend. 'Yes indeed. Thanks for everything Florian. You are a good friend indeed.'

Just at that moment Ollie could see Ben running towards him in the distance, shouting at the top of his voice with Sue and Sam trying to keep up with him.

'Ollie, Ollie,' Ben shouted. He ran as fast as his little legs would take him.

'You mustn't get on that plane!' Ben hurled himself into Ollie. Ollie looked amazed.

'Please don't get that plane!' Ben pleaded

Ollie could see how upset Ben looked.

'Look, pal, I am late for the plane. I will write and send you postcards, just as always Ben. I promise. But I need to get the flight. I'll be back, some time, I promise.'

'No! You don't understand. Aunty Alice says you can't get on the plane she needs to see you.'

Ollie really didn't know what to make of this?

Sue and Sam had now caught up with them. They were both so out of breath they could hardly speak. Sue tried to take in a big breath, 'Ollie, Alice is on her way now, she needs to talk to you.'

Ollie heard the announcement over the Tannoy again. He had to go. He couldn't wait any longer, the plane wouldn't wait.

'Look Sue, I think she just feels bad about us leaving on bad terms. Tell her everything is fine between us. I understand. Now, I need to get the flight.'

Alice had never run so fast; she had never felt such an urgent need to see anyone in her life before. She spotted Ollie turning away from Ben and walking towards Security.

'Ollie, Ollie!' she shouted, 'don't you dare go a step further. If you go a step further, I swear I will, well I…' Alice didn't know what she would do.

Ollie turned around and walked towards her, 'I need to get on this flight, we both know why. No hard feelings, I promise. I wish you and Alistair all the best, I really do.' Ollie gave Alice a kiss on the cheek and turned to walk through security.

Alice had never felt so sick, sick in the pit of her stomach. She couldn't let him go. This was not going to be another *Gone with the Wind* she was determined.

'You stupid man. You have got it all wrong, as per usual, stop, just stop and listen you stubborn man. Yes, I know you saw Alistair and I together but you don't understand. He kissed me but the thing is Ollie, I didn't feel a thing, not a thing. I don't know why I didn't, but I didn't. Then I remembered when you kissed me and as irritating and as annoying and as maddening as you are, I realise that it is you Ollie. I love you, it's as simple as that.'

Ollie looked at her, not quite believing what he was hearing.

Ben came to take Ollie's hand and then Alice's.

'I told you both, you wouldn't listen to me, either of you.' Ben looked very pleased with himself for being right.

Ollie looked at Ben. Alice looked at Ben. Everyone smiled.

Ollie leaned forward and kissed Alice. It was the best kiss Alice had ever known. This just felt so right. Perfect she thought.

Robert and Mr Hughes had finally arrived together.

Robert just stood in disbelief staring at his little sister, 'Gosh this is a bit unexpected, isn't it?'

Sue, Sam, Ben and Florian just tutted and smiled.

Mr Hughes shook his head, 'Well I hope they are not going to spend all day kissing; the car park costs a fortune!'

So that was that. Everyone had been right, Alice and Ollie became the best of friends, lovers and soul mates. Ollie, having been left Mario's café in his will, enjoyed being settled in London. All agreed there was no one better to take over

Mario's café than Ollie. Ben was delighted to have an Uncle and even happier to have two newly adopted cousins, a little older than him, but both with the same passion for football.

Eighteen months came and went and Christmas had arrived yet again. Alice felt proud to be hosting her very first Christmas in her and Ollie's new home.

She looked around the dinner table: Robert and Sue were complimenting Ollie on what a great job he had done on cooking the Christmas dinner. Mr Frobersham was complimenting his new wife on how splendid her Irish Coffees were, tasting so much better without the whisky. The boys were trying to explain the Offside Rule to Nanny Betty who just couldn't quite get her head around it, particularly after all the sherry and wine. Sam grabbed Malcolm to come and join her in the living room and proceeded to teach him how to salsa. Last, but not least, sat Miss Prendergast. Still single, Alice lamented but, after all, tomorrow *is* another day.

THE END

Grateful thanks to

James Essinger, The Conrad Press, for giving me the opportunity to publish my first novel and for all his words of wisdom.

For all their help, support and encouragement.

My sister, Cath Follin.

My walking and afternoon tea buddies: Julia, Lynn, Kate, Chris, Anne, Maria, Rachel, Sue, Sam, Emily, Laura and Alice.